Honoré de Balzac

DOMESTIC PEACE

AND OTHER STORIES

TRANSLATED BY
Marion Ayton Crawford

PENGUIN BOOKS

Penguin Books Ltd, Harmondsworth, Middlesex
U.S.A.: Penguin Books Inc., 3300 Clipper Mill Road, Baltimore 11, Md
AUSTRALIA: Penguin Books Pty Ltd, 762 Whitehorse Road,
Mitcham, Victoria

—

This translation first published 1958

—

Made and printed in Great Britain
by Richard Clay & Company, Ltd,
Bungay, Suffolk

CONTENTS

INTRODUCTION

ALL these stories were first published between 1830 and 1832, with
the exception of the fragment from *A Mysterious Affair*, which first
appeared in 1841. After publishing the first novel to which he set
his name, *Les Chouans*, in 1829, Balzac was exploiting the fashion of
the moment for the story, and wrote quantities of them, very
rapidly, among masses of other work, making use of the short form
to work out his ideas and develop his techniques. These stories are
some of the best in the world's literature. But they are much more
than that. They are organically part of the *Comédie humaine*. The
groups into which Balzac at this time began to classify them together were to form the nuclei around which the *Comédie humaine*
was to grow for the next twenty years. When they were written, the
great novels were still all to come, but they were to add themselves
to and extend a scheme gradually beginning to reveal itself.

It was in 1834 that the frame was put together of what was in
1842 first called *The Human Comedy*. That frame had three parts:
(1) Studies of Manners, (2) Philosophical Studies, (3) Analytical
Studies. Of these, the first, Studies of Manners, was to be built from
six groups: Scenes of Private Life, Scenes of Provincial Life, Scenes
of Life in Paris, Scenes of Political, Military, and Country Life.

The purpose of the notes that follow is to indicate some of the
ways in which the handful of isolated stories translated here, each
complete in itself, belong to the *Comédie humaine*; and also to consider some of the technical means by which Balzac obtained his
characteristic and unique effects.

Walter Scott's success on the Continent had earlier set the French
publishing world looking for a 'French Walter Scott' and a number of writers, in various series, had aspired to the title, without
much success. Balzac, with the same idea, planned a series picturing
the 'manners' of the French people at different periods coinciding
with the great events of French history. For this series only one
novel was completed – *Les Chouans*. The series was abandoned,
but *Les Chouans* became the first volume of the *Comédie humaine*.

The novel deals with the royalist insurrection in Brittany and the
west after the Revolution, and its original title was *The Last Chouan,
or Brittany in 1800*, changed to *The Chouans or Brittany in 1799* when
Balzac revised it and published a new edition in 1834.

The date of its action meant that there were plenty of people alive who had witnessed or taken part in the exciting events of the time, and with this novel Balzac began what later became his invariable custom of questioning eye-witnesses. The action of nearly all the novels and stories of the *Comédie humaine* was to lie between 1792 and 1840, a period in which, although it was so short, everything that was not contemporary was history, by reason of the terrific political convulsions that had taken place, and the social and economic changes; yet documentation of his facts and living survivals of the age that had passed lay all about Balzac.

This limitation of his period meant that Balzac, instead of chronicling history in a straight long line, was exploring it in depth and in every direction within his narrow span, registering such things as changes in fashions of dress, furniture, and speech, in ordinary manners, changing laws, and changing customs, the rise of the new, the survival of the old, in every field, as well as the political, social, and economic changes. The dramatic events of the earlier part of the period were suited to his power of illuminating persons and situations with a bright limelight. In the later part he finds his drama in the movement of social groups and their impingement on the individual life – the secret power of groups of the clergy, for example, or of gossiping old women – and the growing power of money. The *Comédie humaine* was to become one vast historical novel, of a unique kind, and the novels and stories of it which are contemporary in their action are regarded from exactly the same point of view as those of Revolutionary or Napoleonic times. This consistency of point of view is quite clearly seen in the stories of this volume. Balzac's distance from each of them is exactly the same, and enables him, while he may be deeply involved psychologically with the characters, both to chronicle manners and to pass judgement, as a historian, on any period, even his own.

M. Maurice Bardèche in his important book *Balzac Romancier*, which, among much else, deals in detail with contemporary influences on Balzac, notes in *Les Chouans* the first appearance of secondary characters which, like Scott's, have a representative part to play. Each of these characters stands for and typifies a group of actors in the civil war – the nobleman who fights for his king, the republican soldier, the careless, happy-go-lucky volunteer, and the fanatic, the ambitious cleric, and the greedy bourgeois who dare take neither side.

This idea of bringing entire groups and categories into the picture in the person of single individuals may seem obvious enough,

familiar as we are with Scott and with the mass of third-rate historical fiction written since his day, but for Balzac it was a discovery,
and one that was to have very far-reaching results. For soon in his
work there came to be no secondary characters; those that were
secondary to the plot began to be capital to the history, to extending
the range of his exploration of society. The representative persons
are no threadbare conventional types, but very carefully chosen individuals whose every word and gesture is significant of the ways
of thinking, speaking, or acting of some group or section of society.
Each individual is strongly individualized, yet reflects a facet of
history. They were tools in Balzac's hand, enabling him to penetrate the overgrown jungle of society and classify its strange fauna
systematically. And when one individual symbolized a group, the
possibility of representing the whole world of Balzac's chosen time
became conceivable. Examples of such representative characters are
easily found in the stories of this book. Two very minor ones are the
old Duchess, Madame de Lansac, the representative of the disdainful aristocracy surviving into the Empire, in *Domestic Peace*; and
Monsieur de Bourbonne, who typifies the rich Norman landowner
who knows everything and keeps his mouth shut, in *The Abbé
Birotteau*.

This use of what with another novelist would be characters of
slight importance was carried a brilliant stage further when, in 1833,
Balzac had the inspiration of making these characters, with the
places they inhabited or frequented, reappear in subsequent volumes.
The same characters reappear sometimes at a period of their lives an-
tecedent in time to their earlier appearance, sometimes more closely
involved in the story, sometimes only mentioned by name in a list
of guests at a ball. They are related, sometimes as niece or brother
or relative by marriage, or doctor or solicitor or confessor, to more
central characters. But they are recognized as familiar by the reader,
and open up to his view a set of circumstances, a personality and
environment, that do not need to be described, as mention of the
name of an acquaintance calls these to mind in real life.

The stories collected together in this volume were written and
published before the idea of making his characters return occurred
to Balzac. Later he corrected and altered them with subsequent
occurrences in mind, and it is, of course, the amended version that
is translated in this edition. Readers will notice many cross-
references, both within the stories themselves and to later novels.
For example, that Count Malin de Gondreville whose alleged kidnapping gave rise to the complications of *A Mysterious Affair* in

1806, is the host who in 1809 in *Domestic Peace* gives a ball to celebrate Napoleon's triumph in Austria. Derville, in *Colonel Chabert*,
in his recital of the instances of dreadful human wickedness that he
has encountered in his professional work, speaks of the father who
was deserted and left to die in an attic by his daughters to whom he
had given all his money, the story that Balzac was to deal with later
in *Old Goriot*. The perfume shop *Queen of Flowers*, a meeting place
and post office for royalist plotters, from whose steps the Abbé de
Marolles watches Robespierre's accomplices pass on their way to
the guillotine in *An Episode during the Terror*, reappears in later
novels, notably the one that deals with the prosperity and subsequent fall of César Birotteau, a brother of the Abbé Birotteau.

Les Chouans, though a historical novel, brings on the scene no
great historical figure, and the events and passions and calculations
of the civil war which is its subject are not the motive forces which
propel the plot. What matters is the love-affair between the leader
of the Chouans, Montauran, and Marie de Verneuil, the spy who
has been sent to betray him. The history, with which their lives are
intricately intertangled, is important, but Balzac's eye is much more
keenly focused on the persons and their private passions, with much
more intensity and penetration than his model, Scott, was capable
of. Balzac was proud to consider himself a historian, and copying
Scott, who was the first to attempt a history of manners and society
in a given region at a given time, he went further and sought a
reason for the results he had observed, and attempted to classify and
explain them; but he was a novelist first, in his passionate concern
with individual human beings, and in his story-telling genius.

The question in what way and to what extent great historical
figures and well-known historical events are to be introduced into
fictitious narrative is an important and difficult one that faces every
writer of historical fiction at the outset, for the true, our conception
of which has grown with all we have heard or read since early childhood, has a way of making the fictitious seem a hollow sham, or
else itself appears twisted to fit the fiction.

Balzac, in some observations on Eugène Sue's work, in 1840, remarks that the authentic personage introduced into fiction should
do nothing out of character, and that he should be reserved for
great scenes. The total elimination of great historical figures in *Les
Chouans* was too radical a solution of the problem, and only a temporary one. His later practice seems to have been to prepare the
appearance of his great character far in advance, and make his
appearance brief but very striking, as is perfectly exemplified in *A*

INTRODUCTION 11

Mysterious Affair. But there is another and even more successful way in which Balzac makes the existence and importance of his authentic persons obvious – he makes them cast their shadow in men's minds, as in fact they do in life, and shows them to us, not in a mirror, but heightened and coloured by others' experience of them and emotions and thoughts about them while the great person and the great event remain for the most part off-stage.

The historical character of these times who casts the longest shadow is, of course, Napoleon.

'When the Emperor hears of it!' exclaims Victor Marchand, when the Spanish town has risen, his garrison has been slaughtered, and he himself has escaped ignominiously with his life by flight.

'He will want to have you shot,' replies his General, who has just a moment previously absolved Marchand from blame. We note the lively consciousness of Napoleon's officers of their Supreme Commander's direct interest and closeness to them. The mention of Napoleon's name reminds us, too, that this very minor incident of the war in Spain is linked with the tremendous struggle going on all over Europe, of which this war is a part.

'I had a father, the Emperor! ... Our sun has set. We are all cold now.' It is the elegy of a whole era of vanished glory, and in a few words evokes the regret of all the scattered soldiers of the Empire, and their affection for their leader.

Magnificently in place and in character where they occur, these references have much to do with that extension of the existence of the characters, both in space and time, in the mind of the reader, which is so characteristic of the stories and novels of the *Comédie humaine*, and which serves to knit them together, since it is largely the same space and the same time into which the characters send these illuminating glances, though individually they are set in different places and different periods of it. Even Birotteau and Mademoiselle Gamard are described as discussing in 1820, in their credulous way, the gossip about Napoleon's supposed death and Louis XVII's supposed survival, and Birotteau has been a nonjuror priest – a priest who refused to take the oath of allegiance to the Revolutionary government which nationalized Church property. All the characters have a past, of which we are made aware, as well as a future; their present is only a stage, a phase; and their thoughts and remarks are often revelatory of their total experience, which as we read story after story reveals points of contact with that of others, especially in the historical events and reflection of the historical persons of the day.

Balzac's admiration of Napoleon is well known. He possessed a statuette of Napoleon to which he had attached a banner with the inscription, 'What he failed to complete by the sword I shall consummate by the pen.' The Napoleonic legend, we are told, laid its lasting hold upon the minds and imaginations of Frenchmen in Balzac's lifetime, and Balzac himself, with his enormous circulation and far-reaching influence upon other writers, must be held to be to some extent responsible for its spread and growth.

The first story included in this volume, *Domestic Peace*, is set in 1809, when Napoleon was at the zenith of his career.

SCENES OF PRIVATE LIFE (first series)

Domestic Peace

After *Les Chouans* followed many volumes of short stories, and it is to one of the first of these that *Domestic Peace* belongs, to a collection called *Scenes of Private Life*, published in 1830. This is a group of six stories which reflect in a series of pictures of Paris society Balzac's first encounters at about this time with the Countesses, the great ladies and dandies, whom he was to study with such passion. They all touch on some aspect of marriage, and were ostensibly written to warn young girls of the hidden perils that surrounded them in society.

After the introductory setting of the scene in its historical circumstances the story is vividly pictorial and strongly dramatic, and flows without interruption from beginning to end. The characters group themselves and pass individually from one group to another in ballroom or cardroom, dance or converse while they watch, brood fiercely like an evil genius with Martial, or stand enjoying the scene with Montcornet, as if for the eye of cinema cameras. Sometimes the eyes of Martial and Montcornet *are* the eye of cinema cameras. Much of the visual information is given in the dialogue, especially at the beginning of the ballroom scene where Martial and Montcornet are sometimes not so much conversing as indulging in parallel dithyrambic monologue.

A film director today, making a film set in a Paris ballroom in 1809, would hardly avoid making Napoleon its centre, and as a result the other characters would be comparatively dwarfed, and Napoleon himself, if we may judge from films so far made, unlikely to convince. Balzac contrives both to have Napoleon's presence at the ball, in the minds of guests expecting his arrival, and to keep him bodily absent for an extremely plausible reason that refers to a known historical event – his approaching divorce from Josephine; and so leaves the characters free to play out their drama in the limelight, and at the same time ties the story more closely to history. The fact that we know the reason for Napoleon's non-appearance while the company at the ball do not, also makes us feel, illogically but quite naturally, that *both* events on which we are looking back are historical fact, the ball as well as Napoleon's divorce. We are not allowed to forget, either, that the careers and social advancement of both men and women enjoying the pleasures of this ball to celebrate the Peace Treaty, depend on Napoleon. References by Montcornet and Soulanges, and the description of Martial's skill in presenting the face to Napoleon that Napoleon wishes to see, reinforce the impression.

The story is linked at its end to another actual event, in the reference to the fire that occurred on 2 July 1810 at the mansion inhabited by the Austrian Ambassador, whose sister-in-law perished in the flames. This, like an appearance of Napoleon at the ball, is something that any other story-writer or any film-scenario writer, treating a story of that time, would have made climactic: one cannot conceive of anyone else casually mentioning in the last paragraph, apparently purposelessly, the death of one of the chief characters, a young and beautiful heiress, by fire! But Balzac is as little concerned as History itself to neaten the edges of his story. He ties up the threads, but only the threads of an episode, and life is seen to continue beyond it for the characters, or to end for one of them in unforeseen death.

Life continues with a difference, at the end of the story, for the Comtesse de Soulanges. All the characters brilliantly sketch universal human types, and varieties of behaviour, and attitudes to life of the period; but in her Balzac suggests greater depths. She is a development from the young heroine of earlier novels, one of the many young women whom in later books we watch grow in sad experience of life. She has not ceased to love her husband, but she casts his hair, given as a love-token, from her ring; and in the gesture and in her painful reflections, we recognize the thoughts of so many of Balzac's women who see life clearly, and prepare to put the best face on it.

PHILOSOPHICAL STORIES

The Young Conscript and *El Verdugo*

Domestic Peace communicates Balzac's delight in the spectacle the world offers and his acute feeling for its drama. *El Verdugo* and *The Young Conscript* do this too to a certain extent, for they are first and before everything exciting stories, but, as in Balzac's own classification of them, they reveal his constant effort to systematize his observations and reflections, to search not only for immediate causes of what he observed, but also for ultimate reasons. They appeared, with others, under the title *Philosophical Novels and Stories* in 1831, and later, in 1836, in a more extensive collection as *Philosophical Studies*.

All his working life Balzac was haunted by certain questions, and he uses story after story and novel after novel to explore them, to clarify and demonstrate his own ideas about them. Such questions were the nature of mind, the effect of the material in a man's surroundings and in his physical make-up on his mind and soul, the different effects produced by the working out of inherited characteristics under different conditions, the effect of a bias of the mind on a man's destiny and on the destiny of others, the nature of goodness and evil, the manifestations of the divine in supernatural phenomena and the strange unexplored and half-unsuspected 'psychic' powers that man possesses.

The taste of the day was for the sensational. Readers eagerly devoured weird tales designed to fill them with awe and horror and blood-chilling fear of the 'occult', and Balzac during the previous ten years had quite flippantly catered for the appetite. But he had retained his profound serious interest in unexplained phenomena, and he now began to suggest that scientific explanations must exist, and also, realizing that reason and science were inadequate tools, to construct philosophical systems. These were partly founded on direct intuitional experience, for he believed himself to be clairvoyant. He read widely in the scientific literature of the day, attended lectures of the leading scientists at the Sorbonne, was deeply influenced for a time by the French mystic Saint-Martin and the Swedish prophet Swedenborg, 'the Buddha of the North'. Yet at the same time he was preaching the doctrine of salvation through good works, and he never ceased to regard himself, strangely, as an orthodox Roman Catholic.

The question that all the stories of the *Philosophical Novels and*

Stories are concerned with (as Balzac explains in Introductions to the editions of 1831 and 1836, which were written by his friends but inspired by him) is the question whether a life lived intensely, consumed in devotion to some end, is suicidal, whether the true part of wisdom is not to stand apart from life like the sage. 'To desire sears us and power destroys us: but to know leaves our frail organism for ever in a state of peace.' That is the theme of *The Wild Ass's Skin*, the short novel published with the philosophical stories, and all these stories show aspects of it. Thus in *The Young Conscript* Madame de Dey's intense devotion to her son causes her death, and in *El Verdugo* extreme pride of race and devotion to the family cause the death of the girl who might have saved herself by marrying Victor Marchand, and the fate of her executioner brother. It is the theme too of *Louis Lambert*, published in 1832, which is strongly autobiographical and stuffed with Balzac's personal and philosophical ideas. The epigraph placed at the head of *The Young Conscript* is taken from this book.

The effect of these preoccupations of Balzac's was to extend the range of the *Comédie humaine* still further, on different planes. On the one hand, the characters of the *Comédie humaine* are not only men and women of France in the last years of the eighteenth century and the first part of the nineteenth, set in the material and historical circumstances of their day and age. They are men and women of any time who see the familiar material things of this world tremble and dissolve in a shaking of the veils of time and space, who may be in process of becoming angels or devils, who are visibly in many cases making their souls in the course of the story; and Balzac's vision of this is more or less compelling and beyond argument. On the other hand, the story is linked with some vast question, moral, philosophical, social, scientific, which is still in many cases, and by its nature may always be, a matter for serious argument, and which opens wide horizons of a different kind.

Balzac's 'science', which one might expect to be completely out of date, is by no means always so by virtue of the aspects of it that interested him in the interaction of mind and body. The question of how it is possible in certain circumstances for the human mind to abolish time and space, which is posed in *The Young Conscript*, for example, is still a question for scientists. It is called extra-sensory perception now, and experiments are carried out under controlled conditions on the transmission of patterns on cards from person to person, separated in space. Scientists working on the problem have declared that the existence of supernormal phenomena is proved beyond dispute, but that a theory is needed to account for them. In other words, Balzac's words of nearly one hundred and thirty years ago, the science still awaits its man of genius.

Scientific questions may all find an answer in time, but moral questions are perennially subject to debate; for example, the question, in *An Episode during the Terror*, whether one is morally guilty of blood shed in the execution of one's duty. It is not now the burning question that it was just after the War, how far generals and concentration-camp officials were responsible for the war crimes of the Nazi régime, but it has never been satisfactorily and definitively answered, and it was an exactly similar question that troubled the conscience of Sanson, Louis XVI's executioner, to which the Abbé de Marolles could find no answer.

We may admire the calm conviction with which at the end of *The Young Conscript* Balzac claims as an entry for a scientist's notebook a wholly fictitious story which he has himself invented, and he does consistently throughout his work draw conclusions from his own stories. One is reminded of what Dickens says of the engineer Daniel Doyce in *Little Dorrit*: 'He never said, I discovered this adaptation or invented that combination; but showed the whole thing as if the Divine artificer had made it, and he had happened to find it ... so convinced was he that it was established on irrefragable laws.' This of course adds to the appearance of reality of the stories. But one overwhelmingly gets the impression that Balzac was less trying to pull wool over the reader's eyes than using a method of discovering the truth for himself as well as for us.

It was noted earlier how many of the characters in the *Comédie humaine* are representative of groups in society. Similarly the characters of the philosophical stories often represent an idea; thus Madame de Dey stands for motherly love, as members of the Légañès family stand for pride of race. It is the force of unique genius in Balzac that makes such creations come alive, and it is a difficult task to analyse genius. But, especially in the later stories and novels, and already evident in the character of Madame de Dey, one notices the perfect understanding resulting from intense sympathy that gives depth and vivid humanity to very different kinds of person. It is partly owing to the character of Madame de Dey that *The Young Conscript* is a much more appealing story than *El Verdugo*.

Balzac's analysis of the reasons for the strength of the bond that unites Madame de Dey and her son, on which the whole story rests, is made with precision at a point in the action when the tension under which she is living has been established, and the reader's curiosity aroused about the oddness, in her circumstances, of her refusal to see her usual guests. From the beginning all eyes are focused on her and all feeling centres in her. She is held in a tautly-strung web of curiosity and anxieties that cut across one another: anxiety to take advantage of her perilous situation on the part of her suitors, anxiety on her behalf of her well-wishers, and her own over-riding, suddenly unbearably increased, anxiety for her son. The tension is sustained by the nerve-racking reception she holds at her house, while our eyes are turned to watch the young soldier's approach to the town, then rises rapidly to crisis after crisis, and what we by this time feel is the entirely credible end.

A chapter might be written, for which this story would supply some pages, on Balzac's technical use, and entirely natural and acceptable use, of the servants of a household as go-betweens with the outside world, as confidants and reflections of their mistress's or master's states of mind, as interesting characters in their own right. Here Brigitte's cry that it is the stranger that has killed her mistress, humming the detestable *Marseillaise* as he gets dressed and prepares to leave his night's billet, makes us aware of everyday life going on, with its trivial detail and comfortable unconsciousness of other people's tragedies, and makes more impressive by contrast Balzac's restrained statement of what the strange nature of Madame de Dey's death really was.

The period of the story is of course established by the whole framework, gone into in such detail, of Madame de Dey's situation, but our sense of it is reinforced by all sorts of unobtrusive and natural touches – the various conjectures made, so near the truth, as to what she was concealing, which reveal the desperate straits of different classes of Royalist sympathizers; the note that Royalists at that time looked every day to see the Revolution end the next day, which in the light of what we know makes us exclaim at their folly, yet realize how comprehensible their optimism was *at that time*; the appeal to readers to fill out from their experience the details of such circumstances as many of them must remember. It is impossible not to believe, at least while we read, that these events happened as stated in France, in Normandy, in 1793.

With Spain in 1808, in *El Verdugo*, the events take a little more salt to make us swallow them, but there Balzac's aim was rather different: he sought to shock and startle as he did not in the other story. Historically he is justified, for the brutality and bloodshed on both sides of the war in Spain, in which later Napoleon's seasoned soldiers became demoralized and his generals fell to pieces, is a matter of record, and the proud, stiff, unyielding spirit of the Spaniards, here illustrated, had much to do with their success where half Europe had failed. The Duke of Wellington is recorded as saying 'It is true that the result may in part be attributed to the operations of the Allied Armies in the Peninsula: but a great proportion of it must be ascribed to the enmity of the People of Spain'. (*The Conversations of the First Duke of Wellington with George William Chad.* Edited by the 7th Duke of Wellington. Cambridge 1956.) Because the story is a leaf from history, and establishes itself as such, the bloody melodrama of the conclusion is bearable.

By its economy, swiftness of movement, and pictorial vividness, this story squeezes the last drop of drama from the series of dramatic situations that succeed one another at breakneck pace, without ever sliding into bathos. To describe setting and circumstances, interweave a love interest – which is another signpost to the times when a Paris grocer's son finds himself in a Spanish Grandee's castle and dare aspire to the hand of his daughter – bring the English fleet into sight, tell of a ball, a rising, a massacre, and a flight and Napoleon's possible reaction to the news, the punitive march of an avenging force, its dispositions for defence against a landing, and the detailed story of the vengeance exacted, all in such a very few pages, is a considerable feat in itself. The story perhaps suffers a little from being so compressed; and the poetic justice of the dramatic contrast at the conclusion – when the merriment of French officers over their wine rings out to the ears of the Spanish watchers on the execution terrace – is a little too apt, it sounds contrived. It horrifies us, even when the General's stern rebuke to a doubtful officer reminds us of the nature of their situation in that savage country. Yet one can only wonder at the story's phenomenal concentration and technical skill.

The general whose name is transparently concealed in the text is Gautier or perhaps Gauthier. M. Marcel Bouteron and M. Henri Longnon, editors of the monumental French edition of Balzac's collected works, comment that this is possibly the major-general Gauthier whom Napoleon recalled from Spain in April 1809, and sent to the Grand Army's headquarters.

SCENES OF POLITICAL LIFE

An Episode during the Terror

This story was assigned to *Scenes of Political Life* in Balzac's later classification. It first appeared as an introduction to a book manufactured in collaboration with another writer – *Memories of the Execution of Louis XVI*, published in 1830 – a book of which Balzac was ashamed, and which he never acknowledged. The story was first published under his name in 1842 with the title *A Mass of 1793*, and received its present title in 1846.

Balzac actually met and questioned the son and grandson of the Public Executioner Charles Sanson who had guillotined Louis XVI, but not until 1834. Son and grandson had in turn succeeded to his office. In his *Études Balzaciennes*, M. Marcel Bouteron tells us that on a previous occasion at the house of Appert (the well-known philanthropist interested in criminology and prison reform), where Balzac later met him, Henri Sanson, the son, had had this to say about the execution of the King:

> *I stood beside my father when he was forced to execute poor Louis XVI, whom everyone in our family loved. And when he was obliged to take up the head by the hair to show it to the people, as he had been ordered to do, the handsome face still bore its gentle and noble cast, and my father was nearly taken ill at the sight. It was lucky that I was near him, and as I am tall I hid him, and his agitation and his tears were not seen; for certainly at that time they would have led to our being guillotined in our turn....*

The setting of the story in 1793 makes it a companion piece to *The Young Conscript*. It does for Paris what *The Young Conscript* does for the provinces – conveys the very feeling of what it was like to be a member there of an outcast section of society under the Terror. Madame de Dey represents the aristocrats: the characters in *An Episode during the Terror* stand as well for the dispossessed clergy – the nuns, of noble blood, turned out of their convent in the Abbaye de Chelles, and the priest who had escaped when one hundred and sixteen of his fellows had been murdered by the mob in the Carmelite monastery, Les Carmes.

In this story too the impression of surrounding and terrible danger is conveyed from the beginning, and an atmosphere of extreme tension is sustained, heightened, and then relieved without anticlimax. The picture of the panic-stricken old lady, followed by a mysterious man, walking in the dark alone through the snow in the time of the Terror, is sufficiently arresting. When she reaches her goal, the lighted confectioner's shop, and we study her appearance, learn that she has come to pay dearly with her last gold coin for something illegal, and consider the shopkeepers' attitude towards her, several hints are dropped both as to what she may be and what is the prevailing social attitude to such as she, but the mystery of the unknown man is only deepened by the confectioner's unfeigned terror. So when on her solitary walk again, homewards, still followed by him, though she may tell herself that he is after all a friend, the reader can only think that she has dreadful reason to fear him.

At this point, when the lady reaches home, the simple natural dialogue tells us all we need to know of the circumstances of the three inhabitants of the garret, and immediately the tension is heightened by the entrance of the stranger. With the sharpened vision and concentrated attention of these conditions the two women and the stranger observe each other, and a few minutes later the stranger and the priest are confronting each other too.

If all this preparation is not to lead to anti-climax, the stranger's presence must have a striking purpose, and his purpose is striking indeed.

In the description of the celebration of Mass for the dead King in these surroundings, Balzac's gifts of dramatic presentation are displayed at their best. His ability to see in trivial things and unimportant persons representatives or symbols of something of much vaster significance, here finds perfect expression. Under the collapsing roof of that house Balzac is dramatically successful in bringing not only the Monarchy of France and the Revolution which has overthrown it, but God himself.

At the end of the story the glimpse of the tumbril with its prisoners and executioner on their way to the Place Louis XV provides a striking oblique view of a historical happening, closely and intimately weaving the story in with recorded history. The fact that Balzac makes the execution of Robespierre's accomplices occur several months early – in January 1794 instead of July 1794 – apparently by mistake rather than by dramatic licence, does not seem to matter at all.

SCENES OF PRIVATE LIFE (second series)

The *Abbé Birotteau* and *Colonel Chabert*

In 1832 Balzac published a second series of *Scenes of Private Life*, and the stories in this volume, to which *The Abbé Birotteau* and *Colonel Chabert* belong, in several respects show changes and development compared with those in the first series.

To begin with, the stories are generally much longer, partly in order to devote more time and space at the beginning to showing the causes from which the story springs, and preparing the effects which are to follow, partly to give time and space in the action of the story for these prepared effects to unroll and reveal themselves. These stories are much more than what we usually understand by the term 'story'; they are novels in everything but length.

The shorter story makes its effect quickly, sustaining interest by exciting happenings or a nervous tension which cannot be held too long. Here a change of emphasis is seen in a lessened desire to dazzle and surprise, and an increasing concentration on the painting of character, from which spring those dramatic effects previously more often sought in external events.

Lawyers and law-courts begin to play the important part in the lives of the characters that is to be increasingly theirs in the *Comédie humaine*, and society to make its coercive weight and pressure more strongly felt in a time of civil peace.

The *Abbé Birotteau*

The beginning of *The Abbé Birotteau* is delightful, and full of comedy. Like *An Episode during the Terror*, though with a very different effect, it opens with one of the persons walking alone by night through a city, and, as in that story, a great deal of information is imparted to us during that walk, about the nature of the person walking and his circumstances. These are of deadly fear and apprehension in the first case; in Birotteau's case they are less the circumstances of his times than his present state of cosy contentment and hope, and the whole history of how he has reached that state. In both stories, the dwelling at which these persons arrive and the reception they meet is described, and what follows is made the occasion of our learning a great deal that we need to know about the characters' past lives.

Balzac never surpassed the skill with which in the beginnings of some of these stories he created a moving frame of the present, with narrative, incident, dialogue, description, within which our interest is held; while piece by piece the circumstances in the past that have led to that present, and are to produce the future action of the story, are naturally introduced and brought to our attention. He invented the device of the 'flash-back' before the cinema, and used it more cleverly. In the novels, what was introduced into the frame of the present was to be enormously expanded, with a certain loss of pace and lightness, though not of vigour. But the marking of the importance of the day and hour of the reader's entry, as it were, into the story, the spotlight thrown on a chief character when some event of crucial importance is just about to happen, with the revelation immediately afterwards that what the spotlight has picked out is just one point of a continuous process that has its beginnings far in the past, was to become characteristic of Balzac's art and technique.

In this connexion it is worth noting a remark that Balzac made in his well-known laudatory article on Stendhal's novel *La Chartreuse de Parme* in his *Revue Parisienne* of 25 September 1840, which was the first to notice and praise the younger writer's work. Balzac criticized the composition of the work because it relates the story throughout according to the chronological order of events, a fault, says Balzac, which many writers commit, 'taking a subject true in nature which is not so in art'. It is an expression of his view that 'a slice of life' does not make an adequate novel or story. A commentary on this is furnished by a comparison of Colonel Chabert's story of his escape from death and wanderings through Europe in his effort to return home, with the true stories of the wanderings of prisoners escaped from prison camps during the last war. These true records are like stills or sequences from documentary film, where Balzac's story is a work of art; not Chabert's story only, but Balzac's setting of it within its frame.

Because the origins of these later stories of Balzac's lie in the past, and in the natures of the persons, their interest to a great extent is a pleasure of recognition, of understanding, of watching the inevitable happen. Given the knowledge of the persons concerned that we are early given, we know that in any combat between Birotteau and Mademoiselle Gamard it is not Birotteau who will triumph, that Troubert is likely to achieve his dark purpose whatever it may be, that Chabert's desire to regain his identity will be defeated by his wife's whole-minded concentration on her own ends, and by his own generous nature. And simultaneously with our knowledge of the characters, that is of the forces within themselves, we build up our realization of the forces in life and in society against which they are struggling, and of the foredoomed failure of the individual. For they all fail, even Troubert, whose victory is a victory over a dead man and a weakling unworthy of any steel, whose forceful ambitious nature and genius for intrigue, as Balzac is at pains to point out, in another period of history might have been used to the profit of his country and humanity: even Countess Ferraud, who in achieving her ends is very unlikely, as we foresee, to achieve the happiness she seeks.

Balzac's psychological analysis is inextricably mingled with the narrative, dialogue, and description; and instead of diluting the interest and slackening the tension, concentrates and tightens them. This is particularly evident in *The Abbé Birotteau*, which is a study, almost a clinical study, of the effects of celibacy on three individuals representing three different groups in society – a representative old maid and representatives of two different kinds of clergy; and as such is an addition to the classifications of the social zoology that Balzac in his Preface of 1842 represents as one of the aims of the *Comédie humaine*.

Old maids have often been studied, often with malicious unkindness, sometimes with a sentimentality as superficial as the other, never, I believe, so mercilessly as here, yet with such complete sympathetic understanding of the psychological causes, social conditions, and blind selfishness of other individuals that have turned human material into the extremely unattractive specimen of the old maids of Balzac's day, Mademoiselle Sophie Gamard.

The effects of celibacy on men have been examined less frequently. Throughout the *Comédie humaine* Balzac appears to demonstrate that sterility in all its forms is maleficent, first of all to the victim, only secondarily to those victimized through him. The warping of Troubert's nature is due to frustrated ambition, of which Mademoiselle Gamard's frustrated social ambition seems almost a caricature. A married Troubert outside the Church is inconceivable. He is what he is by the interaction of all the circumstances of his nature and his life, and his celibacy must be considered a strongly influential element in these circumstances. There is a fine dramatic irony in putting into Troubert's mouth the justified rebuke to Birotteau that a priest's preoccupation with the spiritual world should make material circumstances indifferent to him. It is not asceticism that Troubert lacks. The quality that the two radically different clergymen and Sophie Gamard all appear to lack, in Balzac's view, is the selfless devotion to others' interests that parents possess, and that some spinsters achieve who become mothers vicariously. 'It is necessary to man', he says, 'that he should experience certain passions to develop in him the qualities which lend his life nobility, extend its range, and still the egotism natural to all created things.'

As well as being a study of three celibates, a genus with three of its species, the story explores the interdependence of individuals and groups in their struggle for existence – a kind of social ecology, if one may use the term. When Birotteau leaves his lodgings in the innocent hope that his landlady's hatred of him will die for lack of fuel, and goes to stay with his friend Madame de Listomère, we find that the position in society which he has taken for granted as so secure, is in reality held in a balance of forces, between friends, who are themselves similarly held and find themselves powerless to help him without destroying their own or their relatives' careers, and enemies, who are themselves striving against forces which thwart and try to keep them down. Madame de Listomère is helpless against the threat to her nephew and brother-in-law that Troubert holds over them. But Troubert has been helpless for years against the dead hand of Chapeloud and the higher clergy's distrust of his ambition; and it is as a representative of another group, the Congregation, that he gains power. To Mademoiselle Gamard and her friends, Birotteau is a weapon in their ceaseless vain struggle to make some impact upon Cathedral society. Everyone is striving against some group or section in society, for some end that means a fuller life for himself; and must instantly make use of any advantage to threaten, restrict, or destroy. Birotteau himself is dumbfounded at the importance of the interests concerned in his small affairs. He repeats Madame de Listomère's words to himself, aghast. ... 'Perhaps with the Archbishop's help we may manage to put an end to this business.' He realizes in the end with pitiful clarity that he is only a straw, and nothing can prevent his being blown away when the wind blows against him.

When in the political, social, and clerical worlds, Balzac finds groups or their representatives 'red in tooth and claw', some of his critics suggest that his mind was so steeped in melodrama that he could not avoid finding it in life where it did not in actuality exist. He was the first novelist fully to conceive of the organization of society as a given external circumstance narrowly conditioning the individual life, and he may have exaggerated the power of the organized groups of like strong political and clerical interests springing up everywhere in France after the Restoration – no one can exactly estimate how great their power was. About the power of social groups we can all make our own estimates. The action of the story is set in 1826 (as for a similar reason is Stendhal's *Le Rouge et le Noir*, written in 1830) because it is the period of the triumph of the 'priest party' backed by Charles X. The *Congregation* of which Troubert is the dreaded representative was formed by one of the clerical parties, which set up a kind of secret police in every town.

When all this has been said, one comes back to the excellence of the telling of the story as the most striking thing about it. Balzac uses a series of petty details to build up not only an illuminating picture of daily existence for Mademoiselle Gamard and her clerical guests, but also a palpable atmosphere of oppressive hatred and intimidation; so that though the fat, comfort-loving little Abbé, radiant in his hope of the canonry within his grasp at last, is comic at first in his concern about the four trifles that disturb his peace of mind: the closed door, the unlit fire, the displaced candlestick, the forgotten slippers, before long the terms in which Mademoiselle Gamard is likened to a bird of prey with hooked and razor-sharp claws ready to plunge into his heart, do not seem exaggerated. Everything about Birotteau is slightly or extremely comic, and the merciless spotlight in which he is held shows up such cosy human weaknesses that the increasingly dark shadows of tragedy gathering round him are darker by contrast, and a deeper pathos is lent to his fate.

Colonel Chabert

The beginning of *Colonel Chabert*, with its description of the solicitor's office, and the half-dozen clerks who work and gossip and rag each other and present a blank face to the griefs of the clients, is an affectionate recollection of Balzac's youthful apprenticeship to the law, and Derville, the solicitor, is probably a representation of Maître Guyonnet de Merville, Balzac's own chief of those days. Derville reappears many times in the *Comédie humaine*, in connexion with the troubled affairs of many of its persons. In bringing Colonel Chabert into this office, with his plain statement that he is a man of whose heroic death on the battlefield everyone knows, Balzac is again employing the device of dramatic contrast, introducing the strange and unexpected, but here in the most plausible fashion, into what the clerks see as an entirely ordinary and matter-of-fact setting, and thus sharpening our perception of both of them.

The setting is entirely matter-of-fact to the clerks, but not to Balzac, to whom indeed nothing ever is, for the gloomy room is seen as representative of all those establishments that batten on the sorrows and troubles of humanity.

In the clerks' joke of telling Chabert the truth, which he is not expected to believe, that Derville sees clients in the small hours of the morning, this scene is linked with the next one, and the way prepared for Derville's return from a ballroom in the dead of night to find this strange awe-inspiring figure awaiting him – 'a Rembrandt without its frame'. Balzac is fond of describing the appearance of his characters by such references, enriching them by the reader's knowledge of and aesthetic pleasure in well-known paintings. But here, in his description of Chabert, and Chabert's story that follows from his own lips, with an originality of technical treatment and a mastery as striking as Rembrandt's, Balzac's achievement in a different medium is comparable with Rembrandt's in some of his greatest canvases. He has painted with the utmost compassion and understanding an old man marked by the vicissitudes of life reflecting on that life, his flesh moulded by the soul within and by the long battle which has worn away everything superfluous from it, and marked it with dreadful experience. Rembrandt's old men are serene, but Chabert has not yet reached serenity. And he is painted in words, his own and Balzac's – his portrait is made by speech. In his case the style is indeed the man.

Chabert and his companion, who have been rolled about the world like pebbles at the mercy of ocean tides, are débris of a war that took place in an almost unimaginably vaster Europe and a wider world than ours. In his narrative, the broken fragments of Napoleon's armies straggle homewards from every quarter of the globe ... 'Egypt, Syria, Spain, Russia .... China, Tartary, Siberia'. On Chabert's tongue they are the ends of the earth.

In military rank and social status Chabert is the equal of Montcornet and Soulanges of *Domestic Peace*, but how different in character, and what a different view of Napoleon we get through his eyes! 'He was fond of me, the Chief.' 'When I think that Napoleon is in Saint Helena I don't care a straw for anything else on earth.' Before Chabert tells Derville that he was a foundling child, we know from his speech that he has been a wanderer from birth, that he is one of Napoleon's devoted soldiers who in the ranks, with any luck, had a Marshal's baton in their knapsacks. He is representative of the new arrivals in society in the new régime, as Soulanges is representative of the aristocrats whom Napoleon wished to fuse with them.

Throughout Chabert's narration of his rising from the dead and years of wandering, Balzac returns us at intervals to the scene he has set. We watch Derville, at first scanning his papers as he listens, becoming wholly engrossed in the fascination of the story. We have the flow of past events held up while Chabert is affected to the point of tears by Derville's consideration and politeness, and Derville is touched and convinced by Chabert's feeling; while Chabert speaks of the lawsuit he wishes to bring and Derville considers practical ways and means. There is a constant fluctuation of time while the reader's attention is turned from the present to the past, on to consideration of the future and back again, following what passes between the old soldier and the young solicitor in the shadowy study. It is another instance of Balzac's framing of the flash-back in a dramatic present, and it adds another dimension to the portrait of Chabert. What Derville says is perfectly in character, and his sceptical remark to his clerk afterwards – that he may have let himself in for a large sum of money, but if it is robbery he does not regret paying for seeing a great actor – focuses the whole thing again from another point of view in the present, not weakening our conviction but rather reinforcing it, for we realize that this hard-headed lawyer, whose whole experience trains him to be sceptical of plausible stories which extract money and require support for lawsuits, is, in spite of his remark, convinced.

Having heard Chabert's story, the reader must learn his wife's, and her present circumstances with her present husband. Derville goes from one to the other, from the Colonel's miserable lodging with the dairyman to the Countess's luxurious surroundings; and while he is in his cab on the way and meditating his plan of campaign, the mass of information is easily conveyed, and is dramatically linked with the interview that follows – ' "There is something very odd about Monsieur le comte Ferraud's position," Derville said to himself, waking from his long reverie'.

Countess Ferraud is one of Balzac's series of hard-hearted women who quickly turn to tigresses if their ambitions are thwarted. She and Sophie Gamard are sisters under the skin. The hardening of the heart in both cases is shown in a comprehensive glance backwards to be a development over a period of years. 'The Colonel had known the Countess under the Empire, he was now seeing a Countess of the Restoration.' The process of change in which human beings, while preserving their identity, ceaselessly alter from day to day is constantly noted by Balzac; and with it the rider to it, that the impression people make on others, even and particularly on those nearest to them, who are blinded by affection, corresponds only momentarily with reality.

Balzac is very successful in conveying the completely feminine cleverness of Countess Ferraud, as well as her unscrupulousness, in her treatment of Chabert and exploitation of his generous nature; for example, in the way in which she uses her real and acute anxiety about the future to make Chabert feel that his existence makes her situation intolerable. Of course her situation *is* intolerable, given her love for Ferraud and her doubts of him. Her passion for Ferraud, Ferraud's ambition, her early circumstances which make her unsuited to help him, her knowledge that he feels this – they explain if they do not excuse her fearful callousness; just as Sophie Gamard's pleasure in vulture-like hoverings over poor Birotteau is accounted for by his unconscious sins against her, and the humiliations she is subjected to by society. Balzac's characters are not *unaccountably* wicked.

Ultimately, throughout the *Comédie humaine*, it is the constitution of society that bears a large proportion of the blame for tragic events. It is Ferraud's social and political ambitions that make his wife's position precarious and so affect Chabert indirectly; but much more immediately he feels himself to be a victim of the weight and pressure of society, whose coherent, impenetrable mass is driving him back underground. 'I have been buried under dead men, but I am buried now under the living, under documents, under facts....' In the end it is his disgust for society and its instrument, the slow, tortuous, spirit-racking workings of the law, with its requirement of money to make it work at all, that leads him to abjure it. He can no longer bear to fight with it for his identity, once he has found out that his wife's tenderness is a sham. He is remarkable as one of the few persons in Balzac's world who renounce the passion that has been their motive force; with him, of course, it has never been entirely wholehearted – 'Sometimes I wish I was not I'. His sun has set with Napoleon, and he is now only a monument of the past, like an old worn-out cannon.

There is a pleasant dramatic surprise in the unexpected answer that Derville and Godeschal get when they pity Chabert as a poor senile old man, and are told that he has merely been celebrating, and the story is related of the Prussian who tried to patronize him and got the answer he deserved. With any other writer the moralizing voice of Derville and Godeschal here would be the voice of the author, and in so far as they speak of the wickedness of the world, they do, of course, speak for Balzac. But the previous jolt given by the old pensioner to their natural enough assumptions, and the way in which Balzac has throughout involved Derville in the action and presented a complexity of points of view, prevent any feeling that these onlookers are only author's mouthpieces and know-alls, themselves godlike above the fight.

SCENES OF POLITICAL LIFE

A Mysterious Affair

Although *A Mysterious Affair* is collected under *Scenes of Political Life*, the episode from it translated here might equally well be placed with *Scenes of Military Life*. It is added to the book partly because the shadow of Napoleon is pervasive of so many of the stories that it seems a pity not to present him in person. Though chronologically last, it is placed here with the shorter stories because, in the period of its action and in its shortness, it seems to belong with them.

It is a magnificent example of Balzac's interweaving of events of historical importance with those of importance only for the individual, making each add tension and reality to the other. The ordered confusion of the movement of armies before Jena, as Laurence drives through them, the rumours of victories reaching her ears, break in upon but do not mitigate the confused violence of her emotions, as she travels upon her errand as a suitor for all she holds dear to the conqueror whom she has hated all her life. And it is through her eyes and ears and all her senses, made more acute by the tension of her feelings, that we are conscious of the presence and movement of the French and Prussian armies facing each other across the Saale, as evening falls and camp-fires are lighted, and we get an impression of the nameless officer on a formless field who quickly resolves himself into the Emperor, with a galaxy of Staff Officers, on a battlefield rapidly taking shape around him. When we meet him again in his humble bivouac we find that we have been insensibly prepared to believe in and accept him.

Throughout the novels and stories of the *Comédie humaine* nothing is static, everything is fluid, is in process of changing, in the lives and natures of the characters, and in the circumstances affecting the classes and societies that they build up; but in this passage the process is put under a spotlight at a moment of crisis. It is symbolized by physical movement in space, by Laurence's barouche laboriously rolling through France and Switzerland and from village to village of Prussia in pursuit of Napoleon, to which the movement of divisions and detachments and units of armies, as it nears and reaches its goal, forms a counterpoint. And it is made visible in minds looking forward to fateful decisions, in the perceptible flow of time in which great events are ineluctably impending to change the fate of human beings and the course of history.

The fate of the five on whom Laurence's heart is fixed is considered for a moment in the light of the fate of thirty thousand who must die on the morrow, yet the five individuals are not diminished and lost in the comparison. Instead, the importance of their possible loss gives scale and a measuring rod to the immense loss and waste of the battlefield, which is a loss of individuals, and which in Napoleon's eyes is scarcely to be weighed against the glory of one's country, as the fate of five men matters little in the upholding of the importance of its law. It is not so much the portrait of Napoleon, celebrated though it is, that reveals genius here, as the conveying to the reader of the physical presence of those masses of soldiers, and the psychological weight of the gathering in that moment of time of their thousands of separate existences.

As Laurence and her companion drive away next morning with the heavy guns grumbling behind them, the heroics of the battlefield are muted. The battle takes place, off, while daily life goes on – to be fundamentally affected perhaps by the results of the battle, but meanwhile entirely set on its own overridingly important affairs.

Notes

The famous Column in the Place Vendôme, to which Colonel Chabert declared that he would appeal for recognition, is faced with the bronze of 1200 cannon taken from the enemy in 1805.

Peers of France, referred to in *The Abbé Birotteau* and *Colonel Chabert*, were members of the Upper Legislative Chamber 1814–48.

The Palais-Royal, where Colonel Chabert first met his wife, means the infamous Wooden Galleries at that place, a kind of bazaar for booksellers and the clothing trade, and a resort of gamblers and libertines.

The Young Conscript is not an exact translation of the French title *Le Réquisitionnaire*. The *réquisitionnaires* were the soldiers raised by the *Réquisitions* of the young First Republic, a levy first made in February 1793 of all unmarried men between the ages of eighteen and twenty-five.

M. A. C.

DOMESTIC PEACE

*

THE episode which this Scene recalls took place towards
the end of November 1809, a time when Napoleon's
ephemeral Empire attained the zenith of its splendour. The
triumphal fanfares for the victory of Wagram were still echo-
ing through the heart of Austria's monarchy. A Peace Treaty
was being signed between France and the Coalition. Kings
and princes came to revolve like satellites about Napoleon,
who took pleasure in sweeping Europe along in his train, in a
magnificent trial of the power which he was to put forth fully
later in Dresden. Never, according to those present at the
time, had Paris seen more brilliant festivities than those that
preceded and followed the marriage of this sovereign power
with an Austrian Archduchess. Never in the greatest days of
the former Monarchy had so many crowned heads swarmed
on the banks of the Seine, and never had the French aristocracy been so wealthy and so eager to display its wealth.
The lavish show of diamonds on women's finery, the gold
and silver braid of military uniforms, in such striking contrast
with the poverty-stricken appearances of Republican days,
seemed to provide the Emperor with a demonstration that the
wealth of the entire globe was circulating in Paris drawing-
rooms.

A general intoxication seemed to have seized this Empire of
a day. All the military men, not excepting their leader, were
newcomers on the social scene, enjoying as newcomers the
spoils won by a million soldiers whose epaulettes were of wool
and whose demands were satisfied with the award of a few
yards of red ribbon. At this period most women paraded the
easy manners and moral laxness which had marked the reign of
Louis XV. Whether it was in imitation of the style of the fallen
monarchy, or whether it was because certain members of the
Imperial family had set them the example, as the critics in the
Faubourg Saint-Germain declared, it is certain that everyone,

both men and women, rushed headlong after pleasure with a recklessness that seemed to presage the end of the world.

But there existed then another reason for this licence. The infatuation which seized women for military men rose to a pitch of something like madness, and was too closely concordant with the Emperor's views for him to wish to apply any restraint to it. The frequent summonses to arms, which made all the treaties drawn up between Europe and Napoleon into so many armistices, made love affairs liable to development as rapid as the speed with which decisions were made by the Supreme Commander of those soldiers with their busbies, short jackets, and shoulder-knots whom the fair sex found so attractive. Hearts, like regiments, lived a nomadic life then. Between a first and a fifth bulletin from the Grand Army a woman might be in turn a girl in love, a wife, a mother, and a widow. Was it the prospect of probable widowhood, of endowment, or the hope of bearing a name destined to live in History, which made soldiers so alluring? Were women drawn to them by the certainty that the secret of their passions would be buried in the battlefields, or is the cause of their fanatic ardour to be sought in the high attraction courage holds for women? Perhaps all these reasons, to which the future historian of Imperial manners and customs will no doubt devote some consideration, counted for something in the facile readiness with which they surrendered themselves to love. However that may be, let us acknowledge the fact here: laurels then covered many a fault, for women ardently sought those intrepid adventurers who appeared to them as veritable fountain-heads of honours, riches, pleasures, and in the eyes of young girls an epaulette, that enigmatical symbol of the future, signified happiness and freedom.

A characteristic feature of that epoch, unique in our annals, was an unbridled passion for everything that glittered or sparkled. Never were there so many displays of fireworks, never were diamonds so highly prized. Men were as avid of these white stones as women, and decked themselves like them. Perhaps the need of holding booty in its most easily portable form made jewels valued in the army. A man did not appear so ridiculous then as he would now with large diamonds on his shirt-front or his fingers. Murat, a man of completely oriental tastes, set the example of a luxurious fashion which in modern soldiers would be found absurd.

The Comte de Gondreville, who was formerly called Citizen Malin and whose kidnapping had made him famous, had become one of the Luculluses of that Conservative Senate which conserved nothing. He had delayed his celebration in honour of the Peace Treaty only in order to pay his respects to Napoleon more strikingly, intending to strain every nerve to eclipse the flatterers who had preceded him. The ambassadors of all the Powers who were friendly to France (with reservations), the most important personages of the Empire, even a few princes, were gathered at this moment in the affluent senator's reception-rooms. Interest in the dance was flagging. Everyone was waiting for the Emperor, whose appearance had been promised by the Count. Napoleon would have made the promise good if it had not been for the distressing scene which had occurred that very evening between Josephine and him, a scene which brought into the open the forthcoming divorce between this august husband and wife. The news of this occurrence, kept very dark then but harvested by history, did not reach the courtiers' ears, and affected the gaiety of Comte de Gondreville's ball only through Napoleon's absence.

The prettiest women in Paris, prompt to crowd the Count's ballroom on the strength of hearsay about him, were at that moment striving to outdo one another in splendour, coquetry, in fashionable display, and in their beauty. Arrogant in their wealth, rich financiers looked down their noses at dazzling generals, the Grand Officers of the Empire, newly gorged with orders, titles, and decorations. These large balls were always eagerly seized upon by rich families as opportunities to display their heiresses to the eyes of Napoleon's praetorian guard, in the crazy hope of bartering magnificent dowries for uncertain favour. Women who believed themselves strong in their beauty alone, without wealth to back it, came to essay its power. There, as elsewhere, the pursuit of pleasure was only a cloak. Serene and laughing faces and calm dignity masked odious calculation, demonstrations of friendship were designed to deceive, and more than one person distrusted his enemies less than he did his friends.

These remarks were necessary in order to make clear the background and development of the little imbroglio which is the subject of this Scene, which paints, in perhaps softened colours, the fashionable manners that ruled then in Paris drawing-rooms.

'Turn your eyes a moment towards that truncated pillar supporting a candelabrum. Do you see a young woman with hair dressed in an oriental style? There, in the corner, to the left. She has blue bell-flowers in the gathered mass of chestnut hair falling back in tresses on her head. Do you not see? She is so pale that you might think she was ill; she is dainty and quite tiny. Now she is turning her head towards us; her blue eyes are almond-shaped and ravishingly soft, they look as if they were made to shed tears. Hold on! she is bending to look at Madame de Vaudremont across the labyrinth of heads in unceasing movement whose high head-dresses intercept her view.'

'Ah! I've found her, my friend. You had only to tell me that she was the whitest-skinned of all the women here and I would have recognized her; I had already noticed her: she has the prettiest colouring I have ever seen. I defy you to pick out from where we are standing the pearls that separate the sapphires in her necklace, against the background of her neck. But she must be prim or a coquette, for the frilling of her corsage hardly allows one to guess at the beauty of her bosom. What shoulders she has! as white as a lily!'

'Who is she?' asked the man who had spoken first.

'Oh, that I don't know!'

'Aristocrat! So you want to keep all the women for yourself, do you, Montcornet?'

'It becomes *you* well to jeer at me,' returned Montcornet, smiling. 'Do you think you have the right to insult a poor general like me because you are Soulanges's fortunate rival, and have only to show the slightest restiveness to alarm Madame de Vaudremont? Or is it because I have only been

here a month, in the promised land? The insolence of you ad-
ministrators who stay stuck to your chairs while we are in the
thick of the fight with shells bursting all around us! Come,
Monsieur le Maître des Requêtes, allow *us* to glean in the field,
which is only yours to hold precariously while we leave it to
you. Hey, what the devil, everyone has to live! If you had any
idea what the Germans are like, my friend, you would do your
best to help me win your dear Parisienne.'

'General, since you have honoured this woman, whom I
have never seen before, with your attention, have the kindness
to tell me if you have seen her dancing.'

'Oh, my dear Martial! where do you come from? If they
send you on a diplomatic mission, I augur ill for your prospects of success. Do you not see three rows of the most hardened coquettes in Paris between her and the swarm of dancers
buzzing under the chandelier, and didn't you have to use your
eyeglass to find her out in the angle of that pillar, where she
seems enveloped in shadow in spite of the candles shining
above her head? Between her and us there are so many sparkling diamonds and so many sparkling glances, so many float-
ing feathers and waving laces and flowers and tresses, that it
would be a real miracle if some dancer should notice her
among all the stars of this galaxy. You surprise me, Martial.
Have you not realized that she must be the wife of some sub-
prefect from the Lippe or the Dyle who is here to try to make
her husband a prefect?'

'Oh! he will become one!' returned the Master of Requests.

'I doubt it,' said the General, laughing. 'She seems to be as
new to intrigue as you are to diplomacy. I'll bet, Martial, that
you don't know how she comes to find herself there.'

The Master of Requests looked at the Colonel of Cuiras-
siers of the Imperial Guard in a way which betrayed both
disdain and curiosity.

'Well!' Montcornet went on. 'She no doubt arrived on the
stroke of nine o'clock, perhaps the first to come and probably
embarrassing Comtesse de Gondreville very much, for she's
a woman who doesn't know how to spin two thoughts together. Rebuffed by the lady of the house, pushed from chair

to chair by each new arrival until she reached the shadows of that little corner, she must have let herself be closed in there, a victim of the jealousy of those ladies, who can have asked for nothing better than to submerge such a dangerous face in that way. She has had no friend to encourage her to defend the seat she must have occupied to begin with, in the front row. Each one of these false-hearted dancers will have intimated to the men of her coterie that they must not have anything to do with our poor friend under pain of the most dire punishment. That, my dear sir, is how these pretty faces, so tender and so candid in appearance, will have formed their coalition against the stranger, and that without any of these ladies saying more than, "My dear, do you know that little woman in blue?" See here, Martial, if you want to bring down upon you more flattering glances and provocative inquiries in a quarter of an hour than you might perhaps normally receive in a whole lifetime, try showing your intention of piercing the triple rampart which forbids access to the queen of the Dyle, the Lippe, or the Charente. You will see whether the most slow-witted of these ladies cannot at once invent a ruse capable of stopping the most determined man from bringing our plaintive stranger into the lime-light. Don't you think she has a rather elegiac air?'

'You really think she is that, Martial? She is a married woman then?'

'Why should she not be a widow?'

'She would be more active if she were,' the Master of Requests said with a laugh.

'Perhaps she is a card widow, with a husband playing bouillotte,' suggested the handsome Cuirassier.

'Indeed, since the Peace Treaty there are plenty of such widows,' Martial said. 'But, my dear Montcornet, we are a pair of idiots. That face is too ingenuous still, there is too much youth and freshness on her forehead, about her temples, for her to be a married woman. The tones of her flesh reveal such youthful vigour! There is no blemish yet in the planes of her face about the cheek-bones and nose. Her lips, her chin, her whole face is as fresh as a white rosebud, although it is clouded and sadness lies like a veil over it. Who can have made this young person cry?'

'It takes so little to make women cry,' said the General.

'I don't know,' Martial went on, 'but she is not grieving because she is sitting there without dancing, her grief is of longer duration than this evening. One can see that she has taken pains to adorn herself for the occasion. She is already in love; I would lay a wager on it.'

Montcornet shrugged his shoulders. 'Perhaps she's the daughter of some German princeling; nobody speaks to her,' he said.

'Ah! how unfortunate a poor girl is,' said Martial. 'Could anyone be sweeter or more full of grace than our little stranger? And yet not one of those shrews around her, though they think themselves very perceptive and full of sensitive feeling, will address a word to her. If she spoke we would see if she has pretty teeth.'

'Bah! so you're ready to effervesce like a saucepanful of milk at the slightest rise in temperature?' cried the Cuirassier, rather piqued at meeting a rival so soon in his friend.

'What!' said the Master of Requests, disregarding the General's remark and turning his eyeglass on all the guests surrounding them. 'What! is there no one here who can tell us the name of that exotic flower?'

'Oh! she is some lady's companion,' said Montcornet.

'Good! a lady's companion wearing sapphires worthy of a queen, and a dress of Mechlin lace. Tell that to the marines, General! You cannot be very strong in diplomacy yourself if you judge a person to be a German princess one moment and a lady's companion the next.'

General Montcornet laid a hand on the arm of a little fat man, whose greying hair and shrewd eyes had been noticeable at every door-corner as he stood watching, or mingled without ceremony with the various groups of guests, who welcomed him with respect.

'Gondreville, my dear friend,' said Montcornet, 'tell me, who is that charming little woman sitting over there under the enormous candelabrum?'

'The candelabrum? Ravrio, my dear sir. Isabey designed it.'

'Oh! I had already recognized your taste and your love of the splendid in the candlestick; but who is the woman?'

'Ah! I don't know her. She is no doubt one of my wife's friends.'

'Or your mistress, you old rogue.'

'No, upon my word! The Comtesse de Gondreville is the only woman in existence capable of inviting people that nobody knows.'

In spite of the acidity of this remark, a smile of inward satisfaction, evoked by the General's guess, hovered around the corpulent little man's lips.

The General rejoined the Master of Requests in a neighbouring group, where the latter was engaged in seeking, vainly, information about the unknown lady. He seized his arm and said in a low voice: 'My dear Martial, take care! Madame de Vaudremont has been staring at you for some minutes with desperate concentration. She is just the woman to guess simply by the movement of your lips what you were saying to me, our eyes have already been only too expressive, she has certainly noticed it and followed their direction, and I think she is more concerned at this moment than we are with the little lady in blue.'

'That's an old stratagem of war, my dear Montcornet! What does it matter to me, anyway? I am like the Emperor, when I make conquests I keep them.'

'Martial, your complacency cries to heaven to teach you a lesson. What! rash civilian, you have the luck to be the husband designate of Madame de Vaudremont, a twenty-two-year-old widow, burdened with four thousand napoleons a year; a woman who adorns your finger with diamonds as fine as that one,' he added, raising Martial's left hand, which the Master of Requests complacently yielded to him, in order to have a closer look at it; 'and you still aspire to be a Lovelace, as if you were a colonel and obliged to keep up the military reputation in the garrison towns! Fie upon you! Just think of all you have to lose.'

'At least I shall not lose my liberty,' Martial replied, with a forced laugh.

He cast a passionate glance at Madame de Vaudremont, who answered it with a smile full of uneasiness, for she had seen the General examining Martial's ring.

'Listen, Martial,' the General went on, 'if you flutter about my young unknown, I shall undertake the conquest of Madame de Vaudremont.'

'As you please, dear Cuirassier, but you won't gain so much as that – –' said the young Master of Requests with a derisive click of his polished thumb-nail against his teeth.

'Reflect that I'm a bachelor, that my sword is all my fortune, and that to challenge me like that is setting Tantalus down before a feast which he will certainly devour.'

'Prrr!'

That scoffing combination of consonants was Martial's only answer to the General's provocative assertion, and he looked his friend over from head to foot mockingly before he left him.

The fashion of the times obliged a man to wear white kerseymere breeches and silk stockings at balls, a becoming dress which displayed Montcornet's well-turned legs to perfection. His height too, obligatory in a Cuirassier of the Imperial Guard, drew the eye, and the handsome uniform enhanced the impression he made of commanding authority. He was thirty-five years old at this time and still young in appearance, in spite of a certain corpulence which he owed to the habit of constant riding. His dark military moustaches set off a true soldier's face, with its broad, open brow, aquiline nose, red lips, and frank expression. Montcornet's bearing and manner, marked with a certain distinction by the habit of command, might easily please a wife who had the intelligence not to wish to make a slave of her husband.

The General smiled in answer to his friend's mockery, looking down amicably from his greater height at the small slim Master of Requests, who had been one of his best friends since his boyhood.

Baron Martial de la Roche-Hugon was a young Provençal,

a protégé of Napoleon's, who seemed marked out for some glittering ambassadorship. He had won the Emperor's favour by an Italian pliancy, by a genius for intrigue, by that drawing-room eloquence, and diplomatic skill and tact in the use of good manners, which so easily take the place of the more substantial qualities of a man of greater depth. Although he was young and lively, his face already possessed the steely impassivity, the brilliant metallic blankness, which is indispensable to diplomatists, enabling them to hide their emotions and disguise their feelings, if indeed this impassivity is not a symptom revealing that no emotion exists and that feeling is dead. Diplomats' hearts may be regarded as an insoluble mystery, since the three most illustrious ambassadors of the period are remarkable for the implacability of their hatreds and their romantic attachments. However that may be, Martial belonged to that class of men who are capable of coolly calculating their future prospects in the midst of their most ardent pleasures. He had already passed judgement on the social world, and concealed his ambitions beneath the fatuous mask of an amorously successful young man, disguising his ability in the common garment of mediocrity, for he had remarked the rapidity of the advancement of people who gave little cause for jealous pique to the master.

The two friends were obliged to part after a cordial handshake, for the prelude which warned the ladies to form sets for a new quadrille was making the men move from the vast dancing-floor where they were chatting in the middle of the room. These remarks had been rapidly exchanged in the usual interval between quadrilles, before the fireplace in the great hall of the Hôtel Gondreville. The questions and answers of this ordinary enough ballroom chatter had been spoken in low voices, and the speakers had stood close together. But the chandeliers and torches set above the fireplace scattered light so lavishly upon the two friends that their faces were strongly illuminated, and could not conceal, in spite of their discreet blankness, the almost imperceptible changes that expressed their feelings, from either the acutely intuitive Countess or the ingenuous stranger. To the idle onlooker one of the pleasures to be found in social gatherings lies in such espionage of their neighbours' thoughts, although so many baffled simpletons are bored to tears at such assemblies, without daring to admit it.

If the interest of this conversation is to be made clear an earlier incident must be described, which was to link together the persons of this little drama, scattered in different corners of the various rooms, by invisible ties.

At about eleven o'clock, as the dancers were taking up their positions for a fresh quadrille, the gathering in the Hôtel Gondreville had seen the most beautiful woman in Paris make her appearance, the queen of fashion, the Comtesse de Vaudremont, the only person absent until then from the splendid assembly. She made it a rule never to arrive at receptions until gaiety was in full swing. In the animation of the ballroom it becomes impossible for women to maintain the freshness of their faces or their toilets for long: so this fleeting moment is the ball's springtide. An hour later, when pleasure has passed and fatigue is on the way, everything is spoiled. Madame de Vaudremont never made the mistake of staying so long at a ball as to be seen with wilting flowers, ringlets out of curl, crumpled lace, with a face like all faces when sleep invites them and they cannot always help succumbing to its blandishments. She took good care not to let herself be seen, like her rivals, with her beauty half asleep. She adroitly sustained the reputation she held for cleverness in dress by leaving a ballroom looking always as radiant as when she entered it. Women whispered to each other, enviously, that she made ready and put on as many changes of gown as she attended balls in an evening. This evening, Madame de Vaudremont was not to have the power of deciding at her pleasure when she should leave the ballroom where she was then arriving in triumph.

Pausing a moment on the threshold, she glanced keenly though briefly at the women, observing and considering their toilets in one swift look, in order to satisfy herself that her own eclipsed them all. The celebrated beauty displayed herself to the admiration of the assembly on the arm of one of the most

gallant colonels of the Artillery of the Imperial Guard, a
favourite of the Emperor's, the Comte de Soulanges. The
momentary and fortuitous juxtaposition of these two persons
was indubitably a rather strange coincidence. When Monsieur
de Soulanges and the Comtesse de Vaudremont were announced, several ladies sitting around the ballroom walls for
want of partners rose to their feet, and men pressed in from
the adjoining rooms to fill the doorways of the principal hall.
A wit among these, member of a class always in evidence at
these crowded gatherings, said as he watched the Countess
and her escort come in: 'The ladies are as eager and curious to
examine a man who remains faithful to his passion, as the men
are to study a lovely woman who will not be pinned down.'

Although the Comte de Soulanges, a man of about thirty-
two, was endowed with the highly-strung temperament from
which, in human beings, spring great qualities, his slight frame
and pale complexion were little calculated to predispose one
in his favour. His dark eyes suggested abundant vitality, but
in society he was taciturn, and there was no sign visible in him
of the oratorical talent which was to scintillate on the Right in
the legislative assemblies of the Restoration. The Comtesse de
Vaudremont was a tall woman with a soft full body and a
dazzlingly white skin, who carried her small head with an air,
and possessed the immense asset of being able to inspire love
by the gracious charm of her manner, and she was one of those
beings who fulfil to the full all that their beauty promises.

This couple, the cynosure of all eyes for the last few moments, did not give curiosity occasion to exercise itself at their
expense for long. The Colonel and the Countess seemed to be
perfectly well aware that chance had placed them in an embarrassing situation. As he saw them come forward, Martial
pushed his way among the group of men posted by the fireplace so that, across the bank of heads that formed a rampart
around her, he could observe Madame de Vaudremont with
the jealous attention which the first fire of passion inspires. An
inner voice seemed to whisper that the success of which he
was so proud might perhaps be precarious; but the coldly
polite smile with which the Countess thanked Monsieur de

Soulanges, and the gesture with which she dismissed him as. she sat down beside Madame de Gondreville, made all the muscles of his face, which had grown tense with jealousy, relax. Yet as he noted Soulanges standing a couple of paces from the sofa on which Madame de Vaudremont was seated, no longer seeming to heed the warning look by which the young beauty had told him that they were both in a ridiculous position, the volcanic-tempered Provençal knitted the dark brows shadowing his blue eyes again, smoothed, to keep himself in countenance, the curls of his brown hair, and, without revealing the emotion which made his heart beat fast, he kept watch on the faces of the Countess and Monsieur de Soulanges while he joked with his neighbours, and as he grasped the hand of Montcornet, who had come up to greet his friend, he listened to him without hearing what he said, his thoughts were so preoccupied elsewhere.

Soulanges was calmly glancing around him at the fourfold border of women that lined the Senator's enormous ballroom, admiring the decorative frame of diamonds, rubies, gold ornaments, and tiara-crowned heads, whose brilliance almost outshone the candle-flames, the crystal of the chandeliers, and the gilding. His rival's careless serenity put the Master of Requests out of countenance. Unable to control his suppressed overmastering impatience, Martial made his way towards Madame de Vaudremont in order to pay his respects to her. When the Provençal appeared Soulanges cast one glum look at him and then rudely averted his gaze. An absorbed silence reigned in the ballroom where general curiosity had reached its highest pitch. All the faces strained to see and hear wore the most peculiar expressions. Everyone was fearful and expectant of one of those explosions that well-bred people take care never to let occur.

Suddenly the Count's pale face became as red as his scarlet facings, and his eyes at once turned downwards to the floor in order not to betray the cause of his embarrassment. Seeing the stranger humbly seated at the foot of the candelabrum, he walked dejectedly past the Master of Requests and took refuge in one of the card-rooms. Martial and the entire assembly believed that Soulanges was publicly yielding his place to him in apprehension of the ridicule which always attaches to deposed lovers.

The Master of Requests proudly raised his head and stared at the stranger; then, after seating himself with relief and some pleasure beside Madame de Vaudremont, he listened to her so absentmindedly that he did not take in what she was saying to him under cover of her fan:

'Martial, I should be pleased if you did not wear that ring which you made me give you, this evening. I have my reasons and I'll explain them to you presently, when we leave. You shall escort me later to visit the Princesse de Wagram.'

'Why did you take the Colonel's hand?' the Baron demanded.

'I met him under the peristyle,' she answered. 'But you must leave me. Everyone is watching us.'

Martial had then joined Montcornet, and it was at that point that the little lady in blue had become the focus of the emotion which was agitating, at the same time and in such different ways, the Cavalry officer, Soulanges, Martial, and the Comtesse de Vaudremont.

When the two friends separated after the challenge with which the conversation ended, Martial hastened to Madame de Vaudremont's side, and was able with her as his partner to join one of the most brilliant quadrilles. Set free by the intoxication with which women are always seized in the joy of dancing and in the animation of a ball, where men no less than women are lent allurement by the meretricious splendour of their best clothes, Martial thought that he could with impunity yield to the spell which drew his eyes to the stranger. Though he may have succeeded in concealing his first stolen glances at the lady in blue from the Countess's uneasily watchful eyes, he was soon surprised in the very act; and though the first absence of mind he betrayed was forgiven him, he could not excuse the rude silence with which he later answered the most beguiling question that a woman can ask a man: 'Do you care for me, this evening?' The more pensive his mood was, the more teasingly importunate the Countess became.

While Martial was dancing, the Colonel passed from group to group in search of information about the young stranger. After fruitlessly exhausting the patience of everyone willing to help him, and even of some who were not very much interested, he was making up his mind to take advantage of a moment when the Comtesse de Gondreville appeared to be disengaged, to ask her herself for the name of this mysterious lady, when he noticed a slight gap between the pillar supporting the candelabrum and the two divans which were placed there. The Colonel seized his opportunity when a dance left vacant a large proportion of the chairs, which formed several fortified lines defended by mothers and women of a certain age, and set off to cross this palisade draped here and there with shawls and handkerchiefs. He set himself to pay compliments to the dowagers; then, passing from lady to lady, from one polite exchange to the next, he at last reached the empty place beside the stranger.

At the risk of getting himself hooked up on the gryphons and chimeras of the huge candelabrum, Montcornet stood his ground under fire from the heat and wax of the candles, to Martial's great discontent. Too adroit to speak to the little lady in blue on his right without further ado, the Colonel began by addressing a majestic lady, a rather ugly one, whom he found on his left:

'This is a very successful ball, Madame! What splendour! What life and gaiety! Upon my word all the women here are pretty! It is really very disobliging of you to disappoint some cavalier by not dancing.'

The Colonel may have begun this banal conversation with the object of making his right-hand neighbour talk, but, silent and preoccupied, she paid not the slightest attention to him. The officer was holding a host of phrases in reserve, which should lead up to a 'What do you think, Madame?' from which he was hoping great things. But he was oddly surprised when he perceived tears in the eyes of the stranger, whose whole mind seemed to have been captivated by Madame de Vaudremont.

'No doubt you are married, Madame?' he began at last, tentatively.

'Yes, Monsieur,' the stranger answered.

'Your husband is no doubt here?'

'Yes, Monsieur.'

'And why, Madame, do you stay in this corner? Is it to make the men seek you out?'

The sorrowful girl smiled sadly.

'Let me have the honour, Madame, of being your partner in the next dance, and I certainly shan't bring you back here! I see an unoccupied ottoman near the fireplace; come, sit there. When so many people are prepared to queen it and sitting on a throne is the passion of the day, I cannot believe that you can refuse the title of queen of the ball, which your beauty seems to claim for you.'

'Monsieur, I do not mean to dance.'

The curtness of her replies was so disconcerting, that the Colonel foresaw that he would be obliged to retreat. Martial, who guessed what the Colonel's last request had been and the rebuff that he had met with, started to smile and stroked his chin, his ring flashing as he did so.

'What are you laughing at?' the Comtesse de Vaudremont asked.

'At the poor Colonel's bad luck. He has just made a blunder....'

'I asked you to take your ring off,' the Countess interrupted.

'I didn't hear you.'

'Though you can hear nothing this evening, Monsieur le Baron, at least nothing escapes your eyes,' retorted Madame de Vaudremont in some pique.

'There's a young man with a very fine brilliant,' said the stranger to the Colonel.

'Magnificent,' he agreed. 'That young man is Baron Martial de la Roche-Hugon, one of my best friends.'

'Thank you for telling me his name,' she said. 'He seems very pleasant.'

'Yes, but he is rather too gay.'

'One would say that he was on very good terms with the Comtesse de Vaudremont,' the lady remarked, turning questioning eyes on the Colonel.

'The very best of terms!'

The stranger turned pale.

'Bless me,' thought the soldier, 'she's in love with that dog Martial.'

'I thought that Madame de Vaudremont was a friend of Monsieur de Soulanges; and had been for a long time,' the young woman persisted, recovering a little from the hidden pain which had for a moment shadowed the beauty of her face.

'For the last week the Countess has been fickle,' answered the Colonel. 'But you must have seen poor Soulanges when he came in: he is still trying not to believe his ill fortune.'

'I saw him,' said the lady in blue. Then she added, 'Thank you, Monsieur,' on an unmistakable note of dismissal.

As the quadrille was about to come to an end at that moment, the Colonel had just time to withdraw in disappointment, saying to himself as he went, by way of consolation: 'She's married.'

'Well, my brave Cuirassier,' cried the Baron, drawing the Colonel into a window embrasure where they could enjoy the fresh air from the garden, 'how far did you get?'

'She is married, my dear fellow.'

'What does that matter?'

'Ah, what the deuce! I'm a moral man,' replied the Colonel. 'I don't want, now, to pay my addresses to any woman that I can't marry. Besides, Martial, she formally announced to me that she did not intend to dance.'

'Colonel, one hundred napoleons to your dapple grey that she will dance this evening with me!'

'Done!' said the Colonel, striking the dandy's hand with his own. 'Meanwhile I'll go and see Soulanges. Perhaps he knows this lady, for she seemed to me to take some interest in him.'

'You've lost your bet, my gallant soldier,' said Martial, laughing. 'I have just met her eyes, and I know what they mean. Dear Colonel, you won't bear malice, will you, if I dance with her after the refusal she gave you?'

'No, no, he laughs longest who laughs last. Besides, Martial, I am a good loser and a fair foe. I warn you that she likes diamonds.'

On this note, the two friends parted. Colonel Montcornet made his way to the card-room, where he observed Soulanges at a bouillotte table. Although the two colonels had only the ordinary feeling of comradeship for one another that is established by the perils of warfare and the traditions of the service, the cavalry officer was concerned to see the artillery officer, whom he knew as a level-headed fellow, engaged in a game which might ruin him. The piles of gold and notes scattered over the fateful table-top bore witness to the heat of the game. A circle of silent men surrounded the seated players. Some words were certainly audible from time to time, such as: *Pass, play, I hold, a thousand louis, taken*: but to the spectator it seemed that the five motionless persons sitting there spoke to one another only with their eyes.

When the Colonel, alarmed at Soulanges's pallor, made his way to him, the Count was winning. Marshal the Duke of Isemberg, and Keller, a well-known banker, rose, completely cleaned out, after losing substantial sums. Soulanges's face grew even more sombre as he pushed together a mass of gold coins and notes – he did not even count them; a bitter disdain curled his lips; he appeared to threaten fortune instead of thanking her for her favours.

'Cheer up,' said the Colonel, 'cheer up, Soulanges!' Then, thinking that he was rendering him a real service in tearing him from the game. 'Come,' he added, 'I have some good news to give you, but on one condition.'

'What condition?' demanded Soulanges.

'That you'll answer a question I want to ask you.'

Count de Soulanges rose abruptly, crammed his winnings into a feverishly twisted and crumpled handkerchief with complete lack of interest in them, and an expression so savage that it occurred to none of the players to take exception to his *doing a Charlemagne*, giving them no opportunity to have their revenge. The faces round the table, indeed, seemed to grow less tense, in relief, when that morose and sullen countenance was no longer held in the luminous circle of light which a card-table lamp sheds.

'These damned soldiers are as thick as thieves!' said a

diplomatist among the onlookers in a lowered voice, as he sank into the Colonel's seat.

A single wan and tired face turned towards the newcomer, and its owner said with a glance that flashed and was gone like a diamond's fire: 'Military manners are not civil manners, Monsieur le Ministre.'

'My dear fellow,' Montcornet said to Soulanges, drawing him into a corner, 'the Emperor was singing your praises this morning, and there's not the least doubt that you're to be given a Marshalship.'

'The Chief has no love for the Artillery.'

'No, but he adores noble blood and you are a *ci-devant*! The Chief said,' Montcornet went on, 'that those who had got married in Paris during the campaign were not to be considered as in disgrace. Well, then?'

This information did not appear to mean anything at all to the Comte de Soulanges.

'Well, that's that,' the Colonel went on. 'Now I hope you'll tell me if you know a charming little woman sitting at the foot of a candelabrum....'

At these words the Count's eyes blazed, he seized the Colonel's hand with startling violence: 'My dear General,' he said in a noticeably shaken voice, 'if anyone but you had asked me that question I would have smashed his skull in with this lump of gold. Leave me alone, I implore you. I feel more inclined this evening to blow my brains out than ... I hate everything I see. I'm going to leave. All this gaiety and music and these stupid smirking faces make me die of exasperation.'

'My poor friend,' Montcornet replied soothingly, tapping Soulanges's hand amicably, 'how fiery you are! What would you say now if I told you that Martial cares so little for Madame de Vaudremont that he has fallen in love with that little lady?'

'If he speaks to her,' cried Soulanges, stammering with rage, 'I will stamp him as flat as his pocket-book, even if the conceited puppy should be in the Emperor's very lap!' And the Count collapsed, almost devoid of sense, on the sofa towards which the Colonel had led him.

The latter walked slowly away. He saw that Soulanges was in a rage too violent for the bracing mockery or soothing friendly attentions of one who knew him only slightly to have any calming effect.

When Colonel Montcornet returned to the ballroom Madame de Vaudremont was the first person who caught his eye, and he noticed that her face, normally so serene, bore traces of ill-concealed agitation. There was a vacant chair beside her, and the Colonel went and sat down in it.

'I would take a bet that there's something worrying you,' he said.

'A trifle, General. I want to leave here. I have promised to appear at the Grande-Duchesse de Berg's ball, and before that I have to visit the Princesse de Wagram. Monsieur de la Roche-Hugon, who knows this, is amusing himself breathing sweet nothings in the dowagers' ears.'

'That's not quite the reason for your anxiety, and I'll wager a hundred louis that you will stay here this evening.'

'Impertinent fellow!'

'I'm right, then?'

'Well, what am I thinking of?' the Countess challenged him, flicking her fan smartly across the Colonel's fingers. 'I might reward you if you guess right.'

'I won't take up the challenge. It's too easy.'

'You presume too far.'

'You are afraid of seeing Martial on his knees before ...'

'Before whom?' demanded the Countess, with an affectation of surprise.

'That candelabrum,' the Colonel replied, indicating the beautiful stranger, and scrutinizing the Countess with embarrassing closeness.

'You have guessed right,' answered the Countess, putting her fan up to her face and then twisting and turning it nervously. 'Old Madame de Lansac, you know she's as fond of mischief as an aged monkey,' she went on after a moment's silence, 'has just told me that Monsieur de la Roche-Hugon is courting danger in running after that stranger who has turned up this evening to be a death's-head at the feast. I would rather see Death himself than that cruelly beautiful face, as pale as a phantom's. It's the face of my evil genius. Madame de Lansac goes to balls only in order to see everything that goes on while she pretends to be sleeping,' she added, with a resentful shrug. 'She has disturbed me horribly. Martial shall pay dearly for this trick he's playing on me. But make him promise, General, since he's your friend, not to vex me like this.'

'I have just left a man who purposes nothing less than to blow his brains out if he courts that little lady. And he's a man, Madame, who keeps his word. But I know Martial; these dangers act as so many encouragements to spur him on. There's another inducement too: we've made a bet on it.' Here the Colonel lowered his voice.

'Can this be true?' said the Countess.

'On my honour.'

'Thank you, General,' said Madame de Vaudremont with a captivating glance.

'Will you do me the honour of dancing?'

'Yes, but in the next quadrille. I want to watch the progress of the intrigue during this one, and find out who this little lady in blue is. She looks interesting.'

The Colonel, seeing that Madame de Vaudremont wished to be alone, went off, satisfied at having so successfully launched his attack.

There are ladies to be met with at these balls who, like Madame de Lansac, sit there like old salts by the sea watching young sailors striving against the storms. At that moment Madame de Lansac, who, it appeared, took an interest in the persons of this scene, could very easily guess the battle raging in the Countess's breast. The young beauty might wave her fan graciously, smile at the young men who greeted her, and employ all the guile a woman can in order to conceal what she was feeling, but all without avail, for the dowager, one of the most perspicacious and malicious duchesses that the eighteenth century had bequeathed to the nineteenth, could read her heart and her mind. The old lady seemed to have the power of interpreting the imperceptible signs that betray the soul's preoccupations. The tiniest line that appeared on that

white, pure forehead, a quivering barely noticeable of the
rounded cheek, the play of eyebrows, the scarcely visible
variation in the curve of lips, whose living coral held no secrets
from the Duchess, could be read like an open book.

From the depths of her capacious armchair, filled to over-
flowing by her billowing dress, the beauty now superannu-
ated, even while she chatted with a diplomat who sought her
company in order to harvest some of the anecdotes she told so
wittily, admired her own reflection in the youthful beauty:
she conceived a liking for her as she watched her mask her
trouble and her aching heart so well.

Madame de Vaudremont indeed was enduring intense pain
while feigning exhilarated gaiety. She had believed that in
Martial she had found an able man on whom she could rely to
adorn her life with the enchanting delights of power. In this
hour she was realizing that she had made a mistake as bitterly
hurtful to her reputation as it was to her pride. In her, as in
other women of the period, the swift onset of the passions
heightened their intensity. Souls that live extravagantly and at
high pressure suffer no less than those that are consumed in a
single affection. The Countess's predilection for Martial was
a thing of yesterday, it is true; but the most inept surgeon
knows that the cutting off of a living member causes keener
pain than the amputation of a diseased limb. There was a
future to look forward to in Madame de Vaudremont's alliance with Martial, while her preceding passion was hopeless,
and poisoned by Soulanges's remorse.

The old Duchess, who was on the watch for the opportune
moment to speak to the Countess, hastened to dismiss her
ambassador, for before lovers' quarrels all other interests
pale, even for an old woman. To begin the contest, Madame
de Lansac cast a sardonic glance at Madame de Vaudremont
which made the younger woman apprehend, with fear, that
her fate might lie in the dowager's hands. There are glances
from woman to woman which are like torches borne in the
dénouements of high tragedy. One would need to have known
the Duchess to appreciate how her expression struck the
Countess with terror.

Madame de Lansac was tall, her features caused people to say: 'There's a woman who must have been lovely once!' She applied so much rouge to her face that her wrinkles were barely visible, but her eyes, instead of gaining a factitious sparkle from this deep carmine colouring, only looked lustreless by contrast. She wore quantities of diamonds and dressed with sufficient taste to lend no handle to ridicule. Her sharp nose suggested her capacity for epigram. A well-made set of teeth preserved unspoiled an ironic grimace which recalled Voltaire's. The exquisite politeness of her manners, however, so successfully softened the impact made by the malicious cast of her mind that she could not be accused of spite.

The old lady's grey eyes lit up; a triumphant look with a smile which said: 'I told you so!' was sent across the room to bring a flush of hope to the pale cheeks of the young woman who was sighing at the foot of the candelabrum. This alliance between Madame de Lansac and the stranger could not escape the Comtesse de Vaudremont's practised eye: she scented a mystery and was concerned to fathom it.

Just then, the Baron de la Roche-Hugon, who had questioned all the dowagers in turn with no success in learning the name of the lady in blue, was despairingly addressing himself as a last resort to the Comtesse de Gondreville, and receiving no more satisfactory answer for his pains than: 'She's a lady that the *ancient* Duchesse de Lansac presented to me.' Chancing to turn towards the chair that the old lady occupied, the Master of Requests surprised the conspiratorial glance cast at the stranger, and, although he had been on rather bad terms with her for some time, he resolved to tackle her. When she saw the gay Baron prowling near, the old Duchess smiled with sardonic malice and looked at Madame de Vaudremont in a way which made Colonel Montcornet laugh.

'If the old character adopts a friendly attitude,' the Baron mused, 'she is probably about to play me some nasty trick. – Madame,' he said, 'they tell me you are entrusted with the guardianship of a very precious treasure!'

'Do you take me for a dragon?' asked the old lady. 'But

whom are you referring to?' she added, with a kindness in her
voice which gave Martial renewed hope.

'That little stranger whom all these coquettes in their
jealousy have kept prisoner over there. You probably know
her family?'

'Yes,' said the Duchess; 'but what do you want of a provincial heiress, married some time ago, a girl of good family
whom you men about Paris don't know, for she goes no-
where?'

'Why isn't she dancing? She is so beautiful! Will you make a
peace treaty with me? If you are pleased to give me information about everything that it concerns me to know, I swear
that a petition for the restitution of the Navarreins woodlands
will find strong backing when the Emperor comes to consider it.'

The younger branch of the Navarreins family quarters the
Lansac arms: *azure, a baton argent between six spearheads three and
three of the second*, and the old lady's liaison with Louis XV had
given her the title of Duchess by Royal Decree; and, the
Navarreins not having returned to France yet, the young
Master of Requests was smoothly proposing barefaced robbery to the old lady, in insinuating that she should demand the
return of property belonging to the elder branch.

'Monsieur,' replied the old lady with deceptive gravity,
'bring me the Comtesse de Vaudremont. I promise you that
I'll unfold the mystery that makes our stranger so interesting,
to her. Look, all the men in the ballroom have reached the
same pitch of curiosity about her as you. Their eyes turn involuntarily towards the candelabrum where my *protégée* has
modestly stationed herself; she reaps all the homage that those
women wanted to deprive her of. Happy the man whom she
takes as a dancing partner!' There she broke off to stare at the
Comtesse de Vaudremont with one of those fixed looks that
say so clearly: 'We are talking of you.' Then she added: 'I
think that you would rather hear the stranger's name from the
lips of your lovely Countess than from mine?'

The Duchess's attitude was so provocative that Madame de
Vaudremont rose, walked across the room to her, sat down on

the chair which Martial offered her; and, without paying any attention to him, said to her with a laugh: 'I think, Madame, you are talking about me; but I confess I'm not very clever at guesswork, I don't know whether your comments are favourable or the reverse.'

Madame de Lansac clasped the young woman's pretty hand with her own old, dry and wrinkled, paw, and with a note of pity in her tone answered in a low voice: 'Poor child!'

The two women looked at one another. Madame de Vaudremont understood that Martial was not wanted, and dismissed him, saying imperiously: 'Leave us!'

The Master of Requests, ill-pleased to see the Countess under the spell of the dangerous sibyl who had drawn her to her side, cast one of those masterful looks at her whose effect is powerful on a blindly infatuated heart, but which appear ridiculous to a woman once she has begun to consider coolly the man whom she has lost her heart to.

'Can you intend to mimic the Emperor?' said Madame de Vaudremont, putting her head on one side and contemplating the Master of Requests mockingly.

Martial was too experienced in the ways of the world, had too much finesse and calculation, to risk a breach with a woman in such high favour at court, whose marriage the Emperor was anxious to arrange; he counted, besides, on awakening her jealousy as the best means of finding out the reason for her coldness, and departed the more willingly as at that moment a new quadrille had set everybody moving. The Baron appeared to be making way for the dancers.

He went to lean against a marble console-table, crossed his arms on his chest, and stayed there with all his attention fixed on the conversation between the two ladies. From time to time his eyes followed the glances that they both several times cast at the stranger. Then, as he compared the Countess with this new beauty whom mystery made so alluring, the Baron gave himself up to the odious calculations which become habitual in men who make conquests easily: he hesitated between a fortune there for the taking, and the gratification of his whim. The reflected lights showed up his care-ridden and sombre face so clearly against the white watered-silk hangings brushed by his dark hair that he could have been compared to some evil spirit. Across the room more than one observer must have been saying to himself: 'There's another poor devil who's supposed to be enjoying himself!'

Colonel Montcornet, his right shoulder lightly supported against the frame of the door leading from the ballroom to the card-room, could laugh unobserved under his ample moustaches: he was enjoying the pleasure of watching the movement and hubbub of the ball. He saw a hundred charming heads turned about, this way and then that, as the caprice of the dance dictated. On some countenances, such as those of the Countess and his friend Martial, he read their secret agitation. Then, turning his head, he asked himself what connexion there was between the melancholy air of the Comte de Soulanges, still sitting on his settee, and the mysterious lady's plaintive face, across which the joys of hope and the anguish of involuntary terror chased each other in turn. Montcornet stood there like the king of all he surveyed. In this animated scene he found a complete conspectus of the social world, and he laughed at it as he harvested the interested smiles of dozens of women, bejewelled and adorned. A Colonel of the Imperial Guard, a position that carried the rank of brigadier-general, was certainly one of the most eligible bachelors in the Army. It was almost midnight. Conversation, gaming, dancing, flirtation, jockeying for advantage, calculation, malicious observation and remark were all warming up to that ardent temperature which impels a young man to exclaim 'What fun balls are!'

'My dear little angel,' Madame de Lansac was saying to the Countess, 'you are at an age when I made many mistakes. When I saw you just now enduring torture it occurred to me to give you some charitable advice. Making mistakes at twenty-two means spoiling one's future, tearing the dress that one will have to wear, isn't that so? My dear, we only learn well on in life to use our dress without crumpling it. Continue, my angel, to gather clever enemies around you and friends without any idea of civilized behaviour, and you will see what kind of nice little life you will come to lead one day.'

'Ah, Madame, it's very difficult for a woman to be happy, isn't it?' cried the Countess naïvely.

'You need to be able to choose between pleasures and happiness at your age, child. You want to marry Martial, who is neither stupid enough to make a good husband, nor ardent enough for a lover. He has debts, my dear; he's a man who could consume your whole fortune; but that would be nothing if he made you happy. Do you not see how old he looks? That man must often have suffered the effects of dissipation; he's making the best of what remains to him. In three years he'll be a finished man. He aspires high, and will take the first steps easily; possibly he may succeed. But I do not think so. Who is he? An adventurer who may possess a marvellously exact sense of the right and profitable thing to do and know how to tattle agreeably; but he is too confident and vain to have real merit, he will not go far. Besides, just look at him! Is it not easy to read his face and see that at this moment it is not a young and pretty woman that he sees in you, but the two millions that you possess? He does not love you, my dear, he makes selfish plans about you, as if you were part of a business transaction. If you want to marry, choose an older man, who has learned consideration and reached the half way milestone on his road. A widow should not make her marriage a light-hearted love affair. Does a mouse get caught in the same trap twice? At this point a new contract should be an investment for you, and you ought when you marry to have at least a prospect of one day finding yourself a Marshal's wife.'

The eyes of the two women turned naturally towards the handsome figure of Colonel Montcornet.

'If you want to play the difficult rôle of coquette and refuse to marry,' the Duchess went on, with genial kindness, 'ah! my poor child, you better than anyone will know how to make tempestuous clouds fill the sky, and how to dispel them. But I adjure you, never to make it your pleasure to disturb a young couple's peace, to destroy family unity, and the happiness of women who are content. I have played that dangerous rôle, my dear. Ah, yes indeed! for a triumph of one's vanity one often murders the happiness of poor virtuous creatures;

for virtuous women exist, my dear, and one creates mortal
enmities. Rather too late I learned that, as the Duke of Alba
put it, one salmon is worth more than a thousand frogs!
Certainly a true affection gives a thousand times greater joy
than the ephemeral passions that one may arouse. Well, I came
here to preach you a sermon. Yes, indeed, you are the cause of
my appearance in this ballroom, which stinks of the vulgar
crowd. Have I not just seen actors here? Once, my dear, we
received them in our boudoir, but as for our drawing-rooms –
unthinkable! Why do you look at me in such astonishment?

'Listen to me,' the old lady continued, 'if you must make
fools of men, only turn upside-down the hearts of those whose
life is not marked out, those who have no duties to fulfil: the
others do not forgive us for the disturbances we create even
though we may have made them happy. Let that maxim, the
fruit of my long experience, be of use to you. That poor Soulanges, for example, whose head you have turned, and whom
you have been intoxicating for the last fifteen months, heaven
knows how! Do you know where your blows have fallen? On
his whole life! He was married two and a half years ago, he is
adored by a charming creature whom he loves and betrays;
she lives in tears and the most bitter silence. Soulanges has had
moments of cruel remorse more intense than the sweetness of
his pleasure. And you, my sly one, you have betrayed him.
Well, come and see your work.'

The old Duchess took Madame de Vaudremont by the hand
and they rose.

'There,' said Madame de Lansac, with her eyes indicating
the stranger, pale and trembling under the light poured down
by the candles, 'that's my grand-niece, the Comtesse de Soulanges. She at last yielded to my entreaties today and consented
to leave the room in which she was sitting mourning, where
the sight of her child brought her only very feeble consolation.
Do you see her? – She looks charming, doesn't she? Well,
my dear little belle, judge what she must have been like when
love and happiness shed their radiance on this now stricken
face.'

The Countess silently turned away her head and seemed to

be gravely reflecting. The Duchess led her to the door of the card-room; then, after glancing round it as if in search of someone: 'And there is Soulanges,' she said, in a tone of deep feeling.

The Countess started when she caught sight in the most ill-lit corner of the room of Soulanges leaning back on his sofa, his features pale and drawn. His limp attitude and blank expressionless face gave an impression of acute suffering: the players came and went before him, paying him no more attention than if he had been dead. The picture presented by these two persons, the wife in tears and the sad and sombre husband, separated from each other in the midst of the ballroom gaiety, like the halves of a tree split by lightning, impressed itself on the Countess's mind, perhaps with a threat of being prophetic. She feared to see in it a reflection of vengeance that the future might hold in store for her. Her heart had not yet grown so callous as to have entirely banished sensibility and kindness. She pressed the Duchess's hand and thanked her with a smile which held a certain youthful grace.

'My dear child,' said the older woman in a low voice, 'from now on remember that it is no more difficult for us to repulse men's homage than it is for us to attract it.

'She is yours, if you don't throw your chances away.'

These last words Madame de Lansac whispered in Colonel Montcornet's ear, while the lovely Countess was lost in compassion as she watched Soulanges, for she still loved him sincerely enough to wish to make him happy, and was declaring in her inner mind that she would use the irresistible power that she still possessed over him, to send him back to his wife.

'Oh! what a sermon I shall preach him!' she said to Madame de Lansac.

'Do nothing of the kind, my dear,' exclaimed the Duchess, settling herself again in her armchair. 'Choose a good husband, and close your door to my nephew. Don't even offer him your friendship. Believe me, child, a woman does not accept her husband's heart from another woman's hands; she is a hundred times happier to believe that she has reconquered it herself. By bringing my niece here, I think I have shown her an excellent means of regaining her husband's affection. All the help I ask from you is that you should go and tease the General.'

And when the Duchess waved her hand in the direction of the Master of Requests' friend, the Countess smiled.

'Well, Madame, do you know the name of the mysterious stranger at last?' the Baron moodily inquired of the Countess when she was alone.

'Yes,' said Madame de Vaudremont, looking at him.

Her expression was mischievous and gay. The smile that curved her lips and rounded her cheek with lively pleasure, the limpid brightness of her eyes, were like the will-o'-the-wisps that mislead the traveller. Martial, who believed that she still loved him, assumed the provocative attitude a man adopts so complacently in the company of someone he loves, and said fatuously:

'And you won't bear me ill-will if I seem to attach a great deal of importance to learning that name?'

'And you won't bear me ill-will,' replied Madame de Vaudremont, 'if, through the last shred and tatter of my love, I do not tell you it? and if I forbid you to make the least approach to that lady? It might cost you your life.'

'To lose your favour, Madame, would that not mean more than losing life?'

'Martial,' said the Countess severely, 'that is Madame de Soulanges. Her husband would blow your brains out, if you have any, that is.'

'Oho!' the coxcomb replied with a laugh. 'The Colonel will allow the man who took your heart from him to live in peace, but would fight for his wife. What a reversal of principles! I implore you, give me your leave to dance with that little lady. So you will have proof of how little love that frozen heart held for you; for if the Colonel does not approve of my dancing with his wife after letting you ...'

'But she loves her husband.'

'Another obstacle in the way that I shall have the pleasure of demolishing.'

'But she is a married woman!'

'That's an odd objection!'

'Ah!' said the Countess, with a bitter smile, 'you punish us both for our sins and our regrets for them.'

'Don't be angry,' said Martial swiftly. 'Oh! I beg you, forgive me. Here, I don't give another thought to Madame de Soulanges.'

'It would serve you right if I sent you to her.'

'I'm off,' said the Baron, laughing; 'and I'll come back more in love with you than ever. You shall see that the prettiest woman in the world cannot seize a heart that belongs to you.'

'Which means that you want to win the Colonel's charger.'

'Ah! the tell-tale,' he replied, laughing and shaking a menacing finger at his friend, who was smiling at them.

The Colonel joined them. The Baron gave up his place by the Countess to him, but said to her sardonically:

'Madame, here's a man who boasts that he can win your favour in an evening.'

He congratulated himself as he walked away on having set the Countess's pride up in arms and done the Colonel an ill turn, but in spite of his normally subtle intelligence he had not guessed the irony that lay behind Madame de Vaudremont's remarks, and did not perceive that she had taken as many steps towards his friend as his friend had towards her, each unknown to the other.

As the Master of Requests approached and hovered about the candelabrum below which the Comtesse de Soulanges, pale and shrinking, seemed to live only through her eyes, her husband appeared at the ballroom door, his eyes blazing with passion. The old Duchess, whose eyes missed nothing, hurried to her nephew's side, and asked for his escort and his carriage home on the pretext that she was dying of boredom, and congratulated herself on thus averting a shocking scene. Before she left she made an oddly conspiratorial sign to her niece, indicating the enterprising gallant who was preparing to speak to her, a sign which appeared to say: 'Here he is, wreak your vengeance upon him.'

Madame de Vaudremont surprised the look exchanged

between aunt and niece; a sudden illumination lit her mind; she was afraid she had been duped by that old lady who was so wily and so practised in intrigue.

'That two-faced Duchess,' she said to herself, 'may perhaps have thought it a good joke to read me a lecture while she was playing me some malicious trick of her own.'

At this thought Madame de Vaudremont's vanity became perhaps even more acutely concerned than her curiosity to disentangle the thread of this intrigue. Her inner preoccupation left her for the moment not entirely mistress of herself. The Colonel, interpreting in his own favour the embarrassment which was evident in the Countess's words and manner, became all the more ardent and pressing. The diplomats, grown too old for pleasure, who enjoyed watching the play of expression on people's faces had never had so many intrigues to follow and guess at. Passions like those which racked the two intertangled pairs of partners were to be seen in different forms at every step in these animated rooms, expressed in a different degree and another colouring on other faces. The spectacle of so many living passions, all these lovers' quarrels, these sweet revenges, these cruel kindnesses, these blazing glances, all this burning life spread out before them, only made them feel the more keenly their own inability to share in it.

At last the Baron had managed to take a seat by the Comtesse de Soulanges's side. He glanced covertly at a dewy neck, sweet-scented as a meadow flower. Now from close at hand he admired beauty which had astonished him at the other side of the room. He could see a well-shod little foot, span with his eye a supple and graceful waist. At that period women knotted the girdle that held their dress just below the breast, in imitation of Greek statues, a pitiless mode for anyone whose figure was not flawless. Martial's stolen glances left him more enchanted than ever with the Countess's perfection.

'You have not danced once this evening, Madame,' he said blandly, in a tone designed to flatter. 'I imagine that it is not for want of partners.'

'I do not go out at all, I am not known in the fashionable world,' Madame de Soulanges replied with chilling indifference. She had not in the least understood the look with which her aunt had just invited her to fascinate the Baron.

To keep himself in countenance, Martial played with the fine diamond that adorned his left hand. The flashing fires of the stone seemed to flash sudden illumination into the young Countess's mind. She blushed and looked at the Baron with an expression difficult to read.

'Do you like dancing?' the young Provençal asked, trying to take up the conversation again.

'Oh! very much, Monsieur.'

At this strange reply, their eyes met. The young man, surprised at her emphatic tone which awoke an undefined hope in his heart, had suddenly questioned the young woman with his eyes.

'Well, Madame, is it perhaps too rash of me to propose myself as your partner in the next quadrille?'

A naïve confusion flushed the Countess's pale cheeks with red.

'But, Monsieur, I have already refused a partner, an Army man.'

'Was it that tall cavalry officer whom you see over there?'

'Yes indeed.'

'Oh! he's my friend, don't be afraid. Do you grant me the favour I hope for?'

'Yes, Monsieur.'

Her voice betrayed emotion so new, and so deep, that the Master of Requests' sated soul was shaken. He felt a schoolboy timidity overwhelm him, lost his self-possession, his southerner's senses catching fire. He sought for something to say; everything he said seemed awkwardly framed and clumsy compared with Madame de Soulanges's polished and pointed replies. Happily for him, the dance soon began. Standing near his beautiful partner, he felt more at ease. For many men dancing is a series of poses: they think by displaying the graces of their persons to impress women's hearts more effectively than they can by the exercise of their intelligence. The Provençal no doubt wished to make use of every possible means of charming, to judge by the studied grace of all his

c

movements and gestures. He had led his conquest to the
set in which, in preference to any other, the most brilliant
women in the room thought it fantastically important that
they should be seen dancing.

While the orchestra played the prelude to the first figure, a
thrill of gratified pride exhilarating beyond belief swept
through the Baron as, passing the dancers lined up in this
formidable set in review, he saw that Madame de Soulanges in
her finery was second to none, not even to Madame de Vaudremont, who by a chance, possibly deliberate, with the
Colonel formed the opposite pair to the Baron and the lady
in blue.

All eyes were fixed for the moment on Madame de Soulanges: a flattering buzz announced that she was the subject of
conversation with each pair of partners. Envious or admiring
glances were focused so relentlessly on her that, abashed at a
triumph which she seemed to deprecate, the young woman
modestly lowered her eyes, blushed, and looked all the more
charming. She raised her white eyelids only to look at her
partner, whose head was spinning, as if she were anxious to
offer up the glory of this homage to him, and to tell him that
she preferred his homage to all others. Innocence was mingled
with her coquetry, or rather she seemed to give herself up to
the naïve admiration which is the first step in love, with the
sincerity only met with in young hearts. When she danced, the
spectators could easily believe that it was only for Martial that
she displayed these graces; and although she was demure and
new to drawing-room arts, she knew as well as the most
skilled coquette how to raise her eyes at the right moment to
his, and lower them with pretended shyness. When the new
figures of a set invented by the dancer Trénis, to which he
gave his name, brought Martial in front of the Colonel: 'I
have won your horse!' he said to him laughing.

'Yes, but you have lost eighty thousand livres a year,' the
Colonel replied, glancing at Madame de Vaudremont.

'And what do I care!' answered Martial. 'Madame de Soulanges is worth millions.'

At the end of this quadrille, more than one whisper buzzed

in more than one ear. The less attractive women moralized disapprovingly for the benefit of their partners, with the dawning liaison between Martial and the Countess de Soulanges as their text. The more beautiful were astonished at such an easy conquest. The men could not understand the good fortune of the little Master of Requests, in whom they could see nothing very fascinating. A few forbearing women said that one should not judge the Countess too hastily; it would be very unfortunate for girls if an expressive glance or a few gracefully executed dance-steps were enough to compromise a woman! Only Martial knew the full extent of his luck. In the last figure, when the ladies had to form the 'mill', his hand held the Countess's, and through the fine scented skin of her gloves it seemed to him that her fingers were responsive to his pressure.

'Madame,' he said, when the dance ended, 'don't go back to that odious corner where your face and your beautiful dress have been buried until now. Is admiration the only harvest you can gather from the jewels which adorn your white neck and your gracefully dressed hair? Come, make a tour of the rooms and enjoy the festive gathering and your own beauty.'

Madame de Soulanges followed her charmer, whose thought was that she would be more surely his if he publicly paraded their interest in one another. Together they took several turns among the groups which thronged the various reception-rooms of the mansion. The Comtesse de Soulanges paused a moment uneasily on the threshold of each room, and stretched her neck to look about at all the men before entering. This fear, which filled the little Master of Requests' cup of pleasure to the brim, appeared to be dispelled only when he said to his apprehensive companion: 'Set your mind at rest. *He* is not here.'

They came in this way to an immense picture-gallery, placed in a wing of the building, where they had a preview of the splendours of a magnificent collation prepared for three hundred persons. As the meal was about to begin, Martial drew the Countess to an oval boudoir giving on the gardens, where exotic flowers and flowering shrubs formed a scented grove under sparkling blue hangings. The hubbub of the ball died away there to a murmur. The Countess hesitated at the entrance and seemed determined not to follow the young man, until, glancing in a mirror, she no doubt saw that there were others present, for she came with a good enough grace to sit on an ottoman.

'This is a delightful room,' she said, admiring a hanging the colour of the sky, sewn with pearls.

'All here is love and pleasure,' said the young man, deeply moved.

Under cover of the mysterious half-light that prevailed in the room he glanced at the Countess, and found her face expressing a mixture of doubt, shyness, and desire which enchanted him. The young woman smiled, and the smile seemed to decide and put an end to the conflict of feelings in her heart. She most beguilingly raised her adorer's left hand, and from his finger took the ring which had arrested her glance.

'What a lovely diamond!' she exclaimed with the naïvety of a girl undisguisedly tantalized by a first temptation.

Martial, stirred by the involuntary but intoxicating touch of the Countess's fingers as she took the ring, turned eyes to her which sparkled like the diamond.

'Wear it,' he said, 'in memory of this hour of heaven, and for love of ...'

She contemplated him with such delight that he could not finish; he kissed her hand.

'You are giving it to me?' she said, in astonishment.

'I wish that I could give you the whole world.'

'You are not joking,' she said again, her voice shaken by a feeling of gratification too keen to bear.

'Do you accept only my diamond?'

'You will never ask it from me again?' she asked.

'Never.'

She put the ring on her finger. Martial, sure of immediate victory, moved as if to place his hand on the Countess's waist. She rose at once and said in a clear voice and quite without emotion:

'Monsieur, I accept this ring with fewer scruples since it is my own.'

The Master of Requests stared, dumbfounded.

'Monsieur de Soulanges took it from my dressing-table recently, and told me he had lost it.'

'You are mistaken, Madame,' said Martial offendedly. 'I have it from Madame de Vaudremont.'

'Precisely,' she answered with a smile. 'My husband borrowed this ring from me and gave it to her. She made you a present of it. My ring has travelled, that is all. This ring will perhaps tell me all the things I don't know, and teach me the secret of how to please always. If it had not been my ring, Monsieur,' she went on, 'you may be sure I would not have risked paying so dearly for it, for a young woman, they say, is in a dangerous position in your company. But, look,' she added, pressing a spring concealed beneath the stone; 'Monsieur de Soulanges's hair is still here.'

She hastened away through the various rooms with such speed that it seemed useless to try to catch her up; and, besides, the discomfited Martial did not find himself in the humour to undertake any such enterprise. Madame de Soulanges's laugh had had an echo in the boudoir, and, looking between two bushes, the young exquisite saw the Colonel and Madame de Vaudremont laughing whole-heartedly.

'Would you like my charger to pursue your conquest?' asked the Colonel.

The good grace with which the Baron bore the teasing which Madame de Vaudremont and Montcornet did not spare him, won for him their discreet silence about this evening when his friend had risked losing his charger but had hoped to win a young, rich, and pretty woman.

The Comtesse de Soulanges traversed the distance that separated the Chaussée-d'Antin and the Faubourg Saint-Germain where she lived with a heart full of the most painful anxiety. Before leaving the Hôtel de Gondreville she had walked through the rooms without seeing either her aunt or her husband, who had left without her. Horrible misgivings then came to torment her unsophisticated soul. As a quiet witness of her husband's suffering from the day when Madame de Vaudremont attached him to her chariot, she had

confidently looked forward to an early repentance bringing her
husband back to her. And so it was with extreme reluctance
that she had consented to the plan that her aunt, Madame de
Lansac, had devised; and now she was afraid that she had
done wrong. This evening had clouded her candid soul with
sadness. She had first been alarmed by the Comte de Soulanges's air of suffering and sombre gloom, then even more
keenly by her rival's beauty; and the world's corruption had
oppressed her heart.

Driving over the Pont-Royal, she threw away the desecrated
hair from under the diamond, given once as a token of pure
love. She wept as she remembered the long days she had had
to endure of such keen suffering, and shuddered more than
once as she reflected that wives who desire to have domestic
peace must bury pain as cruel as hers in the depths of their
heart, without complaint.

'Alas!' she said to herself, 'what do wives do when they are
not in love? Where can they get the strength to be forbearing?
I cannot believe that reason is enough, as my aunt says, to
sustain them in such loyalty in such a plight.'

She was still lost in sad reflection when her footman lowered
the smart carriage-step for her before her house. She hurried
under the porch and went precipitately upstairs; and when she
reached her room, it was with a thrill of terror that she saw
her husband sitting there by the fire.

'Since when, my dear, do you go to the ball without me,
without telling me?' he demanded, in a troubled voice.
'Please note that a woman always looks out of place without
her husband. You were singularly exposed to comment in
that dark corner where you were hiding.'

'Oh, dear Léon,' she said caressingly, 'I couldn't resist the
pleasure of seeing you without your seeing me. My aunt took
me to the ball, and I enjoyed it very much.'

The Count was disarmed by this, and his gaze lost its forced
severity, forced, for he had been reproaching himself sharply,
fearing his wife's return with the information which she had
no doubt received at the ball, of an infidelity he had hoped to
hide from her; and, in the manner of lovers with guilty con-

sciences, he was trying, by blaming the Countess first, to
evade her only too just anger. He silently looked at his wife:
in her ball-dress and brilliant jewels she seemed to him more
beautiful than ever. Happy to see her husband smiling, and to
find him at this hour in a room where for some time he had
come less frequently, the Countess looked at him so tenderly
that she blushed for it and lowered her eyes.

Soulanges found this clemency all the more elating because
the scene followed the tortures he had experienced during the
ball. He seized his wife's hand and kissed it, in gratitude. Is not
gratitude often an element in love?

'Hortense, what is that on your finger that hurts my lip?'
he asked, with a laugh.

'It is my diamond ring that you said was lost, and that I
have found again.'

General Montcornet did not ever marry Madame de
Vaudremont, in spite of the good understanding that had been
established between them shortly before; for she was one of
the victims of the dreadful fire which made for ever memor-
able the ball which the Austrian Ambassador gave, to celebrate the marriage of the Emperor Napoleon to the daughter
of the Emperor François II.

July 1829

THE YOUNG CONSCRIPT

*

Sometimes they saw him, by a phenomenon of vision or movement,
abolish distance in its two forms of time and space.
Intellectual History of Louis Lambert

ONE evening in November 1793 the leading inhabitants of
Carentan were gathered in Madame de Dey's drawing-
room, which was where they were wont to have their *assembly*
every day. Certain circumstances which would have passed
entirely unnoticed in a large town, but were bound to attract
the absorbed attention of a little one, lent this usual meeting
an unaccustomed interest. Two days before, Madame de Dey
had been 'not at home' to her circle, and she had excused
herself from receiving them on the previous evening too,
pleading an indisposition.

Even in normal times these two events would have had the
same effect in Carentan as is produced in Paris by suspension
of the performance at all the theatres. On such days existence
is in some sort incomplete. But in 1793 Madame de Dey's behaviour could have the most deadly consequences. For people
of noble birth to venture to take the slightest unusual step
then, became nearly always a matter of life and death.

If the reader is to understand the lively curiosity and the
close calculation that animated the Norman countenances of all
these persons during that evening, and above all if he is to
share Madame de Dey's secret perplexities, the rôle which she
played at Carentan must be explained to him. Her critical position at that moment was no doubt a position that many people
found themselves in during the Revolution, and the sympathies of more than one reader will fill in and add colour to
this narrative.

Madame de Dey, widow of a lieutenant-general, a *chevalier
des ordres*, had left the Court when people began to flee the
country. As she possessed a considerable estate near Carentan
she had taken refuge there, hoping that there the effect of the

Reign of Terror would be little felt. This expectation, based on an exact knowledge of the country, proved well founded. The Revolution did little havoc in lower Normandy. Although Madame de Dey had been accustomed to see only the aristocratic families of the district when she used to pay visits to her country estates, she had offered hospitality to the chief citizens of the town and the new authorities, as a matter of policy, and did her best to make them proud of having made a conquest of her, without awakening hatred or jealousy in them. She was gracious and kind, and endowed with that indescribable charm which enables a woman to please without being over-conciliatory or insincere, so that she had succeeded in winning general esteem; and the exercise of exquisite tact, and the delicate perception which made its use possible, had allowed her to hold her course along the narrow way within which alone she could meet the requirements of this mixed society, without humiliating the touchy self-esteem of the *parvenus* on the one hand, or shocking the pride of her former friends on the other.

At about thirty-eight years of age she was still beautiful, not with the fresh, plump good looks that distinguish the girls of lower Normandy, but with a refined and, so to speak, aristocratic beauty. Her features were fine and delicate, her figure lithe and active. When she spoke, her pale face seemed to light up and take on animation. Her large dark eyes were full of kindness, but their calm, dedicated expression seemed to make it plain that the mainspring of her life no longer lay within herself. She had been married in her prime to an old and jealous soldier, and the falsity of her position in a gaily amoral Court had no doubt contributed much to the dropping of a veil of grave melancholy over this face where the charm and vivacity of love must have sparkled earlier.

She had been continually forced to repress a woman's impulses and emotions at an age when she is a sentient being rather than a reflective one, and passion still lay unawakened in her heart. And so her most attractive quality was the essential youthfulness which showed from time to time in her expression and which gave her thoughts an innocent colouring of desire. Her reserve compelled respect, but there was always in her attitude, in her voice, a note of eager aspiration towards an unknown future, as there is in a young girl. The most unsusceptible of men easily and early fell in love with her, yet preserved a kind of respectful awe of her, imposed by her polished manners, which held them at a distance. Her soul, great by nature and fortified by cruel struggle, seemed set too far aloof from the common herd, and men did not flatter themselves. For this soul nothing less than a noble passion would do.

And so indeed all Madame de Dey's power of feeling had been concentrated in one single affection, for her son. The happiness and joy she had been deprived of as a wife she found in the intense love she bore this boy. She loved him not only with a mother's unmixed and deep devotion, but with the coquetry of a mistress and the jealousy of a wife. Apart from him she was unhappy; she was anxious about him during his absences, never saw enough of him, lived only in him and for him. To make men understand the strength of this attachment, it will be enough to add that the boy was not only Madame de Dey's only child, but her last living relative, the only human being to whom she could attach the fears, hopes, and joys of her life. The late Comte de Dey was the last scion of his family, and she herself had become the sole heiress of hers. So ordinary human calculations and interests had combined with the noblest needs of her soul, to force the growth in the Countess of an affection already naturally rooted so strongly in women's hearts. It was only with infinite pains that she had succeeded in rearing her son, and this had made him even more precious to her. A score of times the doctors had shaken their heads and foretold that she would lose him. But she had had instinctive confidence, had been strong in her hopes, and she had the inexpressible joy of seeing him safely traverse the perils of childhood, and marvelling at the improvement in his constitution, in spite of the pronouncements of the learned doctors.

Thanks to constant care, this son had grown to manhood, and his development had been so pleasing that at twenty he was regarded as one of the most accomplished young noble-men at Versailles. Finally, by a happy dispensation that does not crown the efforts of every mother, her son adored her. Their souls had a fraternal understanding and sympathy with one another. If they had not been already bound by a natural tie, they would instinctively have felt for each other a friend-ship as between man and man of that kind which is so rarely met with in life. Appointed Sub-lieutenant of Dragoons at eighteen, the young Count had followed the Princes into exile, as it was regarded as a point of honour at the time to do.

Madame de Dey, then, rich, of noble birth, and mother of an *émigré*, did not blind herself to the dangers of her cruel situation. Only because she was anxious to preserve a great fortune for her son had she given up the happiness of going with him; and she saw reason to congratulate herself on this courageous act when she read the rigorous laws in virtue of which the Republic every day confiscated the lands of *émigrés* at Carentan. Was she not, at the peril of her life, the guardian of her son's riches? Then when she learned of the terrible executions decreed by the Convention, she went to sleep at night happy in the knowledge that her only wealth was safe, far from dangers, far from scaffolds. She took pleasure in re-flecting that she had adopted the course best calculated to save all her treasures. In this secret thought she made the conces-sions required by the evil times, without compromising her dignity as a woman or her beliefs as an aristocrat, and she wrapped her sorrows in a veil of reticence and mystery.

She had understood the difficulties which awaited her at Carentan. Did not coming here to fill the leading place mean defying the scaffold every day? But, sustained by a mother's courage, she was able to gain the affection of the poor, reliev-ing all distress without distinction of persons, and make her-self indispensable to the rich by her attentive regard for their pleasures. She received the Procurator of the Commune, the Mayor, the President of the District Court, the Public Prosecu-tor, and even the Judges of the Revolutionary Tribunal. The first four of these persons were bachelors and were courting her; and they hoped to win her hand either by frightening her with the thought of the harm they had the power to do her, or by offering her their protection. The Public Prosecutor, formerly a solicitor in Caen who had once looked after the Countess's interests, was trying to inspire love by behaving with the greatest devotion and generosity. A dangerously subtle approach! He was the most to be feared of all the suitors. He was the only person who knew all the facts about the state of his former client's considerable fortune. His passion was bound to be increased by all the desires of an avarice which was backed by immense power, the right to decide matters of life and death in the district. This man, still young, displayed such admirable nobility of character in his dealings with Madame de Dey that she had not yet been able to form a conclusive opinion about him. But, heedless of the danger of trying to outwit Normans at their own wily game, she was making use of the ingenuity and guile with which women are naturally endowed to play the rivals off, one against the other. She hoped by gaining time to reach the end of her troubles safe and sound. At that period the Royalists who remained in the country looked every day to see the Revolution ended on the day after, and this sure expectation of theirs was the cause of the death of many of them....

In spite of these difficulties the Countess had maintained her independence adroitly enough until the day when, with inexplicable rashness, she had taken it into her head to be 'not at home'. The interest which she inspired was so keen and so genuine that the persons who had come to call on her that evening were filled with a lively concern when they heard that it was impossible for her to receive them. Then, with the frank curiosity that marks country manners, they inquired about the misfortune or sorrow or illness which must be afflicting Madame de Dey. To these questions an old housekeeper, called Brigitte, replied that her mistress had shut herself up in her room and would see no one, not even her household servants.

The, in some ways, cloistral existence led by the inhabitants of a small town creates in them a habit of analysing and explaining other people's actions so naturally unconquerable that when they had compassionated Madame de Dey, without knowing whether she was actually happy or sad, everyone began to consider what the causes of her sudden retirement into seclusion might be.

'If she was ill,' said the first curious inquirer, 'she would have sent for the doctor; but the doctor has spent the whole day at my house, playing chess. He said to me, laughing, that as things go nowadays there's only one illness ... and that unfortunately is incurable.'

This pleasantry was cautiously ventured. Then women and men, old grey-beards and young girls, set themselves to quarter the vast field of conjecture. Everyone thought that he had got wind of a secret, and this secret kept every imagination busy. On the morrow suspicions became inflamed. As life has no privacy in a small town, the women were the first to learn that Brigitte had made more substantial purchases than usual in the market. This fact was incontrovertible. Brigitte had been seen very early in the market square and, an extraordinary thing, had bought the only hare that there was for sale. The whole town knew that Madame de Dey did not care for game. The hare became the point of departure for infinite flights of fancy. As they took their constitutional, old men observed a kind of concentrated activity in the Countess's house, which betrayed itself by the very precautions the servants took to hide it. The man-servant was beating a carpet in the garden; the day before no one would have paid any attention to the fact; but this carpet became a piece of evidence in support of the romances that the whole town was fabricating. Everyone had his own version.

On the second day, when they had learned that Madame de Dey said she was indisposed, the leading citizens of Carentan met in the evening at the house of the Mayor's brother, a married man, a retired wholesale merchant, and a man of integrity who was held in general esteem, and for whom the Countess had a great deal of regard. There, all the aspirants to the rich widow's hand had a story, more or less likely, to put forward; and each of them was thinking of how he could turn the secret circumstance which was forcing her to compromise herself in this way to his advantage. The Public Prosecutor invented a whole drama, bringing Madame de Dey's son to her house under cover of night. The Mayor believed in a nonjuror priest, come from La Vendée and asking for asylum; but he was quite at a loss to explain the purchase of a hare, on a Friday. The President was strongly in favour of a Breton insurgent chief or Royalist leader from La Vendée on the run and closely beset. Others leaned towards an aristocrat escaped from Paris prisons. They all, in fact, suspected the Countess of complicity in one of those generous actions which the laws of the time called crimes, and which could bring one to the scaffold. The Public Prosecutor said, indeed, in a low voice, that they must hold their tongues and try to save the unfortunate woman from the abyss towards which she was rushing.

'If you spread rumours about this business,' he added, 'I shall be obliged to intervene, and make a search of her house, and then!...'

He did not finish his sentence, but everyone understood what was left unsaid.

The Countess's sincere friends were so alarmed on her account that on the morning of the third day the Attorney-Syndic of the Commune caused his wife to write to her, urging her to receive visitors that evening, as usual. The retired merchant, more daring still, presented himself at Madame de Dey's door in the course of the morning. Given courage by the service which he was anxious to render her, he demanded to be shown in to her, and was dumbfounded when he saw her in the garden, busy cutting the last flowers in her flower-beds to fill her vases.

'She must be sheltering her lover,' the old man said to himself, seized with pity for this charming woman.

The singular expression on the Countess's face confirmed his suspicions. Deeply touched by her devotion, a devotion so natural in women, but which we are always moved by because all men are flattered by the sacrifices which a woman makes for one man, the merchant informed the Countess of the rumours which were current in the town, and of the risk she ran.

'For,' he said in conclusion, 'there may be some of our officials ready enough to pardon a heroic action undertaken for the sake of a priest, but no one would sympathize with you if it should come to light that you were sacrificing yourself because your heart was involved.'

When she heard this Madame de Dey stared at him with a wild lost look which sent a cold thrill through him, old man as he was.

'Come,' she said, taking his hand to lead him to her room, where, when she had made sure that they were alone, she drew a dirty tattered letter from her bosom. 'Read it!' she exclaimed making a violent effort to utter the words.

She fell into her armchair, as if fainting. While the old merchant was looking for his glasses and rubbing them, she raised her eyes and looked at him for the first time with curiosity; then in a faltering voice, 'I trust you,' she said gently.

'Haven't I come to have a share in your crime?' the old fellow answered simply.

She gave a start. For the first time in this little town her heart felt sympathy in another's. The old man soon understood both the Countess's feverish tension and her joy. Her son had taken part in the siege of Granville; he wrote to his mother from the depths of his prison and gave her a sweet but desperate hope. He was sure of being able to escape, and named three successive days on which he was likely to appear at her door, in disguise. The fateful letter said goodbye in heart-rending terms in case he should not have arrived in Carentan by the evening of the third day, and he begged his mother to give a handsome reward to the messenger who had undertaken to bring her this note through a host of dangers. The paper trembled in the old man's hands.

'And this is the third day!' cried Madame de Dey, jumping to her feet. She took the letter and began to walk up and down.

'You have done some rash things,' said the merchant. 'Why did you lay in provisions?'

'But he may be arriving dying of hunger, utterly exhausted, and ...' Her voice died away.

'I am sure of my brother,' the old man went on. 'I will go and enlist his sympathies on your behalf.'

Faced with this situation, the merchant found that he had not lost the astuteness which he had once put to good use in his business affairs, and he gave the Countess notably wise and sound advice as to the course she should adopt. When they had agreed on what they should both say and do, the old man, on one easily found pretext or another, visited the principal households in Carentan and announced that Madame de Dey, whom he had just seen, would receive visitors that evening, in spite of her indisposition. In a battle of wits with the Norman intelligences opposed to him, in the interrogation which each family subjected him to as to the nature of the Countess's illness, he successfully put on the wrong scent nearly all the people whose powers of conjecture were busy with this mysterious affair. His first visit worked wonders. He related before an old lady who suffered much from gout that Madame de Dey had nearly died of an attack of gout which had affected her stomach. The famous Tronchin had once in a similar attack recommended the placing of the skin of a hare flayed alive on her chest, and absolute rest in bed without her lifting a finger or moving a muscle; and now the Countess, who had followed this extraordinary prescription of Tronchin's to the letter, after being at death's door for the last two days, found herself sufficiently recovered to receive those who might come to see her during the evening.

This tale had a prodigious success, and the Carentan doctor, a Royalist *in petto*, increased its effect by the weighty gravity with which he discussed the specific. But suspicion had taken too strong a hold in the minds of a few obstinate fellows and a few philosophers to be entirely rooted out; so that, that evening, those who were habitually received by Madame de Dey hastened early and eagerly to her house, some to keep a watch for what they could discover from her face, others in a spirit of friendship, and most people startled by the news of her surprising cure.

They found the Countess sitting at the corner of the great fireplace in her drawing-room, which was nearly as modest as

the drawing-rooms of Carentan. For in order to avoid shocking her guests' narrow-minded ideas of what was fitting, she
had denied herself the luxurious accessories which she had
been accustomed to enjoy. She had left this house as she had
found it. The floor of the reception-room was not even waxed.
She retained the gloomy old tapestries hanging on the walls,
kept the furniture made in the district in use, burned tallow
candles, and followed the ways of the town, embracing a provincial mode of life without shrinking from the most stringent
petty economies or the most disagreeable privations. But,
knowing that her guests would pardon her for splendours designed for their comfort, she left nothing undone that might
contribute to their personal enjoyment; thus she provided
them with excellent dinners. She went so far as to feign miserly
tendencies to please these cheese-paring spirits, and when she
had adroitly led them to express disapproval of some concessions to luxury, gracefully yielded to their ideas.

Towards seven o'clock in the evening, then, the cream of
Carentan's unpolished society was gathered in her house, in a
great circle round the fire. The mistress of the house, sustained
in this trial by sympathetic glances from the old merchant,
submitted herself with extraordinary courage to close questioning by her guests, and their silly and stupid comments.
But at every knock that sounded at her front door, every time
footsteps passed in the street, her agitation must be held in
check, while she talked, raising questions which were of interest and concern locally. She initiated lively discussion and dispute about the quality of ciders, and was so well seconded by
the sharer of her secret that the company almost forgot to keep
a watch on her, as they found her expression natural and her
self-possession imperturbable. The Public Prosecutor and one
of the Revolutionary Tribunal judges remained taciturn, kept
a keen eye open for the slightest changes in her face, lent an
ear to what was happening in the house, in spite of the babble
around them; and several times they shot embarrassing questions at her, to which the Countess replied with admirable
presence of mind. Mothers have so much courage!

When Madame de Dey had arranged card-tables, settled

everybody down to play boston or reversi or whist, she stayed talking unconcernedly and easily with a group of young people, playing her part like a consummate actress. She led up to a request from one of them for a lotto set, declared that she alone knew where it was, and disappeared.

'I'm stifling, my poor Brigitte!' she exclaimed, wiping away the tears which rose irrepressibly to eyes brilliant with feverish impatience and suffering. 'He's not come yet,' she went on, looking around the upstairs room. 'Here I can draw my breath and come to life. A few more minutes and he'll be here! For he is still alive; I'm sure of it. My heart tells me so. Do you not hear anything, Brigitte? Oh! I would give the rest of my life to know if he is in prison, or if he is walking across the fields. I wish I could stop thinking....'

She looked again to see if everything was in order in the room. A good fire burned on the hearth; the shutters were carefully closed; the furniture shone with polishing; by the way in which the bed had been made ready it was clear that the Countess as well as Brigitte had had a hand in the least details; and her hope and expectation were revealed by the loving pains that had been expended on this room, by the tender grace that caressed and laid love's benediction on it, and that breathed in the scent of the flowers. Only a mother could have foreseen a soldier's wishes and provided such complete satisfaction for them. A delicious meal, choice wines, clean linen, slippers – everything that a tired traveller might need or find pleasure in was assembled there so that he should lack nothing, so that the comforts of his home should declare his mother's love.

'Brigitte? ...' said the Countess in a heart-rending voice, moving to set a chair before the table, as if to give actuality to what she longed for, as if to confirm the existence of what she hoped was true.

'Ah! Madame, he will come, he is not far away. ... I'm sure he is alive and on his way,' answered Brigitte. 'I put a key in the Bible and held it on my finger-tips while Cottin read St John's Gospel ... and Madame, the key did not turn!'

'Does that prove it? Are you sure?' said the Countess.

'Oh, Madame, it's well known! I would bet my hope of heaven that he's still alive. God cannot make mistakes!'

'In spite of the danger that's here waiting for him, I cannot help wishing very much that I could see him here.'

'Poor Monsieur Auguste,' exclaimed Brigitte, 'he's no doubt tramping on foot, walking along the roads!'

'And there is eight o'clock chiming from the belfry!' cried the Countess in dismay.

She was afraid of having stayed longer than she should in this room where everything she saw testified to her son's existence and convinced her that he was still alive. She went downstairs again, but before returning to the drawing-room she stayed a moment by the pillared porch above the steps, listening if she might hear some noise awaken the silent echoes of the town. She smiled at Brigitte's husband, who stood there as sentinel, his eyes staring owlishly in his effort to take in the faint whispers of the square and of the night. She saw her son in everything, and everywhere she went. She soon went in, with an assumption of light-hearted gaiety, and set herself to playing lotto with the little girls; but from time to time she complained of headache, and went back to occupy her armchair beside the fire.

Such was the state of affairs and of people's minds in Madame de Dey's house, while on the road from Paris to Cherbourg a young man wearing a brown *carmagnole*, a vest-like jacket worn by Revolutionaries, and a garment indispensable at that period, was making his way towards Carentan. When the first levies of soldiers were first called up, there was little or no discipline. The exigencies of the time hardly allowed of the Republic's equipping its soldiers at once, and it was not unusual to see the roads full of newly-enrolled troops who still wore their civilian clothing. These young men arrived in advance of their battalions at the halting-places, or trailed along in the rear, for their pace depended on their ability to stand the fatigue of a long march. The traveller with whom we are concerned was some distance ahead of the main column of newly called-up men who were on their way to Cherbourg, and whose arrival in Carentan the Mayor was hourly awaiting, in order to assign them to billets. The young man was walking with the heaviness of fatigue, but still steadily and resolutely, and his bearing seemed to show that he had been long familiar with the hard conditions of a soldier's life. Although the moon was shedding its light over the pasture land surrounding Carentan he had taken note of snow-laden white clouds about to release their burden over the countryside, and it was no doubt the fear of being overtaken by a blizzard which made him hasten his step, which now became more rapid than had seemed possible in his state of weariness. He carried on his back an almost empty knapsack, and held a box-wood stick cut from one of the tall, thick hedges that this shrub forms around most estates in lower Normandy.

The solitary traveller entered Carentan, whose towers, fantastically picked out in the moonlight, he had had in sight for some minutes. His step woke echoes in the silent streets, and he met no one. He was obliged to ask the way to the Mayor's house, of a weaver who was working late. The Mayor lived not far away; the soldier soon found himself under shelter in his porch and, after asking for his assignment to a billet, sat down there on a stone bench to wait for it. But he was sent for by the Mayor, appeared before him, and was subjected to a close scrutiny. The soldier was a young man of good appearance who looked as if he belonged to a distinguished family. He bore himself with dignity. His face had the intelligent light which is the gift of a good education.

'What is your name?' asked the Mayor, with a shrewd glance.

'Julien Jussieu,' replied the soldier.

'And you come from? ...' the official said, not repressing an incredulous smile.

'Paris.'

'Your comrades must be far behind?' the Norman went on, in a bantering tone.

'I am three leagues ahead of the battalion.'

'There's no doubt some special attraction to make you hurry to Carentan, Citizen soldier?' said the Mayor, with a knowing air. 'That's all right,' he added, silencing the young man, who was about to speak, with a wave of his hand; 'we know where to send you. Here,' he said, handing him his note of assignment, 'go ahead, *Citizen Jussieu....*'

These last two words were said with a lightly ironical inflection, and the note that the official held out bore Madame de Dey's address. The young man read it with apparent curiosity.

'He knows well enough that he hasn't far to go, and once he is outside it won't take him long to cross the square!' the Mayor ejaculated, talking to himself as the young man went out. 'He's a cool fellow all right! God guide him! ... Yes, but if anyone but me had been here and asked to see his papers he would have been done for!'

At this moment, Carentan's clocks had struck half-past nine; lanterns were being lighted in Madame de Dey's anteroom; servants were helping their mistresses and masters to put on their sabots, their greatcoats, or their cloaks; the card-players had paid their losses or pocketed their winnings, and were now going home in a body, following the established practice in all little towns.

'I see the Prosecutor means to stay behind,' said one lady, noticing that this important personage was not with them, when they were about to separate at the corner of the square to go to their several dwellings, after having exhausted all the formulas of leave-taking.

This terrible official was indeed alone with the Countess, who waited, trembling, till it should please him to go.

'Citizeness,' he said at length, after a long silence which held something terrifying. 'I am here to see that the laws of the Republic are observed. ...'

Madame de Dey shuddered.

'Have you not got something to tell me?' he asked.

'No, nothing,' she replied with astonishment.

'Ah! Madame,' the Prosecutor exclaimed, sitting down close to her and changing his tone, 'for want of a word, on your side or mine, we may bring our heads to the scaffold. I have observed your character too well, your soul, your ways, to be led astray in the way that you have managed to delude your visitors this evening. You are expecting your son. I can have not the slightest doubt of it.'

The Countess involuntarily made a gesture of denial, but she had turned pale, but the muscles of her face had contracted in the effort she found herself forced to make to display a misleading coolness, and the Public Prosecutor's relentless eye missed not a single sign of her disturbance.

'Well, take him in,' the Revolutionary official went on, 'but he must not stay later than seven in the morning under your roof. Tomorrow, at first light, provided with a denunciation which I shall have sent in to me, I shall come to your house.'

She looked at him in a stunned way which would have drawn pity from a tiger.

'I shall demonstrate the falsity of the accusation,' he went on gently, 'by making a thorough search; and the nature of the report I shall make will protect you against all further suspicion. I shall speak of your patriotic gifts, your civic spirit, and we shall *all* be saved.'

Madame de Dey feared a trap; she stood as if turned to stone, her face on fire, and her tongue stiff as if with ice. A knock echoed through the house.

'Ah! ...' cried the mother in terror, falling on her knees. 'Save him! Save him!'

'Yes, let us save him!' answered the Public Prosecutor with a passionate glance. 'Even if it costs *us* our own lives.'

'I am lost!' she exclaimed, as the Prosecutor politely raised her to her feet.

'Oh, Madame!' he replied with a fine eloquence, 'I have no desire to owe you to anything ... except yourself alone.'

'Madame, he's ...' cried Brigitte, who thought her mistress was alone.

At the sight of the Public Prosecutor, the old servant who had burst in, red in the face and full of joy, stood rooted to the spot and turned ghastly pale.

'Who is it, Brigitte?' the official asked mildly, with a look of clear understanding.

'A soldier the Mayor has sent us to put up for the night,' answered the servant, showing him the billeting order.

'That's true,' the Prosecutor said when he had read the paper. 'We have a battalion coming in this evening.'

And he went out.

The Countess needed too greatly at that moment to believe that her former attorney was sincere, to have the slightest doubt of him. She ran quickly up the stairs, scarcely able to endure another second. Then she opened the door of her room, saw her son, rushed fainting into his arms.

'Oh! my boy, my boy!' she cried, sobbing and covering him with kisses, in a sort of frenzy.

'Madame ...' said the stranger.

'Ah! it is not my son!' she exclaimed, recoiling in horror and standing staring wildly at the soldier.

'Holy God, how like he is!' said Brigitte.

There was a moment's silence, and the stranger himself was disturbed at the sight of Madame de Dey's face.

'Ah! Monsieur,' she said, leaning for support on Brigitte's husband, and feeling then the full force of a blow whose first shock had almost killed her, 'Monsieur, I could not bear to stay and see you any longer. ... Please allow my servants to take my place and entertain you.'

She went downstairs to her own room, half-carried by Brigitte and her old man-servant.

'What, Madame!' exclaimed the housekeeper, leading her mistress to a chair, 'is that man to sleep in Monsieur Auguste's bed, wear Monsieur Auguste's slippers, eat the pâté I made for Monsieur Auguste? Even if they were to guillotine me for it, I ...'

'Brigitte!' cried Madame de Dey.

Brigitte said no more.

'Hold your tongue, chatterbox,' said her husband in a low voice. 'Do you want to kill Madame?'

Just then the soldier could be heard moving about overhead, sitting down to his supper.

'I cannot stay here,' exclaimed Madame de Dey. 'I'll go to

the greenhouse. I'll hear better there what's happening outside during the night.'

She was still wavering between the fear that she had lost her son and the hope that she might yet see him appear. The night was dreadfully silent. There was for the Countess one appalling interval when the battalion reached the town and the men individually sought out their billets. Every step outside, every noise, raised hopes only to mock them: then soon the night relapsed into oppressive peace. Towards morning the Countess was forced to return to her room. Brigitte, who was keeping an eye on the Countess's movements, not seeing her come out, went into the room and found the Countess dead....

'She must have heard that soldier getting dressed, marching about in Monsieur Auguste's room singing their cursed *Marseillaise* as if he was in a stable!' cried Brigitte. 'That's what has killed her!'

The Countess's death was caused by something of graver import, no doubt by some terrible vision. At the exact time at which Madame de Dey died in Carentan her son was shot in Morbihan. We may add this tragic happening to all those instances noted of sympathies that defy the laws of space: to those documents which a few men alone in the wilderness are collecting with scientific interest, from which one day there may be extracted the first principles of a new science, a science which today still awaits a man of genius.

Paris, February 1831

EL VERDUGO

*

MIDNIGHT had just chimed from the belfry in the little town of Menda. A young French officer leaning on the parapet above a long embankment bounding the gardens of the Château de Menda, appeared to be sunk in meditation, a depth of thought that seemed quite out of keeping with the happy-go-lucky insouciance of a soldier's way of life; but it must be noted that never were time, place, and darkness more conducive to reflection. The beautiful Spanish sky suspended a dark blue vault above the soldier's head. The sparkling stars and calm light of the moon shone down upon a delightful valley, entrancingly spread at his feet. Leaning against an orange-tree in bloom the major could see, a hundred feet below him, the town of Menda, which seemed to have huddled for shelter from the north winds, at the foot of the great rock on which the château was built. Turning his head he could see the sea whose shining waters contained the land with a broad silver blade. The château was illuminated. The joyous tumult of a ball, snatches of music from the orchestra, an occasional laugh from some officers and their partners reached him, mingled with the distant murmur of the waves. The freshness of the night filled him with new vigour after the fatiguing heat of the day, and, to complete his pleasure, the gardens were planted with trees and flowers so sweet and strongly-scented that he felt as if bathed in their fragrance.

The Château de Menda belonged to a Spanish grandee who was in residence at the time, with his family. During the whole of that evening, the eyes of the elder of his daughters had followed the officer with such sad interest, that the compassion these Spanish eyes expressed might well be the cause of the Frenchman's reverie. Clara was beautiful, and, although she had three brothers and a sister, the Marquis of Léganès' broad lands seemed to give Victor Marchand sufficient reason to suppose that the young woman would have a handsome dowry. But how could one dare to imagine that the daughter of the proudest old man in Spain, who held the most lofty ideas of a grandee's importance, could ever be given to the son of a Paris grocer!

Besides, the French were hated. Because the Marquis had been suspected by General G..t..r, who was Governor of the province, of preparing a rising in favour of Ferdinand VII, the battalion commanded by Victor Marchand had been quartered in the little town of Menda in order to contain the surrounding country, which gave its allegiance to the Marquis de Légañès. A recent dispatch from Marshal Ney had given grounds for anticipating an early landing by the English on this coast, and named the Marquis as a man who was in communication with the Cabinet in London. And so, in spite of the hospitable reception which this Spaniard had given Victor Marchand and his men, the young officer was constantly on his guard.

On his way to this terrace, where he had come to keep a watchful eye on the state of the town and the countryside entrusted to his vigilance, he had been asking himself what interpretation he should put on the friendliness which the Marquis had consistently shown him, and how the tranquillity of the countryside could be reconciled with his General's uneasiness; but for the last minute or two these thoughts had been driven out of the young commanding officer's mind by a phenomenon which had excited his suspicious attention and aroused a very natural curiosity. He had just caught sight in the town of a large number of lights. In spite of the fact that it was the festival of Saint James, he had commanded that very morning that curfew should be observed at the hour he had prescribed. The château alone had been exempted from this rule. He could see the bayonets of his soldiers gleaming here and there at their accustomed posts; but a solemn silence held the town, and there was no sign that the Spaniards had given themselves over to the rowdy delights of festivity. Seeking an explanation of this breach of his regulation by the inhabitants of the town, he found it all the more incomprehensible because he had left officers on duty to police the town and make nocturnal patrols.

With the impetuosity of youth he was about to dash through a gap in the wall and scramble down the rocks by a short cut, to reach more quickly a little guard-house placed on the road from the château at the entrance to the town, when a slight noise stopped him in his tracks. He thought he heard the gravel of the pathways crunch under a woman's light step. He turned his head and saw nothing; but his eyes were arrested by the extraordinary radiance of the ocean. There he suddenly caught sight of a spectacle so ominous that he stood held to the spot, unable to believe his eyes. In the whitening moonbeams he could distinguish sails at a great distance. He shuddered, and tried to persuade himself that the sight was an optical illusion created by the fantastic interplay of shadows on the waves in the moonlight. At this point a hoarse voice called his name, and looking towards the breach in the embankment he saw, slowly rising from below, the head of the soldier whom he had taken with him to the château.

'Is that you, sir?'

'Yes. Well?' said the young man in a low voice, for a kind of presentiment warned him to act with caution.

'Those scoundrels down there are wriggling around like worms, and I came as fast as I could, if you will allow me, sir, to make my little report.'

'Speak,' replied Victor Marchand.

'I have just been following a man from the château, who came this way with a lantern in his hand. A lantern is damnably suspicious! I don't believe that Christian soul needs to light church candles at this hour.... "They want to take a bite out of us!" that's what I said to myself, and I took it into my head to sniff at the fellow's heels. And so, sir, I discovered three paces from here on a pile of rock, sure enough, there's a heap of faggots.'

A terrible cry which rose all at once from the town interrupted the soldier. A sudden light broke in upon the major's mind. The poor soldier fell, a bullet through his head. A blaze of straw and dry wood flared up in a roaring conflagration ten paces from the young man. The music and the laughter in the ballroom were no longer heard. A deathly silence, broken by

groans, had suddenly succeeded the murmur and the music of
the festival. A cannon boomed across the blanched plain of
the ocean.

On the young officer's face cold sweat broke out. He was
unarmed. He realized that his soldiers had perished, and that
the English were about to land. He saw himself disgraced if
he survived, he saw himself arraigned before a court-martial:
then his eyes turned to look down, to measure the fall into the
valley beneath him, and he was about to cast himself headlong
down when Clara's hand seized his.

'Fly!' she said, 'my brothers are coming after me to kill
you. At the foot of the cliff, there, you will find Juanito's
jennet. Go, quickly!'

She urged him on with both hands. The young man looked
at her for a moment, stunned: then, swiftly obedient to that
instinct of self-preservation that never quite deserts even the
most resolute man, he dashed off across the cliff in the direction she had pointed out, scrambling over rocks until then
trodden only by goats. He heard Clara cry to her brothers to
follow him; he heard his assassins' footsteps behind him; he
heard the bullets of several volleys whistle about his ears; but
he reached the valley, found the horse, mounted it, and
vanished at lightning speed.

A very few hours later, the young officer arrived at General
G..t..r's headquarters and found him at dinner with his
Staff.

'I bring you my head!' cried the major, appearing pale and
drawn before him.

He sat down and related the dreadful story of what had
happened. His tale was heard in intimidating silence.

'I find you more unfortunate than criminal,' said the ter-
rible General, at last. 'You are not accountable for the
Spaniards' crime, and, unless the Marshal decides otherwise,
I shall exonerate you.'

These words brought only very meagre consolation to the
unhappy officer.

'But when the Emperor hears of it!' he exclaimed.

'He will want to have you shot,' said the General; 'but we

shall see. Let us speak no more of this,' he added, severely, 'except in order to exact a vengeance which shall strike salutary terror into this country, where they wage war like savages.'

An hour later, a complete regiment, a detachment of cavalry, with an escort of artillery, were on their way. The General and Victor rode at the head of this column. The soldiers, told of the massacre of their comrades, were filled with such rage as they had never felt before. The distance between headquarters and the little town of Menda was covered with extraordinary speed. Along the way the General found entire small towns under arms. These wretched villages were surrounded and taken and their inhabitants decimated.

By some inexplicable fatality, the English vessels had had to heave to, unable to proceed: it was known later that these ships only carried artillery, and had outstripped the other transports. And so the town of Menda, deprived of the defenders whom she was expecting, and whose arrival the English sails had seemed to promise her, was taken by the French soldiers, almost without a blow being struck. The inhabitants, in terror, offered to surrender at discretion.

In one of those acts of self-immolation which have not been rare in the Peninsula, the assassins of the French, foreseeing, as the General's utter mercilessness was known, that Menda would perhaps be delivered up to the flames and the entire population put to the sword, proposed to give themselves up of their own accord to the General. He accepted the offer, stipulating as a condition that the inhabitants of the château, from the least servant to the Marquis, should be placed in his hands. This capitulation agreed, the General promised to pardon the rest of the population and prevent his soldiers from pillaging the town or setting fire to it. An enormous fine was imposed, and the richest inhabitants made themselves hostages to guarantee its payment, which had to be effected within twenty-four hours.

The General took all the precautions necessary for the safety of his troops and the defence of the district. He refused to billet his men in the houses. When they had encamped, he made his way to the château and formally took possession of it. The members of the Légañès family and the servants were put under close surveillance, bound, and locked in the room where the ball had taken place. From the windows of this room one could easily overlook the terrace which looked down upon the town.

The Staff set up its headquarters in a gallery nearby, where the General first of all held a council to decide the measures to be taken to oppose the landing. When an aide-de-camp had been dispatched to Marshal Ney, batteries sent to take up positions on the coast, the General and his Staff dealt with the prisoners. Two hundred Spaniards handed over by the townspeople were shot out of hand on the terrace. After this military execution, the General ordered as many gibbets as there were servants in the château to be set up on the terrace, and the hangman to be sent for from the town. Victor Marchand made use of the time which was to elapse before dinner, to go and see the prisoners. He soon left them and approached the General.

'I have come in haste,' he said in a shaking voice, 'to ask for an act of mercy.'

'*You* ask that!' replied the General in a tone of bitter irony.

'Alas!' said Victor, 'it is a sad favour I have to ask. The Marquis, seeing the gibbets set up, hoped that you might alter the method of execution for his family, and begs you to behead those of noble birth.'

'So be it,' said the General.

'They ask further that they should be granted the succour of religion, and should be freed from their bonds; they promise not to try to escape.'

'I consent,' said the General, 'but you shall be answerable for them to me.'

'The old man, moreover, offers you his whole fortune if you will be pleased to pardon his young son.'

'Really!' was the General's answer. 'All he has is forfeit already to King Joseph.'

He stopped. A contemptuous thought made him raise his eyebrows, and he added:

'I'll do more for them than they ask. I can see the significance of his last request. Very well, he may buy the perpetuation of his name, but let Spain remember for ever his treachery and his punishment! I give his fortune and his life to that one of his sons who shall take on the office of the executioner. ... Go away and don't speak to me of this again.'

Dinner was served. The officers sat down to table and set about satisfying an appetite made keener by fatigue. Only one of them, Victor Marchand, was absent from the feast. After long hesitation he entered the great room where the Légañès family languished, and looked sadly at the spectacle presented by this room where, two evenings before, he had seen the heads of the two young girls and their three brothers outstanding under the lights, as they were carried along and whirled around in the waltz. He shuddered at the thought that shortly these heads were to roll on the ground, severed by the executioner's blade.

Tied to their gilt chairs, the father and mother, two daughters, and three sons, sat completely motionless. Eight servants were standing, their hands tied behind their backs. These fifteen persons looked gravely at one another, and their eyes gave little sign of what their feelings were. A profound resignation and regret at having failed in their enterprise could be read on a few faces. Motionless soldiers guarded them, and respected these cruel enemies in their affliction.

A flicker of curiosity lighted faces when Victor appeared. He gave the order to untie the condemned prisoners, and himself went to loosen the ropes that held Clara prisoner on her chair. She smiled sadly. The officer could not help touching the girl's arm, looking with admiration at her dark hair, her supple form. She was a true Spaniard, with the eyes and colouring of Spain, long curling eyelashes, and an iris darker than a crow's wing.

'Had you any success?' she said with a mournful smile, which yet showed a girl's lively spirit.

Victor could not refrain from groaning. He looked in turn at the three brothers and Clara. One, the eldest, was thirty years old. He was small, not handsome in figure, with a proud

D

and disdainful air, was not without a certain dignity of manner, and seemed no stranger to that delicacy of feeling which
made Spanish gallantry formerly so famous. He was called
Juanito. The second son, Philippe, was about twenty years
old. He resembled Clara. The youngest was eight. A painter
would have seen in Manuel's features something of that
Roman steadfastness that David has given to the children in
his Republican paintings. The old Marquis had a head, with a
wealth of white hair, which seemed to have escaped from one
of Murillo's canvases. As he looked at them the young officer
shook his head, despairing of seeing the General's bargain
accepted by any of these persons; however, he dared confide
it to Clara. The Spanish girl shuddered at first, but then she at
once assumed a calm expression and went to kneel before her
father.

'Oh!' she said to him, 'make Juanito swear that he will
faithfully obey the orders you give him, and we shall be
content.'

The Marquise gave a start of hope; but when, leaning towards her husband, she heard Clara confide the horrible news,
she fainted, in a mother's horror. Juanito grasped all that was
involved: he sprang up like a caged lion.

Victor took it upon himself to send away the soldiers, when
he had obtained the Marquis's assurance of his complete submission. The servants were taken away and handed over to
the executioner, who hanged them. When no one was left to
watch the family but Victor, the old father rose.

'Juanito!' he said.

Juanito replied only by an inclination of the head which was
equivalent to absolute refusal, fell back on his chair, and
looked at his parents with a cold and terrible eye. Clara walked
over to him, sat on his knee, and said cheerfully:

'My dear Juanito,' and she put her arm round his neck and
kissed his eyelids, 'if you knew how sweet death would be,
given by you! I should not have to endure the odious contact
of an executioner's hands. You would save me from the evils
in store for me, and ... my good Juanito, you never wanted to
see me belonging to anyone, well then ...'

Her velvety eyes cast a blazing look at Victor, as if to rouse in Juanito's heart his horror of the French.

'Have courage,' said his brother Philippe; 'otherwise, our virtually royal line becomes extinct.'

Suddenly Clara rose, the group which had gathered round Juanito fell apart, and this rebellious son, rebellious with good cause, saw his old father standing before him, who solemnly exclaimed:

'Juanito, I command you!'

The young Count making no movement, his father fell on his knees. Involuntarily, Clara, Manuel, and Philippe followed his example. They all stretched out their hands towards the one who must save the family from oblivion, and seemed to echo their father's words:

'My son, would you be found wanting in Spanish strength and true sensibility? Do you mean to leave me long on my knees, and ought you to consider *your* life and *your* suffering? – Is this my son, Madame?' the old man added, turning to the Marquise.

'He consents!' exclaimed his mother despairingly, seeing Juanito raise his eyebrows in a sign which only she could interpret.

Mariquita, the younger daughter, still on her knees, threw her frail arms round her mother; and as she wept hot tears, her little brother Manuel came to scold her. Just then, the chaplain of the château entered; the whole family immediately surrounded him; he was led to Juanito.

Victor could not endure this scene any longer. He gestured to Clara and hurried away to make a last appeal to the General. He found him in a good humour, enjoying the banquet, drinking with his officers, whose conversation was beginning to be merry.

An hour later, one hundred of Menda's most respected inhabitants arrived on the terrace to be, in obedience to the General's orders, witnesses of the execution of the Légañès family. A detachment of soldiers was placed to keep the Spaniards in check, and they were formed up underneath the gibbets on which the Marquis's servants had been hanged.

The heads of these prosperous citizens almost touched the feet of the common herd of victims. Thirty paces away stood an executioner's block, and a curved blade shone. The executioner was there, in case Juanito should refuse.

Soon, amidst the deepest silence, the Spaniards heard the footsteps of several people, the measured tread of a picket of soldiers, and the light clank of their guns. These different sounds mingled with the officers' joyous carousal, as, not long before, the dance music of a ball had disguised the preparations for bloody treachery. All eyes turned towards the château, and the aristocratic family was seen advancing with unbelievable assurance. Every face was serene and calm. One man only, pale and shaking, leaned on the priest, who proffered all the consolations religion could afford this man, the only one doomed to live. The executioner understood, as did everyone present, that Juanito had accepted his post for one day.

The old Marquis and his wife, Clara, Mariquita, and their two brothers, approached and knelt down a few paces from the fateful spot. Juanito was led by the priest. When he reached the block, the executioner, touching his sleeve, drew him aside, probably to give him some instructions. The confessor placed the victims so that they could not see the execution. But they were true Spaniards and stood there upright and unflinching.

Clara ran first to her brother.

'Juanito,' she said, 'take pity on my lack of courage. Begin with me!'

As she spoke, hurried footsteps became audible approaching, and Victor arrived on the scene. Clara was already on her knees, her white neck held out, inviting the steel blade. The officer turned pale, but pulled himself together and rushed up to her.

'The General grants your life if you are willing to marry me,' he said in a low voice.

The Spanish girl cast a proud and scornful look at the officer.

'Come, Juanito!' she said, in a voice which came from the heart.

Her head rolled at Victor's feet. The Marquise de Légañès made a convulsive gesture when she heard the sound; it was the only sign of her grief.

'Have I got myself properly in position like this, dear Juanito?' was the question little Manuel asked his brother.

'Ah! you are crying, Mariquita!' said Juanito to his sister.

'Oh, yes!' the girl replied. 'I am thinking of you, my poor Juanito: you will be very unhappy without us!'

Soon the Marquis's tall figure approached. He looked at his children's blood, turned to the mute and motionless on-lookers, stretched out his hands towards Juanito, and said in a firm and resonant voice:

'Spaniards, I give my son my paternal blessing! – Now, *Marquis*, strike without fear, as you strike without reproach.'

But when Juanito saw his mother approach, supported by the confessor:

'She gave me birth!' he exclaimed.

His cry drew a cry of horror from the assembly. The noise of the feast and the joyous merriment of the officers died away at the sound of that terrible outcry. The Marquise understood that Juanito's courage was gone: she sprang at one leap over the parapet and fell to strike her head upon the rocks below. A cry of admiration filled the air. Juanito had fallen senseless.

'Sir,' said a half-tipsy officer, 'Marchand has just told me some things about this execution. I'll warrant you did not order it ...'

'Do you forget, gentlemen,' exclaimed General G..t..r, 'that in a month five hundred French families will be mourning, and that we are in Spain? Do you wish us to leave our bones here?'

After this speech, there was not a person present, not even a sub-lieutenant, who dared empty his glass.

In spite of the honour in which he is held, in spite of the title *el verdugo* (the executioner) which the King of Spain has granted to the Marquis de Légañès as a title of nobility, he is consumed with grief, lives solitarily, and shows himself rarely. Bowed down with the burden of his admirable crime, he seems to be impatiently waiting for the birth of a second son to give him the right to rejoin the shades who are his constant companions.

Paris, October 1829

AN EPISODE DURING THE TERROR

*

ON 22 January 1793, about eight o'clock in the evening, an old lady was walking down the steep hill which flattens out to level ground before the Church of Saint-Laurent, in the Faubourg Saint-Martin, in Paris. The snow that had fallen persistently all day muffled the sound of footsteps. The streets were deserted. The feeling of apprehension which the silence naturally induced was increased by the oppression of the reign of terror under which France was then groaning. The old lady had not yet met a single person on the way. The shortness of her sight, moreover, which had been failing for some time, prevented her from distinguishing in the light of the street-lamps a few passers-by scattered like shadows along the vast expanse of this road. She made her way courageously on alone across the deserted space, as if her age were a talisman which must preserve her from all harm. When she had left the Rue des Morts behind, she imagined that she could hear the firm, heavy tread of a man walking behind her. It occurred to her that this was not the first time that she had heard that sound. She was seized with panic at the thought that she had been followed, and tried to walk still faster in order to reach a passably well-illuminated shop, where she might hope to see by its lights if her suspicions were well-founded. As soon as she had reached the level beam of light that issued from the shop she turned her head sharply, and caught a glimpse of a human form through the haze. This indistinct apparition was enough. She staggered for a moment under the impact of over-whelming terror, for she now had no doubt but that she had been escorted by the stranger since the first step that she had taken outside her own door, and the urge to escape from a spy lent her strength. Urged by blind impulse she quickened her pace, as if she could thus elude a man who must necessarily be more active than she. When she had hastened along for some minutes she reached a confectioner's shop, walked in, and collapsed rather than sat down on a chair set by the cashier's desk.

As the doorlatch rasped under her touch, a young woman busy at her embroidery raised her eyes, recognized the old-fashioned cut and violet silk of the old lady's voluminous mantle through the glass panes of the door, and hastened to open a drawer as if to take something from it which she had ready to give her. The gesture and expression of the young woman showed a desire to be rid quickly of the stranger, as if she were someone unwelcome, and she uttered an impatient exclamation when she found the drawer empty. Then, without looking at the lady she hastily left the counter, hurried towards the room at the back, and called her husband, who appeared at once.

'Where did you put …?' she asked with an air of mystery, indicating the old lady with a glance, and leaving her sentence unfinished.

The pastry-cook could see only the enormous black silk bonnet swathed with violet ribbons which was the stranger's headgear, but he disappeared after throwing a look at his wife which seemed to say, 'Do you really think that I would leave that below your counter? …'

Surprised at the old lady's silence and immobility, the pastry-cook's wife returned and went close to her; and when she saw her felt an impulse of pity, and perhaps also of curiosity. Although this woman's complexion was naturally transparent, like that of a person vowed to private austerities, it was easy to see that some recent agitation had spread an extraordinary pallor over it. Her bonnet was so arranged as to hide her hair, which no doubt age had whitened, for the speckless collar of her dress showed that she wore no powder in it. The lack of relief gave her face a kind of conventual severity. Her features were grave and proud. Formerly, the ways and manners of persons of quality were so different from those of people belonging to the other classes that it was easy to recognize a member of the nobility; and the young woman was convinced that the stranger was a *ci-devant*, a former aristocrat, and had belonged to the Court.

'Madame? ...' she said involuntarily and with respect, forgetting that this title was proscribed.

The old lady did not reply. She kept her eyes fixed on the glass door of the shop, as if some frightening object were silhouetted against it.

'What's the matter, citizeness?' asked the shopkeeper, reappearing almost immediately.

The lady roused from her reverie when the citizen pastrycook held out a small cardboard box wrapped in blue paper.

'Nothing, nothing, my friends,' she replied, in a gentle voice.

She raised her eyes to the pastry-cook's face as if to cast a grateful glance at him, but catching sight of the red cap on his head uttered a cry, 'Ah! ... you have betrayed me! ...'

The young woman and her husband answered with a horrified gesture which made the stranger redden, either with shame at her suspicion of them, or with relief.

'Forgive me,' she said then, with a childish sweetness. Then, drawing a gold louis from her pocket, she presented it to the pastry-cook. 'Here is the price we agreed on,' she added.

There is a poverty that the poor can recognize. The pastry-cook and his wife exchanged a glance and then glanced at the old woman, in the thought that had occurred to both of them. This gold louis must be her last. The lady's hands trembled as she held out the coin, which she contemplated painfully, without cupidity, but seeming to realize the full extent of the sacrifice that she was making. Fasting and poverty were legibly engraved in the lines of that face, as were fear and an ascetic habit of life. Her clothing showed vestiges of former splendour. It was of silk, though worn, a mantle well-cut, though faded, lace carefully mended: in fact the shabby rags of opulence. The confectioner and his wife, torn between pity and self-interest, began to relieve their consciences with words.

'Citizeness, you seem to be faint and weak.'

'Would you not feel better for taking something, Madame?' the woman interrupted her husband.

'We have some very good broth,' the pastry-cook added.

'It's so cold! You have perhaps caught a chill walking, Madame. But you can rest here and warm yourself a little.'

'We're not just devils, you know,' exclaimed the pastry-cook.

Disarmed by the kindly tone of these charitable shop-keepers, the lady confessed that she had been followed by a stranger, and was afraid to go home by herself.

'Is that all?' said the man in the red cap. 'Wait for me, citizeness.'

He handed the coin to his wife. Then, in a grateful impulse of that kind which creeps into a shopkeeper's soul when he is given an exorbitant price for a piece of goods of middling value, he went to dress himself in his National Guard's uniform, took his headgear, put on his short sabre, and reappeared under arms. But his wife had had time to reflect. As has happened with many another heart, reflection closed the open hand of benevolence. Uneasy, and fearing to see her husband drawn into some affair that might turn out badly, the pastry-cook's wife pulled him by his coat-tail and tried to stop him; but obeying his charitable impulse, the worthy fellow offered then and there to escort the old lady home.

'It looks as if the man the citizeness is afraid of is still prowling about in front of the shop,' said the young woman excitedly.

'I'm frightened,' the lady said naïvely.

'Suppose he's a spy? ... suppose it's a plot? Don't go, and take the box from her....'

These words whispered in his ear by the pastry-cook's wife froze the warm burst of courage which had filled him in the impulse of the moment.

'Eh! I'll just have a couple of words with him and get rid of him without more ado!' the pastry-cook exclaimed, opening the door and dashing out.

The old lady, as passive as a child and seeming almost dazed, sank into her chair again. The honest shopkeeper soon reappeared. His face, red enough by nature and further flushed by his oven fire, had suddenly turned a ghastly white. Terror possessed him to such a degree that his legs shook and his eyes started from his head like a drunk man's.

'Do you want us to lose our heads, wretched aristocrat? ...' he shouted furiously. 'Just show us your heels, and never come back here again. Don't think you can count on me to supply you with the raw material for conspiracy!'

As he finished speaking the pastry-cook tried to take back the little box that he had given the old lady, and which she had put in one of her pockets. But scarcely had his rash hands touched her mantle when the stranger, preferring to brave the dangers of the road with no protector save God rather than lose what she had just bought, regained the agility of her youth: she rushed to the door, burst it open, and vanished from the gaze of wife and husband, who stood there dumbfounded and shaking.

As soon as the stranger found herself outside, she started to walk rapidly along; but soon her strength began to fail her, for she heard the spy relentlessly following her, the compressed snow squeaking under his heavy footsteps. She was forced to stop: he stopped too. She dared neither speak to him nor look at him, whether by reason of the fear that possessed her or through inability to handle the situation. She continued on her way, walking slowly: then the man too slackened his pace, so that he remained just near enough to keep watch on her. The unknown watcher dogged her steps like the old woman's very shadow. Nine o'clock was striking when the silent pair passed the Church of Saint-Laurent again.

We are so made that in every soul, even the weakest, a feeling of calm succeeds violent agitation, for if emotion has no limits, our physical capacity has. And so the old lady, finding that her alleged persecutor did her no harm, became inclined to see in him a secret friend anxious to protect her. She gathered together in her mind all the circumstances attending her unknown shadower's apparition as if in search of reasons supporting this comforting view, and it pleased her then to discover in him good intentions rather than evil ones. And so, forgetting the fear that this man had inspired in the pastry-cook a short time before, she walked on resolutely into the upper part of the Faubourg Saint-Martin.

After walking for half an hour she reached a house situated near the angle where the main thoroughfare of the district is met by the road leading to the Pantin gate. This region is still today one of the most unfrequented in the whole of Paris. The north-east wind, passing over the rising ground of Saint-Chaumont and Belleville, whistled across the houses, or rather thatched cottages, scattered over this sparsely inhabited valley, where enclosing fences are built of earth and bones. This desolate spot seemed a natural shelter for wretched poverty and despair. The man tenaciously pursuing the poor creature bold enough to traverse these silent streets by night appeared to be struck by the spectacle that met his gaze. He stood still, pensively and in an attitude of hesitation, dimly lit by a street lamp whose feeble glimmer barely pierced the mist. Fear lent eyes to the old woman, and she fancied she saw something sinister in the stranger's features: she felt her terrors spring to life again, and took advantage of the seeming uncertainty which had brought the man to a halt to slip in the shadows towards the door of the lonely house. She released a spring lock, and vanished at once like a phantom.

The unknown man stood motionless, contemplating the house, which was to some degree a type of the miserable habitations of this outlying district. This ramshackle dwelling, built of rubble, was coated with a layer of blackened plaster so cracked and creviced as to rouse apprehension of its falling at the least gust of wind. The roof, of brown moss-covered tiles, had subsided in several places in a way that made its complete collapse under the weight of snow seem imminent. There were three windows on each floor, whose decaying frames, rotten with damp and split by the action of the sun, gave warning that they offered no protection against the penetrating cold outdoors. This isolated house was like an ancient tower left to moulder, forgotten by time. A pale light shone from the windows set irregularly in the mansard roof which topped this pitiful structure, while the rest of the house was wrapped in total darkness.

The old woman groped her way painfully enough up the clumsy rough stairway with its rope slung alongside to lean on by way of banisters. She knocked mysteriously on the door of the apartment in the attic floor, then sat down precipitately on a chair which an old man pushed out for her.

'Hide! hide!' she said to him. 'In spite of our going out so rarely, our doings are known, our steps are spied on.'

'Has anything fresh happened?' inquired another old woman sitting by the fire.

'The man who has been prowling round the house since yesterday, followed me this evening.'

At this, the three inhabitants of this poor tenement looked at one another with undisguisedly terror-stricken faces. The old man was the least agitated of the three, perhaps because he was in the greatest danger. Under the pressure of a great misfortune, or the yoke of persecution, a brave man begins by making, so to speak, the sacrifice of himself; he considers his days as just so many victories snatched from fate. The eyes that the two women fixed on this old man made it easy to guess that all their keen anxiety centred in him.

'Sisters, why despair of God?' he said in a hollow but impressive voice. 'We were singing His praises amidst the cries of assassins and dying men in the Carmelite monastery. If it was His will to save me from that slaughter, no doubt it was to reserve me for a destiny which I must accept without murmuring. God protects His own, He may dispose of them as He will. It's you, not I, that we must think about.'

'No,' said the old woman who had just come in, 'what is our life, compared with a priest's?'

'As soon as I saw myself outside the doors of the Abbey at Chelles, I thought of myself as a dead woman,' said the other nun.

'Here,' said the first woman, holding the little box out to the priest. 'Here are the holy wafers.... Oh!' she exclaimed, 'I hear footsteps coming upstairs.'

The three persons strained their ears. The noise ceased.

'Don't be frightened if someone tries to reach you here,' said the priest. 'A person whose loyalty we can rely on has had to make all his arrangements to cross the frontier, and is to come to take the letters that I have written to the Duc de Langeais and the Marquis de Beauséant so that they may see about some means of rescuing you from this appalling country, and the death or destitution that awaits you here.'

'Are you not to follow us, then?' cried the two nuns softly, with a kind of gentle despair.

'My place is where there are people suffering,' said the priest simply.

They were silent and looked at their guest with devoted and selfless admiration.

'Sister Marthe,' he said to the nun who had gone to fetch the wafers, 'this messenger is to reply *Fiat voluntas* to the password *Hosanna*.'

'There is someone on the stairs!' exclaimed the other nun, opening up a hiding-place contrived under the roof.

This time it was easy in the deep silence to hear a man's boots scraping on the lumps of hardened mud with which the stairs were covered. The priest crept painfully into a kind of clothes-press, and the nun threw a few articles of clothing over him.

'You can close it now, Sister Agathe,' he said in a stifled voice.

The priest was barely hidden when three knocks on the door made the two nuns start. They looked questioningly at one another, but dared not utter a word. They appeared to be both about sixty years of age. Living isolated from the world for the last forty years, they were like plants adapted to a hothouse atmosphere and unable to survive if taken from it. Accustomed to a convent life, they could conceive of no other. Their grilles having been broken down one morning, they had shuddered to find themselves free. One can readily imagine the kind of seeming imbecility that had been produced in their innocent minds by the Revolutionary happenings. They were quite incapable of bringing their convent-regulated ideas to bear on the problems of life and, not even understanding the situation in which they found themselves, were like children who had been looked after until this moment and who now, deserted by their maternal providence, prayed instead of crying. And so, faced with the danger which they felt this moment held, they remained speechless and passive, knowing no other defence than that of Christian resignation.

The man who was demanding admittance interpreted this silence in his own fashion; he suddenly opened the door and appeared on the threshold. The two nuns trembled as they recognized the person who had for some time been prowling about their house and making inquiries about them. They stood unmoving, looking at him with an uneasy curiosity, like timid children silently examining strangers. This man was tall and thick-set; but nothing in his bearing, attitude, or face suggested that he was a wicked man. He stood there, as motionless as the nuns, and made a leisurely survey of the room in which he found himself.

Two straw mats laid on planks served the nuns as beds. A single table stood in the middle of the room and held a copper candlestick, a few plates, three knives, and a round loaf of bread. A very small fire burned in the grate. The few scanty pieces of firewood piled in a corner, too, made it clear that the nuns lacked money. The walls, washed with a coat of very ancient paint, revealed the bad repair of the roof in stains like brown streaks, where rain had seeped through. A holy relic, no doubt salvaged from the pillage of the Abbaye de Chelles, adorned the chimney breast. Three chairs, two chests, and a shabby old chest of drawers completed the furniture of the room. A door opening near the fireplace indicated that there was another room.

The inventory of this cell was soon made by the individual who had introduced himself so inauspiciously and so alarmingly into the household. His face expressed a feeling of commiseration and he cast a benevolent look at the two women, at least as embarrassed as they were. The strange silence in which the three of them stood did not last long, for the stranger in the end guessed at the inexperience and helplessness of the two poor creatures and said, in a voice which he tried to make gentle:

'I have not come here as an enemy, citizenesses......' He stopped, and then began again. 'If some trouble came to you,

Sisters, believe me I had no hand in it. I have a favour to beg of you.'

They remained wrapped in silence.

'If I am intruding, if I ... annoy you, speak frankly ... I will go away; but let me tell you that I am completely loyal to you, that if there is any service I can render you, you may make use of me fearlessly, and that I and perhaps I alone am above the law, since there is now no king....'

There was such an accent of truth in what he said that Sister Agathe, the nun who belonged to the Langeais family, and whose manner seemed to show that she had once known the brilliance and display of high society and breathed the air of the Court, hastily waved her hand towards one of the chairs as if inviting their guest to be seated. The stranger showed pleasure, with an underlying sadness, as he understood this gesture. He waited till the two worthy women were seated before he took his chair.

'You have given asylum,' he went on, 'to a venerable priest who has not taken the oath, who miraculously escaped the massacre of the Carmelites.'

'*Hosanna!* ...' Sister Agathe interrupted the stranger, looking at him with anxious curiosity.

'I don't think that's his name,' he replied.

'But, Monsieur,' said Sister Marthe quickly, 'we have no priest here, and ...'

'You should be more careful and show greater foresight, then,' the stranger answered gently, stretching out an arm to the table and picking up a breviary. 'I don't imagine that you know Latin, and ...'

He did not finish, for the faces of the two poor nuns were a picture of such extraordinary horror that he was afraid he had gone too far. They were shaking and their eyes were full of tears.

'Set your minds at rest,' he told them with honest bluntness, 'I know your guest's name and yours, and for the last three days I have known of your distress and your devoted care for the venerable Abbé de ...'

'Hush!' said Sister Agathe naïvely, putting her finger to her lips.

'You see that if I had had in my mind the dreadful thought of betraying you, I should have been able to do it already, over and over again....'

When he heard this, the priest extricated himself from his prison and stood revealed in the middle of the room.

'I can't believe, Monsieur,' he said to the stranger, 'that you are one of our persecutors, and I trust you. What do you want of me?'

The priest's saintly confidence, the nobility obvious in every line of his face, would have disarmed assassins. The mysterious person, whose coming had brought animation to this scene of poverty and resignation, for a moment contemplated the group that these three beings formed. Then in the tone of one making a disclosure he spoke to the priest in these terms:

'Father, I came to beg you to celebrate a requiem mass for the repose of the soul ... of ... of a crowned person whose body will never rest in consecrated ground....'

The priest involuntarily shuddered. The nuns, not yet understanding of whom the stranger was speaking, sat with their ears strained, their faces turned towards the two who were conversing in an attitude of curiosity. The cleric studied the stranger: an unmistakable anxiety was depicted on his face and his eyes were ardently beseeching.

'Very well!' answered the priest. 'This evening, at midnight, come back, and I shall be ready to celebrate the only funeral rites it is possible for us to observe in expiation of the crime of which you speak. ...'

The stranger started, but a satisfaction both sweet and solemn appeared to gain the mastery over some hidden grief. When he had bowed with respect to the priest and the two nuns, he vanished, with a kind of mute expression of gratitude which those three magnanimous souls understood.

About two hours after this scene the stranger returned, knocked discreetly at the attic door, and was let in by Mademoiselle de Beauséant, who led him to the second room of this modest lodging, where everything had been made ready for the service. Between two stove pipes the nuns had set the old chest of drawers, and its ancient corners were enfolded in a magnificent altar-cloth of green watered silk. A great crucifix of ebony and ivory hung on the dingy wall with a dramatic and eye-compelling effect against its bareness. Four slender candles, which the Sisters had managed to affix to this improvised altar by sticking them in sealing-wax, shed a pale glimmering light which was barely reflected by the wall. In this feeble light the rest of the room was hardly visible, but striking only on the sacred things, its rays were like rays shed from Heaven on this unadorned altar. The floor was damp. The roof, which sloped steeply down on two sides like a garret roof, had several cracks through which an icy draught blew. Nothing could have displayed less funerary pomp than this mournful ceremony, and yet perhaps nothing could have been more solemn. A deep silence, in which the faintest cry uttered on the Route d'Allemagne would have been audible, laid a pall of sombre majesty on this nocturnal scene. The grandeur of the thing being enacted was in such strong contrast to the poverty of the means that it created a feeling of religious awe. On each side of the altar the two old nuns, kneeling on the floor tiles heedless of the mortal damp, were praying, led by the priest, who, clothed in his vestments, was preparing a golden chalice set with precious stones, a sacred vessel no doubt salvaged from the pillage of the Abbaye de Chelles. Near this pyx, a memorial of royal magnificence, the water and wine destined for the holy sacrifice were contained in two glasses of hardly good enough quality for the humblest inn. In place of missal the priest had laid his breviary on a corner of the altar. A common plate had been prepared for the washing of hands innocent and free from blood. Everything was immense in its implications, though trivial in itself; poor, yet instinct with nobility; at once profane and holy.

The stranger came to kneel devoutly between the two nuns. But when he suddenly noticed the crêpe on chalice and crucifix, for, having nothing to indicate for whom this requiem mass was being offered, the priest had put God Himself in mourning, a memory so powerful overwhelmed him that drops of sweat appeared on his broad forehead. The four silent actors in this scene now looked at one another in mysterious harmony; then their striving souls, working one upon the other, commingled all their feelings and joined together all in a divine compassion. It seemed as if their thoughts had evoked the martyr whose remains had been devoured by quicklime, and that his shade was before them in all his royal majesty. They were celebrating an *obit*, a memorial service without the body of the dead man. Under this roof of collapsing tiles and laths four Christians were going to intercede with God for a King of France, and accompany his body to the grave with no coffined body present. It was an act of the purest possible devotion, of astonishing faith without reservation. It was in God's eyes, doubtless, as the glass of water given in His name which weighs as heavily in the balance as the grandest virtues. The whole Monarchy was there, in the prayers of a priest and two poor women, but perhaps the Revolution was represented too in this man whose remorse-stricken face too plainly showed that he was carrying out the penance imposed by an immense repentance.

Instead of pronouncing the Latin words: *Introibo ad altarem Dei*, etc., the priest, by divine inspiration, looked at the three participants who stood for Christian France, and said, in words that obliterated the poverty of that wretched hovel:

'We are about to enter the sanctuary of God!'

At these words spoken with piercing gravity, a holy awe descended on the stranger and the two nuns. Under the vaulted roof of Saint Peter's in Rome God would not have been more majestically present than He was at that moment in that poverty-stricken dwelling to the eyes of those Christians: so true it is that between man and Him all intermediary pomp seems vanity, and that He draws His grandeur from Himself alone. The stranger's fervour was sincere. And so the feeling in which were united the prayers of these four servants of God and of the King was one. The sacred words fell on the air like celestial music in the midst of the silence. There was a moment when tears overcame the stranger, it was at the *Pater noster*. The priest added this prayer in Latin, which the stranger no doubt understood: *Et remitte scelus regicidis sicut Ludovicus eis remisit semetipse* (And forgive the regicides as Louis XVI himself forgave them). The two nuns saw two great tears trace a wet path down the stranger's harsh cheeks and fall on the floor.

The office for the dead was recited. The *Domine salvum fac regem* (God save the King), sung in a low voice, was found affecting by these faithful Royalists, as they reflected that the child King for whom they were supplicating the Most High at that moment, was a captive in his enemies' hands. The stranger shuddered to think that a fresh crime might yet be committed, in which he would no doubt be forced to have a share. When the funeral service was ended, the priest signed to the nuns, who withdrew. As soon as he was alone with the stranger he went towards him, his expression gentle and sad, and said in a fatherly tone: 'My son, if you have dipped your hands in the blood of the martyr King, trust yourself to me. There is no sin which, in God's eyes, may not be wiped out by a repentance as touching and sincere as yours appears to be.'

At the cleric's first words the stranger started in involuntary terror, but he regained his composure and looked calmly at the surprised priest. 'Father,' he said in a perceptibly strained voice, 'no one is more innocent than I of the blood that has been shed....'

'I am bound to believe you,' said the priest....

There was a pause during which he considered his penitent afresh; then, persisting in his idea that this was one of those timid members of the *Convention Nationale* which voted the execution of the King, who yielded up an inviolable and anointed head so that they might preserve their own, he went on gravely: 'Think, my son, that to be free of guilt of this great crime it is not enough not to have co-operated in it. Those who, with the power to defend the King, left their sword in the sheath will have a very heavy reckoning to answer for before the King of Heaven.... Oh, yes indeed!' added the old priest, shaking his head expressively, 'yes, very heavy! ... for by remaining passive they became involuntary accomplices in that dreadful sin....'

'Do you believe,' the stranger demanded, in stupefaction, 'that an indirect participation will be punished? ... Is the soldier obeying a command who formed one of a firing squad guilty?...'

The priest hesitated. The stranger was elated when he saw this Royalist puritan at a loss for an answer, placed as he was between the dogma of implicit obedience which, according to the partisans of the Monarchy, must rule military codes, and the equally important dogma which makes sacred the person of kings, and hastened to take the priest's hesitation as an answer to doubts which seemed to torment him. Then, to give the venerable Jansenist no longer time to reflect, he said: 'I would be ashamed to offer you a fee for the mass which you have just celebrated for the repose of the King's soul and for the relief of my conscience. A thing of inestimable value can only be paid for by something beyond price. So be pleased to accept, Monsieur, this gift of a sacred relic. ... A day may come, perhaps, when you will understand its value.'

As he said this the stranger presented the priest with a little box which was extremely light. The priest took it, as it were, involuntarily, for the solemnity of the man's words, the tone in which he spoke, the respect in which he held the proffered box, had overwhelmed him with surprise. They then returned to the room where the two nuns were waiting.

'You are in a house,' the stranger told them, 'whose owner, Mucius Scaevola, the plasterer who lives on the first floor, is noted in the section for his patriotism! but he is secretly attached to the Bourbons. He was formerly huntsman to Monseigneur le prince de Conti, and he owes his fortune to him. If you do not leave the house you are safer here than in any place in France. So stay here. Pious souls will care for your needs, and you may await less evil times without danger. A year from now, on the twenty-first of January ...' (as he said these last words he could not suppress an involuntary shudder), 'if you adopt this dismal place as your refuge, I shall return to be with you at a mass in expiation ...'

He left the rest unsaid. He bowed to the silent inhabitants of the garret, cast a last glance around at the evidences of their poverty, and disappeared.

For the two innocent nuns, such an adventure had all the

interest of a romance; and when the venerable Abbé had told them of the mysterious present so solemnly made by this man, they placed the box on the table and three anxious faces, feebly illuminated by the candle, bent over it with indescribable curiosity. Mademoiselle de Langeais opened the box, and took from it a handkerchief of very fine cambric, soiled with sweat, and as she unfolded it they discovered stains.

'That's blood! ...' said the priest.

'It's marked with the royal crown!' exclaimed the other Sister.

The two nuns let the precious relic fall in horror. For these two simple souls the mystery surrounding the stranger was now inexplicable; and as for the priest, from that day he did not even try to seek an explanation.

The three prisoners were not slow to perceive that in spite of the Terror, a powerful hand was extended to aid them. To begin with, they received firewood and provisions; then the two nuns realized that a woman was associated with their protector when they were sent linen and clothing that enabled them to go out, without being conspicuous by the aristocratic fashion of the garments which they had previously been obliged to continue wearing; lastly, Mucius Scaevola gave them two civic cards. Often information necessary to the priest's safety reached him by roundabout ways; and he recognized an opportuneness in the arrival of these pieces of news that could only be due to a source in some person informed of State secrets. In spite of the famine that held Paris in its grip, the proscribed persons found rations of *white bread* at the door of their wretched garret, regularly set there by invisible hands; yet they believed that in Mucius Scaevola they recognized the mysterious agent of these benefactions, which were both ingenious and imaginative.

The unworldly inhabitants of the garret could not be in doubt that their protector was none other than the person who had come to be present at the mass of expiation on the night of the 22 January 1793; and he became the subject of a special cult for these three beings whose only hope was in him, and who lived only by his aid. They had added special petitions for him to their prayers; evening and morning these devout souls prayed for his happiness, his prosperity, his safety; they made supplication to God to free his path of all snares or ambushes, to deliver him from his enemies and grant him a long and peaceful life. Their gratitude being thus, as it were, daily renewed, was necessarily combined with a feeling of curiosity which every day became more lively. The circumstances attending the stranger's apparition were the subject of their conversations, they made endless surmises about him, and the distraction of their thoughts of which he was the cause was a benefaction of a different kind. They promised themselves that they would not let the stranger slip away without some sign of their friendly feelings towards him, when he returned, as he had promised, to mark the sad anniversary of Louis XVI's death.

That night, so impatiently looked forward to, came at last. At midnight, the stranger's heavy footsteps echoed on the old wooden staircase; the room had been adorned to receive him, the altar was prepared. This time the Sisters had the door open in advance of his arrival, and both hurried to bring light to the staircase. Mademoiselle de Langeais even went down a few steps to meet him in order to see her benefactor sooner.

'Come,' she said in a moved and affectionate tone, 'come ... we are waiting for you.'

The man raised his head, cast a sombre look at the nun, and made no reply; she felt as if a cloak of ice had fallen about her, and fell silent; at sight of him gratitude and curiosity died in all their hearts. He was perhaps less cold, less taciturn, less terrible than he appeared to these souls, who in the warmth and exaltation of their feeling were anxious to pour out their friendship for him. The three poor prisoners, understanding that this man wished to remain a stranger to them, resigned themselves. The priest imagined that he saw a smile, quickly repressed, on the stranger's lips when he noticed the preparations which had been made to receive him. He heard Mass, and prayed, and then vanished, after replying politely in a few words in refusal when Mademoiselle de Langeais invited him to share the light repast that had been made ready.

After the ninth Thermidor, the nuns and the Abbé de Marolles might go out in Paris without the slightest risk. The old priest's first outing was made to a perfume shop, at the sign of the *Queen of Flowers*, kept by Citizen and Citizeness Ragon, former Court perfumers, who were still loyal to the Royal family, and were made use of by the loyalists of La Vendée in correspondence with the Princes, and the Royalist party in Paris. The Abbé, dressed as was the fashion of the time, was standing on the doorstep of this shop, situated between Saint-Roch and the Rue des Frondeurs, when a crowd, filling the Rue Saint-Honoré, prevented him from leaving.

'What's this?' he asked Madame Ragon.

'It's nothing,' she replied; 'it's the tumbril and the executioner going to the Place Louis XV. Ah! that's a sight we saw often enough last year; but today, four days after the anniversary of the twenty-first of January, we can watch the horrible procession and not shed any tears.'

'Why?' said the Abbé. 'That's not a Christian thing to say.'

'Well, it's the execution of Robespierre's accomplices. They resisted it as long as they could, but now they're going in their turn where they sent so many innocent people.'

The crowd which filled the Rue Saint-Honoré surged past them. Above their heads the Abbé de Marolles, looking in an impulse of curiosity, saw standing in the tumbril the man who three days before had heard his Mass.

'Who's that? ...' he said, 'the man who ...'

'That's the headsman,' replied Monsieur Ragon, giving the public executioner the name he held under the Monarchy.

'My dear! My dear!' cried Madame Ragon, 'Monsieur l'Abbé is dying.' And the old lady took a flask of vinegar to revive the fainting priest.

'He must have given me,' he said, 'the handkerchief the King used to wipe his forehead when he was going to his martyrdom. ... Poor man! the steel blade had pity when the whole of France had none! ...'

The perfumers thought that the poor priest was delirious.

Paris, January 1831

BEFORE JENA

*

An Episode From *A Mysterious Affair*

Laurence, in her own right Marquise de Cinq-Cygne, has travelled
from France, accompanied by an elderly relative, to find Napoleon
on his European battlefield, to beg him to spare her four Royalist
cousins and Michu, a land-steward and a faithful servant of their
family, who have been falsely accused, through police intrigue,
and sentenced for the mysterious kidnapping of the Comte de Gondreville, a member of the Senate. Once before these men have
been implicated in a Royalist conspiracy, and been pardoned by
Napoleon. Talleyrand has furnished the necessary passports and
dictated the letter which Laurence carries and which the sentenced
men have signed, asking for mercy. As a member of the decimated
despoiled aristocracy, and of a family which suffered greatly in the
Revolutionary events and those that followed them, Laurence has
always held Napoleon in fanatical detestation.

The weariness of the two travellers and their anxiety about the
outcome of their journey, the concern of the Marquis de Chargebœuf for his companion's fatigue, Laurence's bitter thoughts at her
need to sue for favour from a man she hated, had made them obliv-
ous of the magnificent scenery as their barouche rolled across
Switzerland, in these first days of October 1806. – TRANSLATOR'S
NOTE.

ONCE they entered Prussia it would have been very difficult
for the two travellers not to notice the movement of men
and military baggage on an immense scale. The battle of Jena
had begun. Laurence and the Marquis saw the French Army's
magnificent divisions move endlessly past them as if they were
parading before the Tuileries. As she watched this deployment
of military splendour, which only the words and metaphors
of the Old Testament could fittingly portray, the man whose
might had set these masses in movement took on gigantic
stature in Laurence's imagination. Soon a rumour of victory

reached her ears. The Imperial armies had just gained two
signal advantages. Prince Louis Ferdinand of Prussia was
killed on the day preceding that on which the two travellers
reached Saalfeld in their attempt to catch up with Napoleon,
who moved at the speed of a thunderbolt. At length, on the
thirteenth of October, ill-auguring date, Mademoiselle de
Cinq-Cygne found herself travelling along the bank of a river,
surrounded by corps of the Grand Army, confusion all
around her. She had been shuttled from village to village,
from one division to another, and was dismayed to see herself
alone, with only an old man for company, tossed on an ocean
of a hundred and fifty thousand soldiers who faced a hundred
and fifty thousand more. Weary of for ever catching glimpses
of the river beyond the hedges of the muddy road, which led
up rising ground, she asked a soldier what river it was.

'It's the Saale,' he said, and pointed out to her the Prussian
army massed in strength on the other side of the water.

Evening was coming on. Laurence watched fires start to
life and weapons catch reflections of their light. The old Marquis, whose undaunted spirit was chivalrous indeed, himself
drove, with his new servant by his side, the pair of good horses
he had bought the previous evening. The old man well knew
that he would find neither postillions nor horses on a battlefield. Suddenly, the audaciously intruding barouche, an object
of astonishment to all the soldiers, was halted by a gendarme
of the military police who descended at a gallop upon the
Marquis, shouting, 'Who are you? Where are you going?
What do you want?'

'The Emperor,' said the Marquis de Chargebœuf. 'I have an
important dispatch from the Ministers for Marshal Duroc.'

'Well, you can't stay here,' said the gendarme.

Mademoiselle de Cinq-Cygne and the Marquis had little
choice but to stay there, however; the less so as night was
falling.

'Where are we?' Mademoiselle de Cinq-Cygne asked, stopping two officers whom she saw approaching. They were
wearing greatcoats which concealed their uniforms.

'You are in front of the van of the French army, Madame,'

replied one of the officers. 'You certainly can't stay here, for if the enemy showed signs of life, and artillery came into action, you would be caught between two fires.'

'Ah!' she said, indifferently.

Upon this *Ah!* the other officer said: 'How does this woman come to be here?'

'We are waiting for a gendarme,' she replied. 'He has gone to notify Monsieur Duroc, who will provide our safe-conduct and enable us to speak to the Emperor.'

'Speak to the Emperor? ...' said the first officer. 'Do you dream of doing that? ... On the eve of a decisive battle?'

'Ah! you are right,' she said. 'I should wait two days before I speak to him. Victory will make him milder.'

The two officers turned away, but moved to a point only twenty paces off where their motionless chargers awaited them. The barouche was then surrounded by a crowd of generals, marshals, officers all resplendent in gold lace, who left the carriage unchallenged just because it was there.

'God!' said the Marquis to Mademoiselle de Cinq-Cygne. 'I believe we've been talking to the Emperor!'

Laurence then saw a few paces from her, ahead, and alone, the man who had exclaimed, 'How does this woman come to be here?', one of the two officers, in fact the Emperor, wearing his famous greatcoat over a green uniform, mounted on a white horse with very rich gear. He was examining the Prussian army beyond the Saale through field-glasses. Laurence realized then why the barouche was allowed to remain there, and why the Emperor's escort respected it. A gust of emotion shook her: the hour had come. She then heard the hollow rumble of several bodies of artillerymen with their guns taking up their position on this plateau at speed. The batteries seemed to have a language of their own, the ammunition wagons clanked and rattled, the cannon crackled.

'Marshal Lannes will take up his position with his whole force in the van. Marshal Lefebvre will occupy this height,' said the other officer, who was Major-General Berthier.

The Emperor dismounted. At his first movement Roustan, his celebrated Mameluke, ran to take the horse's bridle.

Laurence was in a daze of astonishment, she could not believe
what she saw happening so simply.

'I shall spend the night on this plateau,' said the Emperor.

Just then the grand marshal Duroc, whom the gendarme
had at last succeeded in finding, came up to the Marquis de
Chargebœuf and asked for the reason of his coming. The Marquis replied that a letter written by the Minister for External
Affairs would inform him of how urgently necessary it was
that Mademoiselle de Cinq-Cygne and he should obtain an
audience with the Emperor.

'His Majesty will no doubt dine at his bivouac,' said Duroc,
taking the letter, 'and when I have seen what the matter is,
I'll let you know if that's possible.... Sergeant,' he said to the
gendarme, 'go with this carriage and show the way to the hut
back there.'

Monsieur de Chargebœuf followed the gendarme, and
brought his barouche to a standstill behind a wretched cottage
built of wood and earth, surrounded by a number of fruit trees
and guarded by infantry and cavalry pickets. It might be said
that there the full majesty of war struck the eye in all its splendour. From this height the lines of the two armies were
visible, lit by the moon. After an hour's wait, a time filled with
the endless comings and goings of aides-de-camp, Duroc came
in search of Mademoiselle de Cinq-Cygne and the Marquis de
Chargebœuf, and led them into the cottage, whose flooring
was of beaten earth, like one of our barn threshing-floors. At
a table which had been cleared, before a fire of smoking green
wood, Napoleon sat in a clumsy chair. His boots, smeared
with mud, bore the marks of his activities across country. He
had taken off the famous greatcoat, and his well-known green
uniform jacket crossed by the broad red ribbon of the Grand-
Cordon, sombre against the whiteness of his kerseymere
breeches and white waistcoat, admirably set off his pale and
terrible Caesarian face. His hand lay on a map unfolded across
his knees. Berthier stood before him in his glittering uniform
of Vice-Constable of the Empire. Constant, the valet, was
serving the Emperor with coffee, on a tray.

'What do you want?' he said with assumed brusqueness, his

glance seeming to penetrate Laurence's mind with a piercing light. 'You are no longer afraid to speak to me before the battle, it appears. What is your business?'

'Sire,' she said, fixing him with a gaze not less steady than his own, 'I am Mademoiselle de Cinq-Cygne.'

'Well, what then?' he replied testily, thinking himself challenged by this stare.

'You do not understand? I am the Comtesse de Cinq-Cygne and I beg your mercy.' And falling on her knees she held out the document which Talleyrand had drawn up, and the Empress and Cambacérès and Malin had added a commendatory note to.

The Emperor graciously raised the suppliant to her feet, giving her a shrewd look as he did so, and said: 'Are you going to behave yourself, at last? Do you understand what the French Empire must be?...'

'Ah, just now I only understand the Emperor!' she said, conquered by the kindness with which the man of destiny had spoken these words, which were an intimation that he would pardon.

'Are they innocent?' the Emperor asked.

'Yes, all of them,' she said with fervour.

'All of them? No, the steward is a dangerous man who would kill my senator without asking your advice....'

'Oh! Sire,' she said, 'if you had a friend who had risked his life for you, would you desert him? Would you not ...'

'You are a woman,' he said with a hint of sarcasm in his tone.

'And you are a man of iron!' she answered with an impassioned harshness, which pleased him.

'This man has been condemned to death by the law of the land,' he returned.

'But he is innocent.'

'Child! ...' he said.

He went to the door, took Mademoiselle de Cinq-Cygne by the hand, and led her out on to the plateau.

'Look,' he said with that eloquence which was his alone, which had the power to make brave men of cowards, '... here are three hundred thousand men; they are innocent too! Well, tomorrow thirty thousand men will be dead, dead for their country. There is perhaps among the Prussians a great engineer, a great ideologist, a genius, who will be cut off. On our side we shall certainly lose great men, not yet known. Indeed, perhaps I shall see my best friend die! Shall I reproach God? No, I shall be silent. Learn, Mademoiselle, that one must die for the laws of one's country, as here one dies for its glory,' he added, leading her back to the cottage.

'Come, go back to France,' he said, looking at the Marquis; 'my orders will follow you.'

Laurence believed that this meant commutation of Michu's sentence, and in an effusion of gratitude she knelt to kiss the Emperor's hand.

'You are Monsieur de Chargebœuf?' said Napoleon then, staring at the Marquis.

'Yes, Sire.'

'You have children?'

'Many children.'

'Why should you not give me one of your grandsons? He would be one of my pages....'

'Ah! that's the sub-lieutenant, showing through,' Laurence thought. 'He wants to be paid for his favour.'

The Marquis bowed, without replying. Luckily, General Rapp burst into the cottage just then.

'Sire, the cavalry of the Guard, and the Grand Duke de Berg's cavalry, cannot reach us until tomorrow afternoon.'

'No matter,' said Napoleon, turning to Berthier; 'these are hours of grace for us too, let us turn them to good account.'

At a sign, the Marquis and Laurence withdrew and got into their carriage. The gendarme set them on their way, and went with them to a village where they spent the night. Next day they drove away from the battlefield to the roar of eight hundred cannon, which grumbled throughout the next ten hours, and on their way they heard the news of the astonishing victory of Jena. Eight days later they entered the outskirts of Troyes.

An order of the High Court, transmitted to the imperial prosecutor at the County Court at Troyes, decreed that the noblemen should be set free on bail, pending the decision of the King and Emperor, but at the same time the order for Michu's execution was sent forward by the prosecutor's office.

THE ABBÉ BIROTTEAU

*

ONE night in the year 1826, as autumn was setting in, the Abbé Birotteau, the chief character in this story, was overtaken by a shower as he was on his way back from the house where he had been spending the evening. So he hurried as quickly as the comfortable roundness of his figure permitted, across the deserted little square called the *Close*, which lies behind the east end of Saint-Gatien, in Tours.

The Abbé Birotteau, who was a short little man of apoplectic constitution, about sixty years of age, had already suffered several attacks of gout; so that of all the minor miseries of human existence the one the good priest detested most was that his shoes with their broad silver buckles should be suddenly splashed with rain and have their soles soaked. Whatever he did, in spite of the flannel socks in which he wrapped his feet in any kind of weather, with the care that the clergy always take of themselves, a little moisture was always sure to penetrate. Then next day, without fail, gout gave him some proofs of its constant attachment to him. Still, as the paving-stones of the Close are always dry, and the Abbé Birotteau had won three livres ten sous playing whist at Madame de Listomère's, he resignedly endured the rain, which had begun to fall heavily when he was in the middle of the Place de l'Archevêché. Just then, too, he was indulging in a daydream of his castle in Spain, which was a dream now twelve years old, a clergyman's dream! a dream dreamed anew every evening, which now seemed about to come true. In a word, he was too cosily engaged in wrapping himself in a canon's befurred vestment to feel the weather's inclemency. In the course of the evening the persons who were in the habit of meeting at Madame de Listomère's had practically guaranteed his nomination to the canonry then vacant in the metropolitan chapter of Saint-Gatien, pointing out to him that there was no one who better deserved the position than he did, and that his claims to it, though they had long gone unrecognized, were incontrovertible. If he had lost at cards, if he had heard that his rival the Abbé Poirel had been made canon, the worthy Abbé would no doubt have felt the rain very cold; he might even have had uncomplimentary things to say about life in general. But he found himself in one of those rare conjunctures in life when feelings of happiness put everything else out of mind. When he quickened his step he did so automatically, and to tell the truth, which is of course essential in a history of manners, he gave not a thought either to the shower or to the possibility of gout.

There existed formerly in the Close at the end nearer the Grand'Rue a number of houses, set in an enclosed space, which belonged to the Cathedral and in which several dignitaries of the Chapter lived. Since the alienation of Church property, the town has made the passage which shuts off the houses into a street, called Rue de la *Psalette*, which is an exit from the Close to the Grand'Rue. This name shows clearly enough that the precentor used to live there formerly, with his schools and all those who lived under his dominion. A single house fills the left side of this street, and the flying buttresses of Saint-Gatien cross its walls and are planted in its narrow little garden in a way that leaves it in doubt whether the Cathedral was built before or after this ancient dwelling. But an archaeologist, examining the arabesques and shape of the windows, the arch of the doorway, and the exterior appearance of the time-darkened house, perceives that it has always been part of the magnificent pile to which it is wedded. An antiquary, if there were any such in Tours, of all the cities in France one of the most illiterate in the arts, might even recognize at the entrance to the passage into the Close some traces of the archway which once upon a time formed the portal of these ecclesiastical dwellings, and which must have harmonized in style with the general character of the edifice. Lying to the north of Saint-Gatien the house is never free of the shadows thrown by the great cathedral, over which time has flung his dark mantle, engraving it with the furrows of age, scattering broadcast his damp chill, his lichens, and tall-growing weeds. The habitation is always wrapped in deep silence, broken only by the sound of the bells, by the chanting of offices from within the Cathedral walls, or by the clamour of the jackdaws which make their nests high up in the bell-towers. The place is a desert of stone, a solitude full of character, and it is only beings who have reached a state of complete nullity or who are endowed with prodigious strength of mind who can make their dwelling there.

The house in question had always been occupied by abbés, and belonged now to a spinster named Mademoiselle Gamard. This property had been acquired by Mademoiselle Gamard's father from the nation at the time of the Terror, but as the spinster had let lodgings there to priests for the last twenty years, it occurred to no one to think it wrong that a devout woman should continue to hold national property under the Restoration. Possibly religious people supposed that she intended to bequeath it to the Chapter, while the worldly did not see that the purpose for which it was destined had suffered any change.

The Abbé Birotteau, then, was making his way towards this house, where he had been living for the last two years. His set of rooms had been, as his canonry now was, the object of his desires and his *hoc erat in votis* for a dozen years. To be Mademoiselle Gamard's lodger and become a canon were the two great businesses of his life; and indeed they may be said to epitomize exactly a priest's ambition, for he, seeing himself as a traveller towards eternity, can wish no more in this world than a sound lodging, a good table, suitable clothing, silver-buckled shoes, things that suffice for the needs of the flesh, and a canonry to satisfy the vanity, that ineffable sentiment which will cling to us, so they say, in the very presence of God, since there are ranks among the saints. The Abbé Birotteau's coveting of the rooms he now occupied, however, a mild enough emotion in the eyes of worldly people, had been for him a passion, a passion full of frustration, and like the most reprehensible passions, compact of hopes, pleasures, and remorse.

The capacity of her house and the arrangement of the rooms

did not allow Mademoiselle Gamard to have more than two lodgers. Now, about twelve years before the day on which Birotteau became this lady's boarder, she had undertaken the maintenance in comfort and good health of M. l'Abbé Troubert and M. l'Abbé Chapeloud. The Abbé Troubert was still alive. The Abbé Chapeloud was dead, and Birotteau had immediately succeeded him.

The late Abbé Chapeloud, in his life-time Canon of Saint-Gatien, had been the Abbé Birotteau's intimate friend. On each of the Abbé's visits to the Canon he had never failed to admire the rooms, the furniture, and the library. From that admiration there sprang one day the desire to possess these fine things. The Abbé Birotteau had found it impossible to stifle this desire, which often made him suffer agonies when it occurred to him to reflect that only the death of his best friend could satisfy this covetous greed, which remained concealed but which grew unceasingly.

The Abbé Chapeloud and his friend Birotteau were not rich. They were both peasants' sons and had nothing beyond the meagre remuneration accorded to priests: and their scanty savings had been spent in living through the troubled times of the Revolution. When Napoleon re-established the Roman Catholic cult, the Abbé Chapeloud was appointed Canon of Saint-Gatien and Birotteau was given official duties in the Cathedral. Chapeloud then went to live as Mademoiselle Gamard's boarder. When Birotteau came to visit the Canon in his new lodging, he found the rooms and furniture very well arranged, but saw nothing else worth special notice. The beginning of this lust for suites of furniture was like the beginning of a true love-affair, which in a young man often starts with a cool admiration for the woman whom he will love for the rest of his life.

The rooms, reached by a stone staircase, were in a wing of the building facing south. The Abbé Troubert occupied the ground floor, and Mademoiselle Gamard the first floor, of the main building facing the street. When Chapeloud first went there the rooms were bare and the ceilings smoke-blackened. The chimneypieces of clumsily cut stone had never been painted. For furniture the impecunious Canon installed to begin with only a bed, a table, some chairs, and the few books that he possessed. The flat was like a beautiful woman in rags. Two or three years later, however, an old lady having died and left two thousand francs to Chapeloud, he used this money to buy a large oak bookcase, remarkable for carving good enough to attract artists' admiration, which came from a demolished château pulled down by the Black Band. The Abbé's pleasure in making this acquisition lay less in the good bargain he was making, than in the fact that its dimensions made it fit perfectly into the gallery. His savings now made it possible to restore the gallery entirely: until then it had been left in its neglected, uncared-for state. The floor was carefully polished, the ceiling whitened, and the woodwork painted to represent the tints and knots of oak. A marble chimneypiece replaced the old one. The Canon had sufficient taste to search out and get hold of old chairs of carved walnut. A long ebony table and two Boule pieces completed the transformation of this gallery, whose appearance was now full of character. Within two years the generosity of several persons devoted to the Church and legacies from his devout penitents, small though these sums were, had filled the empty shelves of the case with books. Finally, an uncle of Chapeloud's, a former Member of the Congregation of the Oratory, bequeathed his collection of folios of the Fathers of the Church to him, together with a number of other great works, of value to a clergyman.

Birotteau, more and more surprised by the successive transformation of this once bare gallery, came by degrees to feel an involuntary cupidity. He longed to possess this room, which was so solidly and harmoniously in keeping with the gravity of clerical manners. His passion grew from day to day. As he spent entire days at work in this sanctuary the Abbé was in a position to appreciate its silence and its peace, where he had first of all admired the happy arrangement of the rooms.

During the years that followed, the Abbé Chapeloud made of the study an oratory which his devout flock were delighted to embellish. At a later period a lady presented the Canon with a suite of tapestry-covered furniture for his bedroom. She had

been engaged in working on the tapestry for months under the
amiable Canon's eyes, without his having a suspicion that it
was destined for him. And then the bedroom made the same
impression on Birotteau that the gallery had, he was dazzled
by it. Finally, three years before his death, Chapeloud had
completed the comfort of his rooms by decorating the drawing-room. Although it was simply upholstered in red Utrecht
velvet, the furniture had fascinated Birotteau. From the day
when the Canon's friend saw the red-flowered silk curtains,
the mahogany furniture, the Aubusson carpet which adorned
this vast room, which had been freshly painted, Chapeloud's
rooms became the object of a secret obsession. To live there,
sleep in the bed with its great silk curtains where the Canon
slept, and find all his comforts around him, as Chapeloud did,
was for Birotteau happiness itself: he saw nothing that could
surpass that. Such worldly desires or ambitions as spring in
the hearts of other men, were all concentrated in Birotteau on
the secret profound passion with which he longed for a home
like the one the Abbé Chapeloud had created for himself.
When his friend fell ill, it was undoubtedly sincere affection
that brought Birotteau to see him; but when he learnt of the
Canon's indisposition, and as he kept him company, in spite
of himself there rose a host of thoughts from the depths of his
heart, whose tenor, reduced to its simplest form, was always:
'If Chapeloud died I could have his rooms.' As Birotteau had
an excellent heart, conventional ideas, and a limited intelligence, however, he did not go so far as to conceive means of
inducing his friend to bequeath his library and furniture to
him.

The Abbé Chapeloud, an amiable and indulgent egotist,
divined his friend's passion, which it was not difficult to do,
and forgave him, which may seem a less easy matter for a priest.
And on his side the Abbé Birotteau, his feelings of friendship
unchanged, continued to saunter with his friend every day in
the same promenade along the Mail de Tours, not begrudging
him a single moment of the time consecrated to this walk
throughout twenty years.

Birotteau, who regarded his involuntary desires as sins, in

his contrition would have been capable of the greatest self-sacrifice for Chapeloud's sake. The latter requited what he owed to a brotherly affection so naïvely sincere by saying a few days before his death to the Abbé, who had been reading the *Quotidienne* to him: 'Now, indeed, the rooms will be yours. I feel that it's all up with me.' In fact, in his will the Abbé Chapeloud bequeathed his library and furniture to Birotteau. The possession of these things, so ardently desired, and the prospect of being taken as a lodger by Mademoiselle Gamard, did much to blunt the edge of Birotteau's grief at the loss of his friend, the Canon. He would perhaps not have brought him to life again, but he mourned him. For several days he was like Gargantua, who having lost his wife in child-birth did not know whether to rejoice in his son or grieve at the burying of his good Badbec, and who in his confusion rejoiced at his wife's death and mourned the birth of Pantagruel. Birotteau spent the first days of mourning in checking the works in *his* library, making use of *his* furniture, saying as he examined them, in a tone of voice which it is to be regretted could not be recorded, 'Poor Chapeloud!' In fact his joy and grief occupied his mind so completely that he felt no pain when he saw the position of canon, in which the late Canon Chapeloud had hoped that Birotteau might succeed him, given to another.

Mademoiselle Gamard having taken the Abbé with pleasure as her lodger, the latter participated from that time on in all the material felicities of which the deceased Canon had boasted to him. Privileges beyond computation! According to the late Abbé Chapeloud not one of all the clergy who inhabited the city of Tours, not even excepting the Archbishop, could be the object of such detailed and delicate attentions as those lavished by Mademoiselle Gamard on her two boarders. The first words which the Canon spoke to his friend as they walked along the Mail used nearly always to be a reference to the succulent dinner which he had just enjoyed, and it very rarely happened that during the seven walks of the week he did not say at least fourteen times, 'That excellent woman has certainly a vocation for serving the clergy.'

'Just think,' the Abbé Chapeloud used to say to Birotteau, 'that for twelve consecutive years fresh linen, albs, surplices, bands, have always been ready to my hand. I always find everything in its place, in sufficient number and scented with orris-root. My furniture is polished and kept so well dusted that it is a long time since I have known what dust is. Have you ever seen a single speck of it in my rooms? Then the fire-wood is carefully selected, the least details are excellent; in short it would appear that Mademoiselle Gamard keeps an unceasingly vigilant eye upon my room. I don't remember having had to ring twice in ten years. That is the way to live! To have to look around for nothing, not even one's slippers. To find always awaiting one a good fire and a good table. Let me give you an instance: my bellows irritated me, they had a choke in the larynx. I did not have to complain twice about that. Indeed no. The very next day Mademoiselle gave me a very pretty pair of bellows and these tongs which you see me stoking the fire with.'

In reply Birotteau used to say only, 'Scented with orris-root!' That *scented with orris-root* always struck him. What the Canon said revealed a state of bliss which seemed fantastic to the poor Abbé, whose bands and albs drove him distracted, for he had no sense of method and frequently enough forgot to order his dinner. And so whether he was collecting the offertory or saying Mass, whenever he saw Mademoiselle Gamard in Saint-Gatien he had never failed to cast such a sweet and benignant glance at her as Saint Teresa might have cast at Heaven.

Although the state of comfort and well-being which every human creature desires, and which he had so often dreamed of, had thus fallen to his lot, since nobody, not even a priest, finds it easy to live without some castle in Spain, some hobby-horse, to cherish, for the last eighteen months the desire for a canonry had succeeded the Abbé Birotteau's two satisfied passions. The title of canon had become for him what a peerage must be for a plebeian minister. And so the probability of his nomination, the hopes that had just been given him at Madame de Listomère's, turned his head so thoroughly that it only occurred to him that he had left his umbrella there when he reached his own domicile. Indeed if it had not been for the rain, which was now falling in torrents, he perhaps would not have remembered it at all, he was so absorbed in the pleasure of turning over and over in his mind everything that had been said to him on the subject of his promotion, by the company met at the house of Madame de Listomère, the old lady that he was in the habit of visiting on Wednesday evenings.

The Abbé rang sharply as if to warn the maid-servant not to keep him waiting. Then he squeezed himself into the jamb of the doorway in order to take as much shelter from the rain as possible; but the water dripping from the roof fell exactly on the toes of his shoes, and gusts of wind drove rain in showers against him. When he had let sufficient time elapse, as he calculated, to allow the maid to leave the kitchen and pull the cord which hung behind the door, he rang again in a way that produced a very significant peal. 'They can't have gone out,' he said to himself, hearing no movement within. And for the third time he applied himself to his ringing, which clanged so harshly in the house, and was so loudly taken up by all the Cathedral echoes, that nobody could fail to be wakened up by all this factious clamour. So a few moments later, not without a certain pleasure mingled with ill-humour, he heard the servant's sabots clacking on the courtyard paving-stones. The gouty clergyman's discomfort was not to be ended so quickly as he thought, however. Instead of pulling the cord, Marianne was obliged to turn the great key of the door in the lock and pull back the bolts.

'How could you let me ring three times on such a night?' he said to her.

'But, sir, you can see the door was locked. Everyone is in bed long ago. It has struck three-quarters after ten o'clock. Mademoiselle must have thought that you hadn't gone out.'

'But you saw me go out! Besides, Mademoiselle knows very well that I go to Madame de Listomère's every Wednesday.'

'Goodness, sir, I did what Mademoiselle told me to,' replied Marianne, shutting the door.

The Abbé felt the edge of this rejoinder the more keenly

because of the state of complete happiness which his reverie
had induced. He said nothing, and followed Marianne to the
kitchen, where he supposed that his candlestick had been
placed. But instead of going into the kitchen, Marianne led
the Abbé to his own floor, where Birotteau perceived his
candlestick on a table which stood outside the red drawing-
room door, in a kind of antechamber formed by the staircase
landing which the late Canon had enclosed with a large glass
screen. Speechless with surprise, he went straight to his bedroom, saw no fire in the grate, and called Marianne, who had
not had time to go downstairs again.

'You haven't lit my fire?' he said inquiringly.

'I beg your pardon, sir,' she replied. 'It must have gone
out.'

Birotteau looked at the hearth again and verified the fact
that the fire had been untouched since the morning.

'I need to dry my feet,' he returned. 'Light a fire for me.'

Marianne did what she was told with the prompt obedience
of a person anxious to go to bed. As he looked for his slippers,
which were not placed ready for him in the middle of his bed-
side mat where he was accustomed to find them, the Abbé
made certain observations on the way in which Marianne was
dressed which made it clear to him that she had not risen from
her bed as she had told him. It occurred to him then that for
almost a fortnight he had been deprived of all the little attentions which for the last eighteen months had made life run
so smoothly and pleasantly for him. Narrow minds naturally
tend to look for the reasons behind trifling occurrences, and
so he at once gave himself up to very serious reflection about
these four events which anyone else would barely have noticed,
but which for him constituted four catastrophes. His entire
happiness was threatened, obviously, by the forgotten slippers,
by Marianne's lie about the fire, by the unusual conveyance of
his candlestick to the anteroom table, and by his enforced wait
in the rain outside the door.

When the flames were alight on the hearth, when the night
lamp had been lit and Marianne had left him, without asking,
as she always used to do, 'Is there anything else, sir?', the

Abbé Birotteau let himself gently relax in his dead friend's handsome and capacious armchair, but the gesture with which he lay back suggested sadness. A foreboding of terrible misfortune oppressed the worthy man. His eyes sought in turn the fine clock, the chest of drawers, the chairs, the curtains, the rugs, the four-poster bed, the holy-waterstoup, the crucifix, a Virgin by Valentin, a Christ by Lebrun, dwelt on each of the furnishings of this room, and his face expressed all the grief of the most tender farewell ever made by a lover to his first mistress, or by an old man to the last trees he will plant.

The Abbé had just awakened, a little tardily to speak the truth, to recognition of the signs of a covert persecution which Mademoiselle Gamard had been carrying on against him for nearly three months. Her malevolent intentions would no doubt have been guessed long before by a man more wide-awake. After all, old maids have all a certain faculty for underlining their hate-inspired words and actions. They scratch like cats. Then it is not only the pain of the wound they make that hurts, but the fact that they take pleasure in inflicting it, and in pointing out to their victim that they have torn his flesh. Where a man of the world would not have let himself be scratched twice, it had taken several paw-strokes in the face to make the kindly Birotteau believe in the possibility of ill-will.

At once, with that kind of catechetical shrewdness which priests acquire in their direction of consciences and in sifting trifles in the depths of the confessional, the Abbé Birotteau set himself, as if it were a matter of religious controversy, to the establishing of the following proposition: 'Granting that Mademoiselle Gamard did not give a thought to the fact that it was Madame de Listomère's reception evening, that Marianne forgot to light my fire, that they thought I had come in; in view of the fact that I myself took downstairs this morning, with my own hands! *my candlestick!!!* it is impossible that Mademoiselle Gamard seeing it in her drawing-room could have supposed that I had gone to bed. *Ergo*, Mademoiselle Gamard wanted to leave me standing at the door in the rain, and in having my candlestick taken upstairs again her intention was to make me understand this.

'What!' he cried aloud, quite carried away by the seriousness of the circumstances, as he rose to take off his damp
clothes and put on his dressing-gown and nightcap. Then he
paced to and fro from his bed to the fireplace, waving his
hands and gesticulating as he talked to himself in a voice that
varied in key, but rose to falsetto at the end of each sentence
as if to supply a question mark.

'What in the world can I have done to her? What has she
got against me? It was not Marianne who forgot my fire! It
was Mademoiselle who must have told her not to light it!
Only a child could fail to see by the tone she takes with me
and her manner that I have had the ill-luck to offend her.
Nothing like this ever happened to Chapeloud. I shan't be
able to live with such vexations as this about me.... At my
age....'

He went to bed hoping that in the morning he might gain
some light on the cause of that hatred which was to destroy
irretrievably the felicity which he had enjoyed for two years,
after having had his heart set on it for so long. Alas! the secret
reasons for the grudge Mademoiselle Gamard bore him must
remain for ever concealed from him; not that they were difficult to guess, but because the poor man lacked the good faith
with which great minds and scoundrels can confront and
judge themselves. Only a man of high mental capacity or an
intriguer says to himself: 'I should not have done that.' Self-
interest and some degree of genius are the only counsellors
that are completely conscientious and clear-sighted. Now the
Abbé Birotteau, whose goodness of heart was so extreme as
to be silly, whose knowledge was only a kind of veneer, acquired by hard work, who had no experience of the world or
its ways, who lived between celebrations of Mass and the confessional, deeply engaged in deciding the most trivial matters
of conscience in his capacity of confessor to the boarding-
schools of the town and to a few fine spirits who knew his
worth, this Abbé might be regarded as an overgrown child to
whom the major part of social practices was completely
strange. Only there had insensibly developed in him without
his suspecting it the egotism natural to every human creature,

augmented by the egotism peculiar to the priest, and aggravated by the self-centred narrowness of a provincial life. If someone had found it a sufficiently rewarding task to search the Abbé's soul, and show him that in the infinitely petty details of his existence and the inconsiderable duties of his private life there was an essential lack of that self-immolation which he believed himself to profess, he would have punished himself and done penance with a whole heart. But those whom we offend, even unwittingly, give us little credit for our innocence: they are anxious and able to avenge themselves. And so Birotteau, weak as he was, must submit to the operation of that great retributive Justice which constantly lays it upon the world to execute its sentences, which some fools call *the misfortunes of life*.

There was this difference between the late Abbé Chapeloud and Birotteau, that one was an adroit and perceptive egotist, and the other in his egotism ingenuous and blundering. When Chapeloud became Mademoiselle Gamard's boarder he was able to form a precise judgement of his hostess's nature. The confessional had taught him to recognize all the bitterness created in an old maid's heart by the ill-luck of finding herself excluded from the ranks of society, and so he carefully considered how he should conduct himself in Mademoiselle Gamard's house. His hostess, who was then barely thirty-eight years old, felt that she still had some claims to admiration, a feeling that in demure persons such as she later changes to a towering self-esteem. The Canon understood that if he wanted to live a comfortable life with Mademoiselle Gamard he must display more than Papal infallibility, must never omit to offer her the same unvarying consideration and the same little attentions. In order to achieve this result he allowed only those points of contact between Mademoiselle Gamard and himself which civility absolutely demanded, to become established, in addition to those contacts which necessarily exist between persons living under the same roof. Thus, although the Abbé Troubert and he both regularly ate three meals a day, he abstained from sharing the common breakfast, and had accustomed Mademoiselle Gamard to sending him a cup of coffee with cream in bed. Then he had avoided the tedium of supper, by taking tea every day in the houses where he went to spend the evening. So he rarely saw his hostess at any other time of day than dinner-time, but at that time he always made his appearance a few minutes before the appointed hour. During this kind of courtesy visit, in the twelve years that he spent under her roof, he had addressed the same questions to her and obtained the same replies. Whether Mademoiselle Gamard had slept well or badly the previous night, the lunch she had prepared, the little domestic events of her day, how well she looked, the state of her health, the weather, the length of the Cathedral service, incidents that had occurred during Mass, and the health of Father so-and-so, made all the conversational small change of this periodical social intercourse. During the meal he always employed a method of indirect flattery, invariably proceeding from the quality of a fish, the judicious flavouring of a dish, or the virtues of a sauce, to the qualities of Mademoiselle Gamard, and her virtues as housekeeper and hostess. He was sure of soothing all the old maid's vanities when he lauded the art with which she had concocted or prepared her jams, her gherkins, her pâtés, and other gastronomical creations. Finally, the wily Canon had never quitted his hostess's yellow drawing-room without first remarking that in no other house in Tours would one be offered coffee so good as that of which he had just partaken. Thanks to his perfect understanding of Mademoiselle Gamard's nature, and this science and art of living practised by the Canon for a dozen years, there had never been any occasion for the slightest detail in the running of the house to be discussed. The Abbé Chapeloud had from the very beginning recognized the angles, the asperities, the crabbedness of the old maid, and so controlled and lubricated the action of the jars inevitable between their two personalities, as to obtain from her all the concessions necessary to the happiness and tranquillity of his life. And so Mademoiselle Gamard used to say that the Abbé Chapeloud was a very pleasant man, extremely easy to live with and very intelligent.

As for the Abbé Troubert, the devout landlady said nothing

whatever about him. Troubert had become completely caught up in the orbit of her life, like a satellite circling its planet. To her he was a creature of a species intermediary between the human and the canine. He took a place in her heart immediately before the place reserved for friends, and after that occupied by a fat asthmatic pug which she tenderly loved. She ruled him absolutely, and the identity of their interests became so complete that many people in Mademoiselle Gamard's social circle thought that the Abbé Troubert had designs upon the spinster's fortune, that by exercising constant patience he was making her gradually grow more and more attached to him, and controlled her the more effectively because he appeared to obey her and never showed any perceptible desire to take the lead.

When the Abbé Chapeloud died, the spinster, wishing to find a quiet boarder, naturally thought of the Abbé Birotteau. Before the contents of the Canon's will were known Mademoiselle Gamard was already planning to give the dead man's rooms to her good friend the Abbé Troubert, whom she considered to be unsuitably housed in his rooms on the ground floor. But when Birotteau came to agree the conditions of the contract between them, and she saw that he was so greatly taken with this flat for which he had so long cherished desires whose intensity could now be confessed, she did not dare to speak of an exchange to him, and made affection give place to the requirements of her interest. To console her beloved Canon, Mademoiselle Gamard replaced the large white tiles from Château-Renaud which formed his flooring by a herring-bone parquet floor, and rebuilt a smoking chimney.

The Abbé Birotteau had watched his friend Chapeloud for a dozen years without its ever occurring to him to wonder why he should proceed with such extreme circumspection in his relations with Mademoiselle Gamard. In coming to live with this saintly woman he found himself in the position of a lover on the point of achieving his happiness. Even if he had not been by nature unperceptive, his eyes were too much dazzled by happiness for it to be possible for him to consider Mademoiselle Gamard and reflect on where he should draw a line in his daily relations with her. Seen from a distance and through the prism of the material felicities the Abbé hoped to enjoy as her guest, Mademoiselle Gamard appeared as a perfect creature to him, a completely Christian woman, an essentially charitable person, the woman described by the Evangelists, the wise virgin adorned with all those humble and modest virtues that shed a heavenly fragrance upon life. And so, with all the enthusiasm of a man who attains a long-desired goal, with the ingenuousness of a child, and the silly thoughtlessness of an old man with no worldly experience, he entered Mademoiselle Gamard's life as a fly entangles itself in a spider's web.

The first day that he dined and slept at the spinster's house he was kept in her drawing-room by the wish to make her acquaintance, and also by the unaccountable embarrassment which often afflicts timid people and makes them afraid of appearing rude in interrupting a conversation to take their leave. So he had stayed there all evening. Another spinster, Mademoiselle Salomon de Villenoix, a friend of Birotteau's, came in during the evening. Mademoiselle Gamard then had the joy of organizing a game of boston in her own house. The Abbé, as he went to bed, felt that he had spent a very pleasant evening. As he as yet knew Mademoiselle Gamard and the Abbé Troubert only very slightly, he saw only the surface aspect of their characters. Few people nakedly display their faults at a first meeting. Generally speaking, everyone tries to provide himself with an attractive outer layer. The Abbé Birotteau then conceived the charming plan of devoting his evenings to Mademoiselle Gamard instead of spending them in houses in the town.

The landlady had, years before, formed a wish which was renewed ever more fervently from day to day as time passed. This desire, of a kind which germinates in old men and even in pretty women, had in her become a passion, like Birotteau's passion for his friend Chapeloud's rooms, and was bound more closely to the old maid's heart by the pride and selfishness, envy and vanity, which pre-exist there already in worldly people. This is an often-repeated story: one need only widen a little the narrow circle in which these persons move to find this motive force affecting events which happen in the most exalted spheres of society. Mademoiselle Gamard was accustomed to spend her evenings in six or eight different houses in turn. Whether it was because she regretted being obliged to go out to seek company and thought she had a right, at her age, to demand some return; whether it was that it wounded her vanity not to have a visiting circle of her own; or whether indeed her self-esteem sought the compliments and benefits that she saw her friends enjoy, her whole ambition was to make her drawing-room the centre for a gathering, towards which every evening a certain number of persons would turn their steps *with pleasure*.

When Birotteau and his friend Mademoiselle Salomon had passed several evenings with her, in company with the faithful and patient Abbé Troubert, as she left Saint-Gatien one evening Mademoiselle Gamard said to her friends, the good ladies whose slave she had considered herself until that moment, that people who wished to see her might well come once a week to her house, where a sufficient number of friends met to play a game of boston. She ought not to leave her new boarder, the Abbé Birotteau, alone; Mademoiselle Salomon had not yet missed a single evening in the week; she was at her friends' disposal, and so on ... and so on ... etc., etc. Her words were all the more humbly arrogant and demurely sweet since Mademoiselle Salomon de Villenoix belonged to the most aristocratic society in Tours. Although Mademoiselle Salomon came only through friendship for the Abbé, Mademoiselle Gamard was triumphant at having her in her *salon*, and saw herself, thanks to the Abbé Birotteau, on the point of realizing her grand project of forming a circle of her own, which might grow to be as large and as pleasant as Madame de Listomère's circle, and Mademoiselle Merlin de la Blottière's and those of other devout ladies who were accepted as possessing the right to receive cathedral society. But, alas! the Abbé Birotteau brought Mademoiselle Gamard's hopes to nothing. Now if those who have ever in their lives succeeded once in achieving a long-desired happiness can understand the Abbé's

F

delight in sleeping in Chapeloud's bed, they will also form some slight idea of Mademoiselle Gamard's chagrin at the destruction of her cherished plan. After accepting his good fortune patiently enough for six months Birotteau deserted the house, taking Mademoiselle Salomon with him. In spite of unheard-of efforts the ambitious Gamard had barely recruited five or six guests, the assiduity of whose attendance was very problematical, and it took at least four faithful visitors to make up a game of boston. She was thus forced to make public apology and reparation and return to the friends she used to visit, for old maids find their own company too disagreeable not to seek the questionable pleasures of society.

The reason for this desertion is easy enough to see. Although the Abbé was one of those to whom heaven is one day to belong in virtue of the decree *Blessed are the poor in spirit!* he could not, like many fools, endure the boredom inflicted by other fools. People with no sparkle of wit are like weeds, which enjoy good soil, and they have all the more need to be entertained since their own company bores them. From the boredom of which they are the embodiment, and which afflicts them, and the need they feel to be constantly taken out of themselves, arises that passion for gadding about, that necessity to be constantly somewhere else, which is characteristic of them, as it is of people who lack sensibility, and of those who have failed to achieve their destiny, or who suffer through their own fault. Without exactly plumbing the void, the nullity, of Mademoiselle Gamard, or assessing in his own mind the pettiness of her ideas, the poor Abbé perceived, a little tardily unhappily for him, the faults that she shared with all old maids, as well as those which were peculiar to herself. Other people's noxious qualities are so strikingly obvious, in contrast to their good points, that we nearly always notice them before they can harm us. This moral phenomenon would, if need were, excuse the tendency we all have more or less to speak ill of our neighbours. It is, socially speaking, so natural to mock at other people's imperfections, that we ought to pardon the unkind shafts provoked by our own absurdities, and only raise our eyebrows when we meet with calumny. But the

Abbé's eyes were never clear-sighted to the degree that enables worldly people to see and so promptly steer clear of their neighbours' sharp corners: he could not recognize his hostess's shortcomings until he had received the warning that Nature gives all her creatures, pain! Since old maids have not had to let their character and life be moulded by another's life and other characters, as a woman's destiny requires, they nearly all have an obstinate determination to make everything around them yield to them. In Mademoiselle Gamard's case this wish to rule was degenerating into despotism, but this despotism could only make itself felt in little ways. To take one example among many, the basket of score-cards and counters placed on the boston table for the Abbé Birotteau must remain in the spot where she had placed it, and the Abbé greatly vexed her when he pushed it aside, as he did nearly every evening. Why was she so touchy, so stupidly irritated by trifles, and what did she hope to gain by it? No one could have said. Mademoiselle Gamard did not know herself. Although very sheep-like by nature, the new lodger liked the frequent application of the crook no more than sheep do, especially a crook armed with spikes. It not occurring to him to seek a reason for the Abbé Troubert's endless patience, Birotteau wished to decline the happiness which Mademoiselle Gamard aspired to serve up to him flavoured in her own fashion, for she thought happiness a dish to be concocted as she prepared her jams: but the unlucky man, in the simplicity of his nature, went about the matter very clumsily. And so the separation did not take place without a good deal of friction and some pin-pricks, which the Abbé Birotteau did his best to appear not to notice.

By the end of the first year passed under Mademoiselle Gamard's roof the Abbé had resumed his previous habits, and went two evenings every week to Madame de Listomère's house, spent three with Mademoiselle Salomon and the remaining two with Mademoiselle Merlin de la Blottière. These ladies belonged to the aristocratic party in Touraine society, to which Mademoiselle Gamard had by no means the entry. And so the landlady was bitterly insulted by Birotteau's desertion, which made her feel her own lack of value: every kind of choice implies scorn of the object rejected.

'Monsieur Birotteau did not find our company good enough for him,' the Abbé Troubert said to Mademoiselle Gamard's friends, when she was obliged to give up her evenings. 'He is a man of culture, a gourmet! He needs fashionable society, luxury, sparkling conversation, the gossip of the town.'

These words always led Mademoiselle Gamard to praise the excellence of Troubert's character at the expense of Birotteau's.

'It's not that Monsieur Birotteau has such great abilities,' she used to say. 'Without the Abbé Chapeloud he would never have been received by Madame de Listomère. Oh! what a lot I lost in losing the Abbé Chapeloud. What an agreeable man he was, and so easy to live with! In twelve years I did not have the slightest difficulty with him, nor even the slightest disagreement.'

Mademoiselle Gamard painted the Abbé Birotteau's portrait in a style so little flattering that the innocent boarder passed in this bourgeois group, which was at heart hostile to aristocratic society, for a man essentially hard to please and very trying to live with. Then the spinster for some weeks had the pleasure of being sympathized with by her friends, who without meaning a word of what they were saying endlessly repeated: 'How could you, so kind and so good, have inspired dislike ...?' Or: 'Never mind, my dear Demoiselle Gamard, everyone knows you so well that ...' etc. But, delighted at avoiding a weekly evening in the Close, the most deserted spot in Tours and the one farthest from the centre of the city, everyone blessed the Abbé.

Among people who are constantly meeting, hatred and love incessantly grow; with each moment that passes they find reasons for loving or hating each other more. And so Mademoiselle Gamard soon began to find the Abbé Birotteau insupportable. Eighteen months after she had first taken him as her boarder, at a time when the worthy Abbé believed that he saw the peace of contentment where there was in fact the silence of hate, and was pluming himself on his cleverness in knowing how to *get on very well* with the spinster, to use his own expression, he was for her the object of a covert persecution and a coldly calculated vengeance. Only the four capital circumstances of the closed door, the forgotten slippers, the unlit fire, the candlestick carried upstairs, could bring home to him the frightful hostility whose momentous implications were to strike him only when his mistakes were irretrievable. As he fell asleep, therefore, the good Abbé searched his brain to its depths (to tell the truth he reached bottom very quickly) to find a reason for Mademoiselle Gamard's extraordinarily rude behaviour, but in vain. In fact as he had previously behaved naturally and with complete logic in following the dictates of his selfishness, it was impossible for him to guess how he had wronged his landlady.

If the great events of life are easily understood, simple to describe, life's petty incidents require a great many details. This long introduction was necessitated by the happenings which constitute, as it were, the prologue to this bourgeois drama, in which, bourgeois though it may be, the passions excited are found to be quite as violent as if they had been roused by great interests; and it would have been difficult for an exact historian to condense the detailed story of their development.

The next morning when Birotteau awoke, his mind was fixed so firmly on his canonry that he thought no more about the four circumstances in which the evening before he had discerned the sinister omens of a future full of woe. The Abbé was not a man to rise without a fire; he rang to warn Marianne that he was awake and call her to his room; then, as was his habit, he remained somnolently lost in a day-dream, in the course of which the servant usually roused him gently by the swish and murmur of her interrupting presence and her coming and going as she lit his fire, a kind of music which he found very pleasing. Half an hour passed, and Marianne had not appeared. The Abbé, by now practically a Canon, was about to ring again when he heard a man's step on the staircase and let the bell-pull fall. It was the Abbé Troubert, and after a discreet knock at the door, he entered at

Birotteau's invitation. This visit, as the two clergymen usually visited each other fairly regularly once a month, did not surprise Birotteau at all. The Canon expressed astonishment as soon as he came in, that Marianne had not lighted his fellow-clergyman's fire. He opened a window, called Marianne brusquely, and told her to come to Birotteau's room, then, turning back to his brother, he said:

'If Mademoiselle were to learn that you had no fire, she would scold Marianne.'

Then he inquired after Birotteau's health, and asked him kindly if he had any recent news which gave him reason to hope that he might be made canon. The Abbé explained the steps he had taken, and naïvely told him which were the persons whose interest Madame de Listomère was to engage on his behalf, unaware that Troubert had never been able to forgive that lady for not having received him in her house, him, the Abbé Troubert, already twice designated for the position of vicar-general of the diocese.

The two clergymen offered as great a contrast in form and face as it was possible to meet. Troubert was tall and gaunt, and had a bilious, sallow complexion, while Birotteau was what is familiarly called chubby. Birotteau's round, ruddy face expressed a *bonhomie* untroubled by thought, while Troubert's face, long and engraved with deep lines, at certain times took on a cast of irony or contempt; but one needed to be watching it with attention to discern the expression of these two feelings. The Canon usually presented an appearance of perfect calm, with eyelids nearly always lowered on his orange-flecked eyes, from which he could direct at will a clear and piercing glance. Rust-coloured hair put the finishing touch to this sombre physiognomy, constantly darkened by the veil which intense reflection draws over a face. Several persons at first may have believed him to be absorbed by high and far-reaching ambition, but those who had claims to know him best had in the end demolished this view, painting him as made a dullard by Mademoiselle Gamard's tyranny or worn out by fasts too prolonged. He spoke rarely and never laughed. When, as sometimes happened, his sense of the ridiculous was agreeably stirred, a faint smile escaped him and lost itself in the folds of his cheeks. Birotteau, on the contrary, was all geniality, all expansiveness, loved good things, and laughed at trifles with the simplicity of a man without malice or bitterness. At first sight the Abbé Troubert caused an involuntary tremor of terror, while Birotteau drew a sympathetic smile from those who saw him. When through the arcades and aisles of Saint-Gatien the tall Canon paced solemnly, his head bent, his eye severe, he inspired awe: his stooped figure was in harmony with the dark vaulting of the cathedral, the folds of his cassock had something monumental in their lines, suggesting sculpture. But the good little Abbé trotted about the cathedral unceremoniously, came and went, pattered to and fro, and almost seemed to bounce along.

The appearance of these two men had, nevertheless, affected their careers in a somewhat similar way. Troubert's look of ambition, by giving grounds for fear of him, had perhaps helped to condemn him to play the insignificant part of a minor canon: while, in the same way, Birotteau's character and appearance seemed to destine him to serve the cathedral permanently in a subordinate capacity. The Abbé Troubert, however, who had now reached the age of fifty, by his judicious conduct, his apparently total lack of ambition, by his very ascetic life, had quite dissipated the fears that his suspected ability and his terrible exterior had inspired in his superiors. Since his health had seriously declined during the last year, his early elevation to the vicar-generalship appeared to be even probable. His rivals themselves desired his elevation so that they might better prepare the way for theirs during the short remaining time that a malady become chronic would allow him to enjoy it. Far from holding out the same hopes, Birotteau, with his triple chin, presented to the competitors who disputed the canonry with him all the symptoms of robust good health, and his gout seemed to them, in accordance with the proverb, an assurance of longevity. The Abbé Chapeloud, a man of great good sense, whose charm had made him much sought after by the higher social circles and the different holders of high clerical office in the diocese, had always

opposed, though secretly and with great discretion, the Abbé
Troubert's promotion. He had even very adroitly prevented
his being invited to all the drawing-rooms in which the best
society in Tours met, although throughout his life Troubert
had never failed to treat him with great respect, showing him
the greatest deference on every occasion. This unvarying com-
plaisance had not changed the late Canon's opinion, and he
had said to Birotteau once again during their last walk together: 'Put no trust in that great stick Troubert. He is Sixtus
the Fifth reduced to diocesan scale.' Such was Mademoiselle
Gamard's friend and the guest at her table who came on the
morning after the day she had, as it were, declared war on poor
Birotteau, to visit him and give him visible proof of friendship.

'You must excuse Marianne,' said the Canon as he saw her
come in. 'I think she must have begun her work by coming to
my room. My rooms are very damp, and I coughed a good
deal during the night. – You are very healthily situated here,'
he added, gazing upwards at the cornices.

'Oh! I am lodged like a canon,' Birotteau replied, smiling.

'And I like a curate,' said the humble priest.

'Yes, but you will soon be lodging in the Archbishop's
palace,' said the good Abbé, whose desire it was to see everybody happy.

'Oh! or in the graveyard. But God's will be done!' And
Troubert raised his eyes to heaven in resignation.

'I came to ask you,' he went on, 'if you would lend me the
diocesan book of benefices. You are the only person in Tours
who possesses the work.'

'Take it from my library,' replied Birotteau, all the delights
of his life called back to mind at the Canon's last words.

The tall Canon passed into the library and stayed there during the time it took Birotteau to dress. Soon the breakfast bell
could be heard, and the Abbé, who was so susceptible to gout,
reflecting that if Troubert had not visited him he would have
had no fire to dress by, said to himself, 'He's a good man!'

The two clergymen went downstairs together, each laden
with an enormous folio which they placed on one of the side-
tables in the dining-room.

'What's that?' inquired Mademoiselle Gamard, sharply addressing Birotteau. 'I hope you are not going to litter my dining-room with your old books.'

'They are books that I need,' replied the Abbé Troubert. 'Monsieur Birotteau is kindly lending them to me.'

'I should have guessed that,' she said, a disdainful smile curling her lips. 'Monsieur Birotteau does not often read in those great books.'

'How are you this morning, Mademoiselle?' the boarder asked her in a thin, piping voice.

'Not very well,' she replied dryly. 'You were the cause of my being wakened from my first sleep, and my whole night was disturbed in consequence.' And, taking her seat, Mademoiselle Gamard added, 'The milk is getting cold, gentlemen.'

Dumbfounded at being so acidly received by his landlady when he was expecting apologies from her, but terrified, as timid people often are, at the prospect of a dispute, especially when they are the subject of it, the poor Abbé took his seat in silence. There, recognizing in Mademoiselle Gamard's face the clear signs of ill-humour, he sat uneasily, torn between his common sense, which urged him not to allow his landlady to treat him with such lack of proper respect, and his natural inclination to let sleeping dogs lie. With a mind thus at war with itself and full of anguish, Birotteau, to begin with, set himself to serious consideration of the thick oilcloth covering, printed with long green hatching strokes, that by an immemorial custom Mademoiselle Gamard laid on the table for breakfast, without regard to its worn edges and numerous splits. The two boarders were installed in cane-bottomed chairs facing one another at opposite ends of the table, which was square, after the royal pattern. Their hostess sat between them, and dominated the table from her high, raised chair, filled with cushions, which had its back turned to the dining-room stove. This room and the common drawing-room were on the ground floor, lying below Birotteau's bedroom and drawing-room on the floor above.

When Birotteau had taken his cup of sweetened coffee from

Mademoiselle Gamard's hands, he was paralysed by the profound silence in which he was about to take his breakfast, an occasion normally so cheerful. He dared not look either at Troubert's impassive face or the spinster's menacing one, and to keep himself in countenance turned to the over-fed pug, weighed down with fat, which lay on a cushion near the stove, from which it never stirred, as it found a little dish full of dainties on its left and a bowl of fresh water on its right always at hand to supply its needs.

'Well, my pet,' he said to it, 'you're waiting for your coffee.'

This personage, one of the most important in the house but a little embarrassing to converse with, since he no longer barked and left replies to his mistress, raised his little eyes, which were almost lost to sight in folds of fat, and looked at Birotteau, then slyly closed them. To give its full poignancy to the poor Abbé's suffering it must be said that Birotteau, being gifted with a loquacity empty and emphatic, like the echo from a struck wineglass, used to declare, although he would have been hard put to it to furnish any medical evidence in support of his opinion, that conversation favoured digestion. Mademoiselle Gamard, who agreed with this principle of good health, had never yet failed, in spite of their strained relations, to talk during the meal; but for several mornings now the Abbé had racked his brains in vain to find insidious questions that might succeed in loosening her tongue.

If the narrow limits of this story had allowed of a record of even one of those conversations, which nearly always drew his bitter and sardonic smile from the Abbé Troubert, it would have presented a perfect picture of the unintellectual life of provincial people. Perhaps it would give some bright people a certain amount of joy to hear of the strange twists that the Abbé Birotteau's and Mademoiselle Gamard's personal opinions on politics, religion, and literature took. There would certainly be no difficulty in finding something comic to show them: such as the reasons they both had seriously to suspect in 1820 that Napoleon was dead, or the inferences that led them to believe that Louis XVII was still alive, having been rescued in a large log of wood. Who could have heard them without laughing, as they busily established the facts by a process of reasoning quite obviously their own, that the king of France himself spent all the money brought in by taxes, that the Chambers were assembled to destroy the clergy, that more than thirteen hundred thousand persons had perished on the scaffold during the Revolution? Then they discussed the Press without knowing how many newspapers there were of various points of view, without having the least conception of this modern instrument. And Monsieur Birotteau listened absorbed to Mademoiselle Gamard when she repeated that a man who ate an egg every morning must infallibly die at the end of a year, that it had been known to happen; that a soft roll, taken for several days without anything to drink, would cure sciatica; that all the workmen engaged on the demolition of Saint-Martin's Abbey had died within six months; that a certain prefect had done all he could, under Napoleon, to have Saint-Gatien's towers demolished, and a thousand other absurd tales.

But at that moment Birotteau felt tongue-tied and incapable of utterance. He resigned himself and ate without broaching a subject of conversation. Soon, however, he found the silence too dangerous for his digestion and boldly said:

'This is excellent coffee!'

This courageous act was quite thrown away. When he had studied the narrow space of sky visible beyond the garden between two of Saint-Gatien's dark flying buttresses, the Abbé had the hardihood to speak again.

'It will be a better day today than it was yesterday ...' he said.

In answer to this remark Mademoiselle Gamard contented herself with bestowing the most gracious of her glances on the Abbé Troubert, and then turning eyes laden with terrifying severity on Birotteau, who happily had lowered his.

No feminine creature was better fitted than Mademoiselle Sophie Gamard to show precisely the mournful nature of the old maid; but in order to give an exact portrait of a being whose character lends immeasurable interest to the petty events of this drama, and to the inner life of the persons who are its actors, perhaps the principles whose embodiment is found in old maids should be summed up here. The habits of daily life create the soul, and the soul creates the face. If it is true that everything, in an ordered society as in the world, must be directed towards an end, then there are undeniably certain existences whose aim and utility are inexplicable. Ethics and economics alike reject the individual who consumes without producing, who occupies a place on earth without spreading round him either good or evil; for evil is no doubt a good whose results are not immediately apparent.

It rarely happens that old maids do not of their own accord class themselves with these unproductive units of society. Now, if his consciousness of the work he has done gives the worker a feeling of satisfaction which helps him to endure life, the conviction of being a charge on society, or even only useless, must produce the contrary effect, and lead the idle person to despise himself as others despise him. This harsh social reprobation is one of the causes which, unknown to themselves, help to fill old maids' souls with the chagrin which their faces express.

A prejudice for which there are perhaps some grounds looks with great disfavour, consistently and everywhere, but more especially in France, on the woman with whom no one has been willing to share the good things or endure the evils of life. Girls reach an age when the world rightly or wrongly condemns them for the rejection of which they are the victims. If they are plain, the goodness of their character ought to have made up for nature's imperfections; if they are pretty, there must have been serious reasons for their bad luck. It is hard to know which class better deserves to be cast out. If their celibacy is deliberate, if it is the result of a desire for independence, neither men nor women will forgive their treason against the ideal of feminine self-sacrifice, in their refusal of the passions which make their sex so touching: to renounce the sorrows of their sex is to abdicate its poetry, and no longer deserve the sweet consolations which are always a mother's incontestable rights.

Then the generous feelings and exquisite qualities of a woman develop only with their constant exercise. If she remains unmarried, a creature of feminine sex is an anomaly: a cold and selfish being, she inspires horror. This implacable rule is unhappily too just for old maids not to be aware of the reasons for it. These ideas germinate in their hearts as naturally as the effects of their sad lives are expressed in their features. And so they grow withered, because the constant maturing process or happiness which makes women's faces bloom and adds so much soft grace to their movements has never existed in them. Then they become morose and sour, because a being who has missed his vocation is unhappy; he suffers, and suffering engenders spite. Indeed, before she blames herself for her isolation, a woman will for long blame the world. From accusation to a wish for revenge there is only one step.

Again, the lack of charm evident in their person is another necessary result of their life. As they have never felt the need for pleasing, they remain strangers to elegance and good taste. In themselves they see only themselves reflected. This leads them insensibly to choose things that are convenient to themselves, to the detriment of those that might be pleasing to others. Without quite perceiving why they look different from other women they eventually notice that they do look different, and suffer from the fact. Jealousy is an emotion ever springing in feminine hearts. So old maids are jealous in a void, and know only the distresses of the sole selfish passion that men forgive the fair sex for possessing, because it flatters themselves.

Thus agonizingly frustrated in all their desires, obliged to thwart the development of their nature, old maids always feel an inner tension to which they never grow accustomed. Is it not hard at any age, especially for a woman, to read a feeling of repulsion on faces, when it should be a woman's destiny to awaken in hearts around her only pleasant sensations? And so an old maid's glance is always oblique, less because of modesty than through fear and shame. These beings do not forgive society for their false position because they do not forgive themselves. And it is impossible for a person perpetually at war with herself or at odds with life to leave others in peace and not envy their happiness.

This world of sad complications was there complete in Mademoiselle Gamard's dull grey eyes; and the wide dark rings that encircled them spoke of the long battles of her solitary life. All the lines of her face were straight lines. The structure of her forehead, her skull, and her cheek-bones had a quality of harsh rigidity, a characteristic aridity. She permitted hairs, once dark brown, to grow unchecked on several moles scattered on her chin. Her thin lips barely covered her overlong teeth, which did not lack whiteness. She was of brunette colouring, but her formerly dark hair had been bleached by atrocious headaches. This accident forced her to wear a front of false hair, but as she did not know how to put it on so as to conceal the foundation, there were often slight gaps between the edge of her cap and the black cord which held this rather badly curled half-wig together. Her dress, of silk in summer and merino in winter but light-brown in colour in both seasons, clipped her stiff waist and held her thin arms a little too tightly. Her collar, which she incessantly smoothed down, revealed a neck whose reddened skin was as artistically lined as an oak-leaf seen in full light. Her origin to some extent provided an explanation of her unfortunate build. She was the daughter of a wood merchant, a peasant who had got on in the world. At eighteen she may have been fresh and plump, but no trace remained of the former whiteness of her skin or the pretty colouring which she boasted that she had once possessed. The tones of her flesh had taken on that pallor quite commonly seen in pious church-goers. Her aquiline nose was the feature which best expressed her despotic tendencies, as her flat forehead showed the narrowness of her mind. Her movements had an odd jerkiness which made grace impossible, and the very sight of her drawing her handkerchief from her bag to blow her nose explosively would have enabled you to guess her character and her ways. She was rather tall and held herself very straight, justifying the observation of the naturalist who explained the gait of all old maids physiologically, declaring that their joints unite. As she walked the movement was not distributed equally throughout her body to produce graceful undulations, so attractive in women; she went along all in one piece as it were, and seemed to bob up at every step like the statue of the Commendatore. In her good-tempered moments she would let it be understood, as all old maids do, that she could have married if she had chosen, but she had luckily perceived in time that her lover was unreliable, and thus unconsciously paid a tribute to her shrewdness at the expense of her heart.

This typical figure of the species *old maid* was very suitably framed by the grotesque fantasy of a varnished wallpaper representing Turkish landscapes, with which the dining-room walls were hung. Mademoiselle Gamard normally used this room, which contained two console-tables and a barometer, as her living-room. On the two chairs which the Abbés had adopted as their own there was a little tapestry-covered cushion, whose colours were faded.

The common drawing-room, where she received visitors, was worthy of her. That it was called the *yellow drawing-room*, adequately describes it. The upholstery was yellow; the furniture and the hangings were yellow; on the chimney-piece, over which hung a gilt-framed mirror, crystal candlesticks and a crystal clock sparkled with a brilliance trying to the eyes. As for Mademoiselle Gamard's own particular sanctum, no one had ever been allowed to enter it. One could only surmise that it was filled with those odds and ends, those worn articles of furniture, those bits and pieces that all old maids surround themselves with, and which they prize so highly.

Such was the person destined to exert the greatest influence on the Abbé Birotteau's last days.

Since she could not use the energy which nature provides women with, as nature intended, and since she had to use it somehow, this spinster had brought it to the mean intrigues, the provincial tittle-tattle, the selfish plotting that all old maids in the end come to make the exclusive occupation of their minds. Birotteau, to his undoing, had developed in Sophie

Gamard the only emotion that this poor creature was capable of experiencing, a hatred which, latent until then, by reason of the peace and monotony of a provincial life whose horizons were still further narrowed for her, was bound to acquire greater intensity from the fact that it was to be exercised on little things in a narrow sphere. Birotteau was one of those people who are predestined to have everything to suffer because being able to perceive nothing, they can avoid nothing: everything comes their way.

'Yes, it will be fine,' returned the Canon a moment later, as if awakening from his reverie and wishing to observe the rules of politeness.

Birotteau, horror-struck at the time which had elapsed between his remark and this reply, for he had for the first time in his life taken his coffee without a word being spoken, left the dining-room, where his heart felt as if it were being squeezed in a vice. Feeling his cup of coffee lie heavy on his stomach, he went to walk sadly round the narrow little box-bordered pathways that traced a star pattern in the garden. But as he turned after the first circuit he saw Mademoiselle Gamard and the Abbé Troubert standing silently in the drawing-room doorway, the Abbé erect, with his arms crossed, and motionless as a statue on a tomb, the lady leaning on the frame of the shutters. Both seemed, as they watched him, to be counting his steps as he took them. Nothing is more trying, to begin with, to a naturally shy creature than to be the object of curious scrutiny, but if the scrutiny is made by the eyes of hate, the suffering it causes becomes insupportable torture. Soon the Abbé Birotteau began to imagine that he was preventing Mademoiselle Gamard and the Canon from taking a walk. This idea, inspired both by timidity and by goodness of heart, increasingly took possession of his mind, and finally made him abandon the place to them. He went off, with no thought any longer of his canonry, his whole mind was so absorbed by the distressing problem of the old maid's tyranny. He found, happily for him, that there was by chance a great deal to do at Saint-Gatien, where there were several funerals, a marriage, and two christenings. He was thus able to forget his troubles, and when his appetite announced that it was dinner-time it was not without a sudden sense of alarm that he drew out his watch, for it was some minutes after four o'clock. He knew Mademoiselle Gamard's punctuality, so he hurried to the house.

He saw in the kitchen the used plates of the first course which had been removed from the table. Then when he reached the dining-room the old maid said in a tone that in equal proportions combined the sharpness of rebuke and her joy at finding her lodger in fault:

'It is half-past four, Monsieur Birotteau. You know that we should not have to wait for you.'

The Abbé looked at the dining-room clock, and the position of the gauze covering which protected it from dust made it obvious to him that his landlady had wound it in the course of the morning, and had given herself the pleasure of setting the minute hand forward to make it fast compared with Saint-Gatien's clock. There was no possible comment that he could make. The verbal expression of his suspicion would have brought down upon him the most terrible and the most justifiable of those explosions of eloquence which Mademoiselle Gamard, like all women of her class, well knew how to burst out with in such circumstances.

The thousand and one vexations that a servant can subject her master to, or a wife her husband in the privacy of domestic life, were conjured up by Mademoiselle Gamard, and she heaped them on her lodger. Her conspiracies against the poor priest's domestic happiness were woven with enjoyment in a way which bore the mark of genius, and genius of a most profoundly malicious kind. She so arranged matters that she never appeared to be in the wrong.

Eight days after the moment when this tale begins, the Abbé Birotteau's life in this house and his relations with Mademoiselle Gamard revealed a plot to him that had been devised at least six months before. So long as the spinster had given vent to her desire for vengeance under cover, and the Abbé had been able to bury his head in the sand and refuse to believe in her malevolent intentions, the attack had gained little foothold in his mind. But since the affair of the moved candlestick and the advanced clock, Birotteau could no longer be in doubt that he lived under the sway of a hatred whose eye was ever open upon him. After that he arrived rapidly at a state of despair, as he saw Mademoiselle Gamard's hooked and razor-sharp claws ever ready at any moment to plunge into his heart. The old maid was happy to find herself living in a state of mind as fertile in emotion as an avenger's is, and delighted to hover and brood over the Abbé as a bird of prey hovers and broods over a mule before devouring it. She had long before conceived a plan which the dumbfounded priest could not guess and which she did not delay to put into action, displaying that organizing talent in minor matters often shown by solitary people who throw themselves heart and soul into the trivialities of Church life, since they have little capacity for the large experience of true religious feeling.

The final and very trying aggravation of Birotteau's troubles was that their nature forbade him – an open-hearted man who loved to be sympathized with and consoled – the sweet comfort of telling his friends about them. Such sense of what was fitting as he possessed, and which he owed to his timidity, made him afraid of seeming ridiculous in concerning himself about such silly trifles. And yet these silly trifles made up his whole existence, his sweet, busy, vacant existence, full of activity about nothing at all, that yet kept him entirely occupied, an empty, dim life in which it was a misfortune to have one's feelings stirred too strongly; in which the absence of all emotion was felicity. So the poor priest's paradise changed suddenly to hell. His sufferings at last became intolerable. The prospect of a scene with Mademoiselle Gamard, when he must demand and receive an explanation, caused him a terror which increased from day to day; and the secret misery which was blighting the autumn season of his life undermined his health.

One morning, as he put on his mottled blue stockings, he realized that the circumference of his calf had shrunk by two-thirds of an inch. Stunned by this cruelly irrefutable evidence of his state, he made up his mind to approach the Abbé Troubert and beg him to use his good offices as an intermediary between Mademoiselle Gamard and him.

When he found himself in the Canon's impressive presence, received in a bare room where Troubert had come to meet him, hastily leaving the inner room, filled with papers, in which he worked ceaselessly and which no one was allowed to enter, Birotteau felt almost ashamed to speak of Mademoiselle Gamard's pinpricks to a man who seemed to him to be occupied with such serious matters. But since he had gone through all the tortures of the inner deliberations which humble, vacillating, or weak people find necessary even in trivial affairs, he brought himself to the point, his heavily beating heart seeming to swell within him as he did so, of explaining his position to the Abbé Troubert. The Canon listened with cold, grave attention, with difficulty repressing certain signs of amusement which might have revealed an intimate satisfaction to intelligent eyes. A flame seemed to flicker in his glance when Birotteau, with the eloquence of real feeling, told him the story of the cup of bitterness constantly held to his lips; but the Canon put a hand to his eyes with a gesture familiar enough in thinkers, and preserved his accustomed dignified composure. When the Abbé stopped speaking he would have found it a difficult and perplexing task if he had tried to discover traces on Troubert's face, whose sallow hue was blotched more than ordinarily with bilious yellow, of the feelings he must have excited in this mysterious priest.

After a moment's silence the Canon made one of those sibylline replies whose words required each to be lengthily weighed before all their implications were clear, but which later were to provide reflective people with proof of the astonishing depth of his mind and the force of his understanding. He overwhelmed Birotteau when he told him that these things astonished him, all the more that he would never have noticed them without his brother's confession. He attributed this lack of perception to his weighty preoccupations, to his work, and the tyranny of a certain habit of abstract thought which did not allow him to pay much attention to the details of life. He pointed out to him, but without wanting to appear to censure the conduct of a man whose age and learning called for his respect, that 'formerly solitary men thought little of their food, their lodging, buried as they were in deep solitude, in hermitages where they gave themselves up to saintly meditation', and that 'in our times the priest by the power of thought can make for himself a hermitage everywhere'. Then, turning to what Birotteau had told him, he added that such dissensions were something entirely new to him. In twelve years nothing of the kind had taken place between Mademoiselle Gamard and the venerable Abbé Chapeloud. As for himself, he could no doubt easily act as mediator between the Abbé and their hostess, he went on, because his friendship for her did not overstep the laws which the Church imposed on its faithful servants; but then justice demanded that he should also hear what Mademoiselle Gamard had to say. For his part, he continued, he found no difference in her; she had always been as she was now; he had willingly humoured her in some of her whims, knowing that this respectable lady was goodness and kindness itself. Slight variations in her temper must be ascribed to the pain she suffered from a pulmonary infection which she never spoke of, but resigned herself as a true Christian to enduring. He ended by telling the Abbé that if he stayed some years longer with Mademoiselle he would be better able to recognize and appreciate the pure gold of her excellent character.

The Abbé Birotteau departed in confusion. Obliged by fate as he was to take counsel of no one but himself, he judged Mademoiselle Gamard by himself. The worthy Abbé thought that if he absented himself for some days, the hate this woman bore him might be extinguished for want of fuel. And so he resolved to go, as he used to do once, to spend a few days at a country house where Madame de Listomère was accustomed to pass the last weeks of autumn, a season when Touraine skies are usually clear and the air is mild. Poor man! he was doing exactly what his terrible enemy secretly willed and desired that he should. Her plans could only be frustrated by austere, monastic patience; but he, guessing nothing, not knowing at all where his own interests lay, was bound to succumb like a lamb, under the butcher's first stroke.

Madame de Listomère's property, which was situated on the causeway between the city of Tours and the heights of Saint-Georges, facing south, sheltered by rocky cliffs, combined the delights of country life with all the pleasures of town. In fact, it did not take more than ten minutes to come from Tours bridge to the door of her house, *Larkrise* as it was called, an advantage precious in a part of the world where no one wants to go a step further than he need for any reason whatever, even in search of pleasure.

The Abbé Birotteau had been about ten days at Larkrise when one morning at breakfast the door-keeper came to tell him that Monsieur Caron wished to speak to him. Monsieur Caron was a lawyer who looked after Mademoiselle Gamard's affairs. Birotteau, who did not remember this, and knew of no matter that he might have for litigation with anyone in the world, left the table in some anxiety to look for the lawyer. He found him unobtrusively seated on a terrace parapet.

'Your intention of giving up your lodging with Mademoiselle Gamard having become clear ...' the solicitor began.

'Eh! Monsieur,' the Abbé shrilly interrupted him, 'I have never thought of leaving her.'

'Well, Monsieur,' returned the lawyer, 'you must have given Mademoiselle to understand that such was the case, since she sends me to obtain information as to whether you intend to remain long in the country. The case of a long absence not having been foreseen in your agreement, this may give rise to some matter for dispute. Now, Mademoiselle Gamard understanding that your board ...'

'Monsieur,' said Birotteau, in some surprise, interrupting him again, 'I do not imagine that it should be necessary to employ almost legal means to ...'

'Mademoiselle Gamard is anxious to forestall any difficulty,' said Monsieur Caron, 'and has sent me to come to an understanding with you.'

'Very well, if you will be good enough to come back to-morrow,' the Abbé Birotteau replied, 'I will take advice on my side.'

'Agreed,' said Caron with a bow. And the lawyer withdrew.

The poor Abbé, in dismay at the persistence with which Mademoiselle Gamard pursued him, returned to Madame de Listomère's dining-room looking distraught. When they saw his face, everyone asked: —

'What's happened, Monsieur Birotteau?'

The Abbé, lost in affliction, sat down without a word, so oppressed was he by the shifting faces of his misfortune. But after breakfast, when several of his friends had gathered in the drawing-room round a good fire, Birotteau artlessly told them the details of his experience. His hearers, who were beginning to feel bored in their country retreat, were greatly interested by this intrigue, which was of a kind very characteristic of provincial life. Everyone took the Abbé's part against the old maid.

'What!' said Madame de Listomère, 'don't you see, isn't it clear that the Abbé Troubert wants your rooms?'

Here the narrator should properly sketch a portrait of this lady; but it occurred to him that even those who are ignorant of Sterne's system of *cognomology* could not pronounce the three words MADAME DE LISTOMÈRE without picturing her as she was, aristocratic, dignified, tempering the rigours of her devotion to religion by the old-style elegance of a classic way of life as it was lived under the monarchy, by polished manners; kind, if a trifle stiff; inclined to talk through her nose; permitting herself to read *La Nouvelle Héloïse*, to go to the theatre, and not yet wearing a cap on her hair.

'Monsieur Birotteau must not give way to that old mischief-maker!' cried Monsieur de Listomère, a naval officer spending his leave with his aunt. 'If the Abbé has pluck and will follow my advice he will soon win back his peace of mind again.'

Then everyone set to work to review and criticize Mademoiselle Gamard's conduct with the perspicacity characteristic of country people, who, one cannot deny, have a talent for laying bare the most deeply-hidden motives of human actions.

'You haven't got to the root of the matter,' said an old landowner who knew his Touraine. 'There is something serious underlying this, that I don't grasp yet. The Abbé Troubert's nature is too deep to be plumbed so quickly. Our dear Birotteau is only at the beginning of his troubles. To begin with, will he have a mind at ease, can he be happy, even if he gives up his rooms to Troubert? I doubt it. If Caron has come to tell you,' he went on, turning to the wide-eyed priest, 'that you intend to leave Mademoiselle Gamard, no doubt Mademoiselle Gamard intends to put you out. ... Well! you will have to go, whether you want to or not. People of that kind never take any risks, and only play when they know the game is theirs.'

This old country squire, Monsieur de Bourbonne by name, represented a summary and abstract of provincial ideas as completely as Voltaire embodied the spirit of his age. In the matter of dress the meagre, spare old man exercised the complete indifference of a man of property, whose worth in land is assessed at its exact value in his Department. His face, tanned by the Touraine sun, was not so much wise as shrewd. He was accustomed to weigh his words and plan his actions, but hid his profound circumspection beneath a deceptive simplicity. Yet the most superficial observer could see at once that, like a Norman peasant, he would always have the best of it in any business matter. He knew a great deal about the science of wines, the Touraine man's favourite branch of learning. He had been clever enough to enlarge the meadows of one of his estates by taking in alluvia left by the Loire without getting involved in any action by the State, and because of this feat he was generally accepted as a man of talent. If, charmed by Monsieur de Bourbonne's conversation, you had demanded his life-story from some native of Touraine: 'Oh, that's a downy old bird!' would have been the proverbial answer given by all his jealous rivals, and there were many of them. In Touraine, as in most of the provinces, jealousy gives richness to the vocabulary.

Monsieur de Bourbonne's observation created a momentary silence, while the persons composing this little committee appeared to reflect; and while they were thus engaged Mademoiselle Salomon de Villenoix was announced. The desire to be of service to Birotteau had brought her from Tours, and her news completely changed the aspect of affairs. When she came in, everyone, except the landowner, was advising Birotteau to fight Troubert and Gamard under the auspices of the aristocratic group, which would protect him.

'The Vicar-General, who makes the reports on candidates for Church appointments, has just fallen ill,' said Mademoiselle Salomon, 'and the Archbishop has handed over his duties to Monsieur l'Abbé Troubert. So now the nomination to the canonry depends entirely on him. Yesterday, at Mademoiselle de la Blottière's house, the Abbé Poirel talked about the annoyances the Abbé Birotteau was causing Mademoiselle Gamard, as if he were anxious to justify our good Abbé's being cast out of favour. "The Abbé Birotteau is a man who absolutely needed the Abbé Chapeloud to stand behind him," he said; "and since that estimable Canon died, it's been proved that ... etc." And false suppositions and slanders followed. You understand?'

'Troubert will be vicar-general,' said Monsieur de Bourbonne gravely.

'Come!' cried Madame de Listomère, looking at Birotteau. 'Which would you rather be, canon or Mademoiselle Gamard's lodger?'

'Canon!' everyone exclaimed.

'Well,' said Madame de Listomère, 'you must let the Abbé Troubert and Mademoiselle Gamard win the day. Isn't it plain that they are giving you to understand indirectly by Caron's visit that if you consent to leave them you will be canon? Give and take!'

There were admiring exclamations at Madame de Listomère's acuteness and sagacity from everyone except her nephew, the Baron de Listomère, who said comically to Monsieur de Bourbonne:

'I would have liked a fight, Gamard *versus* Birotteau.'

But, unhappily for the Abbé, the odds were not equal between his aristocratic supporters and the spinster backed by the Abbé Troubert. Soon the struggle was to take shape more openly, loom increasingly larger, grow to vast proportions. On Madame de Listomère's advice and that of most of her adherents, who were beginning to take a hotly partisan interest in this intrigue which had chanced to come to fill a gap in their empty provincial life, a servant was dispatched to M. Caron. The lawyer returned with remarkable celerity, a fact which gave cause for alarm only to Monsieur de Bourbonne.

'We should put off any decision until we are informed more fully,' was the advice of this Fabius in a dressing-gown, who was accustomed by profound meditation to search out and lay bare the higher strategy behind moves on the Touraine chess-board.

He wished to enlighten Birotteau on the dangers of his position. But the 'downy old bird's' wisdom did not serve the passions of the moment, and he obtained scant attention.

The interview between the lawyer and Birotteau did not last long. The Abbé returned, looking scared and bewildered, saying:

'He is asking me for a declaration of *withdrawal*.'

'What's that portentous word?' asked the lieutenant-commander.

'What does that mean?' exclaimed Madame de Listomère.

'It simply means that the Abbé must declare his wish to leave Mademoiselle Gamard's house,' replied Monsieur de Bourbonne, taking a pinch of snuff.

'Is that all? Sign!' said Madame de Listomère looking at Birotteau. 'If you have seriously made up your mind to leave her, there can be no harm in stating that that is your will ...'

Birotteau's will!

'That is true,' said Monsieur de Bourbonne, snapping his snuff-box shut with a dry gesture whose significance cannot be rendered in words, for it was a whole language in itself. 'But it is always dangerous to put things in writing,' he added, laying his snuff-box on the chimney-piece with an air which might well make the Abbé tremble.

Birotteau was so stunned by the upsetting of all his ideas and the rapidity with which one event trod upon another's heels, taking him by surprise and finding him defenceless, by the casual, easy way in which his friends dealt with the most intimate and dearest concerns of his solitary life, that he stood there without moving a finger, as if lost in the moon, thinking of nothing, but listening and trying to understand the cascade of words that everyone poured forth so prodigally. He took the paper from M. Caron, and scanned it, as if the lawyer's wording of the deed was going to receive all his attention; but it was a mechanical gesture. And he signed the document, in which he agreed voluntarily to renounce his right to lodging and board at Mademoiselle Gamard's house according to the agreement made between them.

When he had added his signature, M. Caron took the paper and asked where his client should have Monsieur Birotteau's belongings sent. Birotteau named Madame de Listomère's house, and that lady indicated that she was willing to take the Abbé in for a few days, not doubting that he would soon be appointed canon. The old landowner wished to see this kind of act of renunciation, and Monsieur Caron took it to him.

'Well,' he said to the Abbé when he had read it, 'so there exists a written agreement between you and Mademoiselle Gamard? Where is it? What are the terms of it?'

'The paper is in my rooms,' replied Birotteau.

'Do you know its general purport?' the landowner asked the lawyer.

'No, sir,' said M. Caron, holding out his hand for the fateful paper.

'Ah!' said the old landowner to himself, 'no doubt you know very well, Monsieur Caron, every clause of the deed, but you are not paid to tell us.'

And Monsieur de Bourbonne returned the document of renunciation to the lawyer.

'Where am I to put all my furniture?' cried Birotteau, 'and my books, my handsome bookcase, my fine pictures, my red drawing-room – all my furnishings?'

And the poor man's despair, as he saw himself thus, as it were, uprooted, had such an element of the naïf in it, so well illustrated the innocence and simplicity of his way of living, his ignorance of the ways of the world, that Madame de Listomère and Mademoiselle Salomon, to console him, said, in the tone of mothers promising their child a toy: 'You are not going to let that nonsense trouble you, are you? We'll surely find you a house much less cold and dark than Mademoiselle Gamard's. If we don't happen to find a lodging to your taste, well, one of us will take you as her boarder. Come, let's take out the backgammon board. Tomorrow you shall go to see Monsieur l'Abbé Troubert to ask him to back you up, and you'll see how well he will receive you!'

Weak people are as quickly reassured as they are easily frightened. Poor Birotteau, dazzled by the prospect of living at Madame de Listomère's house, forgot the ruin that had irretrievably overtaken the happiness which he had desired for so long and which he had enjoyed with such pleasure. But that evening, before he went to sleep, with the distress of a man for whom the disturbance of a change of dwelling and new ways was the end of the world, he racked his brain, desperately trying to think where he could find a place to set his bookcase, as well suited to it as his gallery was. Picturing his books astray, his suites of furniture broken up, his household all in disorder, he asked himself over and over again why the first year he had spent with Mademoiselle Gamard had been so sweet, and the second so cruel; and always his misfortune was a bottomless well in which his reason drowned. The canonry no longer seemed sufficient compensation for such unhappiness. He compared his life to a stocking in which one slipped stitch unravelled the whole web. Mademoiselle Salomon remained his friend. But, as he lost his old illusions, the poor priest no longer dared to trust a friendship of recent date.

In the *città dolente* of old maids one meets many, especially in France, whose life is a sacrifice nobly offered every day to noble principles. Some keep proud faith with a heart too quickly torn from them by death; they are martyrs to love, led to find the secret of being true women by their souls. Others yield to family loyalty, which to our shame is now every day declining, and devote themselves to the fortunes of a brother or to orphan nephews: those achieve motherhood, though they remain old maids. These spinsters attain the highest heroism their sex knows, devoting all their womanly feeling to the service of misfortune. Woman's natural stature is made ideal in them, in their renunciation of her destiny's rewards and acceptance only of her sorrows. They live irradiant in the splendour of their devotion, and men bow their heads in reverence before their withered faces. Mademoiselle de Sombreuil has never been a wife; she was and always will be a living poem. Mademoiselle Salomon was one of this band of heroic creatures. Her devotion was in exact terms sublime, in that it could bring her no glory in the end, though it had been a daily martyrdom to her all her life. She was beautiful and young. She was loved and in love. Her future husband lost his reason. For five years, with the courage love gives, she had devoted herself to the material welfare of this unfortunate man, whose madness she had so closely embraced that she did not think him mad. For the rest she was a person of simple manner, frank in her speech, and her pale face did not lack character in spite of its regularity of feature. She never spoke of the events of her life. Only, sometimes, a sudden involuntary shudder when she heard the story of some sad or dreadful accident, revealed that she possessed the fine powers of sympathy which great suffering develops. She had come to live in Tours when she had lost her life companion. She could not be appreciated at her proper value there, and was regarded as a *good-hearted person*. She did a great deal of good, and by preference sought the society of the weak. For this reason the poor Abbé had naturally enough awakened her deep interest.

Mademoiselle de Villenoix, who was going into town early in the morning, took Birotteau with her, set him down in the Quai de la Cathédrale, and left him making his way towards the Close, which he was impatient to reach in order to save at least the canonry from the shipwreck, and supervise the removal of his furniture.

It was not without violent flutterings of the heart that he rang at the door of this house to which he had been in the habit of coming for fourteen years, where he had lived, and from which he was to be an exile for ever, although he had dreamed of peacefully ending his days there, as his friend Chapeloud had done. Marianne was surprised to see the Abbé. He told her that he had come to see the Abbé Troubert, and turned towards the Canon's ground-floor apartments; but Marianne called out to him:

'The Abbé Troubert is not there now, Monsieur l'Abbé; he is in your old rooms.'

These words gave the Abbé an appalling shock. And at last he understood Troubert's character, and the deep-rooted nature of a vengeance calculated so long before, moving so slowly to its purpose, when he found him ensconced in Chapeloud's library, seated in Chapeloud's fine gothic chair, no doubt sleeping in Chapeloud's bed, enjoying Chapeloud's furniture, lodged at Chapeloud's heart, annulling Chapeloud's Will, and finally disinheriting the friend of that Chapeloud who for so long had kept him mewed up in Mademoiselle Gamard's house, blocking the way to all advancement and closing the doors of Tours society against him.

What magic wand had been waved to effect this metamorphosis? Did all this not belong any longer to Birotteau? Certainly, seeing the sardonic air with which Troubert surveyed this library, poor Birotteau believed that the future vicar-general was sure of permanently possessing the abandoned belongings of those that he had so cruelly hated, Chapeloud as an enemy, and Birotteau because in him Chapeloud still lived on. At the sight of Troubert a host of thoughts rose in the good Abbé's heart and plunged him into a sort of reverie. He stood there motionless, as if fascinated by Troubert's eye, and Troubert stared at him stonily.

'I do not think, sir,' said Birotteau at length, 'that you would want to deprive me of articles which belong to me. Though Mademoiselle Gamard may have been impatient to find you a better lodging, she must in all fairness give me time to identify my books and remove my furniture.'

'Sir,' said the Abbé Troubert coldly, his face expressionless, 'Mademoiselle Gamard informed me yesterday of your departure; I am still unaware of the reason for it. If she has installed me here, it is because she had to. Monsieur l'Abbé Poirel has taken my rooms. I do not know whether the articles which are in these apartments belong or not to Mademoiselle, but if they are yours, you know her good faith: the saintliness of her life is a guarantee of her probity. As for me, you are not unaware of the simplicity of my mode of life. I have slept for fifteen years in a bare room without regard to its dampness, which in the long run has shortened my life. However, if you wish to live in these rooms again, I will willingly hand them over to you.'

When he heard these terrible words Birotteau forgot the matter of the canonry. He ran downstairs as impulsively as if he were a young man to find Mademoiselle Gamard, and met her at the foot of the staircase on the wide tiled landing that joined the two wings of the building.

'Mademoiselle,' he greeted her, paying no attention to the sourly mocking smile on her lips or the extraordinary flame which gave her eyes the brightness of a tiger's, 'I do not understand why you did not wait until I had removed my furniture before ...'

'What!' she interrupted him. 'Have your belongings not all been sent to Madame de Listomère's?'

'But my furniture?'

'Have you not read your agreement?' said the old maid, in a tone that would have to be expressed in music to convey the delicate shades of venom that hatred could find skill to infuse in the accentuation of each word.

And Mademoiselle Gamard appeared to grow taller, and her eyes blazed more brilliantly, and her face shone, and her whole person thrilled with pleasure. The Abbé Troubert threw open a window in order to see the pages of a folio more clearly. Birotteau stood thunderstruck. Mademoiselle Gamard screamed in his ears in a voice as shrill as a trumpet, these words:

'Was it not agreed that your furniture should belong to me in the event of your leaving me, to indemnify me for the difference in the sum you paid for your board and lodging and that paid by the venerable Abbé Chapeloud? Well, as Monsieur l'Abbé Poirel has been appointed canon ...'

When he heard these last words, Birotteau bowed feebly, as if to take his leave of the old maid; then he precipitately left the house. He was afraid that if he stayed a moment longer he might grow faint and let these implacable enemies triumph too greatly over him. Walking like a drunken man, he reached Madame de Listomère's house, where in a mean room he found his linen, clothing, and papers packed in a trunk. At the sight of all that was left of his furnishings the unhappy priest sat down and hid his face in his hands to conceal his tears from the servants. The Abbé Poirel was canon! He, Birotteau, was left with no home, no means, and no furniture! Fortunately Mademoiselle Salomon's carriage chanced to pass the house. The door-keeper, who had realized the poor man's despair, made a sign to the driver. There followed a short conversation between the spinster and the door-keeper, and then the Abbé suffered himself to be led, more dead than alive, to his faithful friend, to whom he could speak only incoherently. Mademoiselle Salomon, alarmed at this temporary disturbance in an intellect already far from strong, took him at once to Larkrise. She attributed this incipient mental derangement to the effect that the Abbé Poirel's appointment must have produced on him. She did not know the clauses of Birotteau's agreement with Mademoiselle Gamard, for the excellent reason that he did not himself know what they included. And as it is in the nature of things that the comic is sometimes mingled with the most affecting pathos, Birotteau's strange answers almost made Mademoiselle Salomon smile.

'Chapeloud was right,' he said. 'He's a monster!'

'Who?' she asked.

'Chapeloud. He has taken everything from me.'

'You mean Poirel?'

'No, Troubert.'

At last they reached Larkrise, and the Abbé's friends there showed such concern for his welfare and surrounded him with such generous kindness that towards the evening they succeeded in calming him, and were able to obtain an account of what had happened that morning.

The imperturbable landowner naturally asked to see the document, which since the evening before had seemed to him to hold the key to the enigma. Birotteau took the fateful piece of stamped paper from his pocket and held it out to Monsieur

de Bourbonne, who read it through rapidly, and soon reached
a clause in these terms:

*As there is a difference of eight hundred francs a year between the sum
paid for board by the late Monsieur Chapeloud and that for which the
aforesaid Sophie Gamard consents to take into her house on the terms
above stipulated the aforesaid François Birotteau; in the circumstance
that the undersigned François Birotteau freely declares that he is not
and will not for several years be in a position to give the price paid by
the demoiselle Gamard's boarders, and in particular by the Abbé
Troubert; and finally, in consideration of various advances made by the
undersigned Sophie Gamard, the aforesaid Birotteau undertakes to
leave to her, in order to indemnify her, the furniture of which he is possessed at his death, or when, for whatever reason, he voluntarily, at any
time, leaves the premises presently let to him, and ceases to enjoy
further the benefits stipulated in the engagement undertaken by
Mademoiselle Gamard in his interest, as under …*

'God bless my soul! What a woman!' cried the landowner.
'And what claws the aforesaid Sophie Gamard possesses!'

Poor Birotteau, whose infantile mind was unable to conceive of anything that might one day separate him from
Mademoiselle Gamard, had counted on ending his days in her
house. He had no memory of this clause, whose terms had not
even been discussed, it had seemed so just to him at the time,
when, in his anxiety to belong to the old maid's establishment,
he would have signed any parchment presented to him. This
innocence was so worthy of respect, and Mademoiselle
Gamard's conduct so atrocious, the poor sexagenarian's fate
was so deplorable and his weakness made him so pathetic, that
in the first flush of indignation Madame de Listomère exclaimed:

'I am responsible for your signing the document which has
ruined you. I must restore the happiness I have taken from
you.'

'But,' said the old squire, 'the document constitutes a fraud,
and is actionable …'

'Well, then! Birotteau shall bring an action. If he loses it in

Tours, he will win in Orleans. If he loses it in Orleans, he will win in Paris!' cried the Baron de Listomère.

'If he intends to bring an action,' Monsieur de Bourbonne returned coldly, 'I advise him first to resign his office.'

'We will consult lawyers,' answered Madame de Listomère, 'and we will bring an action if we must. But this affair is too shameful for Mademoiselle Gamard, and may become too harmful to the Abbé Troubert, for us not to obtain some compromise.'

After mature consideration and debate, each person present promised his assistance to the Abbé Birotteau in the battle which was about to be joined between him and all the adherents of his antagonists. A sure intuition, an indefinable provincial instinct, made everyone add Troubert's name to Mademoiselle Gamard's. But none of those who were there at that moment in Madame de Listomère's house, excepting the 'downy old bird', had any very exact idea of the momentous nature of such a conflict. Monsieur de Bourbonne drew the poor Abbé aside into a corner.

'Of the fourteen persons here,' he told him in a low voice, 'there will not be one for you in a fortnight. If you need to call someone to your aid, you will perhaps find only me intrepid enough to dare take your part, because I know the country, the men, affairs, and, more important still, the interests involved! But all your friends, although they are full of good intentions, are setting you on a mistaken course from which you will not be able to turn back. Listen to my advice. If you want to live in peace, resign your appointment in Saint-Gatien, leave Tours. Do not say where you are going, but look for some living far away where Troubert cannot run across you.'

'Leave Tours?' exclaimed the Abbé in indescribable dismay.

For him that was a kind of death. Did it not mean breaking all the fibres by which he had taken root in the world? Bachelors live by their habits, as their powers of response decay. When to this rigidity of mind, which makes them rather travel through life than live, is joined a weak nature, external

G

things take an astonishing hold on them. So Birotteau had
grown to be rather like a plant: to transplant him was to en-
danger his innocent flowering and fruit. Like a tree, which in
order to live has to imbibe the juices from the same soil unceasingly and spread its hair-roots always in the same ground,
Birotteau must never cease trotting to and fro in Saint-Gatien,
must always tread the earth in the vicinity of the Mail where
he was accustomed to take his walks, constantly traverse the
streets through which he normally passed, and continue to
visit the three drawing-rooms where every evening he played
whist or backgammon.

'Ah! I didn't think of that,' replied Monsieur de Bourbonne, considering the priest with pitying eyes.

Everyone in the city of Tours soon knew that Madame la
Baronne de Listomère, the widow of a lieutenant-general, was
harbouring the Abbé Birotteau, one of the minor clergy of
Saint-Gatien. This fact, which many people found hard to believe, placed matters on a clear footing, and defined the sides
that were being taken, especially when Mademoiselle Salomon, who was the first to dare to do so, spoke of fraud and
legal action. With the complex vanity which marks old maids
and their characteristically fanatical egotism, Mademoiselle
Gamard discovered that she was grievously wounded by the
course Madame de Listomère was adopting. The Baroness was
a woman of high rank, who lived with style and elegance,
whose good taste, polished manners, and religious feeling
were unquestionable. In giving Birotteau asylum she gave the
lie in the most formal fashion to all Mademoiselle Gamard's
assertions, indirectly censured her conduct, and seemed to
approve the Abbé's complaints against his former landlady.

To make this story fully understood it must be here explained how much strength was lent to Mademoiselle Gamard's cause by the penetration and analytical spirit with which
old women study other people's actions, and what the resources of her party were. Accompanied by the taciturn Abbé
Troubert, she was accustomed to pass her evenings in four or
five houses where a dozen persons met, who were bound to-

gether by the same tastes and the similarity of their situation.
There were one or two old men who made their servants' passions and idle chatter their own ruling interests; five or six old
maids who spent their whole days sifting the words and narrowly scrutinizing the doings of their neighbours and those
placed socially above them; and finally several elderly married
women, exclusively occupied in distilling scandal, in keeping
exact account of everyone's fortunes, and in taking note of
other people's actions: they forecast the marriages and condemned the conduct of their friends as acidly as they did those
of their enemies.

These persons, living in every quarter of the town and
forming something like the network of a plant's capillary vessels, drank in, with a leaf's thirst for dew, the news, the secrets,
of every household, sucked them up and automatically transmitted them to the Abbé Troubert, as leaves transmit to the
stem the cool moisture they have absorbed. So, every evening
of the week, spurred on by the need for excitement which
every individual feels, these good churchwomen drew up an
exact balance sheet of the state of the city with a shrewdness
worthy of the Council of Ten, and made themselves the armed
police of that wholly efficient system of espionage which is inspired and created by passionately engaged interest. Then,
when they had nosed out the secret reason for some happening, their vanity led them to take upon themselves the wisdom
of their sanhedrin, in order to set the key for the gossip in
their respective zones.

This church community, then, doing nothing, yet active, invisible and seeing everything, unheard and ceaselessly talking,
possessed an influence which the nonentity of the persons
composing it made seemingly harmless, but which could become terrifying when these persons were animated by a major
interest. Now it was long since an event so serious and so
generally important for all of them, as the conflict between
Birotteau backed by Madame de Listomère and the Abbé
Troubert and Mademoiselle Gamard, had occurred in the
sphere in which they had their being. Indeed, as the groups received in the three drawing-rooms of Mesdames de Listomère,

Merlin de la Blottière, and de Villenoix were considered
enemies in the drawing-rooms which Mademoiselle Gamard
visited, at the bottom of this quarrel lay *esprit de corps* and all
its vanities. It was the struggle between the Roman people and
the Senate in a mole-hill, a storm in a glass of water, as Mon-
tesquieu remarked of the Republic of Saint-Marin, where
tyrannical power was so easy to seize that public appointments
were held for only one day. Nevertheless this storm excited as
many passions in the soul as would have supplied motive
power to direct the greatest social enterprises.

Is it not a mistaken idea that it is only when vast schemes
consume people's hearts and fill their lives with turbulence
and commotion that time moves quickly? The Abbé Troubert's hours rushed by with as great an impetus, as charged
with care, as heavy with thought, as ever fled the cruel hours
of the ambitious man, the gambler, or the lover, and were
harrowed by despairs and hopes as poignant. Only God holds
the secret of what the cost to us is of unseen victories achieved
over men, things, and ourselves, in the life force we expend.
If we do not always know whither we are bound, we well
know the fatigues of the journey. Yet, if the narrator may be
allowed to stand aside from the drama which he is relating to
take the rôle of critic for a moment, if he invites you to cast a
glance at the existences of these old maids and the two Abbés
in order to seek in their lives the cause of the unhappiness that
vitiated them at their heart, it will perhaps be demonstrated to
you that it is necessary to man that he should experience certain passions to develop in him the qualities which lend his life
nobility, extend its range, and still the egotism natural to all
created things.

Madame de Listomère returned to town unaware that, for
the last five or six days, several of her friends had been obliged
to refute an opinion expressed about her, which would have
made her laugh if she had known about it, according to which
her affection for her nephew had causes which verged on the
criminal. She took the Abbé Birotteau to her lawyer, who did
not find the proposed law-suit a simple matter. The Abbé's
friends, complacent in their consciousness of the justice of a

good cause, or disinclined to bestir themselves in a legal matter which was not of personal concern, had put off starting the suit until they should return to Tours. Mademoiselle Gamard's friends were thus able to forestall them and tell their story of the affair from an angle not very flattering to the Abbé Birotteau. And so the legal adviser, whose clientèle was exclusively composed of the religious set in the town, much surprised Madame de Listomère by advising her not to be drawn into such a suit, and he concluded the consultation by saying that in any case he would not undertake it, because, according to the terms of the agreement, Mademoiselle Gamard was legally in the right; that in equity, that is beyond the terms of legal justice, the Abbé Birotteau would appear, in the eyes of the tribunal and of honourable people, to lack the peaceable conciliatory character and the forbearance which he had been credited with possessing; that Mademoiselle Gamard, who was known to be a kindly person and easy to live with, had obliged Birotteau by lending him the money he needed to pay the estate duty on his inheritance from Chapeloud, without asking him for a receipt; that Birotteau was not of an age or character to sign a document without knowing its contents or realizing their significance; and that if he had left Mademoiselle Gamard after two years, when his friend Chapeloud had stayed with her for twelve and Troubert for fifteen, it could only be for some purpose plain to himself; that the suit would thus necessarily be considered an act of ingratitude, and so on, and so forth. Leaving Birotteau to walk ahead towards the staircase, the lawyer drew Madame de Listomère aside as he showed her out, and besought her, in the name of her peace of mind, to have nothing to do with this business.

In the evening, however, the poor Abbé, who was as much on tenterhooks as a man in the condemned cell at Bicêtre waiting for the result of his appeal, could not refrain from telling his friends of the result of his visit, as the circle was forming round Madame de Listomère's fireplace before breaking up into card-parties.

'Apart from the Liberal solicitor, I don't know anyone in Tours concerned with litigation who would undertake this

action without intending to lose it,' exclaimed Monsieur de
Bourbonne, 'and I do not advise you to engage in it.'

'Well, it's a shame!' said the Lieutenant-Commander. 'I'll
take the Abbé to this solicitor myself.'

'Go to him after dark,' Monsieur de Bourbonne interrupted
him.

'Why?'

'I have just been informed that the Abbé Troubert has been
appointed vicar-general in succession to the man who died the
day before yesterday.'

'I don't care a fig for the Abbé Troubert.'

Unluckily the Baron de Listomère, a man of thirty-six, did
not notice Monsieur de Bourbonne's glance recommending
him to weigh his words, and indicating a member of the
General Council, a friend of Troubert's. And the Baron
added:

'If Monsieur l'Abbé Troubert is a rascal ...'

'Oh!' interrupted Monsieur de Bourbonne. 'Why bring the
Abbé Troubert into a business which has nothing at all to do
with him?'

'But is he not in possession of the Abbé Birotteau's furniture?' said the Baron. 'I remember visiting Chapeloud and
seeing two valuable pictures. Suppose they are worth ten
thousand francs. Do you believe that it was Monsieur Birotteau's intention to give ten thousand francs for two years'
board and lodging with that woman Gamard, when the library
and furniture are worth about as much again as well?'

The Abbé Birotteau opened his eyes wide as he learned that
he had possessed such an enormous capital. And the Baron
went on hotly:

'By heaven! Monsieur Salmon, the former expert from the
Musée de Paris, is here visiting his mother-in-law. I shall go to
see him this very evening with the Abbé Birotteau, and ask
him to value the pictures. From there I shall go on with the
Abbé to the solicitor.'

Two days after this conversation, the lawsuit had begun to
take shape. The Liberal party's solicitor, now Birotteau's,
brought much disfavour upon the Abbé's cause. Men opposed

to the Government, and men who were known to have no liking for priests or religion – two attitudes which many people confuse – took up the affair, and the whole town talked about it. The former expert from the Musée estimated Valentin's Virgin and Lebrun's Christ, both first-class pieces, to be worth eleven thousand francs. As for the bookcase and the gothic furniture, the taste of the day for that kind of thing, which was becoming increasingly fashionable in Paris, gave them a value for the moment of twelve thousand francs. Finally the expert, after due examination, set a value of ten thousand crowns on the whole of the furniture. Now it was obvious that as Birotteau had not meant to give this relatively enormous sum to Mademoiselle Gamard for the small sum of money which he might owe her in virtue of the stipulated compensation, there were, legally, grounds for reconsidering their agreement; otherwise the spinster would have been guilty of a deliberate fraud. The Liberal solicitor, therefore, initiated the business by applying for an injunction against Mademoiselle Gamard. Although it was very dryly written, this document, fortified by quotations from Supreme Court judgements and confirmed by certain articles of the Code, was none the less a masterpiece of forensic logic, and so clearly condemned the old maid that thirty or forty copies of it were maliciously distributed in the town by the party opposed to her.

A few days after the commencement of hostilities between the spinster and Birotteau, the Baron de Listomère, who was hoping to be promoted to the command of a corvette in the next list of appointments, which had been awaited from the Ministry of Marine for some time, received a letter from a friend, telling him that there was some talk in the department of his being retired. Completely taken by surprise by this news, he left immediately for Paris, and presented himself at the Minister's first 'at home'. His Excellency seemed very astonished at what the Baron de Listomère told him, and laughed at his fears. Next day, in spite of what the Minister had said, the Baron made inquiries at the Ministry. A secretary, by an indiscretion which some men at the top of their profession readily enough commit for the sake of their friends, showed him a document, prepared and ready, which owing to the illness of a chief had not yet been submitted to the Minister, and which confirmed the disastrous news. The Baron de Listomère went at once to one of his uncles, who as a Deputy had immediate access to the Minister in the Chamber, and begged him to find out how the land lay and the Minister's intentions, for it was a matter of life and death for his career. Sitting in his uncle's carriage, he waited for the Chamber to finish its business with the liveliest anxiety.

The Deputy appeared well before the end of the sitting, and said to his nephew as they returned to his house:

'Why the devil must you get mixed up in making war on the clergy? The Minister began by informing me that you had set yourself at the head of the liberals in Tours! You had abominable opinions, you didn't know the Government line, and so on, and so on. He got his sentences tied into as many knots as if he were still declaiming in the Chamber. Then I said to him, "Come, let's hear the facts!" In the end His Excellency let it out that you had got on the wrong side of the clerical hierarchy. To cut a long story short, I tried to gather some information from my colleagues, and heard that you were going about speaking very slightingly of a certain Abbé Troubert, a simple vicar-general, but the most important personage in the province, where he represents the Congregation. I answered for you, my life for yours, to the Minister. My dear nephew, if you have any desire to continue your career, do not make the clergy hostile to you. Go back to Tours at once and make your peace with that confounded vicar-general. Take it to heart that vicars-general are men with whom one must always live at peace. Heaven knows, when we are all trying to re-establish religion on a firm footing, it is not very clever of a lieutenant-commander who would like a command of his own to run down priests. If you do not patch matters up with the Abbé Troubert, don't count any further on me: I will disown you. The Minister for Ecclesiastical Affairs spoke to me just now of this man as a future bishop. If Troubert took a spite against our family he could prevent my being included in the next batch of senators. Do you understand?'

This was a complete explanation for the naval officer of what Troubert's secret occupation was, of which Birotteau used to say foolishly: 'I don't know what he spends all his nights at, or what good it does.'

The Canon's position at the centre of the female senate who so subtly policed the province, and his personal capacity, had made the Congregation choose him from all the clergy of the city to be their secret proconsul in Tours. Archbishop, general, Prefect, great and small lay under his occult dominion. The Baron de Listomère soon made up his mind about the course he should follow.

'I have no desire,' he said to his uncle, 'to receive a second ecclesiastical broadside in my hull.'

Three days after this consideration of diplomatic relations by uncle and nephew, the sailor, returned post-haste to Tours by the mail-coach, on the very evening of his arrival was unfolding to his aunt the story of the dangers to which the most cherished hopes of the Listomère family were exposed, if he and she both persisted in backing *that idiotic Birotteau*.

The Baron had laid a detaining hand on Monsieur de Bourbonne's arm when the old gentleman took his stick and hat preparatory to departure after the rubber of whist. The downy old bird's power of illumination was indispensable for showing up the reefs among which the Listomère family found themselves sailing, and the downy old bird had sought his stick and hat prematurely only in order to hear them whisper in his ear: 'Don't go. We want to talk to you.'

The Baron's prompt return, the serious expression observable on his face at certain moments, in contrast with his normally contented air, had not been lost on Monsieur de Bourbonne, and suggested that the lieutenant-commander had received some reverses in his engagement with Gamard and Troubert. The landowner showed no surprise when he heard the Baron proclaim the secret power of the Vicar-general, representing the Congregation.

'I knew that,' he said.

'Did you?' exclaimed the Baroness. 'Then why did you not warn us?'

'Madame, forget that I have guessed this priest's hidden influence,' he said, with emphasis, 'and I will forget that you know of it too. If we do not keep the secret, we shall be taken for accomplices, we shall be feared and hated. Follow my example and pretend to be hoodwinked; but keep your eyes wide open and watch where you place your feet. I did say a good deal, but you did not understand me, and I was afraid of compromising myself.'

'What on earth are we going to do now?' inquired the Baron.

There was no question of deserting Birotteau. That was a first condition taken for granted by the three in council.

'To beat a retreat with the honours of war has always been the cleverest achievement of the most adroit generals,' Monsieur de Bourbonne replied. 'Give way to Troubert. If his vanity is stronger than his hate, you will make an ally of him. But if you give way too far, he will ride roughshod over you; for, as Boileau has said: "To spoil and destroy is the mind of the Church." Let it be understood that you are leaving the service, and you slip from his clutches, Monsieur le Baron. Send the Abbé away, Madame, and you will give the Gamard woman the victory. Ask the Abbé Troubert at the Archbishop's party if he plays whist. He will say yes. Invite him here, where he would like to be received, for a rubber! He will certainly come. You are a woman, you can win him to serve your interests. When the Baron is Captain, his uncle a peer of France, Troubert a bishop, you will be able to make a canon of Birotteau, just as you please. Until then, give way; but give way gracefully and with an underlying threat. Your family can lend Troubert as much support as he will give you, you will get on like a house on fire. But navigate, sailor, with your sounding-line in your hand!'

'Poor Birotteau!' said the Baroness.

'Oh, deal with him without delay,' replied the landowner, as he prepared to leave. 'If some clever liberal got hold of that empty head he might cause you a great deal of trouble. After all, the courts would pronounce in his favour, and Troubert must be afraid of the verdict. He may still forgive you for having started the fight, but after a defeat he would be implacable. That's all I have to say.'

He clicked his snuff-box shut, went to put on his goloshes, and left.

Next morning after breakfast the Baroness, alone with the Abbé, said to him, not without visible embarrassment:

'My dear Monsieur Birotteau, you are going to find what I ask very unjust and very illogical, but for both our sakes, for yours and for mine, it is necessary that you should first of all break off your action against Mademoiselle Gamard and withdraw your claims, and then leave my house.'

The poor priest turned pale as he heard this.

'I am the innocent cause of your misfortunes,' she went on; 'and I know that had it not been for my nephew you would not have begun this lawsuit, which now constitutes a worry to you and to us. But listen!'

She told him succinctly of the wide ramifications of this affair and explained the seriousness of its consequences. During the night her reflections had led her to guess the probable facts of Troubert's past history, and she was able to show Birotteau, beyond the possibility of doubt, the enveloping web so skilfully woven about him by the hands of vengeance, and reveal his enemy's great capacity and power, tear the veil from his hatred by showing its causes, revealing Troubert crouching for twelve years in front of Chapeloud, and swallowing up Chapeloud, and persecuting Chapeloud still in his friend. The innocent Birotteau joined his hands as if in prayer and wept with grief at this picture of such human horrors as his pure soul had never dreamed of. He listened, as appalled as if he had found himself standing on the edge of a precipice, his eyes fixed and humid, saying nothing, to all his patroness had to say. She concluded with these words:

'I know how painful and wrong it is to desert you, but, my dear Abbé, family claims come before those of friendship. Bow to this storm, as I am doing, and I will give you proof of my gratitude. I say nothing about your interests; I make them my charge. You will be freed from all anxiety about your livelihood. Through M. de Bourbonne, who will know how to preserve appearances, I shall arrange that you lack for nothing. My friend, give me permission to act as a traitor towards you. I shall still be your friend, even if I conform to worldly rules of conduct. Make your decision.'

The poor dumbfounded Abbé exclaimed:

'So Chapeloud was right when he said that if Troubert could come and tweak his toes in his grave he would do it! He is sleeping in Chapeloud's bed!'

'There's more to do than wring our hands,' said Madame de Listomère. 'We have not much time to spare. Come, now!'

Birotteau had too much goodness of heart not to do, in a major crisis, what his unreflecting loyalty suggested to him in the first moment. Besides, in any case his life was now nothing better than misery. He said, giving his patroness a despairing look, which went to her heart:

'I'm in your hands. I'm only a straw in the street now!'

The word he used, *bourrier*, was a word from the Touraine dialect, for which there is no possible equivalent but *straw*. But there are pretty little yellow straws, polished and gleaming, which children delight in; while a *bourrier* is a discoloured muddy straw, rolled in the gutters, driven by the storm, crushed by the feet of passers-by.

'But, Madame, I do not want to leave Chapeloud's portrait to Troubert. It was painted for me, and it's mine. Get them to give it back to me and I will give up all the rest.'

'Very well,' said Madame de Listomère; 'I will call on Mademoiselle Gamard.'

Her tone showed what a desperate effort it took for the Baroness de Listomère to humble herself to flatter the spinster's pride.

'And I shall try to settle everything,' she added, 'though I scarcely dare hope. Go to see Monsieur de Bourbonne and let him formally note your withdrawal. Bring me the document properly drawn up. Then, with the Archbishop's help, perhaps we may manage to put an end to this business.'

Birotteau left the room in a state of stupefaction. In his eyes

Troubert had taken on the dimensions of an Egyptian pyra-
mid. The hands of this man were in Paris and his elbows in
Tours, in the Close.

'A man like him,' he said to himself, 'prevent Monsieur le
Marquis de Listomère from becoming a peer of France? ...
*And perhaps with the Archbishop's help we may manage to put an
end to this business!*'

In the presence of such important interests, Birotteau felt
himself to be a mite; he saw himself as he was.

The news of Birotteau's removal astonished everybody, the
more that no one could learn its cause. Madame de Listomère
gave it out that as her nephew wanted to marry and leave the
service, she needed the Abbé's room to enlarge his apartments.
Nothing was known yet of Birotteau's withdrawal. And so
Monsieur de Bourbonne's instructions were discreetly carried
out. When these two pieces of news reached the ears of the
Vicar-general they were bound to flatter his vanity, showing
him as they did that the Listomère family, if it did not capitu-
late entirely, was at least remaining neutral and tacitly recognized the occult power of the Congregation: did recognition
not imply submission to it? But the lawsuit still remained entirely *sub judice*. That surely meant giving way and threatening
at the same time!

The Listomères had thus adopted an attitude exactly parallel
to the Vicar-general's in this struggle: they held themselves
aloof and could control everything. But a serious event
occurred, which made the success of the plans laid by Monsieur de Bourbonne and the Listomères to conciliate the
Gamard and Troubert party still more difficult of achievement.
The evening before, Mademoiselle Gamard had caught cold
leaving the cathedral, had taken to her bed, and was said to be
dangerously ill. The whole town bewailed her fate and echoed
with insincere cries of commiseration. Mademoiselle Gamard's sensibility was too fine to stand the scandal of that legal
action. In spite of having right on her side, she was on the
point of dying of the shame of it. Birotteau had killed his
benefactress. Such was the substance of the messages sent
out along their capillary network by the grand female

self-appointed commission, and complaisantly repeated by the citizens of Tours.

Madame de Listomère suffered the humiliation of calling on the spinster without reaping any fruit of her visit. She asked with great politeness if she might speak to Monsieur Troubert, the Vicar-general. Troubert was perhaps flattered to receive a woman by whom he had been slighted, in Chapeloud's library, and before the chimney-piece adorned with the two famous pictures in dispute, and he made the Baroness wait a moment or two; then he consented to give her an audience. Never did courtier or diplomat in the discussion of their own individual interests or the negotiation of an international deal exercise more skill, have greater powers of dissimulation to draw on, or profounder depths concealed, than the Baroness and the Abbé when they found themselves at this moment face to face.

Like the sponsor who, in the Middle Ages, armed the champion, and fortified his valour with wise counsel before he entered the lists, the *downy old bird* had said to the Baroness:

'Don't forget your rôle; you are a conciliator and not an interested party. Troubert too is an intermediary. Weigh your words! Study the inflexions of the Vicar-general's voice. If he strokes his chin, you have won him over.'

Caricaturists have sometimes amused themselves by sketching the contrast that frequently exists between *what one says* and *what one thinks*. The interest of the duel fought in words between the priest and the great lady will be fully grasped only if the thoughts that they concealed from one another under apparently insignificant remarks are here revealed. Madame de Listomère began by declaring the regret that she felt at Birotteau's lawsuit; then she spoke of her wish to see the affair concluded to the satisfaction of both parties.

'The harm is done, Madame,' said the Abbé gravely. 'The virtuous Mademoiselle Gamard is dying. ...' (*I care no more for that stupid woman than I do for Prester John*, he thought; *but I would very much like to cast the responsibility for her death upon your shoulders and trouble your conscience about it, if you are foolish enough to worry.*)

'When I heard of her illness, Monsieur,' the Baroness replied, 'I asked Monsieur Birotteau to give me his withdrawal of the action, and I was bringing the document to this saintly woman ...' (*I know your game, you crafty rascal!* That was what she was thinking. *But now we are no longer at the mercy of your whim. As for you, if you take the document you'll stain your fingers, for you will be admitting your complicity.*)

There was a moment's silence.

'The temporal affairs of Mademoiselle Gamard do not concern me,' said the priest at last, lowering his broad eyelids over his piercing eyes in order to veil his feelings. (*Oho! you will not succeed in involving me in the affair! But God be praised! those damned lawyers will not argue a case which might sully my reputation. What can the Listomères want from me to make them do as I wish like this?*)

'Monsieur,' replied the Baroness, 'Monsieur Birotteau's affairs concern me as little as Mademoiselle Gamard's interests do you; but unfortunately religion may suffer because of their differences, and I see in you a mediator, where I myself am acting only to reconcile the parties ...' (*Neither of us will pull wool over the other's eyes, Monsieur Troubert,* she thought. *Do you note the pointed nature of that reply?*)

'Religion suffer, Madame!' said the Vicar-general. 'Religion is set too high for men to strike at it.' (*I am religion,* he thought.) 'God will judge us without being deceived, Madame,' he added. 'I recognize only His tribunal.'

'Well, Monsieur,' she answered, 'let us try to make men's judgements accord with God's.' (*Yes, religion, that means you.*)

The Abbé Troubert changed his tone.

'Your nephew was in Paris, was he not?' (*You had news of me there,* he thought. *I am able to crush you, you who despised me. You have come to surrender.*)

'Oh, yes, Monsieur. Thank you for taking such an interest in him. He is going back to Paris again this evening. He is summoned by the Minister of Marine, who is a very kind friend to us. He does not want to see him leave the service.' (*Jesuit, you shall not crush us,* she thought; *and your quip is understood.*)

A momentary silence.

'I do not approve of his conduct in this affair,' she went on, 'but a sailor must be forgiven for not knowing his way about in legal matters.' (*Let's make an alliance. We shall gain nothing by fighting each other.*)

A faint smile lost itself in the folds of the Abbé's face.

'He has done us the service of showing us the value of these two paintings,' he said, looking at the pictures. 'They will be a fine ornament for the chapel of the Virgin.' (*You shot a barbed remark at me*, he thought. *There are two for you. We are quits, Madame.*)

'If you are going to give them to Saint-Gatien, I shall ask you to let me offer frames worthy of the place and the pictures to the Cathedral.' (*If only I could make you confess that you coveted Birotteau's possessions!* she thought.)

'They don't belong to me,' said the priest, still on his guard.

'But here is a document,' said Madame de Listomère, 'which ends all discussion and returns them to Mademoiselle Gamard.' She placed Birotteau's withdrawal of his action on the table. (*See, Monsieur, how much confidence I have in you.*) 'It will be an act worthy of you, worthy of your fine character, to reconcile two Christians; although I take little interest in Monsieur Birotteau now.'

'But he is living in your house,' he interrupted her.

'No, Monsieur, he does not stay with me now.' (*My brother-in-law's peerage and my nephew's promotion make me commit many mean acts*, she thought.)

The Abbé looked as impassive as ever, but his calm covered the most violent emotions. Monsieur de Bourbonne alone had guessed what lay beneath this serene outward appearance. The priest was triumphant!

'Why then did you bring his act of withdrawal?' he asked, prompted by a feeling analogous to that which drives a woman to have the compliments she has been paid repeated to her again.

'I could not help feeling sorry for him. Birotteau, whose weak nature is known to you, begged me to see Mademoiselle Gamard in order to obtain in exchange for his renunciation of ...'

The Abbé frowned.

'... of *rights* recognized by distinguished lawyers, the portrait ...'

The priest looked at Madame de Listomère.

'... the portrait of Chapeloud,' she continued. 'I leave you to judge of his claim ...' (*Your claim would be rejected if you brought the matter to court*, she thought.)

The emphasis with which the Baroness uttered the words *distinguished lawyers* let the priest see that she knew the enemy's weakness as well as his strength. In the course of this conversation, which continued for some time on similar lines, Madame de Listomère displayed so much diplomatic skill to this connoisseur well qualified to judge of it, that he went downstairs to Mademoiselle Gamard to obtain her answer to the suggested transaction.

Troubert soon returned.

'Madame, this is what the poor dying woman says: "Monsieur l'Abbé Chapeloud showed me too much friendship," those were her words, "for me to part with his portrait." If it were I,' he added, 'if it belonged to me, I would not give it up to anyone. My feeling for the late Canon has always remained unchanged, and gives me grounds for believing that I have the right to fight for his likeness against all comers.'

'Monsieur, don't let us fall out over a bad painting.' (*I care as little about it as you do yourself*, she thought.) 'Keep it; we will have a copy made. I rejoice at having put an end to this unfortunate and deplorable lawsuit, and I shall have personally gained the pleasure of making your acquaintance. I have heard some talk of your talent for whist. You will forgive a woman for being curious about such matters,' she said smiling. 'If you would care to come to my house for a rubber sometimes, you may be sure that you would be very welcome.'

Troubert stroked his chin. (*He is caught! Bourbonne was right*, she thought. *He has his share of vanity.*)

Indeed, at that moment the Vicar-general was experiencing that delicious sensation which Mirabeau could not resist, when, in the days of his power, he saw the gates of a mansion once closed to him swing open before his carriage.

'Madame,' he replied, 'my time is too much taken up with serious matters to permit me to go into society, but for you what is there that one would not do?' (*The old maid is about to be taken off. I shall win over the Listomères, and serve their interests if they serve mine*, he thought. *It is better to have them as friends than as enemies.*)

Madame de Listomère returned home, hoping that the Archbishop would complete a work of pacification so propitiously begun. But Birotteau was not even to profit by his withdrawal of his suit. Madame de Listomère heard the following day that Mademoiselle Gamard was dead. When the spinster's will was read no one was surprised to learn that she had made the Abbé Troubert her sole legatee. Her fortune was reckoned to be a hundred thousand crowns. The Vicar-general sent two cards of invitation for his friend's funeral service and procession to Madame de Listomère, one for her and one for her nephew.

'We shall have to go,' she said.

'That's precisely his intention!' exclaimed Monsieur de Bourbonne. 'It's a test by which Monseigneur Troubert means to try you. Baron, go to the cemetery,' he added, turning to the Lieutenant-Commander, who, unfortunately for him, had not left Tours.

The service took place and was of great ecclesiastical magnificence. One person only wept. That was Birotteau, who, alone and unseen in a chapel apart, blamed himself for this death, prayed sincerely for the dead woman's soul, and bitterly regretted that he had not obtained from her forgiveness for her wrongs.

The Abbé Troubert accompanied his friend's body to the burying ground. At the graveside he pronounced an oration in which, thanks to his skill, the account of the narrow life led by this woman who had bequeathed her possessions to him took on a monumental aspect. Those present remarked these words in the peroration:

'This life filled with days completely devoted to God and her religion, this life adorned by so many fine deeds accomplished in silence, by so many modest and unsung virtues, was broken by a grief which we would call undeserved if here, on the edge of eternity, we could forget that all our afflictions are sent us by God. The numerous friends of this saintly woman, knowing the nobility and candour of her soul, foresaw that she could endure anything except suspicions which threw dishonour upon her whole life. And so perhaps Providence has taken her to the bosom of God to spare her our distresses. Happy are those who can rest here on earth at peace with themselves as Sophie rests now in the realm of the blessed, wrapped in her robe of innocence!'

'When he had finished this pompous oration,' went on Monsieur de Bourbonne, who was relating all that had happened at the funeral, when, the gatherings dispersed and doors closed, he and the Baron were alone with Madame de Listomère, 'picture, if you can, this Louis XI in a cassock sprinkling the last aspergillum of holy water, like this.'

Monsieur de Bourbonne took the tongs and sketched the Abbé Troubert's gesture so graphically that the Baron and his aunt could not help smiling.

'At that point only,' went on the old landowner, 'he gave the lie to his words. Until then his demeanour had been perfect. But I suppose it must have been too much for him when he was locking up this old maid for ever, whom he despised with all his heart and perhaps hated as much as he detested Chapeloud, not to let his delight be betrayed in his gesture.'

Next morning Mademoiselle Salomon came to lunch with Madame de Listomère, and arrived in a state of agitation and upset, saying as soon as she came in:

'Our poor Abbé Birotteau has just received a dreadful shock, and it's obviously a carefully calculated blow aimed at him through hatred. He has been nominated Curé at Saint-Symphorien.'

Saint-Symphorien is a suburb of Tours, situated beyond the bridge. This bridge, one of the finest examples of French architecture, is nineteen hundred feet long, and at each end leads to identically laid out squares and buildings.

'Do you understand?' she went on after a pause, astonished at the coldness with which Madame de Listomère received this news. 'The Abbé Birotteau there will be just as if he were a hundred leagues from Tours, from his friends, from everything. Don't you see that his exile will be all the worse because he is being torn from a city which his eyes will rest on every day, but where he can hardly ever go again? Since these troubles have come upon him he can barely walk, and he would be obliged to walk a league in order to see us. At this moment the unfortunate man is in bed; he has a fever. The parochial house at Saint-Symphorien is cold and damp, and the parish is not rich enough to restore it. The poor old man is going to find himself buried in a veritable sepulchre. It's an atrocious and ingeniously arranged plot!'

Now, to complete this story it will be enough, perhaps, simply to report certain events and sketch a last picture.

Five months later the Vicar-general was raised to a see. Madame de Listomère was dead, and had left fifteen hundred francs a year to the Abbé Birotteau in her Will. On the day when the Baroness's Will was generally known, Monseigneur Hyacinthe, Bishop of Troyes, was on the point of leaving Tours to take up residence in his diocese, but he put off his departure. Furious at having been the dupe of a woman to whom he had given his hand, while she secretly held out hers to a man whom he regarded as his enemy, Troubert again threatened the Baron's career and the Marquis de Listomère's peerage. He let fall in full convocation, in the Archbishop's drawing-room, one of those ecclesiastical remarks heavy with vengeance and full of honeyed forbearance. The ambitious sailor went to see the implacable priest, who no doubt dictated harsh conditions, for the Baron's conduct demonstrated the most complete devotion to the wishes of the terrible representative of the Congregation.

The new Bishop handed over by a legal and binding act Mademoiselle Gamard's house to the Cathedral Chapter. He gave Chapeloud's bookcase and books to the school run by the clergy. He dedicated the two disputed pictures to the Chapel of the Virgin. But he kept Chapeloud's portrait. No-

body could find a reason for this almost complete relinquish-
ment of Mademoiselle Gamard's bequest. Monsieur de Bourbonne imagined that the Bishop secretly retained the liquid
part of it in order to be able to maintain his position with
honour in Paris, if he were raised to the bench of Bishops in
the Upper Chamber.

At last, on the eve of Monseigneur Troubert's departure,
the *downy old bird* could guess the final calculation that lay behind this action, the final fatal blow struck by the most persist-
ent of avenging hates against the weakest of victims. Madame
de Listomère's legacy to Birotteau was contested by the Baron
de Listomère on the grounds of undue influence! A few days
after the preliminary writ was issued the Baron was given
command of a vessel. By a disciplinary order the Curé of Saint-
Symphorien was forbidden to plead. His ecclesiastical superiors
prejudged the issue. (So the late Sophie Gamard's assassin was
a swindler as well!) If Monseigneur Troubert had kept his inheritance from the spinster, it would have been difficult to
censure Birotteau.

As Monseigneur Hyacinthe, Bishop of Troyes, drove by
post-chaise along the Quai Saint-Symphorien on the road to
Paris, the poor Abbé Birotteau was sitting where he had been
placed in an armchair, in the sun on a terrace above the road.
The poor priest, who had been rebuked by his Archbishop,
looked pale and thin. Sorrow had left its imprint on all his features, and completely broken up the picture of gentle gaiety
his face had once presented. Over his eyes, ingenuously lighted
once by the pleasures of good cheer and innocent of the heaviness of thought, illness cast a veil which simulated reflection.
This was no more than the skeleton of that Birotteau who a
year before had trotted through the Close, so empty-headed,
but so content. The Bishop cast a look of contempt and pity at
his victim, then deigned to forget him, and passed on.

Undoubtedly in other times Troubert would have been a
Hildebrand or an Alexander VI. Today the Church is no
longer a political power and no longer absorbs the energies of
solitary men. Thus celibacy presents the capital vice that,
focusing a man's qualities upon one passion, the study of his

own interest, it makes those who practise it either actively harmful or else useless. We live in an epoch when the fault of governments is to have less made Society to fit Man than twisted Man to fit into Society. A perpetual struggle exists between the individual and the system, which is framed to exploit him and which he tries to exploit for his own profit; whereas formerly a man who was in fact more free to do as he chose showed himself more generous in what concerned the public welfare.

The circle within which men act out their lives has insensibly grown larger. The mind which can embrace and synthesize it will never be anything but a magnificent exception; for, ordinarily, in the mental sphere as in the physical, an impulse loses in intensity what it gains in range. Society cannot base itself upon exceptions. Once, a man was simply and solely a father, and his affections were warm and active, concentrated in the circle of his family. Later he lived for a clan, or a small republic; and from that relation sprang the great historical acts of devotion of Greece and Rome. Then he was the man of a caste or a religion, in the service of whose greatness he often showed himself to be sublime; but there the range of his interests was extended by all the intellectual fields. Today his life is bound up with that of a vast stretch of country; soon his family will embrace, so they say, the entire world. But is this conception of the cosmopolitanism of the soul, the hope of Christian Rome, not a sublime mistake? It is so natural to believe in the realization of a noble chimera, in the brotherhood of man. But alas! the human machine is not made on such a divine scale. Souls great enough to embrace a noble sentiment which only the great can feel will never be those of simple citizens or family men.

Certain physiologists think that when the brain is thus extended, the heart must contract. But that is a fallacy! Is not the apparent egotism of men who carry a science, a nation, a system of laws in their breast, the noblest of passions, and do they not, to some extent, bear the life of the masses? To give birth to new nations, to produce new ideas, must they not with their powerful intellects combine the woman's life-giving and nourishing strength and the might of God? The story of men like Innocent III, like Peter the Great, like all the leaders of a century or a nation, would give proof at need, of a very high order, of that tremendous intellectual force which Troubert represented in the depths of the Close, by Saint-Gatien in Tours.

Saint-Firmin, April 1832

COLONEL CHABERT

*

'HULLO! Here's our old box-coat again!'
The clerk who uttered this exclamation belonged to
the species that in solicitors' offices they call *skipjacks*, and at
the moment was attacking a piece of bread with every sign of
a healthy appetite. He pulled some crumb from it to make a
pellet, which he threw derisively through the casement of the
window against which he was leaning. The pellet, adroitly
aimed, bounced back almost as high as the window again,
after striking the hat of a stranger who was crossing the
courtyard of a house in the Rue Vivienne, the residence of
Maître Derville, solicitor.

'Look here, Simonnin, don't play silly tricks like that on
people, or I'll put you out. However poor a client may be,
what the devil! he's still a man!' said the head clerk, looking
up from the statement of costs which he was adding.

The *skipjack* or apprentice is usually, like Simonnin, a boy
of thirteen or fourteen, who in all lawyers' offices is under the
special dominion of the head clerk, whose commissions and
love-letters give him plenty to do, while he is on his way to
carry writs to bailiffs and petitions to the law-courts. In his
manners he belongs to the street-urchins of Paris, and in his
destiny to the law. This child is nearly always completely lack-
ing in regard for other people's feelings, is undisciplined, in-
disciplinable, a stringer together of jeering verses, a mocker, and
both greedy and lazy. All the same, nearly all these little clerks
have an old mother lodged on a fifth floor, with whom they
share the thirty or forty francs which is their monthly portion.

'If he is a man, why do you call him *old box-coat*?' asked
Simonnin, with the air of a schoolboy catching out his master.

And he set to work on his bread and cheese again, leaning
his shoulder against the window-frame, for he took his rest
like a cab-horse, standing, one leg dangling crossed against the
other, supported by the toe-cap of his shoe.

'What trick can we play on the old scarecrow?' said the third clerk, Godeschal, in a low voice, stopping in the middle of the flow of reason which he was producing for a petition which was being engrossed by the fourth clerk, and of which copies were being taken down by two neophytes from the country. Then he continued his improvisation: ... *But, in his noble and beneficent wisdom, His Majesty Louis the Eighteenth* (write that in full hey! you, Desroches our learned friend, in your fair copy), *on taking into his own hands the reins of government of his kingdom, understood* ... (what was it he understood, that joker?) *the high mission to which he was called by Divine Providence!* ... (exclamation mark and six dots: they are religious enough at the Palais de Justice to let them pass), *and his first thought was, as is proved by the date of the decree named below, to make reparation for the misfortunes caused by the sad and terrible disasters of our revolutionary times, by restoring to his many and loyal servants* ('many' is a piece of soap which ought to please the Court) *all their lands which remain unsold, whether now public property, or the ordinary or extraordinary property of the crown, or part of the endowment of public foundations, for we are assured and we hold ourselves ready to uphold that such is the spirit and meaning of the famous and most just decree, issued in* ... – Wait,' said Godeschal to the three clerks, 'that wretched sentence has brought me to the end of my page. Well,' he went on, licking the edge of his sheaf of paper as an aid to turning the thick stamped page, 'well, if you want to play a trick on him, you should tell him that the chief only interviews his clients between two and three in the morning. We shall see if the old villain turns up!'

And Godeschal went back to his half-finished sentence:

'*Issued in* ... Have you got that?' he asked.

'Yes,' cried the three copyists.

Everything made progress together, the petition, the conversation, and the plot.

'*Issued in* ... Hi, Papa Boucard, what is the date of the decree? We must dot our i's, heaven help us! It all adds to the bulk.'

'*Heaven help us!*' repeated one of the copyists, before Boucard, the head clerk, had replied.

'What! Have you put *heaven help us* down?' cried Godeschal, staring at the inexperienced clerk half-severely, half-jeeringly.

'He has indeed,' said Desroches, the fourth clerk, leaning over his neighbour's copy, 'he has written: *We must dot our i's*, and *eavenelpus* without any aitches.'

All the clerks burst into roars of laughter.

'What! Monsieur Huré, you take *heaven help us* for a legal term, and you claim to come from Mortagne!' exclaimed Simonnin.

'Scratch that out completely!' said the head clerk. 'If the judge who considers the documents saw anything like that he would say that we were showing disrespect to the lingo. The chief would get into trouble over it. Come, don't go making mistakes like that, Monsieur Huré! A Norman should not be careless in writing a petition. It's the *Shoulder arms* of the profession.'

'*Issued in ... in?*' said Godeschal. 'Tell me when, Boucard.'

'June, 1814,' replied the head clerk without raising his eyes from his work.

A knock at the door interrupted this sentence of the verbose petition. Five clerks well supplied with teeth, with bright and mocking eyes, and curly hair, raised their noses towards the door, after shouting with one voice, and a precentor's voice at that, 'Come in!'

Boucard kept his face buried in a pile of documents, a morass of law technicalities, known as *whimwham* in the slang of the law-courts, and went on with the statement of costs at which he was working.

The office was a large room furnished with the classic stove which adorns all lawyers' lairs. The pipes crossed the room diagonally to a blocked fireplace, on whose marble mantelpiece was displayed a varied collection of bread, triangles of Brie cheese, fresh pork chops, glasses, bottles, and the head clerk's cup of chocolate. The smell of these comestibles, blended with the odour of the immoderately heated stove, and with the characteristic smell of offices and documents, formed an amalgam such that a fox's stink would not have been noticed in it. The floor was already deep in mud and snow brought in on the clerks' boots. Near the window was set the principal clerk's roll-top desk, beside which stood the little table allotted to the second clerk. The second at the moment was *doing* the law-courts. It might have been any time between eight and nine in the morning. For only ornament the office had a number of those big yellow notices which advertise the attachment of real property, sales, sales by auction in one lot, of property held *indivisum*, for the settlement of minors' estates, final or preliminary findings, the pride of solicitors' offices! Behind the head clerk was a vast rack of pigeon-holes which covered the wall from floor to ceiling, every compartment stuffed with bundles of paper from which hung the innumerable seals and ends of red tape which give their own characteristic appearance to legal papers. The lower pigeon-holes were full of files, yellow with handling, edged with blue paper, on which were written the names of the substantial clients whose juicy affairs were in the pot at that moment. The dirty window-panes let little light through. There are few solicitors' offices, in any case, in Paris, where one can write without using a lamp before ten o'clock in the month of February, for they all suffer from a neglect which is understandable enough. The fact is that everybody goes there, but nobody stays. No personal interest can attach to what is so workaday. The solicitor does not care, nor do litigants nor clerks, that a place which for the clerks is a classroom, for litigants a passage-way, and for the lawyer a workshop, should be elegantly kept. The soiled furnishings are handed down from lawyer to lawyer with such scrupulous care that certain offices still possess boxes for business dealing with residual estates, frames for parchment latchets for holding deeds together, bags which have come down from lawyers working at the *Chlet*, an abbreviation of the word CHÂTELET, a law-court which in the former order of things represented the present court of first instance.

And so this gloomy office, veiled in dust, like all the others, had an atmosphere which repelled litigants, and which made it an example of one of the most monstrous and hideous features of Paris. Certainly if it were not for damp church vestries, where prayers are weighed out and paid for like groceries; if it were not for old women's second-hand clothes shops, where tawdry rags fluttering from the pegs blight all our illusions about life by showing us in what our gaieties end: if these two cesspools where the poetry of life expires did not exist, a solicitor's office would of all markets where the requirements of society are met be the most hideous. But gaming houses, law-courts, lottery offices, and houses of ill repute are hideous too. Why is this so? Perhaps in these places the drama that is being enacted in a man's soul makes his surroundings a matter of indifference to him, an explanation which would account also for the simplicity of the lives lived by great thinkers and ambitious men.

'Where's my penknife?'

'I'm going to have my lunch!'

'Run away and play: there's a blot on the petition.'

'Hush, gentlemen!'

Such were the exclamations that were let fly as the old would-be litigant shut the door with that kind of humility which makes the movements of a man who has had misfortunes so unnatural. The stranger tried to smile, but the muscles of his face relaxed when he had searched the implacably indifferent faces of the six clerks in vain for some sign of response. He was, no doubt, used to judging men, and he addressed himself very politely to the apprentice, hoping that that whipster would reply pleasantly.

'Monsieur, is it possible to see Monsieur Derville?'

The mischievous junior clerk made the poor man no reply, but tapped his ear repeatedly with the fingers of his left hand, as if to say, 'I am deaf.'

'What do you want, Monsieur?' asked Godeschal, swallowing a mouthful of bread big enough to load a small cannon as he spoke, brandishing his knife, and crossing his legs in a fashion which put the foot which he was waggling on a level with his eye.

'This is the fifth time that I have come here, Monsieur,' answered the client. 'I wish to speak to Monsieur Derville.'

'Is it a matter of business?'

'Yes, but I can only explain it to Monsieur Derville himself.'

'Monsieur Derville is sleeping. If you wish to consult him about some difficulty, he does not do any serious business before midnight. But if you would care to tell us your business, we could advise you just as well....'

This awoke no response in the stranger. He started to look unassumingly about him, rather like a dog who has slipped into a strange kitchen where he fears that he will receive blows. Thanks to their circumstances, clerks are never afraid of thieves, so they had no suspicions of the man in the box-coat and let him examine the premises, in which he vainly sought a place to sit down, for he was visibly tired. Of set purpose lawyers leave few chairs in their offices. The ordinary client, getting tired of standing, goes away grumbling, but he does not use time whose expense, as one old lawyer put it, cannot be entered on a bill of costs.

'Monsieur,' he said, 'as I have already had the honour to inform you, I can explain my business only to Monsieur Derville. I shall wait till he gets up.'

Boucard had finished his reckoning. He noticed the smell of his chocolate, rose from his cane-bottomed chair and walked to the fireplace, looked the old man over, stared at the box-coat, and made an indescribable grimace. He probably thought that no matter how this customer was squeezed it would be impossible to extract a centime from him; so he intervened curtly with the intention of ridding the office of an unprofitable client.

'They are telling you the truth, Monsieur. The chief works only during the night. If your business is serious, I advise you to come back at one in the morning.'

The client looked at the head clerk stupidly, and made no move for a moment. The clerks, accustomed to all the varied facial expressions and odd manifestations of indecision and absent-mindedness characteristic of people who go to law, went on munching, champing their jaws as noisily as horses at a manger, and troubled no more about the old man.

'I will come back this evening,' he said at last, tenaciously set, like all unhappy people, on putting humanity in the wrong.

The sole retort open to poverty is to force justice and bene-ficence to unjust refusal. When the unfortunate have convicted society of hypocrisy, they throw themselves the more vehemently upon the bosom of God.

'Isn't that an obstinate fellow?' said Simonnin, not waiting till the old man had closed the door behind him. 'He looks like someone risen from the dead,' he went on.

'He's some colonel claiming arrears of pay,' said the head clerk.

'No, he's an old *concierge*,' said Godeschal.

'I'll bet he's a nobleman,' cried Boucard.

'I bet he has been a house-porter,' Godeschal retorted. 'Only doormen are endowed by nature with box-coats as worn, greasy, and tattered at the hem as that old fellow's. Did you not notice his split and leaking old down-at-heel boots, or his neckcloth which has to do duty as a shirt as well? That man has slept under bridges.'

'He might be of noble birth and yet have answered to "door please!"' exclaimed Desroches. 'Such things have been known.'

'No,' answered Boucard, as everyone laughed, 'I'm sure that he was a brewer in 1789, and a colonel under the Republic.'

'Well, I'll bet a show for everyone that he has never been a soldier,' said Godeschal.

'Done!' replied Boucard.

'Monsieur! Monsieur!' called the junior clerk, opening the window.

'What are you doing, Simonnin?' demanded Boucard.

'I'm calling him back to ask if he's a colonel or a house-porter. After all, he ought to know.'

All the clerks began to laugh. As for the old man, he was already climbing the stair.

'What are we to say to him?' exclaimed Godeschal.

'Leave it to me!' Boucard replied.

The poor man came in timidly, with his eyes lowered:

perhaps he was afraid of looking too greedily at the food, and betraying the fact that he was hungry.

'Monsieur,' said Boucard, 'would you be good enough to give us your name so that the chief may know if ...'

'Chabert.'

'Is that the colonel who was killed at Eylau?' asked Huré, who had said nothing yet, and was anxious to add his plea-santry to all the others.

'The same, Monsieur,' the old fellow replied with the sim-plicity of a former age, and he went out again.

'That puts you in your box!'

'You're pinked!'

'Oh!'

'Ah!'

'Haha!'

'Oh, the old rascal!'

'Tra la la, tra la.'

'That shuts you up!'

'Monsieur Desroches, you shall go to the theatre without paying,' said Huré to the fourth clerk, giving him a slap on the shoulder which might have felled a rhinoceros.

There was a torrent of yells, guffaws, and exclamations which beggars description and renders inadequate all the onomatopoeic words in the language.

'To what theatre shall we go?'

'To the Opéra,' cried the head clerk.

'To begin with,' Godeschal retorted, 'the theatre wasn't mentioned. If I like I can take you to see Madame Saqui.'

'Madame Saqui isn't a show,' said Desroches.

'What is a show?' Godeschal went on. 'Let us first estab-lish the question of fact. What did I bet, gentlemen? A show. What is a show? Something one sees ...'

'But if that's the case, you would pay your debt if you took us to see the water flowing under the Pont Neuf, wouldn't you?' Simonnin interrupted him.

'... Sees after payment of money,' continued Godeschal.

'But you pay to see lots of things which are not shows. The definition is not exact,' said Desroches.

'Will you just listen to me?'

'Your reasoning is faulty, my dear chap,' said Boucard.

'Is Curtius a show?' Godeschal went on.

'No,' said the head clerk; 'that's a collection of wax-works.'

'I'll lay one hundred francs to a sou,' returned Godeschal, 'that Curtius' collection constitutes the combination of things to which the term "show" is applied. It comprises a thing to be seen at various prices according to the different places one may wish to see it from ...'

'And so on, and so on, and so forth,' said Simonnin.

'You look out or you'll get a cuff on the ear!' said Godeschal.

The clerks shrugged their shoulders.

'Besides, there's no proof that that old baboon wasn't pulling our legs,' he said, giving his argument up, defeated by the other clerks' mockery. 'In all conscience Colonel Chabert is well and truly dead, his wife is married again to Comte Ferraud, Councillor of State. Madame Ferraud is one of our clients!'

'The case is stood over until tomorrow,' said Boucard. 'To work, gentlemen! Upon my word, no one does any work here! Set to and finish your petition, it has to be sent in before the sitting of the fourth court. They're doing that business to-day. Come, all shoulders to the plough!'

'If it *had* been Colonel Chabert, wouldn't he have applied his toe to that silly ass Simonnin's bottom when he pretended to be deaf?' said Huré, who considered this a much more conclusive argument than Godeschal's.

'Since we've settled nothing,' Boucard said again, 'let's agree to go the circle of the Théâtre des Français to see Talma in *Néron*. Simonnin can go to the pit.'

Thereupon the head clerk sat down at his desk, and everyone followed his example.

'*Issued in June eighteen hundred and fourteen* (in full),' said Godeschal. 'Have you got that?'

'Yes,' answered the two copyists and the engrosser, and their pens began to scratch on the stamped paper with the

H

rustle of a hundred cockchafers imprisoned by schoolboys in paper cages.

'*And we hope that the honourable Judges of the Court,*' said Godeschal. 'Stop, I must re-read my sentence, I don't understand what I'm saying myself now.'

'Forty-six. ... That can't be a rare occurrence! ... and three makes forty-nine,' said Bouchard.

'*We hope,*' Godeschal went on, after reading the document through, '*that the honourable Judges of the Court will not show themselves less magnanimous than the august author of the decree, and that they will treat the worthless claims of the administrative body of the Legion of Honour as they deserve and determine the matter at issue in the wide sense which we here establish....*'

'Monsieur Godeschal, would you like a glass of water?' said the junior clerk.

'That clown Simonnin!' said Boucard. 'Here, saddle your double-soled horses and go take a waltz with this package as far as the Invalides.'

'... *Which we here establish,*' repeated Godeschal. 'Add: *For and on behalf of Madame* ... (in full) *la Vicomtesse de Grandlieu.* ...'

'What!' exclaimed the head clerk. 'You think fit to make petitions in the affair Vicomtesse de Grandlieu versus the Legion of Honour, which is business for our office already contracted for? Well, you are a bright specimen! Will you kindly put your copies and your draft aside, keep them for the Navarreins suit against the Hospices. It's late. I'm going to do a spot of petitioning, *whereas* and *in as much as*, and I'll go to the courts myself. ...'

That scene represents one of those endless happy hours which make us say later when we think of our youth, 'We enjoyed life then!'

Towards one in the morning the self-styled colonel came to knock on the door of Maître Derville, solicitor, practising at the Inferior Court of the Department of the Seine. The house-porter told him that M. Derville had not come in. The old man pleaded an appointment and went upstairs to the rooms occupied by the celebrated lawyer, who, in spite of his youth, was held to be one of the cleverest men about the law-courts.

When he had rung and entered, the somewhat sceptical client was not a little surprised to find the head clerk busy arranging the numerous files of the cases for the following day in due order on his chief's dining-room table. The clerk, no less surprised, offered him a chair, which he took.

'Upon my word, Monsieur, I thought you were joking yesterday when you named such an early hour for a consultation,' the old man said, with the forced brightness of a man, down-and-out, making an effort to be pleasant.

'The clerks were making a joke of it, but telling the truth too,' answered the head clerk, going on with his work. 'It suits M. Derville to choose this time to consider his cases, note possible lines of action, arrange what is to be done, mark out the *defences*. His prodigious brain is freer at this time, the only time available when he can find the silence and peace he needs for the conception of effective plans. Since he became a solicitor you are the third client he has given an appointment to at this hour in the night. When he comes in the chief will debate every case, read all the documents, spend perhaps four or five hours at this work; then he will ring for me and explain what he intends to do. In the morning from ten o'clock till two he hears what his clients have to say, then spends the rest of the day keeping appointments. In the evening he goes into society in order to maintain his lines of communication there. So he has only the night left for digging at his law-suits, ransacking the arsenals of the Code, and drawing up his plans for battle. He will not allow a single case to go against him; he's in love with his art. He does not undertake any kind of case that comes along, like his colleagues. That's his life, and it's packed with activity. He earns a lot of money, too.'

The old man made no comment on this explanation, and his strange face took on an expression so blank and vacant that the clerk, after one glance, took no further notice of him. A few minutes later Derville came in, dressed for a ball. His head clerk opened the door to him, and hastened to complete his arrangement of the files. The young lawyer was taken aback for a moment at the first glimpse in the dim light of the singular client who awaited him. Colonel Chabert was as completely motionless as any wax figure in Curtius's collection, to which Godeschal had wanted to take his friends. His immobility by itself would perhaps not have seemed so surprising, but it put the finishing touch to the weird spectacle which his whole person presented. The old soldier was gaunt and lean. The deliberate concealment of his forehead by the locks of his shining wig gave an air of mystery to his face. His eyes appeared to be covered with an opaque film, like dirty mother-of-pearl, its bluish lights shimmering in the light of the candles. His pale, livid, sharp-featured face – a hatchet face, if one may borrow the common term – seemed devoid of life. His neck was muffled in a shabby black silk neckcloth. His body below the dark line of this rag was so completely in shadow that an imaginative man might have taken this old head for some chance effect of light and shadow, or a Rembrandt portrait without its frame. The hat-brim shading the old man's forehead threw a patch of black across the upper part of his face. This natural but odd effect threw up in harsh contrast the high-lighted folds, the cold curves, the impression that the natural hue of flesh had altered, in this cadaverous physiognomy. Finally, the absence of all movement in the body, of all warmth in the regard, joined with a certain expression of sad vacancy, with the dehumanized signs that mark dementia, gave this face an indefinable melancholy beyond anything that human words can express. But an observer, and especially a lawyer, would have found over and above this, in this stricken man, signs of profound grief, indications of a wretchedness which had worn this face down, as drops of rain falling on a fine marble statue from the sky in the end disfigure it. A doctor, a writer, a magistrate, would intuitively have felt that a whole drama lay there at sight of that supremely horrifying head, of which the least remarkable aspect was that it resembled the fantastic heads that painters amuse themselves by sketching at the bottom of their lithographic stones, as they talk with their friends.

When he caught sight of the lawyer, the stranger gave the

convulsive start of a poet who has been aroused from a reverie rich in fancies, by an unexpected sound in the silence and darkness of the night. The old man at once took off his hat and rose to greet the young lawyer. Unperceived by him, his wig adhered to the no doubt very greasy leather band lining his hat and left bare his horribly disfigured cranium, whose entire expanse was crossed by a prominent thick cicatrice, formed by a scar which started at the back of the skull and ended above the right eye. At the sudden removal of the dirty wig, which the poor man wore to hide his wound, the two young men had not the slightest inclination to laugh, so dreadful was the sight of that split skull. The first thought that sight of the wound suggested was this: 'By that road reason fled!'

'If he is not Colonel Chabert, he must be a rare old campaigner!' Boucard thought.

Derville said, 'To whom have I the honour of speaking, Monsieur?'

'To Colonel Chabert.'

'Which Colonel Chabert is that?'

'The man who was killed at Eylau,' answered the old man.

The clerk and the attorney exchanged a glance, which meant 'He's a madman!', when they heard this singular reply.

'Monsieur,' continued the Colonel, 'I should like to confide the secret of my situation to you privately.'

It is a fact worth remarking on that lawyers are naturally careless of danger. Whether it be the result of their habitually receiving a great many people, or of a deep-seated consciousness of the protection that the law affords them, or of confidence in the value of the work they do, they go fearlessly everywhere, like priests and doctors. Derville signed to Boucard, who vanished.

'Monsieur,' said the lawyer, 'during the daytime I am not too grudging of my time; but in the middle of the night minutes are precious. So be brief and concise. Give me the facts without digression. I shall ask you myself for such elucidation as I think necessary. Go ahead.'

After motioning his peculiar client to a seat, the young man sat down himself before the table; but while he listened to what the deceased colonel said he perused and turned the pages of his files.

'Monsieur,' said the dead man, 'perhaps you know that I commanded a cavalry regiment at Eylau. I had a large share in the success of Murat's famous charge which was decisive in winning the victory. Unhappily for me, my death is a historical fact published in *Victoires et Conquêtes*, where it is reported in detail. We split the three Russian lines in two, but they immediately re-formed, and we were obliged to ride through them again in the opposite direction. As we were returning towards the Emperor, after scattering the Russians, I encountered a main body of enemy cavalry. I hurled myself upon this stubborn foe. Two Russian officers, two real giants, attacked me at the same time. One of them broke my head with a sabre stroke which crashed through everything, even to the black silk cap I was wearing, and cracked my skull wide open. I fell from my horse. Murat came to my aid. He rode over my body, he and all his company; fifteen hundred men, no less! My death was announced to the Emperor, who took the precaution (he was fond of me, the Chief) of trying to find out if there was not some chance of saving the man to whom he was indebted for that hard-pressed attack. He sent two surgeons to pick me out and carry me to the ambulances, saying to them, perhaps rather too carelessly, for he had work on his hands: "Go and see if by any chance my poor Chabert is still alive!" Those confounded sawbones, who had just seen me trampled underfoot by the horses of two regiments, no doubt spared themselves the trouble of feeling my pulse, and said that I was certainly dead. My death certificate was thus probably drawn up properly according to the rules laid down by military law.'

Hearing his client express himself with perfect lucidity and relate facts of such apparent plausibility, strange though they were, the young lawyer abandoned his files, leaned his left elbow on the table, supported his head on his hand, and looked closely at the Colonel.

'Do you know,' he interrupted him, 'that I act as solicitor for Countess Ferraud, Colonel Chabert's widow?'

'My wife! Yes, Monsieur. And that is why, after I had approached a hundred lawyers to no effect, for they all took me for a lunatic, I made up my mind to come to see you. I will tell you about my troubles later. Let me first set out the facts, explain what must have happened rather than what I know to have happened. Certain circumstances which can be known only to God oblige me to present several of them as hypotheses. For example, from the wounds that I received I must almost certainly have developed tetanus, or been thrown into a coma analogous to that of an illness named, I believe, catalepsy. Otherwise how can it be explained that I was, according to the usual custom in war, stripped of my clothes and thrown into a common grave with other soldiers by the men detailed to bury the dead! Let me here set out a point that I could only have learned after the event which I must call my death. In 1814, in Stuttgart I met a former sergeant of my regiment. This dear man, the only one willing to recognize me, explained the phenomenon of my preservation by telling me that my horse was shot in the flank at the same instant that I was wounded. And so horse and rider tumbled over one another. Falling from the saddle, to right or to left, I was no doubt covered by my horse's body, which saved me from being crushed by the horses or struck by bullets. When I came to myself, Monsieur, I was in a position and an atmosphere of which I could give you no idea if I talked to you till tomorrow. The air which I breathed seemed close and was mephitic. I tried to move and found no room. When I opened my eyes I saw nothing. The lack of air was the most ominous sign and the one that most acutely brought my predicament home to me. I realized that where I was the air did not become renewed, and that I was going to suffocate. That thought wiped out all consciousness of the unutterable pain which had brought me back to waking life. There was a violent ringing in my ears. I heard, or thought I heard for I can swear to nothing, groans uttered by the host of corpses among whom I lay. Although the memory of those moments is very shadowy, although my recollections are very blurred, in spite of the impressions left by still greater sufferings which I was to undergo and which have thrown my thoughts into confusion, there are nights when I believe I can still hear those stifled moans. But there was something more frightful than the cries: a silence the like of which I have never known anywhere, the true silence of the tomb. Raising my hands, groping among the dead, I found a gap between my head and the human mass that lay above. I was able to measure the limits of the space that had been left me by an accident whose cause I did not know. It seems that, thanks to the carelessness or haste with which we had been thrown in pell-mell, two dead men lay across one another at an angle above my head, like two cards placed by a child building a castle. Rummaging hastily, for it was no time for hesitation, I very luckily struck an arm which was not attached to anything, the arm of a Hercules, a good bone to which I owe my salvation. Without this unlooked-for aid I should have perished. But, with a fury which you may imagine, I set myself to work my way through the corpses which separated me from the layer of earth which had no doubt been thrown over us. I say us, as if there were living men there! I went at it with a will, Monsieur, for here I am! But I do not know to this day how I succeeded in penetrating the covering of flesh which set a barrier between me and life. You will tell me that I had three arms! That crowbar which I wielded well won a little air for me from between the bodies that I displaced, and I was careful to breathe it sparingly. At last I saw daylight, but through snow, Monsieur! At that moment I felt that my head was split. By good fortune, my blood or my comrades' blood, or perhaps torn skin from my horse – how can I tell? – had coagulated and covered me with something like a natural plaster. In spite of this protective crust I fainted when my skull came into contact with the snow. What small measure of heat my body still held, however, melted the snow around me, and when I regained consciousness I found myself in the middle of a little opening through which I shouted as long as I could. But the sun was just rising then, so there was little chance of my being heard. Were there already people in the fields? I raised myself by pushing hard with my feet, bracing myself against dead men whose backs were firm.

You appreciate that it was not the moment to say to them, *"Way for the valiant wounded!"* In short, Monsieur, after long hours – oh yes, how long! – in which I had to endure the anguish, if the word can express my rage, of seeing those accursed Germans running away when they heard a voice where they could see no man, I was at last pulled out by a woman bold or curious enough to approach my head, which seemed to have sprouted from the earth like a mushroom. The woman went to fetch her husband, and together they carried me to their poor hut. It appears that I had a cataleptic relapse, if you will excuse this term, used to describe a state of which I know nothing, but which from what my hosts told me I guess must have been an effect of that malady. I lay for six months between life and death, unable to speak, or speaking only non-sense. Finally my hosts got me admitted to the hospital at Heilsberg. You understand, Monsieur, that I had left the earth's womb as naked as on the day that I was born; so that six months later, when one fine morning I remembered that I was Colonel Chabert, and with the recovery of my reason required more respect from my nurse than she was paying to a poor devil, all my companions in the ward thought it a good joke. Happily for me, the surgeon, in a boastful spirit, had answered for my cure and naturally took an interest in his patient. When I spoke to him in a coherent manner about my former existence, this fine fellow, who was called Sparchmann, had affidavits sworn in the legal form of the country, stating the miraculous fashion in which I had risen from the common grave, the day and hour when I had been found by my bene-factress and her husband, the nature and the exact location of my wounds, and added a description of my appearance to these documents. Well, Monsieur, I have not got these important papers, or the declaration which I made before a notary in Heilsberg with the idea of establishing my identity! Since the day when I was forced to fly from that town by the events of the war, I have never ceased wandering as a vagrant, begging my bread, treated as a madman whenever I told my story, without ever finding or earning a sou by means of which I might procure the records which would prove the truth of my statements, and give me back a place in the framework of society. Often the pain of my wounds held me prisoner six months at a time in little towns, where people were exceedingly kind to a sick Frenchman but laughed in his face when he claimed to be Colonel Chabert. For a long time this laughter and incredulity threw me into a rage which was prejudicial to me, and even caused me to be locked up as a madman at Stuttgart. In truth, you can judge from what I have told you that there was sufficient matter in my story to get a man locked up! After a two years' spell of detention, which I had no choice but to submit to, when I had heard my warders say a thousand times, "Here is a poor man who thinks he is Colonel Chabert!" to people who replied, "Poor man!" I was convinced myself of the impossibility of my own experience. I became sad, resigned, calm, and gave up calling myself Colonel Chabert in order to be able to leave my prison and see France again. Oh, Monsieur, to see Paris again! It was a feverish dream that I …'

Here Colonel Chabert fell into a deep reverie, which Derville respected, and left his sentence unfinished.

'Monsieur, one fine day,' the client resumed, 'one day in Spring, they gave me ten thalers and set me free, on the grounds that I talked very good sense on all sorts of subjects and no longer called myself Colonel Chabert. Indeed, at that time, and even today at times, I hate my name. I wish I were not I. My consciousness of my rights wears me out. If my illness had wiped out all memory of my past existence, I should have been happy! I should have re-joined the service under any name, and who knows? I might have become a field-marshal in Austria or Russia.'

'Monsieur,' said the lawyer, 'you turn all my ideas upside-down. Listening to you I think I'm dreaming. For mercy's sake, let us leave the story there for a moment.'

'You are the only person who has ever listened to me patiently,' said the Colonel sadly. 'No lawyer would advance me ten napoleons to send to Germany for the documents I need to bring my suit …'

'What suit?' said the lawyer, who was forgetting his client's present grievous situation as he listened to the tale of his past distresses.

'But, Monsieur, is Countess Ferraud not my wife? She is in possession of an income of thirty thousand livres which belongs to me, and will not give me two farthings. When I say these things to lawyers, to men of common sense, when I, a beggar, propose to bring an action against a count and countess, when I raise my voice, I, a dead man, against a death certificate, a marriage licence, and birth certificates, they show me to the door in one way or another, according to their nature, with the cold politeness that you people can assume to rid yourselves of a poor wretch, or rudely, as men who believe that they have an adventurer to deal with, or a lunatic. I have been buried under dead men, but I am buried now under the living, under documents, under facts, under the whole weight of society, which wants to drive me back underground!'

'Kindly go on with your story now, Monsieur,' said the lawyer.

'*Kindly!*' exclaimed the unfortunate Colonel, seizing the young man's hand. 'That is the first polite word I have heard since ...'

He wept. Gratitude robbed him of speech. The impressive, unutterable eloquence that may be in a look, a gesture, in silence itself, finally convinced Derville and deeply affected him.

'Listen, Monsieur,' he said to his client. 'I won three hundred francs at cards this evening. I can very well employ half that sum to procure a man's happiness. I will do what is necessary to obtain the documents you speak of, and until they come I will make you an allowance of one hundred sous a day. If you are Colonel Chabert, you will be able to understand and forgive the smallness of a sum lent by a young man who has his way to make. Go on with your story.'

For a moment the Colonel sat speechless and dumbfounded. His extreme ill-fortune had no doubt destroyed his former beliefs, his trust in human beings. If he chased after his military renown, his fortune, his identity, it may have been only in obedience to that inexplicable emotional force, the seeds of which lie in every human heart, to which we owe the researches of alchemists, the passion for glory, the discoveries of astronomy and physics, everything that drives man to increase his stature by multiplying his achievement by deeds or in the world of ideas. His *ego*, in his mind, was no more than a secondary consideration now, as the satisfied vanity of triumphing or the pleasure of sweeping in winnings becomes dearer to the man who lays a bet than his original reason for betting.

The young lawyer's words, then, seemed like a miracle to this man who had been rebuffed for ten years by his wife, by justice, by the entire social world created by man. That he should find in a lawyer's purse the ten gold coins which had been refused him for so long, by so many persons, and in so many ways! The Colonel was like the lady who after suffering from a fever for fifteen years thought that she had developed a new malady when she found herself cured. There are strokes of good fortune so great that one cannot believe in them: they arrive like thunderbolts and lay one low. And so this poor man's gratitude was so acute that he could not express it. It would have seemed cold to superficial people, but Derville perceived that whole-minded natural integrity underlay this unresponsiveness. A rascal would have found a voice.

'Where was I?' said the Colonel, with the naïveté of a child or a soldier, for there is often much of the child in a true soldier, and nearly always something of the soldier in a child, especially in France.

'In Stuttgart. You were just leaving prison,' the lawyer answered.

'You know my wife?' said the Colonel.

'Yes,' Derville replied, nodding.

'How is she?'

'As enchanting as ever.'

The old man with a wave of the hand seemed to stifle some secret pang, in the spirit of grave and solemn resignation characteristic of men tried in the blood and fire of battlefields.

'Monsieur,' he said with a kind of gaiety, for the Colonel

was breathing again, poor man; he was rising a second time
from the tomb; he had just melted a depth of snow less easily
thawed than that which had once covered his head so icily,
and he breathed the air like a man escaped from a dungeon.
'Monsieur,' he said, 'if I had been a good-looking fellow,
none of my troubles would have happened. Women believe
men when the word "love" fills out their sentences. They bestir themselves then, they run about, they walk through fire,
intrigue, and publish the facts abroad, and kick up the devil of
a shindy on behalf of the man who takes their fancy. But how
could I have caught a woman's interest? I had a graveyard
face; I was dressed like a *sans-culotte*; I was more like an
Eskimo than a Frenchman – and I was the man who was once
thought to be the handsomest gay spark in town, in 1799! I
was Chabert, a Count of the Empire!

'Well, on the very day that I was thrown into the street like
a dog, I met the sergeant that I was telling you about. The fellow was called Boutin. The poor devil and I made the prettiest
pair of broken-down old screws that I have ever seen. I
noticed him walking about, but although I recognized *him*, he
had not the faintest idea who I was. We went together to an
inn. There, when I told him my name, Boutin's mouth split
open in a guffaw like a bursting mortar. His amusement, Monsieur, gave me one of my bitterest pangs! Without dressing
things up, it showed me bluntly and fairly all the changes that
had taken place in my appearance. So I was now unrecognizable, even by the eye of the humblest and most grateful of my
friends! I had saved Boutin's life once, but that was in return
for what *I* owed *him*. I shall not go into all the facts of how he
came to render me this service. The scene took place in Italy,
in Rome. The house where Boutin saved me from a poignard
in the back was not a house of very good repute. At that time
I was not a colonel, I was an ordinary trooper like Boutin.
Fortunately, in the events of this story there were details
which could only be known to the two of us, and when I reminded him of them his incredulity diminished. Then I related the various mischances of my bizarre existence. Although my eyes and my voice were, so he said, strangely

altered, although I had no hair, no teeth, no eyebrows, and was as white as an albino, in the end he rediscovered his colonel in the beggar, after a merciless interrogation which I came through with flying colours. He related his adventures; they were not less strange than mine. He was just returned from the farthest bounds of China, which he had set out to reach after escaping from Siberia. He told me of the disasters of the Russian campaign and Napoleon's first abdication. This piece of news was one of my heaviest blows! We were two curious bits of wreckage now after being tossed about the globe, like pebbles in the ocean rolled from one coast to another by the storms. Between us we had seen Egypt, Syria, Spain, Russia, Germany, Italy, Dalmatia, England, China, Tartary, Siberia; the only places we had missed were India and America! Well, since Boutin was brisker on his pins than I was, he undertook to go to Paris with the utmost speed he could command to inform my wife of my condition. I wrote a letter to Madame Chabert, giving her full details. It was the fourth, Monsieur! If I had had relatives, all that perhaps would not have happened; but I must confess to you that I am a poor-house child, a soldier who for patrimony had his courage, for family the whole world, for his country France, for sole protector God. No, I'm wrong! I had a father, the Emperor! Ah, if he was on his feet, dear man, and saw *his Chabert*, as he used to call me, in my present state, well, he would fly into a rage. But what can we expect? Our sun has set, we are all cold now. After all, political events might well have justified my wife's silence! Boutin set out. He was a very lucky man! He had two white bears superlatively well trained to earn his living for him. I could not go with him: the pain of my wounds did not allow of my travelling long stages. I wept, Monsieur, when we parted, after I had walked as far as my poor condition allowed me, in company with his bears and him. At Carlsruhe I had an attack of paroxysms of pain in the head, of a neuralgic character, and lay for six weeks in miserable poverty in an inn. I would never come to an end if I had to tell you all the troubles of my beggar's life. Mental suffering, beside which physical suffering pales, excites less pity because no one sees it.

I remember shedding tears in front of a Strasbourg mansion where I had once given a party, and where they gave me nothing, not even a crust of bread. I had agreed with Boutin the route I was to follow, and I went to each post office to ask if there was a letter and money for me. I reached Paris without finding either. How much despair I had to swallow as best I could! "Boutin must be dead," I said to myself. In fact the poor devil had succumbed at Waterloo. I learned of his death later and by chance. His mission to my wife had no doubt been fruitless. Well, I entered Paris at the same time as the Cossacks. For me that was woe heaped upon woe. When I saw the Russians in France I no longer worried that I had neither shoes on my feet nor money in my pocket. Yes, my clothes were in rags. The evening before I reached the city I was forced to sleep out in the woods at Claye. It was no doubt the coolness of the night that gave me an attack of I don't know what malady that overcame me when I was walking through the Faubourg Saint-Martin. I fell almost fainting at an ironmonger's door. When I came to myself I was in bed in the Hôtel-Dieu. There I stayed for a month, happily enough. I was presently discharged. I had no money, but was in good health, and walking the good streets of Paris. With what joy and what haste I went to the Rue du Mont-Blanc, where my wife should be living in a house of mine! Bah! the Rue du Mont-Blanc had become Rue de la Chaussée-d'Antin. I could not find my house; it had been sold and demolished. Speculators had built several small houses in my gardens. I did not know that my wife was married to Monsieur Ferraud, and I could obtain no news of her. Finally I went to look up an old lawyer who had formerly looked after my affairs. The old fellow was dead, and had some time before handed over his practice to a young man. From him I learned, to my great surprise, of the winding-up of my estate, the sale of my property, my wife's marriage, and the birth of her two children. When I told him that I was Colonel Chabert he started to laugh so openly and unrestrainedly that I left him without making any further remark. My detention in Stuttgart made me think of Charenton, and I resolved to act with discretion. Then, Monsieur, since I now knew where my wife lived, I made my way to her home, with my heart full of hope. Well,' said the Colonel with a gesture of concentrated rage, 'I was not received when I had myself announced under a borrowed name, and the day when I took my own I was turned away from her door. To see the Countess returning from a ball or a play, at dawn, I have spent whole nights flattened against a post of her carriage entrance. My gaze searched the carriage that dashed past my eyes like a flash of lightning, and I could barely catch a glimpse of the woman who is mine, and who is mine no longer! Oh, since that day I have lived for vengeance!' cried the old man hollowly, suddenly drawing himself up to his full height before Derville. 'She knows that I am alive: she has had two letters from me since my return, written in my own hand. She cares no more about me! For my part I don't know whether I love her or abhor her: I desire and curse her turn about. She owes me her fortune, her happiness – and she has not so much as arranged for me to receive the slightest help! At times I don't know any more which way to turn!'

As he said this the old soldier sank back into his chair and relapsed into silence and immobility again. Derville said nothing, but sat there contemplating his client.

'It's a serious business,' he said at last mechanically. 'Even granting the authenticity of the documents which must be there in Heilsberg, there is no certainty to my mind that we could win a victory straight away. The suit will go before three courts in succession. A case like this must be reflected upon and considered coolly; it is quite exceptional.'

'Oh!' replied the Colonel coldly, proudly raising his head, 'if I fail I can die, but I shall not die alone.'

It was not an old man who said these words; and they were the eyes of a man in the full vigour of life that gleamed, relighted at the fires of desire and vengeance.

'We shall perhaps have to compromise,' said the lawyer.

'Compromise!' repeated the Colonel. 'Am I a dead man or am I alive?'

'Monsieur,' returned the lawyer, 'you will take my advice, I hope. Your cause shall be my cause. You will soon realize the interest that I take in your situation, which is practically without parallel in legal annals. Meanwhile I am going to give you a line for my notary, who will remit you fifty francs every ten days against your receipt. It would not be proper for you to come here looking for help. If you are Colonel Chabert, you should not be under a compliment to anyone. I will let you have these advances as a loan. You have property to recover, you are a rich man.'

This last touch of delicacy drew tears from the old man. Derville rose abruptly, for it was not perhaps correct form for a lawyer to show emotion. He disappeared into an inner room and returned with an unsealed envelope which he handed to Colonel Chabert. When the poor man held it in his fingers he felt two gold coins through the paper.

'Will you specify the documents and give me the postal address?' said the lawyer.

The Colonel dictated the information and verified the spelling of place-names. Then he took his hat with one hand, looked at Derville, held out the other – a calloused horny hand – and said simply, 'Upon my word, Monsieur, after the Emperor you are the man to whom I am most indebted! You are a capital fellow.'

The lawyer struck the Colonel's hand with his, escorted him as far as the staircase, and lighted him on his way.

'Boucard, I have been listening to a story that may perhaps let me in for twenty-five louis,' Derville said to his head clerk. 'But even if it's robbery I shall not regret my money; I shall have seen the cleverest actor of our times.'

When the Colonel found himself in the street and near a lamp-post, he took the two twenty-franc pieces that the lawyer had given him from the envelope, and looked at them for a moment in the lamp-light. He was looking at gold for the first time in nine years.

'So I shall be able to smoke cigars!' he said to himself.

About three months after this nocturnal interview given to Colonel Chabert at Derville's house, the notary responsible for paying the pension which the lawyer gave his odd client came to see him for a consultation on a serious matter, and began by claiming repayment of six hundred francs handed over to the old soldier.

'So you're amusing yourself by supporting the late army?' this notary said, laughing. He was a young man named Crottat, and had just bought the practice where he had been head clerk. The lawyer whose practice it was had absconded, leaving a lamentable deficit in the funds he was responsible for.

'Thank you for reminding me of that business,' replied Derville. 'My philanthropy does not go beyond twenty-five louis. I begin to have some fears already that my patriotism may have made a fool of me.'

He had barely finished speaking when he noticed the packets on his desk that his head clerk had set there. His eye was caught by the appearance of the stamps, oblong, square, triangular, red, and blue, on a letter that had passed through Prussian, Austrian, Bavarian, and French posts.

'Ah!' he said with a laugh, 'here is the dénouement of the comedy. Now we shall see if I've been bamboozled.'

He took the letter and opened it, but could not read a word; it was written in German.

'Boucard, take this letter yourself, get it translated and come back at once,' said Derville, half-opening his office door and holding the letter out to his head clerk.

The Berlin notary to whom the lawyer had written advised him that the documents whose dispatch he had asked for would reach him a few days after this letter of advice. The papers were, he said, perfectly in order and duly authenticated so that they could stand as proper evidence in a court of law. In addition, he informed him that nearly all the witnesses to the facts sworn to in the affidavits were living in Prussich-Eylau, and that the woman to whom Monsieur le comte Chabert owed his life was still alive and in one of the suburbs of Heilsberg.

'This begins to look like serious business,' exclaimed Derville, when Boucard had finished giving him the substance of the letter. 'But tell me, my boy,' he went on, turning to the notary; '... I am going to need information which must be in your office. Wasn't it that old rogue Roguin ...'

'We speak of the unfortunate, the unlucky Roguin,' Maître Alexandre Crottat interrupted him with a laugh.

'Wasn't it that unfortunate man who has just made off with eight hundred thousand francs of his clients' money and reduced several families to beggary, who was concerned in the winding-up of the Chabert estate? It seems to me that I have seen that in our Ferraud papers.'

'Yes,' replied Crottat. 'I was third clerk then. I copied the instrument and studied it closely. Rose Chapotel, wife and widow of Hyacinthe, surnamed Chabert, Count of the Empire, Grand Officer of the Legion of Honour. They were married without a marriage settlement, so they held their property jointly. As far as I can remember, the assets amounted to six hundred thousand francs. Before his marriage Count Chabert had made a will in favour of the Paris hospitals, bequeathing a quarter of the fortune of which he should die possessed to them; the Treasury would inherit the other quarter. There was a sale, auction, and partition, for the lawyers made short work of it. At the time of the winding-up, the monster who was then ruling France returned the Treasury share by decree to the Colonel's widow.'

'So Count Chabert's personal fortune would only amount to three hundred thousand francs?'

'Just so, as you say, old man!' replied Crottat. 'You solicitors do sometimes hit the nail on the head, even if you are occasionally accused of being ready to see the justice of the cause of either party to a dispute. ...'

Count Chabert, whose address was written at the foot of his first receipt for payment received from the notary, lived in the Faubourg Saint-Martin, Rue du Petit-Banquier, in the house of a former sergeant of the Imperial Guard turned dairyman who was called Vergniaud. When he had gone a certain distance, Derville was obliged to continue the search for his client on foot, for his cab-driver refused to drive into an unpaved street where the ruts were rather too deep for the wheels of a cabriolet. After looking all round him, the lawyer finally discovered in the part of the street nearest the boulevard, an opening in a wall built of earth and rubbish of various kinds, framed by two crudely shaped roughstone rectangular pillars, which, in spite of pieces of wood placed as gateposts, had been damaged by the passage of traffic. The pillars supported a beam, surmounted by a red tiled coping, on which these words were written in red: VERGNIAUD DAIRYMAN. Eggs were depicted in white paint to the right of this name, and a cow on the left. The gate was open, and no doubt stayed open all day. Beyond a fairly spacious yard a house stood, facing the gate; if indeed the word house may be used of one of those shanties of the Paris suburbs, which are like no other habitation, not even the sorriest of country cottages, whose wretchedness they share without possessing their romantic appearance. Cottages surrounded by fields, indeed, have the grace given them by pure air, verdure, the sight of the fields, a hill, a winding road, vines, a living hedge, mossy thatches, agricultural appurtenances and implements. But in Paris poverty is unrelieved or, worse, is aggravated by its own wretchedness. Although this house had been recently built, it seemed on the point of falling to pieces. None of the materials it was made of fulfilled the purpose they were meant for; they all came from demolitions, which are of daily occurrence in Paris. Derville read on a shutter made of part of a sign-board: *Drapery and Fancy Goods*. The windows did not match in size or shape, and were irregularly and oddly placed. The ground floor, which appeared to be the habitable part, stood higher on one side, while on the other the rooms were half sunk in rising ground. Between the gate and the house lay a pool full of dung into which flowed streams of rain-water and drainage from the house. The wall against which this flimsy structure leant, which seemed more substantial than the rest, was fitted with hutches fronted with wire netting in which field rabbits produced their numerous progeny. To the right of the entrance lay the byre with a loft for fodder above it, and between byre and house there was a dairy. To the left were a poultry yard, a stable, and a pigsty, whose roof, like that of the house, had been finished with broken boards of white wood nailed one above the other and clumsily overlapped with rushes. Like nearly all the places where the ingredients of the great meal

that Paris devours every day are prepared, the yard in which
Derville now set foot showed signs of the haste needed to get
things to the city with the requisite punctuality. Battered speci-
mens of the kind of large white-metal containers in which
milk is transported, and jars for cream, were thrown pell-mell
in front of the dairy, with their cloth stoppers. The tattered
rags used to wipe them fluttered in the sunshine, hung on
strings stretched between posts. The stolid horse, of a breed
found only in the milk trade, had taken a few steps away from
his cart and stood in front of the closed door of the stable. A
goat nibbled the shoots of the frail and dusty vine that adorned
the cracked yellow wall of the house. A cat crouched on top of
the cream jars, busily licking them. The hens put to flight by
Derville's approach fled cackling, and the watch-dog barked.

'So this is where the man whose decisive charge won the
battle of Eylau lives!' Derville said to himself, embracing this
squalid scene with one comprehensive glance.

The house had been left under the protection of three
youngsters. One, who had climbed to the summit of a mound
of green fodder piled on a cart, was throwing stones down the
chimney of the house next door, in the hope that they would
fall into the stew-pot. Another was trying to lead a pig up one
of the cart-shafts, which rested on the ground, while the third,
hanging on to the front of the cart, was waiting until the pig
was safely on, to see-saw the cart and raise the pig aloft into
the air. When Derville asked them if it was there that Monsieur
Chabert lived, none of them replied, and the three looked at
him with lively stupidity, if it is permissible to use these two
words together. Derville repeated his questions without result.
Irritated by the sly air of these three rascals, he abused them
chaffingly in the terms that young men think they have the
right to use to children, and the urchins broke their silence
with a rude guffaw. Derville was becoming angry. The
Colonel, hearing him, appeared from a little low-roofed room
near the dairy and stood at his door with an indescribable air
of military phlegm. Between his lips he held one of those
notably *coloured* pipes (to use the smokers' technical expression), one of those humble clay pipes known as *cutties*. He

raised the peak of a horribly dirty cap, saw Derville, and walked straight across the dung-heap in order to reach his benefactor the more rapidly, calling meanwhile amicably to the children:

'Silence in the ranks!'

The youngsters immediately observed a respectful silence which bore witness to the authority the old soldier possessed over them.

'Why did you not send me a note?' he said to Derville. 'Walk along by the byre! There, look, the way is cobbled,' he cried, noticing the lawyer's hesitation, for he did not want to get his feet wet in the dung-heap.

Jumping from one stone to another, Derville reached the door through which the Colonel had come. Chabert showed some distress at having to receive him in the room he occupied. As a matter of fact Derville could only see one chair. The Colonel's bed consisted of a few bundles of straw over which his landlady had spread two or three strips of those old furnishing materials, picked up who knows where, which dairy-women use to cover the benches in their carts. The floor was simply beaten earth. The walls, covered with saltpetre, greenish in colour and cracked, were so damp that the wall against which the Colonel's bed was set was provided with a protective reed mat. The famous box-coat hung from a nail. Two worn pairs of boots were flung in a corner. There was no sign of linen. On the worm-eaten table the bulletins of the Grand Army reprinted by Plancher lay open, and appeared to be the Colonel's reading matter. The Colonel in these wretched surroundings wore a calm and serene expression. His visit to Derville seemed to have altered the lines of his face, and the lawyer found in it the imprint of a happy train of thought, a peculiar radiance shed there by hope.

'Does the tobacco-smoke annoy you?' he asked, offering his lawyer the chair, which lacked half the straw of its seat.

'You are horribly uncomfortable here, my dear Colonel.'

The suspicion natural to lawyers irresistibly prompted this remark of Derville's, and also the deplorable experience that lawyers acquire early because of the shocking dramas, concealed from the general public, which they witness.

'Here is a man,' he said to himself, 'who must certainly have used my money to practise the soldier's three theological virtues – cards, women, and wine!'

'It's true, Monsieur, it's not our luxury that strikes the eye here. This is just a bivouac, its discomfort tempered by friendship; but ...' (Here the soldier threw an intense look at the lawyer) 'I have never wronged anyone, I have never rebuffed anyone, and I sleep with a mind at ease.'

The lawyer reflected that it would hardly be tactful to ask his client to render an account of the sums he had disbursed to him, and he contented himself with saying:

'It did not occur to you to come into Paris, where you could have lived as inexpensively as you do here, and been much better off?'

'But,' replied the Colonel, 'the good people with whom I am at present took me in and fed me *gratis* for a whole year! How could I leave them as soon as I have a little money? Then the father of those three youngsters is an old *Egyptian...*.'

'An Egyptian? What do you mean?'

'That's what we call soldiers who returned from the campaign in Egypt, like myself. It's not only that all those who were there are in some sort brothers, but Vergniaud was then in my regiment, we went shares in water in the desert. Besides, I haven't finished teaching his little chaps to read.'

'He could have lodged you better for your money.'

'Bah!' said the Colonel. 'His children sleep on straw like me. His wife and he have no better bed; they are badly off, don't you see? They have taken on a business which is beyond their means. But if I recover my fortune ... Well, enough!'

'Colonel, I should receive your papers from Heilsberg tomorrow or the day after. The woman who freed you is still alive!'

'Accursed money! To think that I haven't any!' the Colonel exclaimed, smashing his pipe on the ground.

A *coloured* pipe is a pipe precious to a smoker, but it was such a natural gesture, such a generous impulse, that any smoker, and even the Excise, would have forgiven him this treason against tobacco. Angels even might have gathered the pieces.

'Colonel, your case is exceedingly complicated,' said Derville, leaving the room and going to walk in the sun by the side of the house.

'To me,' said the soldier, 'it seems perfectly simple. I was thought to be dead, and here I am! Give me back my wife and my fortune. Give me the rank of General to which I am entitled, for I was promoted Colonel in the Imperial Guard on the eve of Eylau.'

'Things are not done in that fashion in the legal world,' returned Derville. 'Listen to me. You are Count Chabert, I grant you that, but it's a question of proving it legally to people to whose interest it will be to deny your existence. So your documents will be challenged. This will mean ten or twelve preliminary issues to be settled. Everything will be opposed and appealed against up to the Supreme Court, and they will constitute so many costly suits, which will drag out at great length, no matter how much drive I put into trying to push things on. Your opponents will demand an inquiry, which we cannot object to, and which will perhaps lead to a fact-finding commission in Prussia. But suppose everything goes as we wish, granting that the law recognizes at once that you are Colonel Chabert, can we tell how the question which the very innocent bigamy of Countess Ferraud raises, will be decided? In your suit the point at issue falls outside the Code, and can only be decided by the judges according to ethical laws, as the jury decides in the delicate questions which certain odd social relations present in some Criminal Court actions. Now, you have no children of your marriage, and M. le comte Ferraud has two: the judges may annul the marriage where there are fewer family ties in favour of that where the ties are stronger, since the contracting parties acted in good faith. Will you be in a very edifying moral position, wishing to hold on tooth and nail, at your age and in your present circumstances, to a woman who no longer loves you? You will have against you your wife and her husband, two

powerful people who will be able to influence the courts.
So, you see, the suit contains elements likely to make it pro-
tracted. You will have time to grow old, while you suffer
bitterly.'

'And what about my fortune?'

'Do you believe you have a large fortune?'

'I had thirty thousand livres a year.'

'My dear Colonel, in 1799, before your marriage, you made
a will bequeathing a quarter of your estate to hospitals.'

'That's true.'

'Well! When you were deemed to be dead, wasn't it necessary to proceed to the making of an inventory, to realize the
estate, in order to give this quarter to the hospitals? Your wife
had no qualms about cheating the poor. In the inventory she
no doubt took good care not to mention her ready money or
her jewels, there was little mention made of silver plate, and
the furniture was assessed at one-third of its real value – either
to help her or to pay a smaller tax to the Treasury, and also because the valuers are liable for their valuations. The inventory
thus made showed possessions worth six hundred thousand
francs. For her share the widow had a right to half. Everything was sold, rebought by her – she profited by every transaction – and the hospitals had their seventy-five thousand
francs. Then, the Treasury being your heir, as you had not
mentioned your wife in your will, the Emperor by decree returned to your widow the portion which fell to the Treasury.
Now, to what have you a claim? Only to three hundred thousand francs, less costs.'

'And you call that justice?' said the Colonel, staggered.

'Certainly.'

'Justice is a fine thing!'

'That's how justice is, my poor Colonel. You see that what
you thought was easy is not so. Madame Ferraud may even
wish to keep the portion which the Emperor gave her.'

'But she was not a widow; the decree is void.'

'Quite so. But everything is subject to litigation. Listen to
me. In these circumstances I think that a settlement would be
the best solution, both for you and for her. You will gain a

more considerable fortune by it than that which you can claim.'

'It would be selling my wife!'

'With an income of twenty-four thousand francs you will find a wife who will suit you better in your present position than yours, and make you happier. I mean to go to see Madame Ferraud this very day to find out how the land lies, but I did not want to make such an approach without letting you know.'

'Let's both go to see her....'

'As you are at present?' said the lawyer. 'No, no, Colonel, no. You might ruin your whole case....'

'Is it possible to win my case?'

'On every point,' replied Derville. 'But, my dear Colonel Chabert, you are not taking one thing into account. I am not a rich man, my practice is not entirely paid for yet. If the courts award you a *provision* – that is to say, an advance on your fortune – they will only grant it after recognizing your status as Count Chabert, Grand Officer of the Legion of Honour.'

'Yes, so I am Grand Officer of the Legion; I had forgotten that,' he said naïvely.

'Well, until then,' Derville went on, 'you will have to litigate, won't you? Brief counsel, set the machinery of the law in motion, set process-servers to work, and at the same time live? The costs of the preliminary actions will amount, at a first estimate, to more than twelve or fifteen thousand francs. I don't possess that; indeed I find it a struggle to pay the huge interest on the money I borrowed to buy my practice. And where will you find it?'

Great tears fell from the poor soldier's faded eyes and rolled down his wrinkled cheeks. At the sight of these difficulties his heart failed him. As in a nightmare, the worlds of society and the law seemed to lie, a crushing weight, upon his chest.

'I will go to the foot of the Column in the Place Vendôme,' he burst out; 'and I will shout there: "I am Colonel Chabert who broke the Russians' great square at Eylau!" The bronze at least will recognize me!'

'And you will be put in Charenton, no doubt.'

At that dreaded name the soldier's fire was quelled.

'Might there not be a possibility of finding something favourable to my chances at the War Office?'

'The officials?' said Derville. 'Go to them if you like, but with a decree perfectly in order annulling your death certificate. The bureaucrats would not be sorry to have it in their power to destroy a man of the Empire.'

The Colonel stood for a moment speechless, motionless, sightlessly staring, sunk in bottomless despair. Military justice is summary and swift, it decides out of hand, and its decisions are nearly always the right ones: that was the only justice that Colonel Chabert knew. As he perceived the labyrinth of difficulties that he would have to make his way through, as he saw how much money he would need to thread it successfully, the poor soldier was struck a mortal blow in that faculty which belongs to man alone, and which is called the *will*. It appeared to him that as a litigant it would be impossible to live: it was a thousand times simpler for him to remain poor, a beggar, to sign on as a trooper if some regiment would take him. In his physical and mental sufferings, already, the defences of his body had been breached in some of the most vital organs. He was on the verge of one of those illnesses for which medicine has no name, whose seat is, as it were, shifting, as in affections of the nervous system which seems to be the most frequently attacked part of our mechanism, an illness which in his case would have to be called *spleen due to hardship and unhappiness*. However gravely affected he was by this invisible but very real malady, a happy ending would still cure it. But to overthrow the balance of this vigorous organism completely, a new obstacle would be enough, or some unforeseen circumstance which would overstretch the strained and weakened elasticity of his constitution, and produce those hesitations, those uncompleted and not quite intelligent actions, which physiologists remark in human beings destroyed by mental and emotional suffering.

Derville, recognizing the signs of profound despondency in his client, said then:

'Take courage; the outcome of this business can only be

favourable to you. Only consider whether you can give me all your confidence and accept blindly the arrangement that I think best for you.'

'Do as you please,' said Chabert.

'Yes, but you surrender yourself to me like a man going to his death!'

'Am I not going to be left without standing, without a name? Is that endurable?'

'That's not how I understand it,' said the lawyer. 'We will seek, in an amicable spirit, a decree annulling your death certificate and your marriage, so that you may regain your rights. You may even, through Count Ferraud's influence, be placed in the Army cadre as general, and you will no doubt obtain a pension.'

'Go ahead, then,' replied Chabert. 'I place myself entirely in your hands.'

'I will send you a paper, giving me power of attorney, to sign, then,' said Derville. 'Goodbye. Don't lose heart! If you need money, count on me.'

Chabert shook Derville's hand warmly, and stood there, his back against the wall, with no power to follow him except with his eyes. Like everyone with little understanding of legal matters, he found it difficult to face these unforeseen difficulties with courage.

During this discussion the face of a man had several times peered round one of the pilasters of the gate. He was posted in the street, watching for Derville's departure, and he accosted him when he left. He was an old man, dressed in a blue jacket and a white pleated coat like a brewer's and wearing a cap of otter fur on his head. His face was dark, hollow-eyed, and wrinkled, but with red patches on the cheek-bones, set there by hard manual work, and tanned by the open air.

'Excuse me, sir,' he said to Derville, stopping him with hand on his arm, 'if I take the liberty of speaking to you; but I misdoubted when I saw you that you were the friend of our general.'

'Well,' said Derville, 'in what way are you concerned about him? And who are you?' the mistrustful lawyer added.

'I am Louis Vergniaud,' he replied to the second question. 'And I have two words to say to you.'

'So you're the man who has lodged Count Chabert in that fashion!'

'Excuse me, I beg your pardon, sir, he has the best room. I would have given him mine if I had only had one. I would have slept in the stable. A man who has suffered like him, who is teaching my youngsters to read, a general, an Egyptian, the first lieutenant I served under ... no mistake about it! No question, he's the best lodged. I shared with him what I had. Unfortunately it wasn't much, bread, milk, eggs – in short, fortune of war, sir, we have to take things as they come! We're heartily glad to. But he has vexed us.'

'Vexed you?'

'Yes, sir, vexed us, there as you might say, up to the hilt. I have taken on a business that's too big for me; he couldn't help seeing that. He didn't like that, and he used to groom the horse! I said to him, "But General, sir!" "Bah!" was what he said. "I don't want to stand around like a loafer, and it's a long time since I first learned to use a curry-comb." I had given promissory notes to the value of my byre to a man of the name of Grados. ... Do you know him, sir?'

'But, my friend, I have no time to listen to you. Simply tell me, how has the Colonel vexed you?'

'He vexed us, sir, as sure as my name is Louis Vergniaud and that it made the wife cry. He knew, through the neighbours, that we hadn't the first sou of our mortgage. The old campaigner, without saying a word, gathered together all you gave him, was on the lookout for the bill when it came, and paid it. Such a dodge! When the wife and I knew that he had no tobacco, poor man, and was denying himself it! Oh, he has his cigars now, every morning. I would sooner sell myself. ... No, we are vexed. And so I would like to propose that you should lend us, seeing that he told us that you were an honest man, about a hundred crowns against our business, so that we can get him to have clothes made, and furnish his room for him. He thought he was putting us in the clear, true enough? Well, he hasn't, don't you see; he has put us into

debt ... and vexed us! He should not have affronted us like
that. It vexed us; and us friends too! On the word of an honest
man, as sure as my name is Louis Vergniaud, sooner than not
return you that money, I'll enlist....'

Derville contemplated the dairyman, and then took several
steps backwards to stare again at the house, yard, dung-heap,
stable, rabbits, children.

'Upon my word, I believe it is one of the marks of virtue
not to be an owner of property,' he said. 'Well, you shall have
your hundred crowns, and even more! But I am not the man
who shall give them to you; the Colonel will be quite rich
enough to help you, and I do not want to deprive him of the
pleasure.'

'Will that be soon?'

'Certainly.'

'Ah! ... how pleased my wife will be!'

And a beaming smile spread over the dairyman's tanned
face.

'Now,' said Derville to himself, as he climbed into his
cabriolet, 'now to visit our foe. We must not show our hand,
but try to find out what she means to do and win the fight with
a single shot. We shall have to frighten her perhaps. She's a
woman. Now what frightens women most? The only thing
women are frightened of ...'

He set himself to study the Countess's position, and fell to
meditating, as high politicians do, when they give their minds
to devising plans and try to divine the secrets of opposition
cabinets. Of course lawyers are surely statesmen of a kind, responsible for private affairs instead of public ones. Here we
must cast a glance at the situation in which M. le comte Ferraud and his wife stood, if we are to appreciate the lawyer's
cleverness.

Count Ferraud was the son of a former judge of the High
Court in Paris. He had emigrated during the Reign of Terror,
and though he saved his head, had lost all his money. He returned under the Consulate, and remained consistently faithful
to the interests of Louis XVIII, in whose entourage his father
had been before the Revolution. This meant that he was a

member of that section of the Faubourg Saint-Germain which loftily resisted Napoleon's enticements. The reputation for great ability which the young Count, then called simply Monsieur Ferraud, created for himself, made him a target for the blandishments of the Emperor, who was often as pleased with his conquests among the aristocrats as he was with winning a battle. The Count was promised that his title and such part of his property as had not been sold would be restored to him. He was given a glimpse of the chance of future ministerial office, of a seat in the Senate. But the Emperor had no success.

At the time of Count Chabert's death Monsieur Ferraud was a young man of twenty-six, blessed with charming manners, who had had his successes and whom the Faubourg Saint-Germain had adopted as its pride and joy, but he had no money. Madame Chabert, however, had been able to turn the settlement of her husband's estate to such good account that after eighteen months of widowhood she possessed nearly forty thousand livres a year. Her marriage with the young Count was not welcomed at first by the coteries of the Faubourg Saint-Germain. Napoleon was pleased with the marriage, which was in conformity with his ideas about the fusion of discordant elements, and he returned to Madame Chabert the part of Colonel Chabert's estate that fell to the Treasury; but Napoleon's hopes were once more to be dashed. Madame Chabert had fallen in love, not only with her lover in this young man, but with the seductive prospect too of becoming a member of that haughty social class which in spite of its humiliation dominated the Imperial Court. All her vanities as well as her passions were gratified by this marriage. She was going to be *a woman of fashion*. When the Faubourg Saint-Germain knew that the young Count's marriage was not a defection, the *salons* opened their doors to his wife.

Then came the Restoration. Count Ferraud's political rise was not rapid. He understood the difficulties of the position in which Louis XVIII found himself, he was among those initiates who were waiting until *the revolutionary chasm closed over*, for a political meaning underlay these royal words which liberals jeered at so much. Still, the decree cited in the long clerkish sentence with which this story opens had restored two forests to him, and a piece of land whose value had considerably increased since its sequestration. At present although Count Ferraud was a Councillor of State, he considered his position to be only the beginning of his political career. Because of his preoccupation with the demands of a consuming ambition, he had attached to himself as secretary a former lawyer, now penniless, named Delbecq, a man who was more than clever, who had an admirable knowledge of how the resources of the law could be used, to whom he left the conduct of his private business affairs. The wily attorney had understood the position he held in relation to the Count clearly enough to be honest by policy. He hoped to achieve some office through his employer's influence, and gave all his care to promoting his employer's fortunes. His behaviour was in such obvious flat contradiction to his previous reputation that he was regarded as a man who had been slandered. With the tact and finesse which all women have a share of, more or less, the Countess, who had fathomed her steward's character and intentions, kept a watchful eye upon him and managed him adroitly, so adroitly that she had already been able to use his abilities to very good purpose in the augmentation of her private fortune. She had been able to persuade Delbecq that Monsieur Ferraud was governed by her, and had promised to have him made President of a court of first instance in one of the leading cities in France if he devoted himself entirely to her interests. The promise of an unassailable position which would permit him to marry advantageously, and later to rise to high position in a political career when he had become a Deputy, made Delbecq the Countess's tool. He had let her miss none of the opportunities that the movements of the Bourse and the rise in value of land offered to wide-awake people in Paris during the first three years of the Restoration. He had tripled his patroness's capital, all the more easily that any means appeared good to the Countess that would build up a huge fortune for her rapidly. She employed the emoluments of the positions the Count occupied for the household expenses, in order to be able to treat her income as capital, and

Delbecq lent himself to her avaricious plotting without concerning himself about her motives. People of his kind are only anxious to learn secrets where knowledge is necessary to their interests. Besides, he found a very natural explanation of the Countess's greed in the thirst for gold that most Parisian women suffer from, and such a large fortune was needed to back Count Ferraud's aspirations that the steward sometimes imagined that her cupidity must be the result of her devotion to a man with whom she was still in love. The Countess had buried the secret reasons for her actions in the depths of her heart. There lay secrets of life and death for her, and precisely in them lay the knot of this story.

At the beginning of the year 1818 the Restoration seemed to rest on immovable foundations; its doctrines of government, as understood by intellectual and idealistic people, seemed to them destined to inaugurate an era of new prosperity for France. Parisian society at that time altered its aspect. Madame la comtesse Ferraud found that in making a love-match she had by chance married money and found an outlet for ambition too. Still young and beautiful, she played the part of a woman of fashion and lived in the atmosphere of the Court. She was rich in her own right, rich through her husband, who, lauded as one of the most capable men of the Royalist party and the friend of the King, seemed marked out for some Ministry, she belonged to the aristocracy, she shared in its splendour. In the midst of this triumph she was stricken by a mortal disease of the spirit.

There are feelings that women intuitively divine, whatever care men may take to hide them. When the King had first returned, Count Ferraud had conceived some regrets for his marriage. Colonel Chabert's widow had brought him alliances with no one; he was alone, without friends to back him, and must find his own way in a career full of hidden dangers and beset by enemies. Then, perhaps, when he had been able to consider his wife in cold blood, he had realized that certain deficiencies in her education made her unsuited to second him in his plans. A remark of his *à propos* of Talleyrand's marriage enlightened the Countess, to whom it was made clear that if his marriage were still to make, never would she be Madame Ferraud. What woman would forgive the harbouring of such regret? Surely every insult, every crime, every repudiation is essentially contained in that one. But consider what an open sore that remark must remain in the Countess's heart if it be supposed that she was afraid of seeing her first husband reappear! She had heard that he was alive: she had rejected him. Then during the time when she had heard no more mention of him she had lulled herself with the thought that he was dead at Waterloo with the Imperial eagles, like Boutin. Nevertheless, she had had the idea of binding the Count to her by the strongest of ties, a chain of gold, and desired to be so rich that her fortune would make her marriage indissoluble if Colonel Chabert should chance to turn up again. And he had turned up, and she had no information to explain why the struggle she dreaded had not already begun. Illness, the hardships he had endured, had possibly delivered her from this man. Perhaps he was half mad; Charenton might yet deal with him for her. She had not wanted to take Delbecq or the police into her confidence for fear of putting herself in someone's power or precipitating the catastrophe. There exist many women in Paris who, like Countess Ferraud, live with a monstrous secret in their hearts, or try to keep their balance on the edge of a yawning chasm: they grow a hard callosity to protect their vulnerable spot, and can still laugh and enjoy themselves.

'There is something very odd about M. le comte Ferraud's position,' Derville said to himself, waking from his long reverie as his cabriolet stopped before the door of the Ferraud mansion in the Rue de Varennes. 'How is it that rich as he is, favoured by the King, he has as yet no seat in the Senate? It is true that it may perhaps be the King's policy, as Madame de Grandlieu told me, to give the senators a rarity value by not creating too many of them. Besides, the son of a judge of the High Court in Paris is by no means either a Crillon or a Rohan. Count Ferraud can only slip into the Upper Chamber surreptitiously. But if his marriage were dissolved, might he not make himself heir to one of those old senators who have an only daughter? The King would be delighted. Here's a fine bogy to pull out of the bag to frighten our Countess with,' he told himself as he climbed the steps.

Derville had, without knowing it, put his finger on the secret wound, penetrated deeply to the cancer that was consuming Madame Ferraud.

He was received by her in a pretty winter dining-room, where she was playing as she breakfasted with a monkey chained to a miniature set of posts adorned with lengths of iron rod. The Countess was wrapped in an elegant morning gown. Curls escaped from her carelessly knotted hair, under a cap which gave her an archly roguish look. She was fresh and gay. Silver, gilt, and mother-of-pearl sparkled on the table, and about the room exotic flowers were set in magnificent porcelain vases. When the lawyer saw Colonel Chabert's wife, enriched with plunder stripped from him, lapped in luxury, at the pinnacle of social success, while her unfortunate husband lived in a poor dairyman's house, surrounded by cattle, he said to himself, 'The moral of this is that a pretty woman will never want to recognize her husband or even her lover in a man in an old box-coat, a tow wig, and split boots.' A malicious, ironical smile showed his thoughts, the half-philosophical, half-mocking thoughts bound to occur to a man so well placed for observing what lies beneath the surface, in spite of the deceits by which most Parisian families keep that concealed.

'Good morning, Monsieur Derville,' she said, and went on feeding the monkey with coffee.

'Madame,' he said brusquely, for he was shocked at the frivolous way in which the Countess had said: *Good morning, Monsieur Derville*, 'I am here to speak to you about a serious matter.'

'I am *exceedingly* vexed, Monsieur le comte is not at home.'

'For my part, I am delighted, Madame. It would be *exceedingly* vexing if he were present at our discussion. Besides I know, through Delbecq, that you like to manage your affairs yourself, without troubling Monsieur le comte with them.'

'Well, I'll have Delbecq called,' she said.

'He could not help you, in spite of his cleverness,' returned

Derville. 'Listen, Madame, one word will be enough to make you take things seriously. Count Chabert is alive.'

'Is it with quips of that kind that you mean to make me take things seriously?' she said, breaking into a peal of laughter.

But the Countess was suddenly subdued by the singularly clear-sighted gaze with which Derville interrogated her and seemed to read her soul.

'Madame,' he replied, with a cold and cutting gravity, 'you are unaware of the magnitude of the dangers that threaten you. I need not talk to you about the incontestable authenticity of the documents, nor about the clearness of the proofs that attest Count Chabert's existence. I am not a man to take on a worthless case, as you know. If you oppose our application to have the death certificate declared null, you will lose this first case, and with that question decided in our favour we shall win all the others.'

'Then what are you anxious to talk to me about?'

'Not about the Colonel, nor about you. I shall say nothing either about the matters for consideration that skilled counsel might advance, with the curious facts of this case to give them point, or the capital that would be made out of the letters that you received from your first husband before the celebration of your marriage with your second.'

'That's a lie!' she said, with all a fine lady's vehemence. 'I have never received a letter from Count Chabert; and if anyone says he is the Colonel, he can only be an adventurer, some freed convict like Cogniard perhaps. It makes me shudder even to think of it. Can the Colonel come to life, Monsieur? Bonaparte sent his aide-de-camp to congratulate me on the manner of his death, and today I receive a pension of three thousand francs, granted to his widow by Parliament. I have had every reason to reject all the Chaberts who presented themselves, as I shall reject all those who present themselves in future.'

'Happily we are alone, Madame. We can tell lies without constraint,' he said coldly, taking pleasure in goading the Countess to a sharper anger to make her speak unguardedly, a tactic well known to lawyers, who are all accustomed to keeping calm while their adversaries or clients lose their tempers.

'Very well; we'll fight it out!' he said to himself, and immediately thought of a trap which should show her how much at his mercy she was.

'Proof of the sending of the first letter exists, Madame,' he went on aloud; 'it contained securities....'

'Oh! there were no securities in it.'

'So you received that first letter?' returned Derville, smiling. 'You are caught in the first trap a lawyer sets for you, and you think you can fight against justice....'

The Countess blushed, turned pale, hid her face in her hands. Then she shook off her feeling of shame and retorted with the coolness natural to women of her type:

'Since you are the alleged Chabert's lawyer, be good enough to ...'

Derville interrupted her. 'I am still, now, your lawyer as much as the Colonel's, Madame. Do you think that I want to lose professional business as valuable to me as yours? But you are not listening to me....'

'Go on, Monsieur,' she said graciously.

'Your fortune came to you from Monsieur le comte Chabert, and you have rejected him. Your fortune is colossal and you let him beg his bread. Madame, barristers can be very eloquent when causes speak for themselves: there are circumstances here that might very well rouse public opinion against you.'

'But, Monsieur,' said the Countess, losing patience at the way in which Derville, having placed her on the gridiron, was grilling her first on one side and then on the other, 'granting that your Monsieur Chabert exists, the courts will uphold my second marriage on account of the children, and all I shall have to do is to pay two hundred and twenty-five thousand francs to Monsieur Chabert.'

'We do not know to which side the sympathies of the courts may incline regarding the question of sentiment. If on one hand we have a mother and her children, on the other we have a man overwhelmed by adversity, aged by your rejection. Where is he to find a wife? Then, can the judges act counter to the law? Your marriage with the Colonel has legality on its side, and priority. Then if you are shown up in odious colours, you might find that you have an adversary that you are not expecting. There, Madame, is the danger from which I should like to preserve you.'

'A new adversary!' she said. 'Who?'

'Monsieur le comte Ferraud, Madame.'

'Monsieur Ferraud is too warmly attached to me, and has too much respect for the mother of his children....'

'Don't talk such nonsense,' Derville interrupted her, 'to lawyers accustomed to reading the depths of the heart. At the moment Monsieur Ferraud has not the slightest desire to break up your marriage and I am sure he adores you, but suppose someone came to tell him that his marriage may be annulled, that his wife will be indicted as a criminal before public opinion. ...'

'He would defend me, Monsieur!'

'No, Madame.'

'What reason would he have for deserting me?'

'The hope of marriage with the only daughter of a peer of France, to whose peerage he would succeed by the King's decree.'

The Countess turned pale.

'It's in our hands!' Derville said to himself. 'Good. I have you now. The poor Colonel's battle is won.'

'Besides, Madame,' he went on aloud, 'he would have the less compunction in doing so in that a man who has covered himself with glory, a general, a count, a Grand Officer of the Legion of Honour would not be a change for the worse, and if that man should demand that his wife be restored to him. ...'

'That's enough!' she said. 'I shall never have anyone but you for my lawyer. What can we do?'

'Come to terms!' said Derville.

'Does he still love me?' she asked.

'I don't see how it can be otherwise.'

At this the Countess raised her head. A gleam of hope shone in her eyes. She was calculating perhaps that she might yet win her case by some feminine ruse, counting on her first husband's tenderness to fight for her.

'I shall await your instructions, Madame, to hear if we must give you formal notice of our documents, or if you wish to come to my office to discuss the terms of a settlement,' said Derville, with a farewell bow to the Countess.

A week after Derville's two visits, on a fine morning in June, the husband and wife whom an almost supernatural chance had parted came from the opposite corners of Paris to meet in the office of their common lawyer. The money which Derville had generously advanced to Colonel Chabert had allowed him to dress in a fashion befitting his rank. The dead man drove up in a smart cabriolet. He wore a wig which set off his features and concealed his head. He was dressed in blue cloth with appropriate white linen, and below his waistcoat wore the red ribbon of Grand Officers of the Legion of Honour. In once more adopting the style of living of the comfortably off he had put on again his former soldierly elegance. He held himself upright. His grave and mysterious face, in which could be read the signs of happiness and all his hopes, appeared rejuvenated and brushed in in broader, richer strokes, to borrow one of its more picturesque turns of expression from painting. He no more resembled the Chabert in the old box-coat than a copper resembles a newly minted forty-franc piece. Passers-by might easily have recognized in him one of the fine survivors of the army we once had, one of those heroic men in whom our national glory is reflected, and who show it off as a splinter of ice lit by the sun seems to reflect all its rays. These old soldiers are in themselves both paintings and books.

When the Count left his carriage to climb Derville's stair, he jumped down lightly like a young man. His cabriolet had barely turned when a pretty coupé painted with a coat of arms arrived. Madame la comtesse Ferraud, dressed simply but in a style cleverly designed to display her youthful figure, got out. She had a charming bonnet lined with rose-colour which was a perfect frame for her face, softening its contours and lending it freshness.

If the clients were rejuvenated, the office had not changed, and presented the same scene as that described at the beginning of the story. Simonnin was eating his lunch, leaning against

the window, which was open now, and watching such blue
sky as could be seen through the opening provided by this
courtyard, surrounded as it was by four blocks of dark
buildings.

'Ah!' cried the junior clerk. 'Who would like to take a bet
against me for a show that Colonel Chabert is a general and
Knight of the Order of Saint Louis?'

'The chief is a famous magician,' said Godeschal.

'Is there no trick to play on him this time?' asked Desroches.

'His wife, Countess Ferraud, will take care of that!' said
Boucard.

'So Countess Ferraud,' said Godeschal, 'will be obliged to
be two....'

'Here she is!' Simonnin broke in.

Just then the Colonel came in and asked for Derville.

'He is in, Monsieur le comte,' said Simonnin.

'So you're not deaf, eh, you young rascal?' Chabert said,
seizing him by the ear and pulling it, while the clerks looked
on laughing, enjoying his discomfiture, and contemplated the
Colonel with the curious interest due to such a singular personage.

Count Chabert was with Derville when his wife came into
the outer office.

'My word, Boucard, there's going to be a fine scene in the
chief's room! There's a wife who can spend odd days with
Count Chabert and even days with Count Ferraud.'

'In leap-years,' observed Godeschal, 'the Count will get
even.'

'Hush, gentlemen! You can be heard,' said Boucard
severely. 'I have never seen an office where the clerks made
jokes about the clients the way you do.'

Derville had sent the Colonel to the bedroom when the
Countess presented herself.

'As I did not know if you would be pleased to see Monsieur
le comte Chabert, Madame,' he said, 'I have separated you.
However if you would like ...'

'That is a kindness for which I thank you, Monsieur.'

'I have prepared a draft instrument for you and Monsieur Chabert to discuss its conditions immediately. I shall go from one to the other to present your respective views to each.'

'Well, proceed, Monsieur,' said the Countess with an impatient gesture.

Derville read.

'Between the undersigned,

'Monsieur Hyacinthe, *surnamed Chabert*, Count, Brigadier-General, and Grand Officer of the Legion of Honour, residing in Paris, in the Rue du Petit-Banquier, on the one hand,

'And the lady Rose Chapotel, wife of the aforenamed Monsieur le comte Chabert, *née* ...'

'Go on,' she said, 'leave the preamble, pass on to the conditions.'

'Madame,' said the lawyer, 'the preamble briefly explains the position in which you severally find yourselves. Then in the first article you recognize in the presence of three witnesses (two notaries and the dairyman at whose house your husband has been living, whom I have told of your business in confidence, and who will preserve the most complete silence on the subject), as I was saying, you will recognize that the person whose signature is attached to the documents herewith, and whose status is moreover attested by a declaration of identity prepared by your notary Alexandre Crottat, is Count Chabert, your first husband.

'In the second article Count Chabert pledges himself in the interests of your happiness to make use of his rights only in certain cases provided for in this agreement. And these cases' said Derville, in parenthesis, 'are nothing but the non-execution of the clauses of this secret agreement. On his side,' he went on, 'Monsieur Chabert consents, in private agreement with you, to seek a judgement annulling his death certificate and declaring the dissolution of his marriage.'

'That doesn't suit me at all,' said the Countess in astonishment. 'I don't want a law-suit. You know why.'

'By the third article,' continued the lawyer with imperturbable phlegm, 'you pledge yourself to settle on Hyacinthe, Count Chabert, an annuity of twenty-four thousand francs, invested in that name in the funds, of which the capital will return to you on his death. ...'

'But that's much too much!' said the Countess.

'Can you make a better bargain?'

'Perhaps.'

'What do you want, then, Madame?'

'I want, I don't want a law-suit, I want ...'

'Him to stay dead,' interrupted Derville sharply.

'Monsieur,' said the Countess, 'if it's a question of twenty-four thousand francs a year we'll fight it out in the law-courts.'

'Yes, we will fight it out in the law-courts!' cried a hollow voice and the Colonel flung open the door and suddenly stood before his wife, one hand thrust into his waistcoat, the other pointing downwards towards the floor in a gesture to which the memory of his experiences lent a fearful force.

'It is Chabert!' the Countess said to herself.

'Too much!' the old soldier went on. 'I have given you nearly a million, and you haggle over my misfortune. Very well! I want you now, you and your wealth. We hold our property jointly, our marriage is still valid ...'

'But you, Monsieur, are not Colonel Chabert!' exclaimed the Countess in feigned surprise.

'Ah!' said the old man, in a profoundly ironical tone, 'would you like proofs! I took you from the Palais-Royal ...'

The Countess turned pale. As he watched her grow white beneath her rouge the old soldier was affected by the acute pain which he was inflicting on a woman once ardently loved, and he stopped; but he received such a venomous look from her that he at once went on:

'You were staying with ...'

'For God's sake, Monsieur,' the Countess said to the lawyer, 'agree that it is time I left this place. I did not come here to listen to such horrors.'

She rose to her feet and went out. Derville rushed after her into the outer office. The Countess appeared to have found wings and flown. Returning to his sanctum the lawyer found the Colonel striding up and down in a violent rage.

'In those times everyone took his wife where it pleased

him,' he said. 'But I had the bad luck to choose badly, to trust to appearances. She is heartless!'

'Well, Colonel, was I not well-advised when I begged you not to come? At least, I am certain now of your identity. When you showed yourself the Countess started, and there was no mistaking what she thought. But you have lost your suit, your wife knows that you are unrecognizable!'

'I'll kill her ...'

'Madness! You would be taken and guillotined like any criminal. Besides you might miss your aim! That would be unpardonable, one should never miss one's wife when one wants to kill her. Go away and leave me to mend the damage your folly has done, my overgrown child. Be careful: she is quite capable of taking you in some trap and shutting you up in Charenton. I am going to give her formal notice of our documents to guard you against any surprise.'

The poor Colonel did as his young benefactor told him, and went out, stammering excuses. He walked slowly down the dark stairs, lost in sombre thoughts, overcome perhaps by the blow which he had just been struck, which for him indeed was the most cruel he had received, striking home most deeply to his heart; when, reaching the last landing, he heard the swish of a dress and his wife appeared.

'Come, Monsieur,' she said, taking his arm with a gesture familiar to him often in the past.

Her action and the tone of her voice, full of graciousness once more, were enough to dissipate the Colonel's anger, and he let himself be led to the carriage.

'Well! Get in!' said the Countess when the footman had finished letting down the step.

And he found himself, as if by magic, seated beside his wife in the coupé.

'Where to, Madame?' inquired the footman.

'Groslay,' she said.

Off they went, and drove right across Paris.

'Monsieur!' the Countess said to the Colonel in a tone which betrayed her emotion, such an emotion as is rarely felt in the course of a life-time, and which when it comes stirs everything within us. At such moments, heart, fibres and nerves, countenance, soul, and body, everything, every pore of our skin even, is affected. Life no longer seems contained within us: it leaves us, springs from us, it is communicated like a contagion, is transmitted by a look, by the sound of our voice, by a gesture, and imposes our will on others. The old soldier gave a start when he heard this one word, this first, this portentous *Monsieur!* For it was at once a reproach, a prayer, an act of forgiveness, a hope, an expression of despair, a question, a reply. The word comprehended everything. Only an actress could have thrown such eloquence, such feeling, into a word. What is genuine is not so perfectly expressed, it does not reveal everything: it leaves it to be perceived how much remains unseen. The Colonel was overwhelmed with remorse for his suspicions, his demands, his anger, and lowered his eyes to hide his confusion.

'Monsieur,' the Countess began again after an imperceptible pause, 'I recognized you at once!'

'What you say, Rosine, is the only possible thing that could heal and make me forget my misfortunes,' said the old soldier.

Two great tears fell hotly on his wife's hands, which he pressed in expression of a fatherly tenderness.

'How did you not guess,' she went on, 'how horribly painful it was for me to appear before a stranger in a position as false as mine is? If I must blush for my situation let it at least be within the family circle. Should this secret not have remained buried in our hearts? You will not blame me, I hope, for seeming indifferent to the misfortunes of a Chabert in whose existence I had no reason to believe. I received your letters,' she added swiftly, reading an objection in her husband's face; 'but they reached me thirteen months after the battle of Eylau. They were open, dirty, the handwriting was unrecognizable, and I was bound to believe, when I had obtained Napoleon's signature on my new marriage contract, that a clever adventurer was trying to make use of me. If I were not to disturb Monsieur le comte Ferraud's peace of mind, not to weaken family ties, I had to take precautions against an imposter. Had I not some justification, tell me?'

'Yes, you were justified. I am an idiot, a donkey, a fool, not to have been better able to foresee the consequences of your being placed in such a situation. But where are we going?' the Colonel asked, seeing that they had reached the Chapelle gate.

'To my country estate, near Groslay, in the valley of Montmorency. There we can consider together what is the best course for us to follow. I know where my duty lies. If I belong to you in law, I am no longer yours in fact. Can you want us to become the laughing-stock of Paris? We surely don't need to inform the public of this situation, which where my position is concerned has its ludicrous side. Let us preserve our dignity. You still love me,' she went on, bestowing a sad and tender look on the colonel; 'but on my side, was it not permissible for me to form new ties? In this singular situation of mine an inner voice bids me trust in your goodness, which is so well known to me. Should I be acting wrongly in taking you for sole and unique arbiter of my fate? Be judge and protagonist both. I trust myself to the nobility of your character. Your heart is kind enough to forgive me the consequences of sins committed in all innocence. I will confess to you, I love Monsieur Ferraud. I believed I had the right to love him. I do not blush before you in making this confession: if it offends you, it does not dishonour us. I cannot hide the facts from you. When chance left me a widow, I was not a mother.'

The Colonel with a wave of his hand imposed silence on his wife, and they drove for more than a mile without uttering a word. Chabert was picturing the two small children, and felt their presence with him.

'Rosine!'

'Monsieur?'

'So it's quite wrong of dead men to return?'

'Oh, no, no! Don't think so hardly of me. Only you find a lover, a mother, where you left a wife. If it no longer lies in my power to love you, I know all I owe you, and can still offer you all a daughter's affection.'

'Rosine,' the old man said gently, 'I no longer feel any resentment against you. We will forget all that,' he added, with a smile of such grace as is always the reflection of a noble soul. 'I am not so indelicate as to exact the semblance of love from a woman who no longer loves me.'

The Countess threw him a look filled with such gratitude that it made poor Chabert feel ready to return to his common grave at Eylau. There are some magnanimous men capable of devotion of this degree, and they find their recompense in the knowledge that the happiness of a person they love is their creation.

'My dear, we will talk of all this later and calmly, with minds at rest,' said the Countess.

The conversation turned into other channels, for it was impossible to go on talking for long on that subject. Although husband and wife often returned to their strange situation, by allusion or serious reflection, they both found their journey delightful as they recalled the events of their past union and happenings under the Empire. The Countess well knew how to lend a nostalgic charm to these reminiscences, and gave the conversation a tinge of melancholy that maintained its seriousness. She brought love to life again, without reviving desire, and gave her first husband a glimpse of how her mind had developed and been stored, as she tried to make him grow accustomed to the idea of limiting his happiness to the pleasure a father enjoys in a cherished daughter. The Colonel had known the Countess under the Empire, he was now seeing a Countess of the Restoration.

At last they arrived by way of a side road at an extensive park, situated in the little valley which separates the heights of Montmorency from the pretty village of Groslay. The Countess possessed a delightful house there, and when they reached it the Colonel saw everything made ready and prepared for his stay and his wife's.

Adversity casts a kind of spell, whose property it is to reinforce our original propensity: it increases the malice and mistrust of certain men and adds to the goodness of others whose heart is sound. Misfortune had made the Colonel still more ready to be kind, more sympathetic than he had been before, so that he was able to begin to understand the secret of feminine griefs which most men have no idea of. Still, in spite of his disinclination to entertain distrust, he could not help saying to his wife:

'You were very sure that you would bring me here?'

'Yes,' she replied, 'if I found Colonel Chabert in the claimant.'

Her air of frank truthfulness in this answer dissipated the slight suspicion which the Colonel now felt ashamed of having conceived.

During the next three days the Countess treated her first husband with the most admirable consideration. By her tender care and constant gentleness she seemed to be trying to efface the memory of the suffering which he had endured, to gain forgiveness for the unhappiness which she, as she declared, had innocently caused. She took pleasure in displaying for his benefit, although with a kind of sadness which she let him perceive, the charms for which she knew his weakness; for we are all more susceptible to the appeal of certain aspects of personality, certain graces of heart or mind which we find irresistible. She was anxious to obtain his sympathetic concern about her situation, to move him to such pity that she could gain possession of his mind and dispose of him as she saw fit. Resolved to stop at nothing to gain her ends, she did not yet know what she was to make of this man, but certainly she meant to annihilate him socially.

On the evening of the third day she became conscious that, in spite of all she could do, she could not disguise the uneasiness she felt as to the outcome of her manoeuvres. In order to find a moment's relief she went up to her own room, sat down at her writing-table, laid down the mask of tranquil composure which she kept in place before Colonel Chabert; like an actress returning exhausted to her dressing-room after a devastating fifth act, sinking down half dead, leaving behind her in the auditorium an image of herself which she no longer resembles. She set herself to finish a letter which she had begun to Delbecq, telling him to go to Derville and ask in her name to see the documents which concerned Colonel Chabert, to copy them and come at once to meet her at Groslay. She had scarcely finished when she heard the sound of the Colonel's step in the passage. Anxious and uneasy, he had come to find her.

'Alas!' she said aloud. 'I wish I were dead! My situation is intolerable! ...'

'Well, well! What's the matter?' the worthy soldier demanded.

'Nothing, nothing,' she said.

She rose, left the Colonel and went downstairs where she could speak to her maid without being overheard. She sent the woman to Paris, enjoining her to give the letter which she had just written into Delbecq's own hands, and to bring it back when he had read it. Then the Countess went to take her seat on a garden bench, where she was sufficiently in evidence for the Colonel to find her there as soon as he wished. The Colonel, who was already looking for his wife, hastened to her and sat down by her side.

'Rosine,' he said, 'what is the matter?'

She did not answer. The evening was one of those magnificent calm evenings in June when the hidden harmonies of nature lend such serenity to the sunset. The air was clear and the silence profound, so that in the farther reaches of the park some children could be heard, whose voices added a kind of melody to the sublimities of the landscape.

'You do not answer me?' the Colonel said.

'My husband ...' said the Countess and then stopped, made an impulsive gesture which she interrupted to turn to him, blushing, and ask – 'What am I to say when I speak of Monsieur le comte Ferraud?'

'Call him your husband, my poor child,' replied the Colonel kindly; 'isn't he your children's father?'

'Well,' she went on, 'if Monsieur Ferraud asks me what I am doing with myself here, if he learns that I have shut myself up here with a stranger, what am I to say to him? Listen, Monsieur,' she went on, drawing herself up with great dignity, 'decide my fate. I am resigned to anything....'

'My dear,' said the Colonel, taking his wife's hands, 'I have made up my mind to sacrifice myself entirely to your happiness . . .'

'That's impossible,' she exclaimed with an involuntary convulsive start. 'Think, you would have to renounce your identity, and in a legally incontestable way ...'

'What!' said the Colonel. 'Is my word not enough?'

The phrase *legally incontestable* fell heavily on the old man's heart and awoke involuntary suspicions. He cast a glance at his wife that made her blush; she lowered her eyes, and fear seized him that he might find himself forced to despise her. The Countess was afraid that she had shocked the sensitive feeling for what was fitting, the strict integrity of a man whose generous nature and fundamental virtues were known to her. Although these thoughts had cast some shadows on their faces, harmony was quickly re-established between them, and in this way. A child's cry was heard some way off.

'Jules, leave your sister alone!' the Countess called.

'What! Are your children here?' said the Colonel.

'Yes, but I forbade them to bother you.'

The old soldier understood the delicacy, the feminine tact, that had prompted such a considerate action. He took the Countess's hand and kissed it.

'Let them come,' he said.

The little girl ran up to complain of her brother.

'Mamma!'

'Mamma!'

'He was the one who ...'

'It was her ...'

Their hands were stretched out to their mother and the two childish voices were mingled. It was an unexpected and charming tableau!

'Poor children!' exclaimed the Countess, no longer holding back her tears. 'I shall have to leave them; to whom will the law award them? It can't divide a mother's heart. I want them!'

'Are you making Mamma cry?' said Jules, casting an angry look at the Colonel.

'Hush, Jules!' his mother said imperiously.

The two children stood silently examining their mother and the stranger with a curiosity impossible to paint in words.

'Oh, yes!' she went on, 'if they separate me from the Count, let them leave me the children and I will agree to everything ...'

This was the plea which decided the matter, which obtained all the success that she had hoped of it.

'Yes,' exclaimed the Colonel as if he were finishing some statement which he had begun in his mind. 'I must go back underground. I had told myself that already.'

'Can I accept such a sacrifice?' the Countess replied. 'If some men have died to save their mistress's honour they have given their life only once. But in your case you would give up your life every day! No, no, it's impossible. If it were only your existence it would be nothing; but to sign a statement that you are not Colonel Chabert, recognize that you are an imposter, give away your honour, act a lie every hour of the day, human devotion could not go so far. Just think of it! No. If it were not for my poor children I should have fled with you already to the world's end.'

'But,' said the Colonel, 'could I not live here, in your little lodge, as one of your relatives? I am finished, like an old worn-out cannon. I only need a little tobacco and *Le Constitutionnel*.'

The Countess dissolved into tears.

There was a battle of generosity between Countess Ferraud and Colonel Chabert, in which the soldier came off the victor. One evening, seeing this mother surrounded by her children, the soldier was wholly won over by the affecting grace of a family scene, set in rural surroundings, amid the shadows and the silence; he made up his mind to remain dead, and no longer balking at the legal incontestability of a document, he asked what he must do to ensure irreversibly the happiness of this family.

'Do as you please!' was the Countess's reply. 'I declare to you that I will have nothing to do with this business. I ought not to touch it.'

Delbecq had arrived some days before, and in accordance with the Countess's instructions, given verbally, the steward had made it his business to win the old soldier's confidence. Next morning, then, Colonel Chabert set out with the former lawyer for Saint-Leu-Taverny, where Delbecq had had prepared at a notary's a document, which was framed in such crude terms that the Colonel left the notary's office abruptly when he had heard it read.

'By thunder! a fine rogue I should be! I should be taken for a forger!' he exclaimed.

'I don't advise you to sign too quickly, Monsieur,' said Delbecq. 'In your place I would make at least thirty thousand livres a year out of this action, for Madame would give that.'

When he had blasted this practised rascal with the luminous glance of offended honour, the Colonel fled in a whirl of contradictory feelings. In turn he was filled with suspicion, with indignation, grew calm again, only to feel fresh waves of suspicion invade his mind. At last he entered Groslay park through a breach in the wall and walked slowly to a small study fitted out on the ground floor of a summer-house overlooking the road to Saint-Leu, to rest and reflect in peace. The path was laid with the kind of yellowish sand which is replacing river gravel, and so the Countess, sitting in the little drawing-room of the lodge, did not hear the Colonel, for she was too preoccupied with thoughts concerning the success of her fight to heed the slight noise of her husband's approach. Neither did the old soldier perceive his wife above him in the little summer-house.

'Well, Monsieur Delbecq! Has he signed?' asked the Countess, seeing her steward standing alone on the road beyond a haha hedge.

'No, Madame. And I don't even know where our man has got to. The old horse got up on his hind legs.'

'We'll have to end by putting him in Charenton,' she said, 'since we hold him.'

The Colonel suddenly found that he had recovered the agility of youth, jumped the haha, and appearing in the twinkling of an eye before the steward, applied two of the finest slaps to his cheeks ever planted on a lawyer's face.

'Add that old horses can kick,' he said.

His anger spent, the Colonel felt that he no longer had the strength to jump the ditch again. The truth had been revealed

in its nakedness. The Countess's remark and Delbecq's reply
had laid bare the plot of which he was destined to be the victim. The kindness which had been so generously shown him
was bait to take him in a snare. That conversation was like a
drop of some subtle poison which induced the return of all the
old soldier's suffering, both physical and mental. He made his
way back to the summer-house by the park gate, walking
slowly like a man oppressed. So there was to be neither peace
nor truce for him! From that moment he must take up against
this woman the hateful war of which Derville had spoken;
he must enter upon a life of litigation, feed on gall, drink every
morning from a chalice of bitterness. Then, frightening
thought, where was he to find the money needed for the preliminary suits? Such disgust of life overwhelmed him, that if
there had been a lake or a river near him he would have thrown
himself into it, if he had had pistols he would have blown his
brains out.

Then he sank back into the state of uncertainty and doubt
that had affected him after his conversation with Derville at
the dairyman's dwelling. Reaching the summer-house at last
he climbed the stair to the airy room from whose walls rose-
windows looked out on every side over the ravishing perspec-
tives of the valley. The Countess was looking out over the
country with an expression of calm composure, displaying the
impenetrable self-possession of a woman determined to stick
at nothing. She wiped her eyes as if she had been shedding
tears, and played absently with the long rose-coloured ribbon
that encircled her waist. In spite of her apparent assurance,
however, she could not prevent herself from trembling when
she saw her venerable benefactor stand before her, his arms
crossed, his face pale, his brow severe.

'Madame,' he said after a moment, when he had gazed at her
fixedly and forced her to change colour, 'Madame, I do not
curse you, I despise you. Now I am thankful for the chance
which parted us. I do not even feel a desire for vengeance, I no
longer love you. I want nothing from you. Live in peace on
the security of my word, it is worth more than the scrawls of
all the notaries in Paris. I will never claim again the name to

which I have perhaps added some lustre. I am now only a poor devil called Hyacinthe who asks no more than a seat in the sun. Goodbye....'

The Countess threw herself at the Colonel's feet and tried to hold him back by grasping his hands, but he pushed her away with disgust and said, 'Don't touch me!'

The Countess's gesture as she listened to her husband's departing footsteps is indescribable. Then with the acute perspicacity which is the gift of deep-dyed villainy or the fierce egotism of the worldly, she perceived that she could live in peace on the promise and the contempt of that loyal soldier.

Chabert disappeared, in fact. The dairyman went bankrupt, and became a cab-driver. Perhaps the Colonel at first turned his hand to some occupation of the same kind. Perhaps like a stone cast down a precipice he rolled by leaps and bounds to find the lowest level in that living detritus dressed in rags which swarms in the streets of Paris.

Six months after the events described above, it occurred to Derville, who had heard no more either of Colonel Chabert or Countess Ferraud, that they had probably made some agreement between them which the Countess, in revenge, had had legally secured in another office. So, one morning, he computed the sums advanced to the aforesaid Chabert, added his costs, and requested the Countess to claim from Monsieur le comte Chabert the total amount of this bill, assuming that she knew where her first husband was to be found.

The very next day Count Ferraud's steward, recently appointed president of a court of first instance in an important town, dispatched the following crushing note to Derville:

Monsieur,
    Madame la comtesse Ferraud asks me to inform you that you were completely deceived in your client, and that the individual representing himself as Count Chabert has acknowledged that he wrongfully made use of a title to which he has no claim.

                                        Believe me, etc.
                                            Delbecq.

'Upon my word there are people in this world who are just a bit too much. Nothing is sacred to them!' cried Derville. 'Be humane, generous, philanthropic, and a lawyer, and you get made a fool of! There's a business that's let me in for more than two thousand francs.'

Some time after the receipt of this letter Derville was in the law-courts looking for a barrister whom he wished to speak to, who had business in the police-court. As chance had it, Derville entered the sixth court when the magistrate was sentencing the accused, one Hyacinthe, to two months in prison as a vagrant, and making an order that he should thereafter be detained in the poor-house at Saint-Denis, which, as police prefects understand the law, was equivalent to a sentence of perpetual detention. At the name Hyacinthe, Derville looked at the delinquent seated between two policemen in the dock, and in the sentenced man recognized his alleged Colonel Chabert. The old soldier was calm, unmoved, almost absent. In spite of his rags, in spite of the signs of wretched poverty marked on his face, his countenance expressed a noble pride. His look revealed a stoic endurance which a magistrate should not have mistaken; but when a man falls into the hands of the Law, he becomes nothing more than an abstraction, a question of law or fact, in the same way that in statisticians' eyes he is no more than a unit.

When the soldier was led back to the clerk's office to await his later removal with the batch of vagrants who were being examined at the time, Derville, making use of a lawyer's right to go where he likes in the law-courts, went to the office with him and watched him for a few moments, and the queer band of beggars he was with.

It is a great pity that no legislator, nor philanthropist, no painter, nor writer, comes to study such a spectacle as the clerk's anteroom then presented. Like all the workshops of chicanery, this anteroom is a dark and stinking room. Its walls are lined with benches whose wood is blackened by the perpetual passage of the unfortunate men who come to this assembly-point of all society's outcasts, where no type of wretchedness lacks its representative. A poet would say that daylight hides its face in shame, and dares not look upon this drain through which so many unhappy persons pass! There is not a single seat that has not held some crime, in germ or consummated; not a single place which has not known some man who, driven to despair by the brand inflicted on him by justice at his first infraction of the law, has started on the road at the end of which lies the guillotine or the crack of a suicide's pistol. All those who fall on Paris streets are brought up against these massive, dingy walls, on which a philanthropist, not necessarily a man of speculative mind, could decipher enough to justify the host of suicides deplored by hypocritical writers incapable of taking a step to prevent them. Their justification is plain, written in this anteroom, which is, as it were, the prologue to the dramas of the Morgue and the Place de Grève.

Colonel Chabert sat down among these men of vigorous appearance, dressed in the horrible uniform of poverty, talking in low voices or falling silent now and then, for three policemen on duty patrolled the room, their sabres clanking on the floor.

'Do you recognize me?' Derville said, standing in front of the old soldier.

'Yes, Monsieur,' replied Chabert, rising to his feet.

'If you are a man with a sense of decency,' Derville went on in a low voice, 'how could you have remained in my debt?'

The old soldier blushed, as a girl might, accused by her mother of a clandestine love-affair.

'What! Has Madame Ferraud not paid you?' he exclaimed loudly.

'Paid indeed!' said Derville. 'She wrote to me that you were an adventurer.'

The Colonel raised his eyes in a gesture of horror and imprecation, as if appealing to heaven at this fresh evidence of deceit.

'Monsieur,' he said, in a voice of strained calm, 'ask the police to allow me to go to the office of the clerk of the court. I am going to sign a cheque for you which will certainly be honoured.'

When Derville had spoken a word to the sergeant he was allowed to take his client to the office, where Hyacinthe wrote a few lines addressed to Countess Ferraud.

'Send that to her,' said the soldier, 'and you will be repaid the money you advanced to me and your costs. Believe me, Monsieur, if I have not shown the gratitude I owe you for your good offices, it is none the less there,' he went on, putting his hand on his heart. 'Yes, it's there, in full and complete. But what can poor devils do? They can feel devotion, that's all.'

'How is that?' said Derville. 'Did you not stipulate that some income should be paid to you?'

'Don't talk to me about that!' the old soldier replied. 'You cannot guess what deep contempt I feel for the life of external material things most men think so much of. I have suddenly been stricken by a sickness: disgust of humanity. When I think that Napoleon is in Saint-Helena, I don't care a straw for anything else on earth. I can't be a soldier any more; that's my whole trouble. Anyhow,' he added, with a boyishly mocking wave of the hand, 'it's much better to enjoy luxurious self-respect than luxurious clothing. I don't need to fear anyone's despising me.'

And the Colonel went, and sat down on his bench again.

Derville left the place. When he reached his office he sent Godeschal, now his second clerk, to Countess Ferraud, who, when she had read the note, immediately had the sum due to Count Chabert's lawyer paid.

In 1840, towards the end of June, Godeschal, now a qualified solicitor, was on his way to Ris, in the company of Derville, his predecessor. When they reached the avenue which leads from the main road at Bicêtre, they noticed under one of the wayside elms one of those hoary and infirm old men who have been awarded the beggars' Marshal's baton and live at Bicêtre, as indigent women live at La Salpêtrière. This man, one of two thousand poor wretches lodged in the Old Men's Almhouse, was sitting on a boundary stone, and seemed to have his whole attention concentrated on an operation well known to pensioners, the drying of their tobacco-stained handkerchiefs in the sun, perhaps to save washing.

This old man had an interesting face. He was dressed in the overall of reddish material that the Almshouse presents its guests with, a very unattractive uniform.

'Look, Derville,' Godeschal said to his travelling companion. 'Look at that old man. He's like one of those grotesque figures they send us from Germany. And he's alive, and enjoying life perhaps!'

Derville took out his eye-glass, looked at the old man, and made a sudden gesture of surprise. He said:

'That old man, my friend, is a whole epic in himself, or what the romanticists call a drama. Have you ever met Countess Ferraud?'

'Yes, a very intelligent and charming woman, but a little too religious,' Godeschal replied.

'This old almshouse inmate is her legal husband, Count Chabert, the former Colonel. She has no doubt had him placed here. If he is in this almshouse instead of living in a mansion, it is solely because he reminded the charming Countess that he took her like a cab from the public square. I still remember the tigress's glance she shot at him at that allusion.'

This opening aroused Godeschal's curiosity, and Derville told him the story related above.

Two days later, on Monday morning, when the two friends were on their way back to Paris, they glanced at Bicêtre, and Derville suggested that they should go to see Colonel Chabert. Half-way up the avenue the two lawyers found the old man sitting on a tree-stump. He held a stick in his hand, and was amusing himself drawing lines with it in the sanded pathway. When they looked more closely they perceived that he had had other refreshment than that the institution provided.

'Good-day, Colonel Chabert,' said Derville.

'Not Chabert! Not Chabert! I'm called Hyacinthe,' the old man answered. 'I'm not a man now; I'm a number – Number one hundred and sixty-four, Room seven,' he added with trembling anxiety, with a childish and an old man's fearfulness. 'You are going to see the man sentenced to death!' he said after a moment's silence. 'He's not married! He's a lucky man!'

'Poor man,' said Godeschal. 'Would you like some money to buy tobacco?'

With all a Paris street-urchin's single-minded directness the Colonel held out his hand eagerly to each of the strangers in turn, and they gave him twenty francs. He thanked them with a blank look and said:

'Stout campaigners!'

He made the gesture of shouldering arms, took aim, and cried beaming:

'For two coins, two-gun salute! Long live Napoleon!' And he traced a fanciful arabesque in the air with his stick.

'It's the nature of his wound that has affected him like this and made him fall into second childhood,' said Derville.

'Him in second childhood!' exclaimed an old inmate who had been watching them. 'Ah! there are days when one had better not tread on his toes. He's a shrewd, knowing old devil full of philosophy and imagination. But today he's been on the spree, that's how it is. Monsieur, he was an inmate here a long ago as 1820. One day at that time a Prussian officer chanced to pass by on foot while his carriage was being driven up the hill at Villejuif. Hyacinthe and I were standing by the roadside. This officer was chatting as he walked with another, a Russian or some creature of that sort, and seeing the old man, the Prussian, in a chaffing sort of way, said, "Here's an old soldier who may well have been at Rosbach." "I was too young to be there," he replied, "but I was old enough to fight at Jena." And the Prussian made off, without another word.'

'What a destiny!' exclaimed Derville. 'He came from the Foundling Hospital and has come back to die in the Old Men' Almhouse, having in the span between aided Napoleon to conquer Egypt and Europe. – Do you know, my friend,' he went on after a pause, 'there are three classes of men in our society, the priest, the doctor, and the lawyer, who can have no high opinion of the world. They wear black gowns; perhaps it's in mourning for all virtue, all illusions. The most unhappy of the three is the lawyer. When a man seeks out a priest he is driven by the need for repentance, by remorse, by belief which make him interesting, add to his stature, and consol he intermediary's heart, cause the task he has to perform to be not without a certain joy, for he has to cleanse, redeem, reconcile. But we lawyers see the same evil feelings recurring again and again, and nothing changes them, our offices are sewers that no one can clean out. What things have I not learnt in the course of my professional business! I have seen a father die in an attic without a penny to bless himself with, deserted by two daughters to whom he had given an income of forty thousand livres. I have seen wills burnt. I have seen mothers defrauding their children, husbands robbing their wives, wives killing their husbands, making use of the love they inspired to drive them into madness or imbecility, so that they might live undisturbed with a lover. I have seen women educing the child of a first marriage to acquire tastes which must lead to his death, in order to enrich the child born of love. I cannot tell you all I have seen, for I have seen crimes against which the law is powerless. Indeed, all the horrors which story-tellers imagine they are inventing, nowadays fall far short of the truth. You will soon become acquainted with these pleasant things. As for me, I'm going with my wife to live in the country ; Paris horrifies me.'

'I have seen plenty of them already, in my time with Desoches,' replied Godeschal.

Paris, February–March 1832

*Two other French classics
are described on the
remaining pages*

BALZAC

OLD GORIOT

Translated by M. A. Crawford

L17

Old Goriot is the tale of a young man's temptation by the world, the flesh, and the devil. The devil is represented by a character founded on the criminal Vidocq, who later became Chief of the Paris Sûreté; the world and the flesh by Paris in the early nineteenth century, and the lovely aristocratic women of the Faubourg Saint-Germain.

It is also the tale of a working-class Lear whose daughters, to whom he had given his all, left him to die in poverty while they lived in the world of fashion.

These are the chief among many threads of the story, which are intertwined through the intersecting lives of a group of people who by various chances came to live in a boarding-house in an old but obscure corner of Paris.

FLAUBERT

MADAME BOVARY

Translated by Alan Russell

LI 5

Flaubert's 'story of provincial life' in nineteenth-century Normandy has been something of a legend ever since it was first published in 1857. Or rather it has been two legends. The first is that of Emma Bovary, the embodiment of desires yearning beyond their inimical environment; failing to escape it, and finally breaking themselves upon it. The second is the legend of Gustave Flaubert, saint and martyr of literature, who shut himself up for over four years in his room at Croisset to make of Emma's story a novel that should be also a model of stylistic perfection.

'Style' to Flaubert was no mere pretty play with words, but a search in words for the very tone and texture of life. 'The form of a thought is its very flesh.' In that search the writer must 'become' whatever he writes of, as Flaubert 'became' not only 'the lovers in the wood' but 'the leaves, the wind, the horses'. . . .